WIDE IS THE GATE I.

"Wide is the gate, and broad is the
way, that leadeth to destruction."

World's End	1913 - 1919
Between Two Worlds	1919 - 1929
Drangon's Teeth	1929 - 1934
Wide is the Gate	1934 - 1937
Presidential Agent	1937 - 1938
Dragon Harvest	1938 - 1940
A World to Win	1940 - 1942
Presidential Mission	1942 - 1943
One Clear Call	1943 - 1944
O Shepherd, Speak!	1943 - 1946
The Return of Lanny Budd	1946 - 1949

Each volume is published in two parts: I and II.

WIDE IS THE GATE I.

Upton Sinclair

LCCN: 43000162

ISBN: 1-931313-04-0

Dis tributed by Ingram Book Com pany

Printed by Light ning Source Inc., LaVergne, TN

Pub lished by Si mon Pub li ca tions, P.O. Box 321 Safety Har bor, FL

When I say "his to rian," I have a mean ing of my own. I por tray world events in story form, because that form is the one I have been trained in. I have sup ported my self by writ ing fic tion since the age of six teen, which means for forty-nine years.

… Now I re al ize that this one was the one job for which I had been born: to put the pe riod of world wars and rev o lu tions into a great long novel. …

I can not say when it will end, be cause I don't know ex actly what the char - acters will do. They lead a semi-independent life, being more real to me than any of the people I know, with the single exception of my wife. … Some of my char ac ters are peo ple who lived, and whom I had op por tu nity to know and watch. Oth ers are imag i nary—or rather, they are com plexes of many people whom I have known and watched. Lanny Budd and his mother and fa ther and their var i ous rel a tives and friends have come in the course of the past four years to be my daily and nightly com pan ions. I have come to know them so in ti mately that I need only to ask them what they would do in a given set of cir cum stances and they start to en act their roles. … I chose what seems to me the most re veal ing of them and of their world.

How long will this go on? I can not tell. It de pends in great part upon two pub lic fig ures, Hit ler and Mus so lini. What are they go ing to do to man kind and what is man kind will do to them? It seems to me hardly likely that ei - ther will die a peace ful death. I am hop ing to out live them; and what ever happens Lanny Budd will be some where in the neigh bor hood, he will be "in at the death," ac cord ing to the fox-hunting phrase.

These two foxes are my quarry, and I hope to hang their brushes over my mantel.

In the course of this novel a number of well-known persons make their appearance, some of them living, some dead; they appear under their own names, and what is said about them is factually correct.

There are other characters which are fictitious, and in these cases the author has gone out of his way to avoid seeming to point at real persons. He has given them unlikely names, and hopes that no person bearing such names exist. But it is impossible to make sure; therefore the writer states that, if any such coincidence occurs, it is accidental. This is not the customary "hedge clause" which the author of a *roman à clef* publishes for legal protection; it means what it says and it is intended to be so taken.

Various European concerns engaged in the manufacture of munitions have been named in the story, and what has been said about them is also according to the records. There is one American firm, and that, with all its affairs, is imaginary. The writer has done his best to avoid seeming to indicate any actual American firm or family.

...Of course there will be slips, as I know from experience; but *World's End* is meant to be a history as well as fiction, and I am sure there are no mistakes of importance. I have my own point of view, but I have tried to play fair in this book. There is a varied cast of characters and they say as they think. ...

The Peace Conference of Paris [*for example*], which is the scene of the last third of *World's End*, is of course one of the greatest events of all time. A friend on mine asked an authority on modern fiction a question: "Has anybody ever used the Peace Conference in a novel?" And the reply was: "Could anybody?" Well, I thought somebody could, and now I think somebody has. The reader will ask, and I state explicitly that so far as concerns historic characters and events my picture is correct in all details. This part of the manuscript, 374 pages, was read and checked by eight or ten gentlemen who were on the American staff at the Conference. Several of these hold important positions in the world of troubled international affairs; others are college presidents and professors, and I promised them all that their letters will be confidential. Suffice it to say that the errors they pointed out were corrected, and where they disagreed, both sides have a word in the book.

Contents:

BOOK FOUR: TRUTH FOREVER ON THE SCAFFOLD

BOOK ONE

Into the Lion's Mouth

1

Dust to Dust

I

FREDDI himself wouldn't have wanted an elaborate funeral or any fuss made over his broken body; but funerals are not for the dead, only for the living. Here was his devoted Jewish mother, aged not so much in years as in feelings, and a prey to terror as well as grief. The calamities which had fallen upon her family and her race could not be blind accidents, they must have a cause; somebody must have done something, and what could it be save that her people had again departed from the ways of their faith and incurred the wrath of that most jealous of Gods, who visits the iniquity of the fathers upon the children unto the third and fourth generations of them that hate Him? It was Jahweh, Lord God of Sabaoth, it was El Shaddai, the Terrible One, thundering as He had done all down the centuries. Know therefore and see that it is an evil thing and bitter, that thou hast forsaken the Lord thy God, and that My fear is not in thee, saith the Lord of Hosts.

The Lord God of Hosts had given to Leah Robin, formerly Rabinowich, a husband and two tall sons, and to them two lovely wives, and to one of these a son; all blessings beyond price. But husband and sons and daughters-in-law all five had dared to treat with contumely the Law and the Prophets, to call themselves "modern" and to prate about "Reform," presuming to decide for themselves what was good and proper, regardless of all those commands which the Lord God of Israel had laid down in His holy books. The mother, though anxious in soul, had permitted herself to be dragged along; trying to keep her family about her and to avoid dissension, she had seen one ancient custom after another dropped and forgotten in her home.

2

El Shaddai the Implacable had waited, for such is His way. The Lord is slow to anger, and great in power, and will not at all acquit the wicked: the Lord hath His way in the whirlwind and in the storm, and the clouds are the dust of His feet. He rebuketh the sea, and maketh it dry, and drieth up all the rivers. . . . The mountains quake at Him, and the hills melt, and the earth is burned at His presence, yea, the world, and all that dwell therein. Who can stand before His indignation? and who can abide in the fierceness of His anger? His fury is poured out like fire, and the rocks are thrown down by Him.

Beyond anything which had confounded Job were the calamities which had fallen upon this happiest of Jewish families. The dreadful Nazis seizing first the father and then the younger son and throwing them into prison; robbing the family of everything in the world, torturing the son in unspeakable ways and finally throwing him out of their land a piteous wreck. A mother who had been taught from earliest childhood that the fear of the Lord is the beginning of wisdom could draw only one conclusion from such a chain of events; Jahweh was behaving according to His nature: the Lord God Omnipotent, who had cast out Adam and Eve and pronounced His terrible dooms, that in sorrow shalt thou bring forth children, and cursed is the ground for thy sake!

The inheritor of these dooms was now fleeing back to the ark of her covenant. Her son had been a poor strayed sheep, a "pink" sheep, tinged with Marxist hues, and it was too late to help him in this life, but at least she could prepare him for that resurrection to which the Orthodox look forward. He must be buried according to sacred tradition, with no concession to those fatal delusions known as "Reform." The stricken household was in a panic, and the estate upon which they lived was thrown into turmoil; for the mother believed that a Jewish corpse was dishonored if it was left above ground more than twenty-four hours, and it might not be buried after dark.

II

Rahel Robin, the young widow, had tended and watched over her husband for a couple of months; she had heard him pleading for death and had made up her mind that that was the way of mercy for him. She had no idea whatever that this so cruelly tortured body would ever rise from the grave, whether in its present distorted shape or restored to its original perfection. But there was no restraining the hysteria of the older woman. Mama wept and wrung her hands and tore her garments; at the same time she rushed hither and thither, trying to perform those offices which decency requires for Jewish dead.

There were many of her race on the French Riviera, but they were for the most part rootless persons, parasites and pleasure-seekers, as much tainted with skepticism and exposed to the wrath of Jahweh as the Robin family. Who among the devotees of fashion would understand how the fingernails of a dead person have to be trimmed? Who among bridge-playing ladies would know how to prepare a "meal of condolence"? Who among tennis-playing gentlemen would see to it that the mourners returning to the home washed their hands and forearms in accordance with the Talmudic formula?

There was a synagogue in Cannes, but Mama would have none of it; it was "Reformed," and the rabbi was so fashionable that he might as well have been an Episcopalian. But in the Old Town of the city there lived in direst poverty a few families from Russia and Poland, earning their bread by such labor as peddling, collecting rags, patching old clothes. They were real Jews, as Leah had once been; they had a sort of hole in the wall where they worshiped, and Leah had gone among them doing charity and had met the head of their synagogue. His name was Shlomo Kolodny, and he was no French rabbi of the Coast of Pleasure, wearing a big black armband at funerals, but a real scholar, a melamed, or teacher of the young; also he was the cantor, and the shammas, or sexton, and the shohet, or ritual butcher; in case of need he would be the undertaker according to the ancient code. After laborious days he spent his nights poring over sacred Hebrew texts and disputing in his imagination with learned

ones whom he had known in Poland, concerning thousands of minute points of doctrine and practice which had been raised during
twenty-five centuries of dealings between Jahweh and His Chosen
People.

So now the chauffeur of Bienvenu drove in haste to the city and
came back with this Shlomo of all trades, wearing a long black beard
and a badly stained Prince Albert which he probably thought looked
like an old-style caftan. In a Yiddish slightly mixed with French he
assured the bereaved mother that he knew everything and would
do it in style, and no "Reform" tricks whatever—"*Pas de tout*, Frau
Robin, *niemals, niemals* will I drain the blood from a good Jew or
put any poisons into him." He rubbed his hands together and purred,
for he knew all about this lady whose husband had been one of the
richest men in Germany and who was still important enough to be
a guest on one of the finest estates of the Cap d'Antibes.

A great consolation he was to Mama. He hastened to assure her
that she need not worry because her dear one was buried so far from
home; if she so desired, a little forked stick could be put in the grave,
wherewith he could dig his way to Palestine when the last trumpet
blew; and of course the screws in the coffin lid would be left loose
for him. As for the mutilations which evil men had done upon his
body, they would all be repaired, and a noble young Jew would
arise, transformed into an angel shining like a star. His broken fingers
would be mended and he could play his clarinet for the greater glory
of the Most High. Meanwhile his soul was comfortable in a sort of
dove-cot in Hades, with an immense number of tiny compartments
for the containing of righteous souls. This wasn't exactly accepted
doctrine, but Shlomo had read it in some ancient text and Mama
found it most comforting.

There are some of the old ways which are utterly impossible in
modern days. The cemetery was up in the hills, and while city
people have not forgotten how to walk, they have forgotten that it
is possible to do so. The coffin and the mourners would have to be
transported in automobiles, but the men would ride in separate cars,
followed by the women, and when they came to the gates of the
cemetery everybody would enter on foot. Tactfully the melamed

mentioned that in his flock were a number of poor women who would make excellent mourners; they would expect to be paid only a few francs each, plus a meal, and they would weep copiously and make a truly impressive funeral. It was too much to expect that all the Jews of Cannes or even of the village of Juan-les-Pins would stop work and follow the cortege; alas, they wouldn't even know that if they met it on the street they were in duty bound to turn and accompany it a distance of at least four cubits. Who could even tell them how much a cubit was?

There was the question of the *hesped*, the funeral eulogy. Shlomo was competent to pronounce it, but he had never met the deceased, and somebody would have to tell him what to say. At this point the young widow dried her tears and broke into the discussion. The person who should deliver the oration was the dead man's dearest friend, the one who knew him best and had risked his life to get him out of Naziland. This friend was in Paris, and Rahel had telephoned to him; he had promised to hire a plane and arrive in Cannes before the day was over. Surely Mama must know that it would be Freddi's wish to have the wonderful Lanny Budd speak the last words over his grave.

This was embarrassing to the master of ceremonies. To be sure, there was nothing in the Torah to forbid a *goy* to speak at a funeral; but it would seem very "modern," and would trouble the Orthodox, into whose hands the mother wished to entrust her son's fate. Nevertheless, Rahel insisted: not merely would it be Freddi's wish, but also that of his father and his elder brother. They, alas, were in South America, and there was no way to consult them; but Rahel knew their minds, and Mama knew that they looked with disfavor upon her most cherished ideas. So there would have to be two orations; Shlomo would speak the proper conventional words and then dear kind Lanny Budd would say whatever came from his heart. Everyone who attended the funeral, Jew or Gentile, would know how much the two young men had meant to each other, how many clarinet and piano duets they had played, and for how many months Lanny had labored to get his friend out of the clutches of Adolf Hitler and Hermann Wilhelm Göring.

III

It was a mild day in early October, and Lanny's plane should arrive in time. The hour for the ceremonies was set as late as possible, and the bereaved women summoned friends by telephone. By various means word was spread among all Jews, rich and poor, who might be willing to attend; for it is necessary to the honor of the deceased that there shall be a procession, accompanied by convincing demonstrations of grief.

Rahel took a step which came near to spoiling the occasion for her mother-in-law; she sent a message to a Spanish Socialist who was employed in Cannes and who ran the workers' school which Freddi and Lanny had helped to finance. Yes, indeed, Raoul Palma would attend the funeral, and many of the comrades would find ways to leave their work and pay the last tribute to a brave and loyal soul. The funeral ought to have been delayed for several days so as to give the anti-Fascists of the Midi an opportunity to make a demonstration of it. But since Moses hadn't known about refrigerants and formaldehyde, the comrades would do their best at short notice and later would hold a memorial meeting with music and Red speeches.

Toward the middle of the afternoon the motor-cars began to assemble in the driveway which circled the pink stucco villa of Bienvenu. Some parked their cars and waited decorously outside the gates, ready to take their places in the procession, and not realizing how this would mix things up. It was hard for modern people to understand that men must precede the hearse and women follow it. Such has been the fate of the most holy customs in these evil days— people don't even know that they exist!

Six pallbearers carried the plain wooden coffin to the hearse and then took their places in a car preceding it. In front went the car with the melamed and the little five-year-old son of the deceased. His mother would have preferred to spare him this ordeal, but the grandmother insisted that duty required him to become familiar with grief, and on the way the melamed would teach him the words of a Hebrew prayer which would be helpful to his father's soul.

Next rode the men friends, taking with them various Jewish males

who were too poor to have cars of their own. Behind the hearse rode
the mother and the widow, heavily veiled; no one would see their
faces or that of Freddi, which had been distorted by pain beyond
power of an undertaker's art. Next rode the women friends of the
family, these also taking a few poor women, to symbolize the fact
that in the eyes of Jahweh all are the same; all are commanded to
appear before Him in white grave-clothes of the same humble and
unpretentious cut.

Slowly the cortege proceeded into the city of Cannes, and everywhere, according to the French custom, passers-by stopped and the
men bared their heads respectfully. But apparently not one of them
knew that he should walk four cubits, a distance of six feet, with the
procession. It went by appointment to the school, where quite a
company had assembled; at least fifty men and women, but they had
no idea that the sexes should be separated. They were working
people, with a few intellectuals; some were black-clad and others
had armbands of crape; several carried wreaths, again being ignorant
of ancient Jewish prejudices. They stood respectfully until the last
car had passed, and then they fell in behind, carrying a red banner
having two clasped hands and the initials E.T.M., École des Travailleurs du Midi.

IV

So into the beautiful hills which line the Côte d'Azur. When they
came to the gates of the cemetery the cortege stopped, and the pallbearers bore the coffin to the grave. Three wealthy and fashionable
friends of the family did not enter the cemetery grounds, but
watched the procedure from outside, reading the prayers which they
could not hear. The reason was that they belonged to the tribe of
the priests, the Cohanim, who are not permitted to enter a burial
ground, a place contaminated and perhaps a haunt of evil spirits.

Frequently the pallbearers stopped and set down their burden;
this was not because they were weary, but because it was a part of
the ritual. As they walked, the melamed recited the Ninety-First
Psalm, full of assurances to those who put their trust in the Most

High. Surely He shall deliver thee from the snare of the fowler, and from the noisome pestilence. He shall cover thee with His feathers and under His wings shalt thou trust: His truth shall be thy shield and buckler. Thou shalt not be afraid for the terror by night; nor for the arrow that flieth by day; nor for the pestilence that walketh in darkness; nor for the destruction that wasteth at noonday. A thousand shall fall at thy side, and ten thousand at thy right hand; but it shall not come nigh thee. So spoke the psalmist; he mentioned plagues and stones and lions and adders and dragons—but nothing about Nazis!

Several times male friends came forward at the pauses and replaced the pallbearers, for this is a way to do honor to the deceased. Lanny Budd had arrived at the cemetery in a taxicab and waited at the gates; when a friend of the family explained the custom in a whisper, Lanny stepped up and did his share. He had known the Robin family for twenty years, and had heard poor Mama wailing over her darling's dreadful fate. He would have done whatever she wished, even if it had included the most ancient custom of having the pallbearers walk barefoot, lest they should stumble over the latchets of their sandals.

The bier arrived at the grave, and the rabbi recited the *Zidduk ha-Din,* a Hebrew prayer; very few knew what it meant, but it had fine rolling sounds. When the coffin had been lowered to its appointed place the Orthodox ones came forward, plucking bits of grass-roots and earth from the ground and throwing them upon the coffin as a symbol of the resurrection. They said a Hebrew formula which means: "And they of the city shall flourish like the grass of the earth." Some of the Gentiles threw flowers, and had to be excused because they didn't understand the proprieties. The Jewish people wept loudly, because it was good form and also because they felt themselves at one with the bereaved women, exiles in a strange land and heirs of the man of Uz. When the dark-eyed, pale little son of the dead man stepped forward and with tears on his cheeks recited the *Kaddish,* part Hebrew and part Aramaic, there were few dry eyes in the assembly.

Shlomo Kolodny delivered his *hesped.* He said about the **son of**

Johannes Robin the same things he had said about a thousand other Jewish men in the course of his long service. He laid stress upon the young man's piety, a virtue in which Freddi had been lacking—unless you chose to give a modernized meaning to the word. He laid stress upon Freddi's dutifulness to his parents and to his wife and child—virtues especially commanded by Jewish law. The melamed said another rolling Hebrew prayer, and then it was the turn of a young Gentile to speak for the Socialist portion of this oddly assorted procession.

V

Lanny Budd at this time was thirty-four but looked much younger. He had pleasant and frank American features and well-tanned and well-nourished skin; he wore a neatly trimmed little brown mustache, and a brown tropical worsted suit of a fashionable cut. He had no claim to being an orator, but had talked to the workers at the school and to other groups and didn't mind doing it when he had something to say. He understood clearly that funerals are for the living, and now his words were for Mama and Rahel and a few others who had really known the deceased; also for those workers for whom Freddi had often played music at the school.

The victim of the Nazis had been twenty-seven, and Lanny had corresponded with him since he was a little boy and had known him since he was a youth. In all those years Lanny had never known him to speak an unkind word or perform a dishonorable action. "He was as near to being perfectly good as one could ask of a human being; and I do not say that just because he is dead—I said it many times and to many people while he was living. He was an artist and a scholar. He knew the best literature of the land which he had made his own. He earned a doctoral degree at the University of Berlin, and he did this not for the honor nor yet for a livelihood, but because he wanted to know what the wisest men had learned about the causes and the cure of poverty."

Dr. Freddi Robin had called himself a Socialist. This was not the place for a political speech, Lanny said, but those who had known and loved him owed it to his memory to study his ideas and understand them, not letting themselves be confused by calumny. Freddi had been done to death by cruel forces which he himself had understood and had refused to bow to. Others also would have to learn about them, and find out how to save the world from hatreds and delusions which are the root of wars. If we would do this, we would be serving this dead man's memory and be worthy to meet him in whatever future abode the Creator of us all may have prepared.

That was all, and it wasn't much of a speech. The Socialists had come expecting more, and some would have been glad to supply it if invited. But this was a Jewish funeral, centered upon two sobbing women. Those who knew the proper way to behave at funerals formed two parallel lines leading back to the cemetery gates, and as the chief mourners walked between these lines everyone recited a formula beginning *"Hamokom yenahem,"* meaning: "May God comfort you in the midst of all those who mourn for Zion and Jerusalem." Just inside the gates of the cemetery stood the melamed with a collection-plate, and no one failed to drop in a coin. This was for charity, of great importance to every Jew. *"Tzedaka tatzil mimavet,"* recited Shlomo, meaning: "Charity delivereth from death."

Lanny stepped into the waiting taxicab, and when he reached Bienvenu he found servants at the porte-cochère of the house with several basins of clean water and towels. It was necessary for every person who attended the funeral to cleanse the hands before entering. This was supposed to be done in a special ritual way, by letting the water run three times from fingertips to elbows, but only the melamed knew this, and the reason—that evil spirits cannot pass running water and so can be kept from entering the house of mourning.

After that the family and their friends sat down with the melamed and recited seven times certain passages from the Book of Lamentations. Then they ate the "meal of condolence," which consisted of any non-alcoholic beverage, with bread and hard-boiled eggs, the last being symbols of life. Leah and Rahel Robin would eat these meals and none others over a period of seven days; wearing slippers, and with their dresses cut in such a way as to indicate that they had torn them in grief, they would sit on the floor or a low stool and read from the Book of Job. This is known as the *shiv'ah*, and during it they would receive consolatory visits and they and their friends would discuss only the virtues of the dear departed.

For eleven months they would not dance or take part in any form of recreation. There was a Talmudic reason for this precise period— if you mourned a full year, it would imply that you thought the deceased had been a bad man and was in Gehenna, that is, hell; you didn't quite wish to admit that, but you thought it wiser to take no chances, so you came as near to a year as propriety allowed. During this period the *Kaddish* must be recited every day for the benefit of the man's soul, and there was only one member of this household who was expected to say it—the five-year-old son. The prayers of women do not count, so little Johannes must say this long prayer, of which he wouldn't understand a single word.

VI

Lanny strolled about the grounds of Bienvenu, his home since he could remember. Always it seemed smaller after he had been visiting in châteaux and *hôtels particuliers*, but he loved it and brought his smartest friends to it with pride. Now it was his duty to look things over and see what repairs might be needed to any of the three villas on the estate. He must consult with Leese, the Provençal woman who had risen from the post of cook to an informal sort of steward. It would be his duty to report matters to his mother, who was visiting in England, but would be coming back after Christmas to take her part in the gaieties of a new Riviera season. He played with the dogs, of which there were always too many, because nobody could bear to dispose of them.

Lanny had a visit from Raoul Palma, a handsome young Spaniard —at least Lanny thought of him as young, just as he thought of himself. Hard to realize that Lanny was going to be thirty-five next month and that Raoul was past thirty! He wanted to get up a meeting in memory of Freddi Robin and wanted Lanny to come and make a good Socialist speech about him. But Lanny explained that his father was in Paris on one of his brief flying trips; also, Lanny had a wife and child in England whom he had been neglecting for the greater part of a year while getting his Jewish friends out of the clutches of Hitler and Göring. Lanny wrote a check to pay the cost of a hall, and told the grateful and attentive schoolmaster some of the things to say about Freddi.

They talked about the progress of the school and about the political situation in France and other countries. That was the way a "parlor Pink" got his education and kept his contacts with the workers. Lanny apologized for his own way of life: as an art expert, advising the rich about the buying of paintings, he had a reason for traveling to all the cities and towns of this old and fear-tormented continent; as an American he was assumed to be a neutral in Europe's quarrels, and it was the part of wisdom for him to keep that position. Thus he could meet the great ones, enjoy their confidence, and gain information which he could pass on quietly to working-class persons who could make use of it. The Spaniard was one of these; he had been born in a peasant hut and had been a humble clerk in a shoe-store; but with a small subsidy from Lanny he had become a leader, attending conferences, making speeches, and furnishing news to the Socialist and labor press of the Midi.

VII

Raoul talked for a while about events in his native land, from which he had fled, driven by a cruel despotism which lined working-class rebels against the wall and shot them without ceremony. But three years ago the wretched King Alfonso had been dethroned; Spain had become a republic and its government had received an overwhelming vote of support from the people. Raoul Palma had been so excited he had wanted to go back, but Lanny had persuaded him that his duty lay with the school he had helped to build.

Now it was just as well, for the teacher was deeply discouraged about his own country. It was the old tragic story of party splits and doctrinal disputes; the factions couldn't agree on what to do, and the amiable elderly college professors and lawyers who composed the new government found it fatally easier to do nothing. The Spanish people continued to starve; and for how long would they rest content with the most well-meaning "Liberalism" which gave them neither bread nor the means of producing it?

Lanny didn't know Spain very well—only from stops on a yachting-cruise and a plane trip. But he knew the Spaniards here on the Riviera; they came to play golf and polo, to dance and gamble and flirt in the casinos, or to shoot pigeons, their idea of manly sport. They read no books, they knew nothing, but considered themselves far above the rest of mankind. Alfonso of the jimber-jaw and the unpleasant diseases liked to be amused, and when on holiday he had unbent with the rich Americans of this Coast of Pleasure. Lanny had played tennis with him, and wasn't supposed to beat him, but had disregarded this convention. Now the ex-monarch was in Rome, intriguing with Mussolini to be restored to his throne.

"You ought to go to Spain!" insisted Raoul. "You ought to know the Spanish workers—they haven't all been killed. They have seen the light of modern ideas, and nothing will be able to blind them again."

Lanny replied that he had often thought of such a trip. "There are pictures there I want to see and study. But it might be better to wait till you have got through expropriating the landlords, and then I can pick up a lot of bargains."

He said this with a smile, knowing that his friend would understand. Whenever the young organizer came to him for funds, Lanny would say: "I've just sold a picture, so I can afford it." Or he'd say: "Wait till next week; I've got an oil princess in tow and expect to sell her a Detaze." Raoul knew that in a storeroom on this estate were a hundred or more of the paintings of Lanny's former stepfather, and whenever a purchaser came along, the École des Travailleurs du Midi could have a mass meeting or a picnic with refreshments and speeches. But don't say anything about Lanny's part in it!

VIII

This was in October of 1934, and Adolf Hitler had held power in Germany for not quite two years. He was the man who dominated Lanny Budd's thoughts; he was the new center of reaction in Europe, dangerous not merely because of his fanaticism, but also because he had in his hands the industrial power of Germany and was proceeding to turn it into military power. "It isn't only what he has done to the Jews," said the art expert. "He has done things much worse to the Socialists and to the whole labor movement in the Fatherland; but you don't hear so much about it in the capitalist press of France."

They talked about this on their way into Cannes, where Lanny was taking the evening train for Paris. He drove his friend in the family car, with the chauffeur in the back seat to bring the car back. Lanny, who had met Hitler and heard him talk, warned Raoul that he was only half a madman and no fool whatever, but on the contrary a trickster of infinite cunning, who had managed to get the German people behind him by a program of radical social changes which he had no slightest intention of carrying out. "We can't ignore him and his purposes," the American insisted. "We can't shut our eyes to him and go ahead with our plans just as if he didn't exist. He is a reactionary and a slave-driver, and he has said in his book that his program requires the annihilation of France."

This was hard doctrine for Raoul Palma, an internationalist preaching disarmament and brotherhood. Here was his friend and patron insisting that the time for such ideas was past; nobody could trust Adolf Hitler in any agreement, and only prompt and united action could keep him from rearming Germany. Frenchmen of all parties had to get together on this program before it was too late. "But, Lanny," objected the school director, "the French capitalists would rather have Hitler than have us!"

"That's because they don't know Hitler," was the reply.

IX

They talked about the disquieting state of the country in which they lived. The head of the French government was a round elderly gentleman wearing an old-fashioned white imperial; a former President of the Republic who had become Premier during a crisis in which nobody would trust anybody else. The mainspring of his being was a childish vanity, and he took delight in addressing the people of France over the radio as if they were his own progeny. But they were a stubborn brood, and by loud clamor had managed to keep Premier Doumergue from interpreting the constitution of the nation so that he could act independently of the Cabinet. What he wanted to do with his power was suspected by Raoul and confirmed by Lanny, who knew that the Premier of France held secret conferences with Colonel de la Roque, head of the Croix de Feu, the leading organization of the French Fascists.

The American felt less anxiety about the situation because of the Foreign Minister, Louis Barthou, a Frenchman of the old school who had learned to distrust any and every sort of German and therefore was not to be fooled by Adolf Hitler's wiles. This was a new point of view to Raoul, who looked upon Barthou as just one more politician and pointed to his reactionary utterances on domestic affairs; but Lanny felt sure he knew what was in the little round head with the high dome and the gray mustache and beard beneath. "He has some fine pictures and showed them to me, and a shelf of the books he has written—including lives of Danton and Mirabeau. You see he really knows the old revolutionary traditions."

"They all learn about them," replied the skeptical schoolman; "the better to fool the workers and sell them out—exactly as Mirabeau did."

"Barthou will never sell out France to Germany. When I met him was before Hitler took power, but the little Gascon realized exactly what the Führer meant. He said: 'Hitler is the man who is going to dominate our political life for as long as he lives.'"

Lanny reminded his friend of the "grand tour" which Barthou had recently made in the Balkans, to rally Yugoslavia and other states to an alliance against the new German counter-revolution. His success had been made plain by the effort the Nazis had made to bomb his train in Austria. "That's the way you tell your friends nowadays," added the American, and went on to point out that the determined little lawyer had been willing to drop his antagonism to the Soviet Union in the face of a greater peril; he had helped to bring Russia into the League of Nations last month and was working hard to prepare public opinion for a military alliance between that country and France.

X

The American was in a somber mood, the funeral having brought back to his mind all the horrors he had witnessed since the Nazi Führer had seized the mastery of Germany. Lanny told of his meeting with Freddi Robin in Berlin, a fugitive from the Nazis, sleeping in the Tiergarten or in a shelter for the unemployed; then the broken and shuddering figure he had helped to carry across the boundary line between Germany and France, when at last it had pleased the fat General Göring to release his prey. Dreadful, unspeakably wicked men the Nazi chieftains were, and Lanny was haunted by the idea that it was his duty to give up all pleasures and all other duties and try to awaken the people of Western Europe to a realization of the peril in which they stood.

So he spoke with repressed feeling; and then, when they reached the station, he bought an evening paper to read on the train. Glancing at its banner headlines he gave a cry. "LE ROI ALEXANDRE ET BARTHOU ASSASSINÉS!"

Quickly Lanny's eyes ran over the story, and he read the salient details to his friend. The King of Yugoslavia had come for a visit of state to France, to celebrate the signing of their treaty of alliance; he had landed at Marseille, and the Foreign Minister had met him at the dock. They had been driven in an open car into the city, through cheering throngs. In front of the stock exchange a man had run out from the crowd, shouting a greeting to the king, and before the police could stop him he had leaped upon the running-board and opened fire with an automatic gun, killing the king and fatally wounding Barthou, who tried to shield his guest.

The crowd had beaten the assassin to death, in spite of the efforts of the police to save him. He had been identified as one of a Croatian terrorist organization; but Lanny said: "You'll find the Nazis were behind him!" So it proved, in due course. The reactionary conspirators had been publishing a paper in Berlin, with funds obtained from the head of the foreign policy department of the Hitler party. The assassin had been traveling on a forged passport, obtained in Munich, and the weapon he had used bore the trademark of Mauser, the German munitions firm.

Such was the new technique for the conquest of power. Fool those who were foolable, buy those who were buyable, and kill the rest. It was the third Nazi murder of foreign statesmen within a year. First, Premier Duca of Rumania had been shot to death. Then a band of gangsters had broken into the office of Chancellor Dollfuss of Austria, the Catholic statesman who had been responsible for the slaughter of the Socialist workers in Vienna and the bombardment of those blocks of model apartments which Lanny had so greatly admired. And now both signers of the Yugoslav-French agreement had been wiped out.

"Good God!" exclaimed Raoul. "How much more will the people need to wake them up?"

"A lot more, I'm afraid," was Lanny's heartsick reply. "You and I, Raoul, chose a bad time to be born!"

2

Indoctus Pauperiem Pati

I

IN HIS youth Lanny had attended St. Thomas's Academy in Connecticut, and one of the subjects forced upon him was Latin. He had got so far as to translate several of the odes of Horace, and in his mind there remained a simile about a merchant whose vessels were wrecked, and he, "untaught to bear poverty," refitted them and sent them forth again. Lanny thought of that when he sat at luncheon in the Hotel Crillon with another merchant, a Roman though he did not know it, and heard him planning with eagerness a new expedition of his ships. In nineteen hundred years the world had changed and now they were ships of the air, but that made little difference in the psychology of the merchant.

Robbie Budd was entering his sixties, but was still driven by pride and ambition, still determined to prove that nothing could lick him. Five years ago the Wall Street crash had knocked him clean over the ropes, but he had picked himself up and wiped the blood out of his eyes and come in for round after round. The fact that his father had not named him as successor to the presidency of Budd Gunmakers Corporation, the fact that the great concern was no longer a Budd family affair, these blows might have finished a less sturdy fighter; but here was Lanny's father ready to start all over again and show them the stuff he was made of. By "them" he meant his family, his friends, his business associates and rivals; more especially his older brother, who had fought him all his life for control of Budd's, and the Wall Street banking crowd who had taken over the family name and the institution which for close to a century had been the family pride.

Robbie's contract as European representative of Budd Gunmakers still had more than a year to run, but Robbie was on the point of dropping it. He had been willing to work for his stern old Puritan father, but he couldn't be happy serving a bunch of interlopers, no matter how greatly they valued his services and how careful they were of his feelings. Robbie was reviving the dream of his early years, of a magnificent new fabricating plant to be built on the Newcastle River above the Budd plant. The land was still there, and could be bought more cheaply than ever—for, whatever the New Deal had accomplished by the end of 1934, it hadn't brought back land values and wasn't likely to.

The sentimentalists and cranks had had their way, and America lay disarmed in the face of a world of enemies—so Robbie declared. Budd Gunmakers was producing mostly hardware and what Robbie called "notions," meaning everything from hairpins to freight ele-

vators. What the salesman now had in mind was the weapon of the
future, and the means of transport of the future, the plane. All the
world was taking to the air; the nations which wished to survive
would be driven to it; and behind the sheltered and well-protected
waters of Long Island Sound Robbie would erect an airplane factory. Before long he would make it into the greatest in the world,
and give the name of Budd's a new and better meaning.

An expert in aerodynamics had showed up, and in an abandoned
warehouse near the Newcastle docks had done a lot of experiment-
ing; Robbie had helped him with a few thousand dollars, and they
had got an important new design for an internally braced flying
wing. Also Robbie had discovered a fellow with patents for an air-
cooled radial engine that was going to add another hundred miles
to the speed of planes, and if they could do that they would own the
world. Robbie was on fire with enthusiasm about it; he had organized a company and gone the rounds among his friends, those who
had put their money into New England-Arabian Oil with him and
done very well. Business was picking up and people had money, but
good investments were scarce, because the government was putting
out most of the bonds. So Robbie had had no trouble in selling stock
in Newcastle, and had taken an option on the land. Now he was in
Paris to talk with Zaharoff and with Denis de Bruyne and some of
Denis's associates; later he was going to London to see investors
there; he was doing it all privately—the Wall Street crowd wasn't
going to get a look-in. "Believe me, son, I'm not going to stay a poor
man." *Indoctus pauperiem pati!*

II

Robbie sat at the well-appointed *table à deux*, enjoying his *sole
meunière* and his Chablis, dry and well chilled. Business didn't interfere with his appetite, quite the contrary; he had always taken the
good things of life as they came along, and in spite of his graying
hair and hard work he was robust and rosy. He enjoyed telling about
his affairs; not exactly boasting, but speaking with quiet assurance,
pointing out how he had been right and forgetting when he had been

wrong. He had studied the field thoroughly and convinced himself that aviation was the industry of the future, the only one that wasn't overbuilt. It held the advantage that it was both a peace and a war industry; you could turn out "flivver planes," and then with only a few changes in design you could be turning out training planes and perhaps fighters. "Our country is asleep," declared the ever-vigilant patriot; "but the day is coming when everybody will be grateful to a few men who have learned to design high-speed planes and to make them in a hurry."

The promoter had an appointment with the one-time munitions king of Europe for the following morning and he wanted to have his son come along. "You know how to handle that old spider better than I do," he said, meaning it for a compliment. "You might sell him a Detaze; but don't try it until I get through with my deal. If I get this thing going, you'll never need for money."

"I don't need for it now," said Lanny, amiably.

Robbie didn't notice this unhelpful remark, but went on to say that Denis de Bruyne and his elder son were to dine with them in the evening; he had taken the liberty of assuming that Lanny wouldn't mind having the matter put before Denis. Robbie phrased it tactfully, as if the husband of Lanny's former *amie* were Lanny's own special property.

"Denis is a business man," the son replied. "If he puts his money into anything, he'll look into it carefully."

Robbie inquired about the funeral, and when Lanny described the ceremonies he couldn't keep from smiling, even though he felt deeply for the bereaved family. "It's hard to understand how people would want to go through such a rigmarole," he commented. "But I suppose that when they suffer too much they lose their balance."

"It's what Mama was brought up in," replied Lanny. "It helped her in a crisis, so it's all right."

"No use expecting women to be rational," added the father; it was one of his oft-repeated formulas. Following an obvious train of thought, he added: "Beauty's coming over from London to see what she can do with some of her friends."

Lanny knew what that meant without asking any questions. From

they comforted each other, forming a clan against both the demagogues and the younger generation.

Denis was past seventy, a handsome gray-haired man with a thin
aristocratic face. His vices, which had broken up his marriage, hadn't
seemed to injure his health. Lanny had been told that he had an unfortunate hankering for virgins; but Denis had never mentioned the
subject. To his father Lanny had expressed a mild curiosity on the
subject of an elderly Frenchman's affliction. How did one find virgins? Were there, in the lush underworld of Paris, merchants who
made a specialty of this commodity? Or did one advertise in the
newspapers: "Wanted virgins; highest prices paid; references required"? Having lived most of his life in the *beau monde*, Lanny had
come to understand that a dignified and even austere appearance,
the best *tournure* and the most gracious and benevolent manners did
not exclude the possibility of secret practices, amusing or disgusting
according as you chose to take such matters.

IV

The dinner was served in the drawing-room of Robbie's suite, in
order that the four men might be able to talk privately. Denis was
a hard-headed person, and it wasn't necessary to use finesse with him.
As soon as the waiter had departed Robbie said: "I have a project
which I think will be of interest to you." The other replied: "Tell
me about it, by all means."

Robbie launched on his "spiel," an exposition to which he had
given as much care and study as Daniel Webster or Jean Jaurès
would have devoted to an oration. He had practiced it many times,
varying it to fit the audience. It wasn't necessary to point out the
importance of aviation in the modern world, for the Frenchman had
more than once expressed himself on the subject; indeed, Robbie
tactfully indicated that Denis's opinion had been one of the factors
causing him to take up this project. He had come to France because
he knew how deep was his friend's anxiety over the inadequacy of
the country's air defenses and what Lanny had told him of the re-

armament campaign of General Göring, Commander of the German Air Force.

Said Robbie: "One thing you can be sure of, there will never be war between your country and mine; so, if I should succeed in building the world's best airplane factory in a part of the world where Göring cannot get at it, that would be a good thing for *la patrie* as well as for the individual investors. It is possible that I could go to the Germans with my proposition; but you know my feelings for France and how much I would prefer helping her to helping her enemies."

Robbie didn't say what he would do in the event that French capitalists didn't back him. On the other hand he didn't say that he wouldn't under any circumstances go to Germany; that would have seemed to him sentimental, out of keeping with the character of a business man—and besides, Denis wouldn't have believed him. Business men talked on the basis of the open market, which modern techniques had broadened to include the world. Budd-Erling—that was to be the name of the new concern—would make planes for the world market, and no favorites played. We have our price and our terms of payment, and the rule is, first come, first served; your money is as good as the next fellow's, and we don't ask about your nationality or your politics or your religion, the color of your flag or of your skin.

The owner of Paris taxicabs said it seemed to him that Robbie had a sound proposition. He asked many questions and Robbie answered them fully. The American had the whole set-up in a folder, and the Frenchman said to leave it with him and he'd study it and decide what he could do. He offered to put it before some friends, and Robbie said he'd come back to Paris after he had got through in London. So everything was all right, and they went to talking politics—where a great many things were far from right.

The killing of Barthou had thrown French affairs into turmoil. The Foreign Minister had been one of the few real patriots left in the country, and who was going to take his place? Conferences were under way and wires were being pulled; Denis explained that he would have to leave early because he had to do his share of the pulling. It was a time of real peril for France—the mad Hitler was rearming his country rapidly, and his agents were busy intriguing and stirring up revolts in every nation, big and little. Meanwhile France was torn by domestic strife, and where among politicians would she find a friend and protector?

Once more Lanny Budd gazed down into the boiling pit of *la haute politique;* once more he smelled the rather nauseous odors which rose from it. Alas, Marianne, *la douce, la belle,* no longer seemed to Lanny the shining, romantic creature he had imagined in his happy boyhood; then he had loved her, and all her children, rich and poor, on that lovely Azure Coast where stood his home. But now Marianne was taking on an aspect somewhat drab; her honor was sold in the market-place, and the clamor of the traffickers spoiled the day and the night. French politicians were creatures of the Comité des Forges, of the great banks, of the *deux cents familles;* the head of one of these ruling families poured out details as to what prices had been paid and what services were being rendered. He was full of bitterness against upstarts and demagogues— save those whom he himself had hired.

Denis reported that the talk was of Pierre Laval as Barthou's successor, and apparently this was a politician with whom de Bruyne had had experience. Like most of the pack, the innkeeper's son had started far to the left, and as soon as he got power had set out to line his pockets. When he was in danger of being exposed in one of the ever-recurrent scandals, he had saved himself by turning informer on his fellows. He had purchased a chain of papers all over France, and now was getting radio stations, useful in support of his financial and political intrigues. He had become as conservative as even Denis could have wished; indeed, so eager to preserve his property that he was an easy mark for the Nazi blackmailers. A man so wealthy could no longer think about France, but only about his own fortune.

Having told all this, and gone into detail about it, de Bruyne added: "I have to excuse myself now; I have an appointment with that *fripon mongol*"—that Mongolian rascal.

V

Next morning Beauty Budd arrived on the night train from Calais
and Lanny went to meet her at the Gare du Nord; he was a dutiful
son, and adored his full-blooming mother, even while he laughed
at her foibles. There she was, descending from a *wagon-lit;* pink and
gold fluffiness in a gray traveling-dress with fur boa to match. When
he kissed her she said: "Don't muss me any worse—I look a fright."
But Lanny, unfrightened, replied: "You are the eternal rose, and
not one petal out of place."

Don't ask how old she was—it would be too unkind. She was
the mother of a son who would be thirty-five next month and she
discouraged the celebration of these recurrent calamities. She was
gradually reducing in her own mind the age at which she had borne
him, and she had been cheered by reading in the newspapers about
an Indian girl in Peru who had produced a son at the age of five.
When you have been so beautiful that you have been named for it;
when you have seen all the men in restaurants and hotel lobbies turn
to stare at you; when you have been many times immortalized by
the most celebrated painters—when you have enjoyed all these
glories too long, you look into your mirror in the morning and the
tears come into your eyes and you begin to work frantically with
the tools of the cosmetician.

For one thing, you have to choose between *embonpoint* and
wrinkles; and fate had chosen for Beauty Budd. The cream-pitcher
remained her worst enemy; while a million women in London and
Paris strove in vain to get enough food, she failed mournfully in
her efforts not to get too much. She was always trying new diets,
but the trouble was they left her dizzy, and she had to have a few
chocolates in between meals of one lamb chop with pear and cucum-
ber salad minus dressing. She told about it, and then asked about
the funeral. She had to reach for her delicate *mouchoir,* for Mama
and Rahel had been her dear friends and yachting-companions,
and she was the kindest of souls; if she had ever done harm to any
human being it was because the social system was too complicated
for her to understand the consequences of her actions.

Robbie Budd had supported her upon a lavish scale, ever since he had fallen in love with her as a very young artist's model in this city of pleasure. He had acknowledged her son, in spite of the opposition of his Puritan family. So how could she fail to do everything she could for him? By her combination of beauty, kindness, and social charm she had won the friendship of rich and important persons; and if Robbie wanted to meet them and make deals with them, why shouldn't she lend her aid? Robbie never cheated anybody; what he sold was what they wanted to buy. If it was guns and ammunition, how could he help that? If now it was going to be planes, well, he would give them their choice, for peace or for war. Nobody could hate death and destruction more than Lanny's mother; she had spoken boldly and had made enemies by it, but had not been able to change the destiny of this old Continent.

Robbie was a married man, and a grandfather several times over. Beauty was a married woman, and a grandmother once, which was enough. She had her separate suite in the hotel, and when she met Robbie they shook hands as old friends and behaved with such propriety that the gossips had long ago lost interest in them. Beauty would have herself made presentable, and then she would get busy on the telephone, and soon would be in a round of events. Wives of retired capitalists and widows of elderly bankers would learn that Robbie Budd, the American munitions man, was in Paris, planning a new enterprise which might be of vital importance to French defense and incidentally might be paying dividends of twenty or thirty per cent in a year or two.

VI

Meanwhile, Lanny was motoring his father to the Château de Balincourt, once the home of King Leopold, misruler of the Belgians, and now the retreat of Sir Basil Zaharoff, retired munitions king of Europe and not retired Knight Commander of the Bath of England and Grand Officier de la Légion d'Honneur de France. The old gentleman was in his middle eighties, and saw very few people, but Lanny Budd possessed the key to his castle and his heart. Not merely had he known the noble Spanish lady who had been the old man's wife, but he had received her messages from the spirit world through a Polish medium whom he had discovered. Sir Basil would be most happy to see Mr. Budd and his son, so the secretary had said over the telephone; would they be able to bring Madame Zyszynski along with them?

Robbie talked about the strategy of approach to one of the most wary of men. "Talk to him about the duquesa," said the father. "Can't you recall something that will get him warmed up?"

"Beauty has been getting some interesting messages purporting to come from the Caillards," replied the son.

"Fine! Tell him about them; and if you can say that the spirits are riding in airplanes, that would really fetch him!" Robbie said that with a grin. He didn't exactly ask that his son should make up some story about Zaharoff's dead wife in the other world, yet if Lanny had proposed doing that, his father wouldn't have objected. It is all right to have scruples, but they should be used with discretion, and not while dealing with an old spider, an old wolf, an old devil, who for more than a generation had played with the nations of Europe as casually as other men play with chessmen on a board.

The lodgekeeper came out and looked them over; evidently he had his orders, and the gates swung back, and they drove up a broad driveway to the stone château—two stories, rather squat, but with wide-spreading wings. A turbaned Hindu servant admitted them; all the servants were from Madras. It was a damp and chilly day, and the master, wearing a green smoking-jacket, sat before the fireplace in his very grand library, which went up the two stories and had a balcony with heavy bronze railings. All those books, at which Lanny gazed hungrily; he doubted if half a dozen of them were opened in the course of a year. The old man no longer had any hair on the top of his head, but still had the white imperial below it; his skin was drawn and yellowish brown like old parchment. He did not rise from his seat or offer one of his palsied hands, but put cordiality into his tone as he told them to take the seats which had been placed for them.

"Sir Basil," said Lanny, at once, "have you heard that 'Birdie' is coming through?"

"Nobody troubles to tell me anything any more," was the sad reply.

"My mother wishes me to tell you about it." Beauty Budd and the Knight Commander of the Bath had both been guests of Lady Caillard in London not long before she had "passed over." She had been an ardent spiritualist and had made the usual promises to communicate with her friends from the other side. She had lived surrounded by mediums, and of course it was inevitable that these would begin getting messages from her. "Birdie," as she was known, had been strong on emotions but weak on brains, and it was to be expected that her words from the spirit world should bear that same character. "Vinnie" was Sir Vincent Caillard, who had been Zaharoff's business partner in Vickers-Armstrong and had been no fool, even if he had thought himself a maker of music as well as of munitions. Zaharoff knew his mind and thousands of things that had been in it. Now he listened attentively while Lanny told what he could remember of the séances.

"Oh, God, how I wish I could believe it!" exclaimed the lonely old man. His beard waggled as he talked, and he leaned forward, thrusting his hooked beak forward as if he thought he could smell the younger man's real thoughts. Lanny knew the one idea that was in his mind: was he ever going to see his beloved duquesa, the only person for whom he had really cared in a long life? He wanted so to believe it—and yet he hated so to be fooled! He wanted to hear that Lanny believed it; and yet, even if he heard it, he wouldn't be sure whether Lanny was being honest with him. When one has been outwitting other people for three-quarters of a century, how can one believe that anybody is being straightforward?

They sat close together, and their eyes met in a long stare. It was as near as they could ever come to intimacy. "Tell me, Sir Basil," asked the younger man, "have you any religion?"

"None, I fear," was the reply. "I have wished that I might. But how can a God permit what I have seen in this world?"

"A God might be leaving men to work out their own destiny."

"A God who made them what they are?"

"You believe, then, that you are an accident?"

"That seems to me the politest supposition I can make about the universe." It might have been humor, and it might have been tragedy; Lanny guessed that it was some of each.

VII

Not for a large amount of money would Robbie Budd have interrupted this conversation. He listened and watched and thought, like the practical psychologist he was. He was interested not in the question of where Sir Basil was going to spend his future years, but only in what he was going to leave behind him. Anyone who didn't like Robbie would have said that his motive was greed, but Robbie would have treated such a person with quiet contempt; he had his answer, which Lanny had known by heart from his earliest days: Robbie wanted to get things done, and money was the means of doing it.

An engagement was made for Madame Zyszynski, the medium, to come to Balincourt for another visit, so that Sir Basil might find out if "Birdie" wished to talk to him. After which the old man must have realized that he wasn't being quite polite to the older of his guests; he turned, saying: "Well, Mr. Budd, what are you doing these days?"

It was an opening, and Robbie was prompt to take it. He replied: "I have come to ask for advice, Sir Basil." His host said that he would give it if he could, and Robbie went on: "I have been studying the world situation, on the basis of the best data I can get, and have come to the conclusion that the industry of the future is aviation. I believe it will be for the next generation what the automobile was for the last."

The older man listened and nodded now and then as Robbie elaborated this thesis. Yes, it was true; he wasn't going to be here to see it, but it was bound to happen; any nation that didn't take to the air might as well give up before the next war started. If Mr. Budd knew sound aviation shares, those were the things to buy.

"That is not exactly what I am thinking of, Sir Basil." Robbie went on to tell about his dream of a perfect place for a perfect fabricating plant. "Airplane factories have been scratch affairs so far, and their techniques are based on small-scale operations. What I have in mind is to apply the principles of mass production to this new job; I want to put airplanes on a belt."

"That is a pretty large order, Mr. Budd."

"Of course; but if the industry is to be large, the order must be the same. Sooner or later somebody is going to become the Henry Ford of the air. He tried it himself, but has given up—just when success had become possible."

It was Lanny's turn to listen and watch and think; he, too, was something of a psychologist, though hardly a "practical" one. This aged plutocrat took on suddenly the aspect of a white-bearded gnome, sitting on a heap of treasure and watching with fear-stricken eyes every creature that came near. He had by now made sure that Robbie Budd wanted his money, and a lot of it, and he had lost every trace of that expansiveness which conversation about Vinnie and Birdie had produced. This was danger!

But still he couldn't quite bear to break off the interview. The visitor was talking about profits, dividends of old-time magnificence. The Knight Commander and Grand Officer had known Robbie Budd for thirty years, and judged him a solid and capable fellow; no speculator, no fly-by-night promoter, but one who put money to work and himself to work with it. At the Genoa Conference, where Robbie had been Zaharoff's agent, he had acted with competence; later, when Zaharoff had gone in on New England-Arabian Oil, he had got the better of Robbie—but not enough so that he would look on his associate with contempt.

You couldn't ignore what a man like that was telling you. You couldn't help but be aroused, even if only by the memories which his voice and manner recalled. Those had been the days, and Zacharias Basileos Sahar or Zahar, who had been born of Greek parents in a peasant hut in Turkey and had become the real behind-the-scenes master of Europe, he was one who could say with the ancient Greek hero that much had he seen and known: cities of men, and manners, climates, councils, governments; himself not least, but honored of them all. If he couldn't exactly say that he had drunk delight of battle with his peers far on the ringing plains of windy Troy, at least he could claim to have sent a hundred thousand other men to drink that dubious delight. Those windy plains were near to the village of Mugla, where Zacharias Basileos had started his career, and also to the scene where twelve years ago his personally financed Greek army had been slaughtered by the Turks.

VIII

Robbie Budd expatiated upon the defenses of Montauk Point, and the safety of Long Island Sound and its tributary rivers as a nesting-place for war industries; he told about railroad connections, and steel that was brought from the Great Lakes through the Erie Canal and the Hudson River. He pictured the factory of steel and glass he was going to build, air-conditioned, a twenty-four-hour-a-day plant. He showed the drawings of his air-cooled radial engine to Zaharoff, who had owned tens of thousands of engines. In its lighter parts Robbie was going to use magnesium, a metal which the industry had slighted. Small shavings of it are explosive, but he had a method of gathering them up automatically. Instead of hammering the cast parts into place he was going to freeze them in liquid air and set them, and when they had returned to normal temperature they were there for life. When he was running tests on his engines he was going to hitch them up to generators and so make electricity for his plant.

So many new ideas this hard-driving Yankee had, and the retired munitions king watched him as a fascinated cobra watches its Hindu charmer. "I am an old man, Mr. Budd," he pleaded, pathetically. "My doctors tell me that I must avoid the slightest strain. I have my safe investments, and find that it disturbs me to think about shifting them."

"Yes, Sir Basil," agreed the promoter; "but this is the sort of thing that comes only a few times in a long life. Here is the one really live industry, the one that is going to shove everything

out of its way. We shall make our turnover every few months—
I don't want to exaggerate, but I have studied the field thoroughly,
and I cannot see how we can fail to make enormous profits."

The operation of greed in this aged Greek trader's psychology
was something automatic. He was like some old toper who has
sworn off, but cannot resist the sight and smell of his favorite
beverage; like Rip Van Winkle: "This time don't count!" Lanny,
watching him, saw a light gleaming in the cold pale-blue eyes; the
palsied fingers seemed reaching out for the treasure and the old
white imperial seemed waggling with excitement.

What did he want with more money? What could he imagine
himself doing with it? Here he was, with all but one or two toes
in the grave, and, whatever else he might believe about the future,
he couldn't expect to take Budd-Erling stock with him. The industrial empire he had formed had been broken up and its fragments
were in the hands of others. He had given small amounts to charity,
but he had no interest in what had been done with them. He still had
several billions of francs, yet he had to have more; it was the nature
of his being.

Robbie had him at a disadvantage, because he knew so much
about the old man's affairs: his staff, his attorneys, the advisers he
trusted. Robbie had already talked to one of them, and perhaps—
who could say?—promised him a *douceur*, a "sweetener." He knew
how easy it would be for Zaharoff to order the sale of a million
dollars' worth of bonds, and the buying of Budd-Erling preferred,
with an equal number of common shares for bait. Robbie waved
this bait in front of Sir Basil's prominent nose, and it followed this
way and that. Lanny saw that there was going to be a "killing,"
and the procedure made him faintly sick, but he decided that this
was sentimentality. Who would worry about the fate of an old
spider, an old wolf, an old devil? .

After all, Zaharoff would get real value for his money. There
was really going to be this wonderful building, with a long line of
objects moving along slowly and being constantly added to by parts
taken from overhead conveyors, until each in turn became recog-
nizable as an airplane and finally rolled off on its own wheels, ready

to mount upon the air. All this would continue, long after Sir Basil
had gone to his duquesa; as long as civilization endured, with its
paper titles of ownership, his descendants would be entitled to dividend checks payable at the First National Bank of Newcastle, Connecticut.

The upshot was that Sir Basil took a copy of Robbie's "set-up,"
promising to study it, and if he found it according to Robbie's statements, to come in on the deal; he wouldn't say for how much, but
would let Robbie know in a couple of days. The promoter was in
high spirits on the drive back to Paris. It was the best day's work
he had done since the depression, he said; you can't keep a good
man down!

IX

Lanny ought to have been a true son of his father and done his
share in the making of this new Budd glory. Robbie had cherished
that hope for many years, but had had to give it up. He had two
sons by his wife in Connecticut; solid fellows, nearing thirty, they
would be his right hand and his left. Lanny would sell a block of his
securities and put the money into his father's enterprise, and then
he would go back to playing the piano, advising purchasers of art
works, and dreaming of seeing the world a less cruel place.

What he did now was to go for an afternoon stroll along the
pleasant streets of Paris in the pleasantest season of the year. There
was a visit he wanted to pay, and he wasn't going to tell his father
about it. His mother, perhaps—she couldn't very well object to his
visiting her brother, who had befriended her and had never done her
the least harm. But with Robbie it would mean the starting of an
argument, and what was the use? Lanny wouldn't tell his wife,
either, for that would mean another argument, and of even less use.

Lanny Budd, good-looking, rich, and called a darling of fortune,
was a man with a secret vice; and like many such unfortunates,
having learned what other people thought of his weakness, he had
evolved subtle devices to protect himself. He didn't enjoy lying,
so when he stole away to practice his vice he would include in his

journey some innocent occupation such as looking at pictures; then when Irma asked him what he had been doing, he would answer: "Looking at pictures." He would learn to keep silent on all subjects that might possibly be connected with his vice and bring it to his wife's mind. What you don't know won't hurt you—such is the maxim of erring husbands.

The fact that he refused to recognize his vice for what it was made a difference to him, but, alas, it made none to Irma; and he had had to learn the lesson that if what you do brings unhappiness to someone you love, the question of vice or virtue is a mere matter of words. They had said all the words it was possible to say on the subject, and it hadn't made any difference; so now Lanny had walled off a portion of his life and mind from most of his friends, including the woman who was dearest to him.

Lanny's vice was that he liked to talk to "Reds"; he liked to meet them, and hear them discuss the state of the world and what they were proposing to do about it. Whenever he expressed his own opinion, he got into an argument with them, too, but he took that as part of the fun. He didn't mind if they denounced the system under which he enjoyed a delightful leisure; he didn't even mind if they denounced him, calling him an idler, a playboy, a parasite. He didn't mind if they got his money and then refused to pay the tribute of gratitude, saying that it wasn't really his money, he had no right to it, it belonged to the wage-slaves, the disinherited of the earth—in other words, to themselves. These things infuriated Irma, but Lanny took them all with a grin.

There was some kind of queer streak in him which Irma and her friends couldn't make out; some called it "yellow," though not often in Irma's hearing. The grandson of Budd's had somehow got fixed in his mind the notion that he wasn't entitled to his money and, worse yet, that Irma wasn't entitled to hers. It was like a thorn buried deeply in his conscience; it festered there, and no surgery had been able to extract it. This caused him to take an apologetic attitude toward disturbers of the social peace and made him their predestined victim; a soft-shell crab in an ocean full of hard-shell creatures. Irma had her own ideas about "parasites"; she thought they were the grumblers and soreheads, the crackpots and cranks who wrote letters to her husband and laid siege to his home, in the effort to dump their sorrows into his heart and their burdens onto his shoulders.

Irma had tried to be good-natured about these annoyances, up to the last year or two; but the episode of the Robin family had broken her patience. She blamed all the misfortunes of that family upon the doings of the Red Hansi and the Pink Freddi and the failure of the head of the family to control his wayward sons. She went further and blamed all the troubles of Europe upon the activities of the Bolsheviks. It was their threats of class war and wholesale robbery which were responsible for the development, first of Fascism in Italy and then of Nazism in Germany. When the well-to-do classes found they could no longer sleep safely in their beds, naturally they hired someone to protect them. Hadn't Irma and Lanny themselves done it, for the safety of their "twenty-three-million-dollar baby"? Irma was quite willing to admit that Mussolini and Hitler and Göring were not the most agreeable types of people, but perhaps they were the best the well-to-do classes had been able to find in the emergency. Thus spoke, vigorously and frequently, the daughter and heiress of J. Paramount Barnes, one-time utilities king.

X

Uncle Jesse Blackless still resided in the apartment in the working-class neighborhood where Lanny had grown used to visiting him. The fact that he had become a deputy of the French Republic hadn't made any difference in his life—except that it might have had something to do with his decision to marry the French Communist who had been his "companion" for ten years or more. The living-room of his apartment was still a studio, one corner of it packed solid with his paintings; he was busy making another when Lanny knocked on the door. He had a little *gamin* for his model, and when he saw his nephew he gave the youngster a few francs and sent him along, then lighted his old pipe and settled back in his old canvas chair to "chew the rag."

They had plenty to talk about: family affairs, the news that Beauty was in Paris and that Robbie was going to become a millionaire all over again; the news about pictures, what Lanny had bought and what was to be seen in the autumn Salon; then political events, the killing of Barthou, and the chances of Laval's taking his place—Lanny told what Denis de Bruyne had said about this *fripon mongol*, and it was data that Jesse would use in his next Red tirade in the Chamber. Of course without hinting at the source of his information.

Bald, lean, and wrinkled Jesse Blackless was what is called a "character"; perhaps he was born one, but now he clung to it as a matter of principle. The income he enjoyed from the States was sufficient to have enabled him to wear a clean new smock, but he chose to be satisfied with one which revealed all the different colors he had had on his palette for several years. And it was the same with many of his habits; elegance was a sign of caste, and he chose to be one of the "workers"—although he had never worked at anything but making pictures and speeches. He chose to believe that everything the workers did was right and that everything the rich did was wrong, this being in accordance with the doctrine of economic determinism as he understood it.

Lanny hadn't been able to find many formulas which satisfied him, and it amused him to pick flaws in his Red uncle's. They would wrangle, both taking it as a sort of mental boxing-match. Jesse sounded quite fierce, but basically he was a kind-hearted man who would and frequently did give his last franc to a comrade in distress. What he wanted was a just world, and the preliminary to this was for the rich to get off the backs of the poor. Since dialectical materialism demonstrated that they wouldn't, the thing to do was to throw them off.

The funeral of Freddi Robin had been reported in both *Le Populaire* and *L'Humanité*, the former celebrating it as a Socialist event and the latter treating it as an anti-Nazi event. This provoked the painter to declare the futility of attempting to overthrow the Nazis except by Communism; which in turn made it necessary for Lanny to declare the futility of attempting to achieve the goal without the co-operation of the middle classes. Jesse said that the middle classes were being ground to pieces by the economic process, and to hell with them. Lanny said statistics showed the middle classes increasing in America, despite all Marxist formulas. And so on.

If Irma Barnes had heard her husband arguing she might have imagined that she had converted him; but no, if she had been here, he would have been driven to take the side against her. This wasn't perversity, he would insist; he was trying to see the problem from all of its many sides, and argued against all persons who wanted to see only one side. He dreamed of a just social order which might come without violence; but apparently everything in this old Europe had to be violent!

XI

The newly established mistress of this household came in, and the argument was dropped, for Françoise, hard-working party member, lacked the American sense of humor and would be annoyed by Lanny's seeming-flippant attitude to the cause which constituted her religion. Lanny chatted for a polite interval and then excused himself, saying that he had an engagement to dine with his father. He went out to walk in the pleasant streets of Paris at the most pleasant hour of sunset, and stopped in a couple of art-shops whose dealers were acquainted with him and were pleased to show him new things. This would keep his record clean—he had been "looking at pictures."

The ladies of the *trottoir* manifested an interest in a handsome, well-dressed, and young-looking man. In fact, walking alone on the streets of *la Ville Lumière* was no easy matter on this account. Lanny liked women; he had been brought up among them and was sorry for them all, the rich as well as the poor; he knew that nature had handicapped them, and this was no world in which to be weak or dependent. He would look at the thin pinched faces of those who sought to join him; their paint did not deceive him as to the state of their nutrition, nor their artificial smiles as to the state of their hearts. He saw their pitiful attempts at finery, and his own heart ached for the futility of these efforts at survival.

There came one, more *petite* and frail than usual, and with a manner showing traces of refinement. She put her arm in Lanny's, saying: "May I walk with you, Monsieur?" He answered: "*S'il vous plaît, Mademoiselle—vous serez mon garde du corps.*" One would keep the others away!

He took out his purse and gave her a ten-franc note, which she crammed hurriedly into her sleeve. She didn't know what he meant, but it sufficed for a start, and as they strolled along he asked her where she came from, how she lived, and how much she earned. Like so many others she was a *midinette* by day; but work was uncertain in these terrible times and one couldn't earn enough to pay for food and shelter, to say nothing of clothes. She perceived that this was a kind gentleman; and Lanny understood that if she wasn't sticking exactly to the facts, this also could be explained by the formulas of economic determinism. Anyhow, she was a woman, and the tones of her voice and the pressure of her hand on his arm told him a good deal.

Their stroll brought them to where the Rue Royale debouches onto the Place de la Concorde. Lanny said: "We have to part now. I have an engagement." She replied, this time doubtless with entire truth: "*Je suis désolée, Monsieur.*" She watched him enter the Hotel Crillon, and knew that a big fish had got away. However, the ten francs would buy her a dinner and leave enough over for a scanty breakfast.

XII

Lanny went into the hotel, in whose red-carpeted and marble-walled lobby great events had happened during the Peace Conference of fifteen years ago. For the grandson of Budd's the place would be forever haunted by the ghosts of statesmen, diplomats, functionaries of all sorts, some in splendid uniforms, others in austere black coats. Many were now dead and buried in far corners of the earth, but the evil they had done lived after them; they had sowed the dragon's teeth, and already the armed men were beginning to rise out of the ground, in Italy, Germany, Japan; in other places the ground was trembling and one saw the round tops of steel helmets breaking through. Lanny and others who thought they understood dragon agriculture predicted a bumper crop, perhaps the biggest in history.

He went to the desk for his mail. There was a letter, a poor-looking letter in a cheap envelope, not usual in this haven of the rich. But it was common enough in Lanny's life, he and his wife being targets for begging letters. This one was postmarked London and addressed to Bienvenu, from which place it had been forwarded; the handwriting was foreign, apparently German, and Lanny didn't recognize it. He opened the envelope as he walked toward the *ascenseur*, and found a note and also a little sketch on a card the size of a postcard. He looked at it and saw the face of the dead Freddi Robin; it caused him to stop in his tracks, for it was extraordinarily well done.

He glanced at the signature, "Bernhardt Monck," and did not know the name. He read:

Dear Mr. Budd:

I have a communication which I am sure will be of interest to you. I came to England because I understood that you were here. I hope this letter will find you and I thank you kindly to reply promptly, because the circumstances of the writer are not permitting of a long wait. It is a matter not of myself but of others, as you will understand quickly.

The stranger signed himself, "Respectfully," and had put in the envelope this little password, this shibboleth or countersign, which had the power to send cold chills up and down Lanny's spine. To an art expert this simple pencil drawing, which bore not even an initial on it, was the surest means of identification and the most secret message that could be contrived. Every line of the drawing cried aloud to him: "Trudi Schultz!" The date on it, October 1934, with a black line drawn around it, said to him: "I have learned of Freddi's dying condition, and have sent a messenger to see you." The young artist Trudi had been one of the teachers at Freddi's school in Berlin, and her style was not to be mistaken.

If Lanny had been a discreet person, if he had learned thoroughly

the lessons which life was apparently trying to teach him, he would
have put this little drawing away in a portfolio with other art treasures, including a sketch of himself by Jacovleff and several by John
Sargent; as for the letter, he would have torn it into small pieces
and sent them down into those sewers of Paris which have been
so vividly described in *Les Misérables*. He thought of these prudent
actions, to be sure; he thought of his wife and what she would
make of this situation. He argued with her in his mind. He hadn't
promised her that he would never have anything more to do with
Reds or Pinks; he hadn't said that he wouldn't receive any more
messages from Germany or give any more thought to the struggle
against the Nazis. All he had said was: "I will never again get into
trouble with the Nazis, or cause you unhappiness because of my
anti-Nazi activities." Surely it couldn't do harm if he saw a messenger from a young artist of talent and found out what had happened to her, and to her husband, and to the other friends of himself and Freddi Robin in Germany.

So the toper says to himself: "I am reformed now; everything is
settled and safe; I will never again touch liquor in any form; but
of course a glass of beer now and then, or a little light wine at mealtimes, cannot do me any harm!"

Lanny had the sketch framed and carefully packed, and sent it
by registered mail to Mme. Rahel Robin, Juan-les-Pins, Alpes-
Maritimes. Also he wrote a note on the stationery of the Hotel
Crillon to the mysterious Mr. Bernhardt Monck, stating that he
expected to be in London in two or three days and would get in
touch with him. Without mentioning the matter, he enclosed a
one-pound banknote with the letter, thus making sure that Mr.
Monck wouldn't perish of starvation in the meantime.

3

A Young Man Married

I

BIDDING temporary farewell to his parents, Lanny Budd set out early on a damp and chilly morning to motor to England. Not far off the route lay the Château les Forêts, home of Emily Chattersworth, and he detoured to pay a duty call on her. This old friend of the family was not so well or so happy; the leading art critic who had been her *ami* for a quarter of a century had decided that a younger woman was necessary to his welfare, and when that happens the older woman does not find joy in even the finest landed estate. Emily had stood by Beauty Budd when her son was born out of wedlock, and she had been a sort of informal godmother to Lanny; having helped to make his match with a famous heiress, she was always interested to hear how it was coming along. After the fashion of this free and easy world of wealthy expatriates, she discussed the troubles of her heart with the young man, and he kept no secrets from her.

There was news to be exchanged concerning the people they knew and what they were doing. Lanny told about Freddi's funeral, and about Lady Caillard's "coming through," and about the success of the concert tour which Hansi Robin and Lanny's half-sister Bess were making in the Argentine. He told about the Salon at which he had spent the previous day, and described a painting he had bought for one of his clients. Emily wanted to know about Robbie's affairs, and he advised her: "Keep away from him; he's in one of his high-pressure moods." That always awakens the curiosity of the rich—they are used to being run after and are impressed when they are run from. Emily talked about the state of the market, and said it was shocking the way her income had fallen off; however, she couldn't bear to think of changing her investments while the prices of all her holdings were so low. Lanny said there was no use remembering that they had ever been higher.

She really wanted to hear about Robbie's project, so Lanny reported on it. He perceived that a white-haired chatelaine was a victim of the same tropism as an aged Levantine trader; he teased her about it, and she made the answer which the rich always make—they have so many taxes, so many dependents, such a variety of expenses which cannot be cut down; whatever their income, they are always "strapped." Lanny said: "You know I'm no promoter, but it looks as if Robbie's going to make a lot of money." Emily responded: "Do you suppose he'll come out to see me if I phone him?"

II

On to Calais, the town full of memories never to be erased; it was there that Lanny had waited for the Robin family to arrive on their yacht, and had learned that the Nazis had seized them. He drove his car onto the packet-boat, and paced the deck watching the busy stretch of water which he had crossed with Marie de Bruyne, then with Rosemary, Countess of Sandhaven, and of late with Irma Barnes; he thought of each in turn, experiencing those delicate thrills which accompany the recollection of happy loves. Here, too, he had crossed with his father in wartime, through a lane made by two lines of steel nets held up by buoys, with destroyers patrolling them day and night. People of Lanny's sort now spent much time discussing the question whether such things were likely to be seen again, and if so, how soon.

There were no fields of clover when Lanny went up from Dover. The green was beginning to fade from the landscapes, and a soft drizzling rain veiled every scene, making it look like an old painting whose varnish has turned brown. Lanny enjoyed this season of mist and mellow fruitfulness, and observed with the eyes of an art connoisseur the thatched cottages and moldy-looking roofs, the hedges, the winding roads—but watch your reactions, for it's tricky when you drive one-half the day on the right and the other half on the left! He by-passed London bound for Oxfordshire and home; he had wired Irma, and Mr. or "Comrade" Monck would have to wait a day or two longer.

They were living in a villa which Irma had rented from the Honorable Evelina Fontenoy, aunt of Lord Wickthorpe. It was called "small," but was large, also modern and comfortable, in contrast to Wickthorpe Castle, whose estate it adjoined. It had a high hedge for privacy, and very lovely lawns; the drive made a turn when it entered, so that passers-by couldn't see the house at all. When Lanny came up the drive at twilight he heard a shout, and here came a small figure with brown hair streaming—little Frances, dressed in a raincoat and overshoes, and let out in care of a groom to await the arrival of that wonderful father, almost as rare as Santa Claus. He stopped the car and she clambered in beside him, to drive a hundred feet or so; there was a present for her in the seat, but she mustn't unwrap it until she got her wet things off.

The "twenty-three-million-dollar baby" so much publicized by the newspapers was now four and a half years old, and wise care had averted most of the evils which might have been predicted for one in her position. She hadn't been kidnaped, and hadn't been too badly spoiled, in spite of two rival grandmothers. A trained scientist had had the final say about her, and had said it with effect. Frances Barnes Budd was a fine sturdy child, and was going to grow up a young Juno like her mother. She had been taught to do things for herself, and nobody had been permitted to tell her that she would some day be abnormally wealthy.

Irma came to the head of the stairs when she heard the child's excited cries. Lanny ran up, two steps at a time, and they embraced; they were in love with each other, and a week's absence seemed long. She wore an embroidered red silk kimono in honor of his coming—her blooming brunette beauty could stand such adornment. She led him into her sitting-room, and the child took a perch upon his knee and unwrapped his present, a picture book with pastel drawings of that gaiety which the French achieve by instinct. She wanted it read to her right away, but Irma said that she and Lanny had much to talk about, and sent the little one off to the governess, whose accomplishments included French.

Then they were alone, and there was the light of welcome in Irma's eyes, and they were happy together, as they had been so many times, and might be forever, if only he would let it happen. At least, so it seemed to Irma; but even while she still lay in his arms, fear crept into her soul like a cloud over a blue sky. She whispered: "Oh, Lanny, do let us be happy for a while!" He answered: "Yes, darling, I have promised."

But his tone meant that the cloud was still there. When lovers have had a clash of wills and unkind words have been spoken, these words are not forgotten; they sink into the back of the mind and stay there, having a secret life of their own, generating fear and doubt. Especially is this so when the cause of the disagreement has not been removed; when the clash of wills is fundamental, a difference of temperaments. The lovers may try to deny it, they may cry out against it, but the difference goes on working in their hearts.

A duel carried on in secrecy and darkness! Lanny thought: "She is trying to put chains upon me; she has no right to do it." Irma thought: "He will think I am trying to put chains upon him; he has no right to think that." But then, in her fear, she thought: "Oh, I must not let him get that idea!" Lanny, in his love, thought: "I must not let her know that I think that! I have caused her too much unhappiness already." So it went, back and forth, and each watched for the signs of stress in the other, and suspected them where they were not actually present, resenting them even while resolving not to cause them. So it is when a ray of light is caught between two almost parallel mirrors and is reflected back and forth an endless number of times, or when a wave of sound is thrown into a tangle of rocky hills and echoes are set rolling back and forth as if evil spirits were mocking the source of the sound.

III

Lanny talked about his trip. Not much about the funeral, for Irma wanted to forget all that as quickly as she could. But she was interested in Robbie and his project, and in the visit of Zaharoff and its outcome. She said: "Lanny, that ought to prove a big thing."

"I believe it will," he replied.

"Doesn't Robbie want me to come in on it?"

"You know how he is—he's shy about putting it up to you."

"But that's silly. If he has a good thing, why shouldn't I have a chance at it?"

"Well, he said he wouldn't mention it unless you asked him to."

"He ought to know that I have confidence in him, and that it's a family matter. I would be hurt if he left me out."

"I'll tell him," said Lanny; and so that was settled most agreeably. Would that it had all been as easy!

"I'm glad you got home early," remarked Irma. "Wickthorpe is having the Albanys to dinner and asked us over in the evening. I said we would come if you got back."

"Fine," replied the husband. "And by the way, would you like to run up to town with me tomorrow? I have a letter from a man in Ohio, asking if I can find him a good Sir Joshua. I think I know where there's one."

What the art expert had said was true; he was determined never to lie to his wife. If Irma had asked: "Did you see Uncle Jesse?" he would have answered "Yes" and told her what they had talked about. But she didn't ask; she knew that she didn't have the right to expect him not to meet Beauty's brother. He, for his part, knew that she must have known that he would go there, and perhaps meet other Reds, and perhaps make them promises of the sort they always tried to get from him. They would unsettle his thoughts, make him discontented with his life, cause him to be moody and to make sarcastic remarks to his wife's friends. The wild echoes were set flying in their hearts again; but neither spoke of them.

IV

Gerald Albany was a colleague of Lord Wickthorpe in the British Foreign Office; they had been through Winchester together and were close friends. Albany was the son of a country clergyman and had to make his own way; perhaps for that reason he was more proper and reticent than other members of the diplomatic set whom Lanny had met. He was a tall lean man with a long serious face, and had found a wife who matched him perfectly, a large-boned lady wearing a dark-blue evening costume which was doubt-less expensive but looked extremely plain. The half-starved little *fille de joie* with whom Lanny had strolled on the boulevards had more *chic* than Vera Albany could ever have or perhaps wish to have.

The husband was a carefully studied model of a British diplomat, cold in manner and precise in utterance; yet, when you knew him, you discovered that he was a sentimental person, something of a mystic, knowing long stretches of Wordsworth by heart—he had even read the *Ecclesiastical Sonnets*, not once, but many times, and was prepared to defend them as poetry. He was conservative in his opinions, but tried hard to be open-minded or at least to believe that he was; he would permit Lanny to voice the most unorthodox ideas, and discuss them in such a carefully tolerant way, with so much suavity, that unless you knew his type of mind you might think he half agreed with you. Yes, of course, we are all Socialists now; we are enlightened men and we understand that the world is chang-ing. The ruling classes must be prepared to give way and permit the people to have a larger say about their affairs; but not in India or Central Africa, in Hong Kong or Singapore. Above all, not in too much of a hurry; right now only the Conservatives understand the situation and are able to guide the ship of state in perilous seas!

Irma was deeply impressed by this conscientious functionary, and wished that her husband might be; she tried in a way which she thought was tactful to bring this about. But Lanny, the impatient one, thought that the world ought to be changed right away. He said that the difference between a Bolshevik and a Tory was mainly

one of timing; the toughest old die-hard in the Carlton Club could
be got to admit that maybe in a few thousand years from now the
dark-skinned races might be sufficiently educated to manage their
own affairs both political and industrial. But, meanwhile, we have to
carry the white man's burden, placed upon our shoulders by that
God of our fathers so intimately known of old.

V

Lanny had been on a scouting expedition, as it were. His friends
were pleased to hear what a French financier thought about political
prospects in his country and what an ex-munitions king, a Knight
Commander of the Bath, had to say about the state of Europe.
Pierre Laval had just become Foreign Minister of France, and
Lanny told what he had heard about him; speaking in the privacy of
the home, the Englishmen agreed that he was an unscrupulous and
undependable fellow. That was the difficulty in relations with
France; the governments changed so rapidly, and policies changed
with them; you could never be sure where you stood. British foreign policy, on the other hand, changed very slowly; in funda-
mentals it never changed at all. Britain had a Prime Minister who
was a Socialist, yet everything remained as it had been. Politicians
may come and politicians may go but the old school tie goes on
forever.

These friends knew all about Lanny's misadventures in Germany
and made allowances for his extreme views on the subject of Nazism.
But they were not prepared to change the fixed bases of their
empire's policy because an American playboy with a pinkish tinge
to his mind had got thrown into the dungeons of the Gestapo—nor
yet because a family of wealthy German Jews had been blackmailed
and plundered. Wickthorpe was prepared to admit that the Nazis
were tough customers; an irruption from the gutter, he called
them; but they were the government of Germany, *de facto* and *de
jure*, and one had to deal with them. They might be made to serve
very useful purposes: for one thing, as a counterweight to French
political upstarts who had a tendency to become extremely arrogant,

on account of their country's great store of gold; and for a second thing, as a check upon Russia. "Oh, yes!" exclaimed Lanny. "Hitler is to put down the Bolsheviks for you!"

Wherever an American art expert traveled, in Europe, in England, in America, he found the privileged classes, his own kind of people, hypnotized by the Führer's flaming denunciations of Communism and the Red Menace. The ex-painter of postcards voiced their thoughts completely on this subject; he was their man and promised to do their job. In vain Lanny tried to make them realize that no slogan meant anything to Hitler, except the gaining and keeping of power; political opinions were an arsenal of weapons from which he picked up those which served his need at a certain moment of conflict. When conscientious, God-fearing English gentlemen stood upon a platform and made promises to their electorate, they meant at least part of what they said; and how could they imagine that Hitler, Göring, and Goebbels would change their entire "line" overnight if it suited their political or military purposes?

Lanny was frightened about it, and sad about the state of opinion in all the countries he knew. But there is a limit to the amount of arguing and protesting you can do in the drawing-room of even your best friends; if you keep it up, they will stop inviting you; and long before that happens, your wife will be pointing out to you that you are making yourself socially impossible. Lanny, well trained from childhood and now provided with a thoroughly competent wife, had to sit and listen while Lord Wickthorpe proceeded to "adumbrate"—so he said—the future of world history in accord with the best interests of the British Empire. "Good God, man, don't you suppose that Hitler knows what you are expecting? And why should he oblige you?"—so Lanny wanted to cry out; but he knew that if he did he would get a scolding on his way home.

VI

The master of this ancient chilly castle, a sight for tourists and a home for bats, was slightly older than Lanny, but, like Lanny, appeared younger than his age. He had pink cheeks, fair wavy hair, and a tiny pale-brown mustache; how he had managed to remain a bachelor had been a mystery to Irma since the first day she had met him at the Lausanne Conference. He had elegant manners and an assured mode of speech. His was a civil service job, and he had had to pass very stiff examinations, so he knew what to do and say in every eventuality. He would listen courteously to what you had to report, and then, if he thought it worth while, would explain to you where you were mistaken. If he didn't think it worth while, he would turn and talk to someone else.

Irma thought him one of the best-informed men she had ever met, and sometimes she cited him to her husband as an authority. Irma loved the romantic gray-stone castle, in spite of its portable bathtubs which she called "tin." She loved the respectful tenants who always tipped their hats to her if they were men and "bobbed" if they were women. She liked English reserve, as contrasted with French volubility. She liked living in a world where all the people knew their places and everything had been happening just so for hundreds of years. She wished that Lanny could be dignified, instead of bohemian, meeting all sorts of riffraff, rubbing elbows with "radicals" in smoke-filled cafés and letting them argue with and even ridicule him.

In short, Irma liked a world without confusion whether domestic or intellectual. She had seen, first in Russia and then in Germany, that if you played with dangerous ideas you presently began to witness dangerous actions. She thought that Lanny was old enough to have sowed his cultural wild oats, and she yearned for him to settle down and take care of her and her fortune and her child. She found in Lord Wickthorpe the perfect model of what she would like her husband to be; and while she was too tactful to put it in plain words, Lanny could gather it without difficulty. He wasn't in the least jealous, but he couldn't help thinking now and then how pleasant it would be if his wife could agree with him about the things he considered important. His effort to keep his annoying thoughts to himself was resulting in a sort of split personality, and as time passed the hidden part of him was becoming the larger and more active.

VII

Emily Chattersworth had persuaded Irma that it was important for her to take a serious interest in her husband's occupation and to let him have the manly sensation of earning his own money, however small the amount. So Irma would go with him to look at old masters and would gravely offer her opinion upon their merits and prices. She wanted to be cultured, and this was a part of it. Many of the paintings really were beautiful, and now and then when Lanny came upon a bargain Irma would buy it herself and have it stored until the time when she had her own palace, either in England or France, she wasn't sure which.

Sir Joshua was an especially interesting master, because he had done so many beautiful aristocratic ladies and their children. Irma herself was such a lady, and Lanny had told her that he was looking for the right man to do a life-size portrait of her. So now she saw herself in these duchesses and countesses, and studied poses and costumes, in order that when the time came she would be able to tell the artist exactly what she wanted. That is the way to meet life, she had decided: know how to spend your money, say what is your pleasure, and hold the respect of those you deal with, from the humblest slavey who brings in your coal-scuttle to the proudest nobleman who invites you to grace his drawing-room.

Lanny was conscientious about serving his clients. When the owner of a ball-bearings plant in Ohio wrote that he wanted a good Sir Joshua for his collection, Lanny didn't pick up the first one the fashionable dealers offered; he didn't say: "That fellow has so much money it doesn't matter what he pays." No, he would consult his card-file and list all the Sir Joshuas of which he had been able to learn; he would get photographs of each, and send them to his client, with a long letter detailing the qualities of each and discussing the possible prices.

"I advise you to let the matter rest for a few weeks," he would write, "until word has got round about the inquiries I have made. You understand that the market for old masters is a small world, full of busy and eager traders, and they gossip among themselves like a hive of bees. They regard Americans as their proper prey, and invariably ask fifty per cent more than they would ask of an Englishman. I have succeeded in impressing them with the view that I am not an easy mark; I worry them with the idea that my client prefers some other picture, and usually in a few days they call up and invite me to dicker, and try to get me to set a price, which I refuse to do until I hear from some other dealer on some other picture. All this is very sordid, but it's the way paintings are bought, and there's no use letting yourself be plucked."

Such a letter would impress the manufacturer, for it was the way he would proceed when placing an order for steel ingots. When he got his painting at last he would appreciate it much more because he had had to worry about it. He would say to his friends: "That chap Lanny Budd got it for me—you know, Budd Gun-makers; he's married to Irma Barnes, the heiress, so it's really a labor of love with him." The arrival of the painting would be celebrated in the local newspapers, and not merely would the painting be reproduced, but also a photograph of the proud owner; so the other steel men of the district would learn that art pays, and the wife of one of them would get Lanny's address and inquire if there was anything really first class now on the market. Lanny would get his ten per cent out of all this, and it provided him with pocket money and made an amusing sort of life.

VIII

After Irma had looked at several paintings she always got tired, and remembered various things which ladies have to do when they visit a great city; hairdressers, manicurists, masseuses, milliners, dressmakers, furriers, jewelers—all sorts of shrewd purveyors who are busy day and night thinking up schemes to persuade them that it is impossible to live worthily and romantically without such services. After lunch Irma said: "I want to go to So-and-so's," and they made an appointment for later in the afternoon to have tea and dance for a while. Lanny, having known that this would happen, had telegraphed Mr. or "Comrade" Monck at what hour he would call upon him, in a very poor neighborhood in Limehouse, near the docks. Here were rows and rows of two-story slum dwellings, laid end to end and exactly alike, each with its two chimneys emitting wisps of soft-coal smoke. With the help of hundreds of factory chimneys they formed a pall which had enveloped the district for a hundred years and brought it to the appearance of a vast dustbin.

In such a neighborhood a fancy sport-car would be a phenomenon; so Lanny, taught by his experience in Germany, spotted the house and then drove around the corner and parked. When he knocked on the door there came a slattern old woman, in features and voice completely Cockney. When he asked for Mr. Monck she said: "Ow, yuss," and as she led him up the narrow stairs she said it was a nice dye, sir; he was quite sure that, whatever Nazi or anti-Nazi plotting might be going on here, the lydy of the 'ouse 'ad nuffin to do wiv it. Lanny hadn't failed to consider the possibility that he might be dealing with the Gestapo; they might have got Trudi Schultz in their clutches and be using one of her sketches as a means of trapping her friends and getting information. He had read of their kidnaping persons from Austria and Switzerland; the brother of Gregor Strasser had been one of their near-victims; but he didn't think it likely they would go that far in London—not quite yet!

The woman, grumbling about her rheumatism, didn't really have to climb the stairs and knock on the door of the rear room; Lanny guessed that she was curious about her foreign lodger and the "toff" who had come to see him. A man inside answered the knock, took one glance, and said, quickly: *"Bitte, keinen Namen!"* Lanny said not a word, but stepped in. The lodger shut the door in the landlady's face and carefully hung a coat over the knob so as to cover the keyhole; he signed Lanny to the sole chair in the small and dingy room, and said, in a low voice: *"Besser wir sprechen Deutsch."*

Lanny had been imagining some sort of "intellectual," but a single glance told him that this was an outdoor man, used to hard and tough labor. His frame was stocky and filled out like a boxer's, and his neck went up straight and solid in the back. His face was weatherbeaten, his hands gnarled; his clothes were those of a laborer and his dark hair was cropped short in Prussian style. Lanny thought: "A sailor or perhaps a longshoreman." He had met the type among the Socialists in Bremen as well as on the Riviera: the man who has labored by day and read at night. His education is narrow, but he has forged it into a sharp sword for his purposes. He knows what he wants, and his speech is direct. If he is middle-aged, he is probably a Socialist; if he is young, he is more likely to be a Communist.

IX

The stranger seated himself on the edge of the narrow bed, not more than three feet from Lanny, and, gazing straight into his face, began, in a voice with a strong North German accent: "The name I gave you is not my real name, so there is no harm in your speaking it; but I will try not to speak your name, and let us not name any of our friends or any places. There are, you understand, extremely important reasons."

"Have you reason to believe that you are being watched here?" inquired the visitor, speaking low, as the other had done.

"I have to assume it always. That is the only way to survive. I sent you something in the way of credentials. Did you recognize it?"

"I believe I did," replied Lanny.

"Let us refer to the woman in the case as Frau Mueller. Let that be for both speaking and writing in the future."

Lanny nodded. He thought: "A miller instead of a village magistrate," that being the meaning of the name Schultz.

The stranger continued: "Frau Mueller and I are associated with others in some work or the utmost importance, and we have one rule, we do not reveal anything about it except in case of absolute necessity. I hope that you will not question me too much, and will not take offense if I say: I cannot answer this or that. It is not merely our own lives that are at stake."

"I understand," replied Lanny.

"We do not under any circumstances name any other person. I know the names of those with whom I deal, she knows the names of those with whom she deals, but I do not know her associates, and so on. We keep nothing in writing, anywhere. So, if we are captured, our enemies have only us; and even if they torture us, and we should break down and wish to betray others, we cannot do much."

"I understand," responded Lanny, again.

"It is my hope that you will trust me on the basis of what you know about Frau Mueller, who gave me your name and sent me to you. She has told me about you, and assured me that you are a comrade and a man of honor; also that you have had experiences which enable you to know what our enemies are and how serious a matter it is to us if we are betrayed or even talked about in a careless way. I ask that you will not mention this meeting to anyone under any circumstances. May I count upon that?"

"You may do so. Of course I can't say how far I might go along with you."

"We need friends outside our own country, and we hope that you will help us and perhaps find others to help us. We can accomplish very important work if we can get help. We represent a people's movement, for the deliverance of our people from a slavery which is intolerable to them and at the same time is a deadly danger to the outside world. I take it you agree with that, and do not require any proofs or discussion."

"Quite so, Herr Monck."

"You know what Frau Mueller was in the old days. I was the same and still am. Secrecy and intrigue are not of our choice; they are forced upon us by brutal tyranny. Our work is educational; we are not terrorists, and are determined not to become such under any circumstances. A great civilized people is being blindfolded, and we are trying to strip the bandages from their eyes. We take that as our duty, and are willing if need be to give our lives, and to risk torture in order to do it. What methods we are using to spread information is our secret, and we are sure you will understand that we do not speak any unnecessary word about them."

"I understand everything that you say."

"You know Frau Mueller and trust her as a comrade. There are reasons why she could not come. My position is such that I can enter and leave the country, and so I am serving as her messenger. I hope you will accept me as you would accept her."

Lanny had been studying the face so close to his own, weighing every tone of the voice and trying to make up his mind concerning the personality behind them. He said: "It will be necessary for us to speak with entire frankness, now and in our future dealings, if we are to have any."

"Quite so, Herr—what shall I say?"

"Schmidt," suggested Lanny—adding one more occupation to the miller and the village magistrate.

"*Einverstanden. Herr Schmidt.*"

"The woman you speak of is one I would trust without question. But I cannot forget the possibility that cunning enemies might have seized her and her papers, and might have sent one of their well-trained agents to me, knowing exactly how to pose as a member of her group."

"You are entirely right, and I expect you to question me and do whatever you find necessary to satisfy yourself. But if I prefer not to answer some questions, do not take it as a sign of guilt. If I were an agent of the enemy, I would answer freely."

Lanny couldn't help smiling. "An enemy might be more subtle," he remarked.

X

The grandson of Budd's didn't fail to realize that this was an important moment in his life. He had been expecting something like this ever since he had come out of Germany, and he had thought hard about how he was going to meet it. Now he said: "There are many things already known to me about Frau Mueller, and if you possess detailed knowledge about these, it will help to convince me that you really know her well and are her friend."

"I will tell you all that I can think of," replied the stranger. Speaking slowly and carefully, like one searching his memory, he began: "Frau Mueller is what is called a blond Aryan. She is, I should say, under thirty, and rather tall for a woman. Her voice is deep in tone. I have only known her about a year, and do not know how she used to look, but she is now thin and pale; her features are extremely delicate and you feel that she is a consecrated person. She has a strong sense of duty, and lays more stress upon personal qualities than most Marxists do. She has fair hair, rather wavy—naturally so, for she concerns herself very little with her appearance. She draws quickly and with accuracy; since I know nothing about art, I can only wonder at it. Also I might mention that she has a strawberry mark just above her right knee."

"I am sorry, I do not know her well enough to confirm that." Again Lanny couldn't keep from smiling.

The other replied, gravely: "Last summer her friends perceived that she was working and worrying too hard, and would persuade her to go to one of the lakes for a few days, and go in swimming; that is how I came to see the mark. She is utterly devoted to the memory of her husband and clings stubbornly to the idea that he is still alive and that she will some day help to set him free."

"You have not been able to find out about him?"

"No one has heard a word since he was taken away. We are all sure that he was murdered and secretly disposed of."

"You might tell me about his arrest, if you can."

"He was arrested with the young relative of yours, the Jew who played the clarinet and who had come to the Mueller home because of sudden illness—he had eaten some food which must have poisoned him. Frau Mueller went out to do some marketing, and when she returned she found that the home had been raided and her husband and your relative had been taken away."

"That is in accord with what she told me. Let me ask, did she tell you about her last meeting with me?"

"She was coming out of a tailor-shop carrying a bundle of clothing, when you came up to her and insisted on recognizing her in spite of her not wishing to be known. You told her that your relative was in Dachau and promised to try to find out whether her husband was there also. But she never heard from you."

"Did she tell you how she expected to communicate with me?"

"You were to come to a certain street corner, and she went there at noon every Sunday for quite a while, but you did not appear."

"Did she say I gave her anything?"

"You gave her six one-hundred-mark notes, and she wishes you to know that they were turned over to the group and used for our work."

"I never had any doubts about that," replied the American. "That is all convincing, Herr Monck; and now tell me what you wish me to do."

"We need more of those notes, Herr Schmidt. You understand that in the old days the workers' movements were strong because they could collect dues from millions of members; but now our group is small, and every time we make a new contact we risk our lives. It is hard for workers in our country now to earn enough to buy food, to say nothing of saving anything for literature. We must have help from comrades abroad, and it is the hope of Frau Mueller that you will consent to act as our collection agency."

Lanny hadn't needed to ask his last question; he had known what was coming, and his conscience had begun to ache, as it had done many times before. People expected so much of Mr. Irma Barnes, who drove expensive cars, dressed in the height of fashion, and lived in elegant villas in the most delightful parts of the earth!

Doubtless Comrade Monck also knew what was going on in that well-shaped and well-cared-for head. He went on quickly: "We have a cause, for which we are risking not merely death, but the most cruel torture which fiends in human form have been able to devise. It is not merely our cause, but yours; for if these fiends whom you know well are able to turn the resources of the country to armaments, you will be in just as great danger as we. Therefore we have a right to claim the support of decent and right-thinking men. I have taken a long and dangerous journey here and I do not feel embarrassed to put it up to you. I am not a beggar, I am a comrade, and

I present it as a matter of honor, of duty which a man cannot refuse without shame. You have seen innocent blood shed, and the blood of your murdered friend calls out to you—not for vengeance, but for justice, for the truth to be spoken, for a long and hard and dangerous job of truth-telling to be done."

XI

There it was: a voice from outside Lanny Budd, speaking the same words which his inner voice had been speaking day and night, haunting him and tormenting him, not letting him rest even in the most fashionable society, even in the arms of the ardent young Juno who influenced him so deeply. It was a commanding voice, and he thought: "If this rough workingman is an agent of the Gestapo, they certainly have a first-class school of elocution and dramatics!"

Poor Lanny! He had to begin the "spiel" which he had repeated so many times that he had got tired of hearing himself. "Genosse Monck, I don't know whether Tru—that is, Frau Mueller realizes it or not, but my money resources are not what people think. I have to earn what I spend; and while I spend a good deal, it is because I earn my money from the rich, and there is no way to go among them unless you live as they do. I have a wealthy wife, but I do not have the spending of her money; she does not share my political beliefs, and it is a matter of pride with me to keep my independence."

"I accept what you say, Genosse; but I cannot have any pride, because I am a hunted man, and I have not only my own fears, but those of millions of working people, whose need is so great that no one can exaggerate it. I am not using wild words, but telling you the plain truth when I say that to take my country out of the hands of the bandits is the most important cause in all the world today. Nothing else matters; literature, art, civilization itself—everything is gone if we fail. Surely what you have been through and seen must make it impossible for you to escape that truth!"

"How do you know what I have seen?" asked Lanny, with sudden curiosity.

"That is one of the questions I ought not answer. People wear masks in my country today, and they speak in whispers, but these whispers keep going all the time, and news spreads with great speed. That is why a few pieces of flimsy paper, which cost so little in money, can do such a tremendous work; they can start a fire which will never be put out. Believe me, I know the state of mind of our workers, and what can be done. Give us what money you can spare, and go out and help raise more for us."

"I have many rich friends"—Lanny was continuing his "spiel"— "but few who would put up money for the cause we are talking about. I fear that what I give you I shall first have to earn."

"Do what you can—that is all we ask. We balance our lives against your time."

"This is what I will do," said Lanny. "I will give you five hundred dollars today—it is all I can spare at the moment; but I will give you a thousand or two now and then, as I am able to earn it by selling pictures. I ask only one condition as to future amounts: I shall have to see your friend Frau Mueller and hear her tell me that this is what she wishes me to do."

"That will be very hard to arrange, Genosse."

"Not so hard, I believe. I am willing to come to your country. An hour ago I would have said that nothing could induce me to re-enter it; but I will come for the sake of this work."

"Will you be permitted to enter?"

"I feel quite sure there will be no interference with my movements. I have my business, which is *bevorzugt*—it brings foreign exchange to your country. I have been careful to preserve my status, and I know important and influential persons. Let me add this: I am keeping your secrets, and I expect you to keep mine. You may tell Frau Mueller about me, but no one else."

"I would not think of doing otherwise."

"*Sehr gut, abgemacht!* Let Frau Mueller write me a little note, in her handwriting, which I think I know, and signed 'Mueller.' Let her set a time, day or night, to be at the place where she was previously to meet me. I remember it well and have no doubt that she does. Tell her to set it a week ahead, which will give me time to make my plans and arrive there. You may assure her that I will take every precaution and make certain that no one is following me. She does not have to walk or drive with me, if she thinks it unwise; it will suffice if I see her clearly, to be sure of her identity, and hear her voice say two words: 'Trust Monck.' Surely that is not an excessive demand."

"*Das wird sich tun lassen!*" declared the visitor, with decision. "And let me add, Herr Schmidt, that I admire your way of doing business."

XII

So here was Lanny "putting his foot in it" again; indulging that vice, displaying that weakness which was the despair of his three families; that inability to say No to persons who prated about "social justice" and promised compensation to the poor at the expense of the rich. What did Lanny really know about this tough-looking customer? He used the language of revolutionary idealism with genuine-seeming eloquence; but what did that mean? The British Museum contained thousands of books filled with such language, and any day you might see bespectacled individuals, drably dressed and in need of haircuts, poring over these volumes, storing these ideas in their minds. They were repeated in thousands of pamphlets which might be bought for a few pence at bookstalls in working-class districts. Anybody could learn this lingo—just as anybody could learn to make explosives and to construct bombs!

Lanny argued the question with his wife and his mother—a silent, mental argument as he drove away from the rendezvous in Limehouse. Lanny wasn't at all sure of his own position, and was exposed to the assaults of these two persons and others who had claims upon him: Irma's mother, Emily Chattersworth, Sophie, Margy, all the other fashionable friends. "Why on earth should you give your trust to this man?" they would demand. "He says he isn't a terrorist; but what a small lie that would seem to him if he was! You say that Trudi Schultz is a Socialist; but a year and several months have passed since you saw her, and how do you know she hasn't changed under the stress of persecution? You say you wouldn't die of grief if they made a bomb and killed Hitler; but would you be prepared to have the Gestapo wring the truth out of them, and have the newspapers of the whole world publish the story that the grandson of Budd Gunmakers, otherwise known as Mr. Irma Barnes, had put up the money for the bomb? And what do you think will be our feelings when we are named as the mother, the wife, the mother-in-law, the friend, of this starry-eyed comrade of assassins? Have the rich no rights that a young Pink is bound to respect?"

Thus the ladies who surrounded Lanny; and then the men, better informed as to politics, would take up the argument. "Even granting that this powerful self-educated sailor or roustabout who calls himself your '*Genosse*,' your devoted comrade in Socialism, is really what you believe, what then? Maybe he will be the Ebert of the coming revolution, but again, maybe he'll be the Kerensky—the Socialist lawyer who took power in Russia, but couldn't hold it and was ousted by the Bolsheviks. Are you prepared to see that pattern repeated in Germany? If so, let us know, so that we may understand what sort of son, or half-brother, or in-law we have got!"

All this clamor, this tumult in Lanny's mind while he drove to the fashionable hotel where he had stayed on various occasions. It was after banking-hours, but the hotel management knew that his check was good and had no hesitation in handing him out ten ten-pound and two one-pound banknotes. From there he went to a near-by establishment which offered European and American currencies at a slight discount, and changed the notes for twelve one-hundred-mark and five ten-mark notes. With these rolled up and safely stowed in his breast pocket he went for a stroll along the Strand, where presently he was approached by a roughly dressed workingman who walked by his side and might have been saying: "Please, Mister, will yer give a poor bloke tuppence for a bite to eat?"—but he wasn't. Lanny slipped him something which might have been a pack of cigarettes, but wasn't. Genosse Monck presumably set out for Germany, and Lanny set out for the nearest art dealer's, so that he would be able to say to his wife with perfect truth: "Well, I saw another Sir Joshua, and it can be bought for something less than ten thousand pounds."

4

When Duty Whispers

I

THE day after Lanny's return from London he drove to the home
of the Pomeroy-Nielsons to tell a lame ex-aviator as much as he was
free to tell about his plans and his uncertainties. The Reaches, as the
place was called, was on the Thames River, a small stream at an early
stage of its career, but good for swimming and punting, and for tow-
boats on the other side where there was a path. The Pomeroy-Nielson
home was old, and built of red brick, added to through the years,
with many gables and dormer windows and one battery after another
of chimney-pots. Even so it was chilly, and American visitors shivered from early autumn to late spring. Lanny, having been raised in
Europe, didn't mind.

The head of the household was Sir Alfred, a crotchety but soci-
able old baronet with white hair, and mustaches still dark, who
had difficulty in paying his debts but was happy collecting materials
on the twentieth-century English drama. (This, he said, was something everybody else would overlook until it was too late.) His
children had gone out into the world, all except the eldest son,
whose family lived in his parents' home; an arrangement not always
successful, but this was a big rambling place, difficult to keep up,
and Rick's mother, who wasn't well, leaned more and more on his
wife for help in carrying the burden. The crippled son had had his
parents' support through the years while he was struggling to be a
writer, and now that he had made good as a dramatist he helped
pay the family debts and tried to keep his father from spending
more than he would ever have.

Another day of mist and light rain, and Lanny sat in his friend's study in front of one of those delightful fires such as they have in English grates, made of chunks of soft coal which sputter and emit oily juices and burn with large varicolored flames. The door was shut, and there was no chance of spies in this Englishman's castle, but even so, Lanny spoke low, because it was becoming an instinct. "Rick," he said, "I've got a contact with the underground movement in Germany."

"Indeed?" said his friend, his interest awakened at once. "Tell me about it."

"I had to give my word not to reveal any details. It's a message from some of the people I used to know there; you can guess if you choose. They want money, of course."

"Are you sure it's the real thing?"

"Pretty nearly; but I mean to make absolutely sure before I give much. I think I'll be going into Germany."

"The devil you do!" exclaimed his friend; then right away: "What's Irma going to make of that?"

"It'll have to be on some picture deal; or maybe you could ask me to get some material for an article."

"Look here, Lanny, you're not going to find it so pleasant living a double life."

"I know, but there're a lot of unpleasant things going on. I can't turn those comrades down flat, can I? After all it's our fight, too."

"Irma's bound to find out about it; and she'll raise bally hell."

"I know; but I'll try to spare her as long as I can."

A smile broke over the older man's face. How characteristic of Lanny—trying to spare Irma, not himself! Being an Englishman, Rick wouldn't say all that he felt, but his heart ached for this friend of his boyhood who was so kind and generous and had chosen such a very bad time to be born. Also, of course, Rick was interested professionally, for he had used Lanny's problem as the basis for a drama of class conflict, and the way things were going he might do it again. One cannot be a writer without thinking about "copy."

II

What Lanny wanted to talk about was not his marital situation, which Rick had known for a long time, but the services he might render to the cause they both had at heart. He enjoyed an exceptional position for several reasons. Being an American, he was supposed to be neutral in the quarrels of old Europe; also, being the type which Hollywood has chosen for its heroes, he carried to many people some of the glamour of the screen. His rich wife gave him access to the great and powerful, and his genuine occupation of art expert provided him with reasons for traveling from one capital to the next. Such a man ought to be able to give real help to the cause of social justice.

"I'm no writer or speaker," he said; "I guess I've had too easy a life, and I'll never be anything but an amateur. But I can get information, and there ought to be some place where I could bring it and have it put to use."

"Wickthorpe and Albany would give you a liberal expense account," declared the Englishman, with a bit of mischief in his eye.

"No doubt," said Lanny; "they've already sounded me out. But what use would they make of the information I brought them? All they want to do with Hitler is to set him to fighting Russia, and I can think of better uses for him."

"What, for example?"

"Well, let him fight Mussolini over Austria."

"Have Robbie get you a diplomatic post," suggested Rick, "and you can enjoy yourself setting all your enemies at one another's throats!"

"In the first place, my father will be the last man in America to have any influence in Washington; and as for our State Department, from what I hear it's going ahead just like your Foreign Office—business as usual. I want to take my information to some place where it will serve our cause."

Up to this time the best Lanny had been able to think of was to help Eric Vivian Pomeroy-Nielson to write plays, and occasional articles for those few newspapers and weeklies which were open to

ideas of a pinkish tinge. That was the tragedy of both men's position: when you adopted such ideas you condemned yourself to
futility; you became a voice crying in the wilderness, and you
might as well have been crying to the hawks and the buzzards, for
all the attention you got.

It had become worse than ever since Adolf Hitler had seized
power in Germany, nearly two years ago. Before that time Lanny
and Rick had had a party they could believe in and a press they
could help: the Socialist party of France and the Labor party of
Britain, groups which stood for peace and international understanding, the cutting down of exploitation and the power of financial
oligarchies. But how could anybody be for peace, with the Nazis
turning all the power of Germany to armaments, with General
Göring setting out to build an air force that would terrorize Europe? Lanny and Rick, pointing this out, were scolded by their former comrades and told that they were crazy. Rick found himself,
to his great embarrassment, on the side with Winston Churchill, reso-
nant imperialist, while Lanny Budd found himself agreeing with the
Army and Navy League!

Rick said: "Do you still have the idea that you can go into Germany and pose as a friend of Göring?"

"I don't know," Lanny said. "It won't do any harm to try. He
can only order me out."

"Surely he must know your record by now, Lanny!"

"I kept thinking that the last time; but you know how it is—
every bureaucracy commits boners. Also, you must remember, the
fat Hermann is so corrupt it's hard for him to believe that anybody
is honest. The offers he made to me must seem to him irresistible.
He may be thinking: 'Well, if the fellow has accepted, and is going
ahead, he'd have to be posing as a Leftist in England and France.'
That's the way the game is played; wheels within wheels and
treachery piled on treachery."

"You're poorly equipped for it, Lanny," warned the friend who
knew him best.

"I'm not so sure," was the reply. "The honest man may be very
successful as a liar when nobody believes a word he says. The

Nazis may be convinced that I'm deep, and they won't ever be quite sure how deep I am—how many levels there are to my tricks! All I want is to have one person who knows what I'm really up to."

"It seems to me you're starting on a darned uncomfortable career," declared the playwright.

III

It was a Friday afternoon, and Rick's eldest son came home for the weekend. Alfy, as he was called, was nearly ready for his career as an undergraduate at Magdalen College, which the English so unaccountably pronounce Maudlin; he had taken a bus from Oxford, and had had to walk quite a distance, so he arrived with shoes muddy and trousers wet, but with the glow of good health in his cheeks; he was just seventeen, tall and slender like his father, also his grandfather for whom he was named; dark eyes, dark wavy hair, a thin serious face. He was precocious, as he had to be in such a family; a conscientious student, much more to the left than his father had been at seventeen.

"Topping!" he said when Lanny asked how he was, and "Righto!" when his father suggested that he change to something dry. Lanny had promised to drive him some forty miles to the fashionable school where Marceline Detaze was a boarder, to bring the girl over for Sunday. Lanny didn't mind dashing about the country like that, regardless of weather. He was fond of this eager intelligent youth and ready to do his share in helping along the match which he had suggested when the two babies had made their appearance in a world torn by universal war. Beauty's daughter had been left fatherless a few months after her birth, and Rick's son had very nearly become a half-orphan before his eyes saw the light. Now it seemed to both Rick and Lanny that the dark shadow of conflict was looming over the world again; but no use to say it, for people didn't want to believe it and they knew how to believe what they chose. Perhaps some deep-hidden instinct guided the young people, causing them to pair off early and fulfill their chief function before it was too late.

It amused Lanny to discover that he was an elder; he didn't feel it, but Alfy did and looked up to him with great respect, as a person who had traveled widely, met the great ones of the earth, and had adventures concerning which it perhaps wasn't sporting to question him too closely. Was it really true that he had been taken into the dungeons of the Nazis and seen them beating a poor old Jewish banker to make him give up his money? "Do you think we'll have to fight those beggars some day? And is it a fact that we are letting them outbuild us in planes?" Lanny realized that here was somebody who took his statements seriously and didn't regard him as slightly daffy. "I'm taking more mathematics than I properly should," revealed the baronet's grandson. "I've an idea it'll be needed in our air service. But don't speak of that when the mater's around because you know how it would trouble her."

Poor Nina! Something shivered inside Lanny Budd at the thought that she might some day have to go through that agony again. One time was enough for any woman's life! He was moved to repeat to this lad the story of the strange experience which had befallen him when he was just at Alfy's age, living with the Robbie Budd family in Connecticut while Rick was flying in the battle of France; how Lanny had awakened at dawn, at the very hour that Rick had crashed and all but died, and Lanny had seen what he thought was his friend standing at the foot of the bed, with a red gash across his forehead—the same scar which the ex-aviator bore to this hour. "Your mother nursed him back to life," said Lanny. "It'll be deuced hard on her if she has to do it again." That was as far as English good form permitted you to go.

IV

Here came Marceline, dancing; she always seemed to be dancing, so happy, so young, so full of energy. She was a month or two younger than Alfy, but, after the way of the female, she had left him far behind; she was a full-blooming young lady while he was a gawky boy—so he felt himself, and was helpless in her hands. The daughter of Beauty Budd couldn't fail to be something special to look at, and this had been made doubly certain when her father had been so handsome a man as Marcel Detaze. The child had been well provided with mirrors and had listened to the talk of the ladies and the women servants of her household, so she knew what she had and what she was going to do with it. A slender, graceful figure, in accord with the fashions of the time; lovely blond hair with glints of gold; and that feature with which Lanny had been familiar in her father, eyebrows much darker than her hair, lending an unusual touch to her bold, high-colored charms. She was half American and half French, having the vivacious temperament of her father's people and the self-reliance she had got from a mother who had run away from a Baptist preacher's home and become an artist's model when no older than Marceline now.

Yes, indeed; poor Alfy, very much in love, and with a lack of worldly graces, was going to be hard put to it to hold her. She was the only child of a great painter whom everybody talked about, who, indeed, was on his way to becoming an "old master"; out of the proceeds of his toil Marceline was going to enjoy comfort and perhaps luxury. She knew there was London and Paris, she knew there were palaces and yachts, and that all such delights were within her reach. That was the way she had been brought up. Lanny, who would have had it different if he could, had to take the position of a spectator, here as in so many other places in that *beau monde* which enveloped and conditioned him, he was forced to remain silently acquiescent.

This Beauty-in-the-Budd, as Rick called her, sat wedged in the front seat between the two men, and Lanny drove and listened to her chatter. Words poured out in floods, because life was so wonderful it could not be restrained. Her talk was all about persons: about girls in the school whom Alfy knew or should know, about boys who were coming to The Reaches for the weekend dances and parties. When they got together they all chattered like this, at least the girls did. They remembered what they had said in other places and repeated what they had heard others say, and it was like the conversation of a family of chickadees in the hedge. Quite a contrast between this and the talk which Lanny had been carrying

on with Alfy; he wondered: "Did women all have to be chickadees
or was it simply the way they were trained?"

This young couple were in love with each other, but in their
own competitive way which outsiders could not regulate. Marceline
resented having her destiny decided, and insisted upon starting all
over again on her own terms. She said that Alfy was as solemn as
an old owl, and persisted in teasing him into activity and making him
miserable in the process. She hadn't the slightest interest in such
matters as politics and only the vaguest notion as to what mathematics might be; but there was nothing she didn't know about the
arts of coquetry, and she practiced them on every personable young
man who came in sight—generally those who were older than Alfy
and therefore more likely to throw him into a panic. It was all rather
cruel, but it was nature, and doubtless it was better to settle these
affairs with quips and teasing than for the young men to butt each
other like the stags in the forest.

V

Back at The Reaches they had dinner, and afterward young
friends from the neighborhood came in. Things were just the way
they had been in Lanny's boyhood, when he had first visited here
and met Rick's playmates, including Rosemary, who had become
his first sweetheart and had sat out in the moonlight while Kurt
Meissner played the piano and they dreamed wonderful dreams.
Now it was a new generation, sons and daughters of Lanny's playmates, but they seemed exactly the same. Fashions hadn't changed
much—they came in cycles; skirts were short, and then they were
longer, and the same with haircuts. Love was the same, only they
talked about it more freely; laughter was the same and no less of
it, in spite of wars past and others on the way. Lanny's first visit
to this home had been in the spring of 1914, and nobody had been
worrying; he wondered now, in the autumn of 1934, would they be
worrying next summer or the one after that?

They moved the rugs and furniture from the center of the drawing-
room, and put on phonograph records and danced. "Hot jazz" had

come from America, and now a new thing called "swing," and the young people shivered with delight, cherishing their favorite records and raving over them endlessly. They had forgotten that the old dances existed—all but a few like Marceline, to whom Lanny had taught everything he knew. When he danced with her, the others were apt to stop and watch; this had happened in many a drawing-room and even on the floor of a casino; they could have got engagements and made their living that way if they had cared to. When Marceline danced, something arose inside and possessed her; she became a creature of music and motion, expressing delight and at the same time knowing that she was doing so, exulting in the attention she was getting. Joy and pride in equal measure, each stimulated the other.

It had been that way from earliest childhood, the first toddling steps that Lanny had watched her discovering for herself; he had praised and encouraged her, and others had done the same, and so they had made a dancer. She would dance alone for the pure delight of it, but she would find a mirror to practice before, and would be thinking of those who would be watching her later on. She came by this honestly, for her mother had loved to be looked at, first as a model and then in the world of fashion; she had been what was called a "professional beauty." Marceline's father had painted pictures to be looked at; and while he had professed to be indifferent to praise and had refused sternly to promote his own work, Lanny suspected it was because he had met with so many disappointments that he had been forced to paint for himself. Surely the primary purpose of art is to communicate to others, and not alone to the artist!

VI

Back in Wickthorpe Lodge, as his temporary home was called, Lanny settled down to normal domestic life, something he had denied himself for a long time. He enjoyed the society of his lovely young wife; he dressed himself properly and took her to social affairs, carefully avoiding the expression of any ideas with which she might disagree. He reminded himself that after all she was only twenty-six, and her mind wasn't entirely matured; it was no use expecting her to know everything or even to wish to know it. He played with his little daughter, teaching her dance steps and going with her to see the new kittens. He played the piano, and read books he was interested in; he went over his card-files and carried on his business correspondence with the help of a stenographer who came when summoned. He enjoyed peace and quiet, and thought with an ache in his heart: "If only men would learn to let one another be happy!"

But all the time he was like a man waiting for a court to pass sentence upon him and for a bailiff or sheriff to come and take him away. He counted the days and tried to guess when Genosse Monck would probably get back to Berlin and a letter from Trudi Schultz, alias Frau Mueller, might be expected. He felt certain that she would write; the conspirators would need all the money they could get, and she would hardly leave him in uncertainty. If no letter came, it could only mean that Monck was some kind of fraud.

As the days passed, Lanny fell to guessing about that—what kind of fraud would he be? A terrorist—and had he now bought his gas-pipe and his nitroglycerin, or whatever it is that bombs are made of nowadays? And who would it be? Hitler or Stalin or Trotsky, Hermann Göring or Pierre Laval, or—God forbid!—Ramsay MacDonald or King George of England? Lanny couldn't believe that this man of intelligence and force was a common swindler who would spend the money on wine and women; no, he was some sort of revolutionary, or else a well-trained agent—in which case Lanny ought to get a letter from Trudi Schultz that would be written under duress or else would be a forgery. Rather difficult to lose yourself in the music of Liszt or Chopin while speculations such as these were haunting your mind!

At last, a letter with a German stamp and a Berlin postmark! A plain envelope, with no sender's name; Lanny shivered, knowing that it was the court sentence. He went to his own study to open it, and standing in the middle of the floor he read:

Dear Mr. Budd:

I have many new sketches which I believe will interest you, and would like to have your help in marketing them. If you are in Berlin on Nov. 6 I would be happy to meet you and show them. If that date is not convenient, any date thereafter will do.

Respectfully yours,
Mueller

A careful and proper note that could not excite the suspicions of any Gestapo man, or of a wife who might have an impulse to pry into her husband's mail. The writing, of German type, might have been a man's or a woman's. Lanny, having had some correspondence with Trudi at the time he arranged for her drawings to be published in *Le Populaire*, now got her letters from his files and sat down and studied them with a lens. More important yet, there were two little sketches with the letter; one was a head with which Lanny was most familiar, his urbane self in his most coming-on mood. Trudi, heart-broken and terror-racked, was saying: "Bright and shining one, dwelling in safety in a happy land—that fortress built by Nature for herself against infection and the hand of war!"

The other picture was of Hansi Robin with his violin, and that, too, had its magic. Ludi and Trudi Schultz, a pair of pure-blooded Aryans, had been invited to the palace of Johannes Robin, Jewish *Schieber*, to listen to Hansi and his New England wife playing the music of the German Beethoven and the Jewish Mendelssohn, the French César Franck and the Hungarian Reményi. This bright little sketch was a reminder of that evening; its message was that of Schiller's hymn and the Ninth Symphony, that all men become brothers where the gentle wing of joy is spread.

Of course it might be possible that a skilled draftsman had imitated Trudi's style; a signature can be forged, and many an expert has been humiliated by a clever imitation of a painting. But Lanny thought this was the young woman's work. He studied the sketches under a glass and saw that the lines were clear and clean, which would hardly have been the case if she had been working under duress. He had what he had been looking forward to for more than a year, a chance to meet her and perhaps to ask her some questions.

For that and that alone he would be willing to go into Naziland again.

VII

Lanny had now come to a parting of the ways in his dealings with his wife. Should he go to her and say, straight out: "I have established a contact with the underground movement in Germany and I propose to go there to make sure about it"? That was the course he would have preferred to take; but was it consistent with his pledge of secrecy, with the protection he owed to people who were risking their lives? It had been all right to tell Rick, who was a comrade, and would keep his lips sealed without even being warned. But would Irma keep a secret when she didn't want to and didn't think that she ought to? When she considered herself being greatly wronged and ardently disliked the persons who were wronging her?

Fanny Barnes, Lanny's large and aggressive mother-in-law, was talking about paying them a visit. Would Irma, nursing a grievance against her husband, fail to pour it out to her mother? Would Fanny feel enjoined against telling it to her brother Horace and to her brother-in-law Joseph Barnes, one of the three trustees of the Barnes estate? Would she even withhold it from those inquisitive dowagers with whom she went about in London? Of course she wouldn't, and the story would be all over town in a few days.

The American heiress and her prince consort were conspicuous people; the eyes of gossip were watching them day and night and the tongues of gossip were busy with them, not merely over teacups and telephone, but by the medium of high-speed rotary presses. Let Irma speak a cross word to her husband at the breakfast table and the footman would whisper it to Irma's maid, and she would pass it on to the maid of the Dowager Lady Wickthorpe at the castle, who in turn would tell it to her best friend in London and it would appear in the *Tatler* before the end of the week. Perhaps not with the names, but so indicated that all the world would know who was meant. "A popular American lady of many millions whose husband amuses himself as an art expert is being made unhappy because he persists in consorting with the Pinks and making leftish remarks in the most exclusive drawing-rooms. Just now it is said that he is distributing the commissions on his picture sales to those '*Genossen*' who are secretly opposing the German Führer. Friends of the Nazi regime in London—and there are many of them, highly placed—are reported making sharply pointed remarks on the subject."

No, that wouldn't do; either Lanny had to keep the secret from Irma or else give up his project altogether. But did he have a right to give it up? Did he owe no debt to those who were sacrificing everything for the cause he professed to believe in? Is a man's only obligation to his wife? Can it even be said that a man's *first* obligation is to his wife rather than to what he believes is the cause of truth and justice? Does a marriage ceremony give a woman the right to take charge of a man's thinking and tell him what is true and what is false? Has a woman the right to try to do that, no matter how rich she is or how sure of her opinion?

Whatever her rights may be, it is certain that she has the power to make him uncomfortable if he persists in making her uncomfortable. Lanny wasn't the first man to have made that discovery—the telephones and rotary presses of ancient Athens had spread the report that the left-wing philosopher Socrates was in hot water all the time, and there were even rumors concerning the head of the state, the august and ultra-fashionable Pericles. As for the grandson of Budd's, who was neither philosopher nor statesman, but only a playboy trying his best to grow up, he didn't want to hurt anybody in the world and was truly thinking about the happiness of his wife when he argued that he wasn't going to get into any trouble and that it was really a kindness to keep her from knowing things which would cause her so much needless anxiety.

He was so scrupulous that he took the trouble to make sure that every statement he made to her should be the exact literal truth. It was true that Germany was an excellent hunting-ground for old masters at the present time. The aristocracy was impoverished, and so were many kinds of business men; taxes were rising, and the only persons who were prospering were those who controlled the raw materials and the plants needed for the making of war goods. Americans, on the other hand, were having a New Deal. Robbie Budd and other soreheads said it was "inflation," and maybe they were right, but anyhow it was paying dividends to some groups, and a few of them had learned to think of rare and famous paintings as a safer form of investment than even gold or government bonds.

Zoltan Kertezsi, Lanny's friend and associate who had initiated him into this distinguished business, happened to be in Paris. Knowing him well, Lanny had figured how to get exactly what he wanted from him. He sent a wire: "You may recall that I mentioned having learned of a delicate small Hubert van Eyck in Germany I believe same might be purchased but there are social reasons why I hesitate to make the approach if I had a wire from you inquiring for such a picture it would facilitate matters will divide commission."

That would sound perfectly natural to Zoltan, who possessed a battery of harmless devices for making contacts with broken-down Erlauchten and Durchlauchten and causing them to think they were performing a cultural service by permitting their art treasures to be added to some famous American collection at a high price. Zoltan had remarked that such people must be handled as if they were made of wet tissue paper; so, before the sun had set, Lanny received a reply from Paris: "I have possible market for small Hubert van Eyck and recall that you once mentioned having seen such a picture in Germany would it be possible for you to enable me to see a good photograph of it and possibly get a price?"

VIII

This telegram the schemer took to his wife, who was, as he expected, much upset. "Why, Lanny! You said that nothing would ever induce you to set foot in Germany again!"

"I know, but I've been thinking it over. It appears that Hitler is going to stay in power for a long time, and whether I go in or stay out isn't going to make any difference. It seems foolish to give up the best market I have—to say nothing of all our friends there."

"But will the Nazis let you in?"

"If they pay any attention to me at all, they'll know that I'm bringing them foreign exchange which they need badly. If they don't want me, they'll refuse me a visa and that'll be that."

"Lanny, it terrifies me to think of your walking into that trap again. I know how you feel about conditions there and what you'll be doing and saying."

He had foreseen this and given careful study to his reply. "If I go there on a business trip, I'm certainly not going to say anything to offend my customers, and I certainly don't want any unfavorable publicity. Also, if I have you with me, I'll be under obligation not to do anything to spoil your pleasure."

"Why don't you tell Zoltan where the picture is, and let him attend to it himself? You surely don't need the money."

"I doubt if Zoltan could handle this deal. It's a matter of some delicacy—the picture belongs to an aunt of Stubendorf, and you know how it is with the old nobility, especially the females. She has met me, but probably doesn't remember my name, and I'll have to get Seine Hochgeboren to introduce me all over again. We could run out and see Kurt, if you wouldn't mind."

"Lanny, it makes cold chills run all over me! Would you still expect to make Kurt think you're a Nazi sympathizer?"

He smiled. "Kurt and I were friends long before the Nazis were invented, and he won't mind if I tell him I've lost my interest in politics. He'll think that's natural enough, now that the Robin family is out of Germany. Remember, I presented Kurt with a whole library of four-hand piano compositions—enough to keep us busy for a full week if we try them all."

Making playful remarks and evading like a lively young eel, Lanny managed to get through this difficult conversation. Irma was so concerned to have him do what she called "behaving himself" that she grasped at every straw of hope. More than three months had passed since he had come out of Naziland, and during that time he hadn't done anything indicative of madness. It had been his family duty to attend Freddi's funeral, but he hadn't revealed any deep emotion over it, and now it was possible for Irma to think that, having got his near-relatives safe, he might consider his duty done and give his wife a chance to enjoy the happiness which was her birthright.

Also, he was proposing a trip; and it was a part of Irma's upbringing, it was the psychology of everybody in the world she knew—they were always ready to take a trip. They had the newest and sportiest cars, and kept them supplied with gasoline and oil, water and air, each in its proper place; they had fancy leather bags, and valets and maids to pack them at an hour's notice. At home they would say: "Let's run down to Miami and drop in on Winnie," or: "Let's drive out to California and see how Bertie's getting along with his new wife." Over here it would be Biarritz or Florence, Salzburg or St. Moritz—it didn't matter so long as it was some place to go. If you didn't have much to do when you got there, you could always move on to some other place.

Now it was Berlin. The time of the year was pleasant; a bit chilly, but bracing, and Irma had lovely furs. They would take the night ferry to the Hook of Holland, and from there a one-day drive. They would visit Stubendorf in Upper Silesia and be guests at the Schloss, which seemed romantic to them both. In Berlin there was the Salon, and the concerts, and a social season getting under way. Yes, it was possible to think of many agreeable things to see and do. Irma said, as usual: "Let's go"; but then, frowning, she added: "Listen to me, Lanny. I mean it—if you do anything to make me miserable the way you did, I'll never forgive you as long as I live!"

IX

They waited only to see Robbie, who was due in London. He arrived, outwardly calm, inwardly exultant over his successes. Zaharoff had agreed to take a million dollars' worth of Budd-Erling shares and had given Robbie permission to mention this to several of his former English associates. Denis de Bruyne had taken three million francs' worth and was getting up a syndicate of his friends. Also Emily Chattersworth was coming in; and now Robbie, at request, sat down with Irma and laid the proposal before her. She said that she owed as much to the Budd family as any old Greek spider or wolf or devil; she wrote to her uncle Joseph, instructing him to descend into that vault where her treasures were stored. It was far beneath a Wall Street bank building, protected by layers of steel and concrete and having spaces between filled alternately with water and poison gas; a place which met all the biblical requirements, where neither moth nor rust could corrupt nor thieves break through and steal. From the many large bundles of securities Mr. Joseph Barnes was ordered to select half a million dollars' worth of those which had brought in the smallest returns during the present year; he was to sell them at the market and replace them with Budd-Erling preferred plus common as a bonus.

Irma wasn't supposed to come into full control of her fortune until she was thirty; but she had taken to expressing her wishes, and so far the trustees had not found it necessary to oppose her. Uncle Joseph couldn't find any fault with the business reputation of her father-in-law or with her desire to promote the fortunes of her acquired family. Of course, Robbie's capable ex-mistress saw to it that the news of Irma's action was spread among her fashionable friends, and Margy, Dowager Lady Eversham-Watson, and Sophie, former Baroness de la Tourette, and all the other ladies with large incomes and still larger appetites were eager to hear about this opportunity of enrichment. "Son," exclaimed the promoter, "we've got the world by the tail!"

He was surprised to learn that Lanny was going into Germany again, but he didn't say much about it, because he was wrapped up in his own affairs and never too curious about other people's. He took it as natural that his son should have decided not to cut off his own nose to spite his face; it wouldn't do Hitler any harm or Lanny any good. Robbie took the projected trip as a sign of returning sanity and so expressed himself to the young wife, thus confirming what she was trying so hard to believe. "Encourage him to make all the money he can," said the father. "He'll manage to find uses for it, and it ought to be at least as much fun as playing the piano."

So Irma's own father would have told her if he had been alive. Missing him greatly, she was moved to take Lanny's father as a substitute. She told some of her troubles, not in a complaining way, but as one asking for guidance, and Robbie, who had had the same troubles with a too trusting idealist, helped her to understand his foibles. "We all think we're going to change the world when we're young," he explained. "When we get older we realize what a tough proposition it is, and in the end we have our hands full taking care of ourselves and those for whom we are responsible. Lanny's pink measles are lasting longer than most cases; but be patient with him—he has to cure himself."

"I know," responded Irma. "People won't let you tell them things. Maybe I'm that way, too."

"Remember this," added the shrewd man of affairs. "Lanny doesn't make so much money selling pictures, but it's an intellectual and artistic occupation and brings you into contact with interesting people."

"I know that, Robbie. Don't think I'm regretting my marriage."

"You understand how I feel about it. I've always left Lanny free to follow his own path, but I haven't given up hope that he may come to take an interest in my affairs. I thought I was training him for that. Now, here's a new opportunity—if he could be brought to see it and come in with me, I could push him right to the top in a year or two. You know what a quick mind he has."

"Oh, indeed!" assented the wife. "And I'd be glad if it could be managed. But it would never do for me to suggest it."

"Bear it in mind and perhaps find a chance to drop a hint. Just think what he could do for us in Germany, if only he could get over his political notions and learn to take business as business. You know what connections he has; and you could help him, as Beauty has helped me so many times."

Irma shook her head. "I'm afraid it's no go, Robbie. Lanny hates the Nazis with a sort of personal hatred."

"He's been too close to them. If he'd seen the other governments of Europe getting started he'd understand there isn't much choice among them. They all put their opponents down with brutality, because they're afraid; but when they're safe in the saddle, they settle down and you can hardly tell them apart. In a few years the Nazis will all be wearing frock-coats."

"I can't argue with Lanny," said the young wife, sadly. "He's read so much more than I have, and he thinks I'm just a dumb cluck."

"You have a lot more influence than you know, and between us we may get him interested in airplanes." Robbie said that, and then after a moment added: "Give him time. There are no perfect husbands, you know."

Irma nodded. There were unspoken thoughts between them. She had been taught the value of her money and understood why Robbie valued her so highly as a wife. But they were both of them well-bred persons, who would act on what they called "common sense" but wouldn't put it into words.

BOOK TWO

Some Hidden Thunder

5

Des Todes Eigen

I

IN GERMANY the highways are smooth and straight and lined with well-kept trees, many of them fruit-bearing. New roads were being started, and some of these were wonderful—four-track model *Autobahnen* with all the crossroads over- or underpassed. Lanny said these were military roads, intended for the invasion of the bordering countries; he added that they were built with American money, borrowed by the German Republic and by its member states and cities. Lanny rarely lost an opportunity to make some disapproving remark about what was going on in Hitlerland, and Irma had learned not to comment, because if she did an argument might start and Lanny would overwhelm her with facts and figures.

What she saw in this country was clean, well-kept streets and houses, and the people in them the same. Everybody appeared well fed, and working from dawn to sunset; a peaceful and industrious land if ever there was one. Adolf Hitler was carrying out literally his promise to provide work for everybody; factory chimneys were smoking day and night—but don't point this out, because if you do, Lanny will say that it's preparation for war, and anybody can do that if he means to make war, but what is the good of it if he doesn't? And all these Stormtroopers marching and singing war-songs! Irma doesn't know the words of the songs, and it is enough for her that the men are young and good-looking, well dressed and happy, singing in tune and marching in step. But don't say that, either!

Irma has lived all her life in free countries, and finds it hard to realize that there are any other sort. She has never witnessed an act of violence in her twenty-six years on earth, and she has difficulty in

84

making real to herself the idea that such acts are frequently committed. To be sure, she knows that the Robins were plundered of
their possessions, and she cannot go so far as to think that Lanny
was having a nightmare when he saw old Solomon Hellstein being
beaten with whips in one of the dungeons of the Gestapo. But Irma
finds reasons if not excuses for these events. She knows that Johannes
Robin, in spite of his being their friend and very agreeable company,
was an unconscionable *Schieber*, a speculator in the currency of the
German Republic. That seems to her a different thing from getting
rich by building up public utility corporations after the fashion of
the late J. Paramount Barnes. If you should mention such matters as
stock-watering and the pyramiding of holding-companies, Irma
would stare at you blankly, perhaps thinking you some sort of an-
archist; for she has been taught that these are the processes out of
which the prosperity and greatness of America were built.

Also, the misfortunes of the Robins were brought on them by
those two sons. Hansi, the out-and-out Red, asked for the worst of
trouble and escaped it only because Lanny and his wife managed to
lure him out of Germany in time. The Communists had had no
mercy on their class enemies, and why shouldn't Hitler dose them
with their own medicine? As for Freddi, who called himself a Socialist, Irma was willing to admit that he had been harmless, like her
own husband; but she considered them both dupes of shrewder men,
who were using them for a while and would throw them aside when
the time for action came. If in the confusion of a great social change
some of the innocent had got mixed up with the guilty, that was a
tragic accident, and what Irma had got from it was an intense desire
to keep her husband from putting his head into a bear-trap.

II

It was evening when they arrived in Berlin. They had telegraphed
the Adlon for reservations, and they found newspaper reporters waiting; they were prominent people, well known in the city, and their
coming would be made much of by the Nazi-controlled press. The
"blood purge" of last summer had pretty well killed the tourist traffic,

so important to the German economy, and the *Regierung* wished to establish the idea that all this was ancient history, an unfortunate necessity at the time, but now to be forgotten by everybody both at home and abroad.

Two shining American *Zelebritäten* would be interviewed amid the popping of flashlight bulbs and would have their opinions on art questions taken seriously. They had come with commissions to buy old masters and prepared to pay precious American dollars. They were expecting to run out to visit their old friend General Graf Stubendorf, also Herr Budd's boyhood friend, Kurt Meissner, the composer. They would be interested to visit the autumn Salon, conducted under the personal supervision of the Führer in order to exclude degenerate modernist stuff. Herr Budd agreed with the Führer on this subject—he was the stepson of a French painter, a sound representational artist, and had had the honor of showing to the Führer personally one of the best-known Detaze portraits. All of this had been published before and was in the *Archiv* of the newspapers, so the reporters had it prepared in advance. When, in answer to a question, Herr Budd stated that he was a non-political person, that pleased everyone, for the Nazis wanted all the world to be non-political except themselves.

Lanny telephoned to Stubendorf and made certain that both their friends were at the estate. Seine Hochgeboren renewed his invitation, and next morning they set out for Upper Silesia over another of the fast highways. It is a coal-mining region, and great numbers of factory chimneys were pouring smoke into the chilly air of approaching winter. The district of Stubendorf had been a part of Poland ever since the Versailles treaty, and if you asked why all the coal was burning and factory wheels turning in this vicinity, any German-speaking person would tell you that no German wanted war, but every German was determined to get back into the Fatherland. The arming and drilling—one of the commonest sights of the countryside —was for the purpose of making clear the German will to the whole non-German world. If they wanted war, they could have it; if they wanted peace, let them get out of German lands.

This was an old problem for Lanny Budd; he had listened to it being discussed at the Paris Peace Conference, day and night, from every possible point of view. He had seen with his eyes the elder statesmen known as the "Big Three"—Wilson, Lloyd George, and Clemenceau—crawling round on their hands and knees over a huge map spread on the floor, trying with colored pencils to mark out some solution of an insoluble problem. The various sorts of people were all mixed together, and if you tried to work on the principle of self-determination, you would have districts and even villages chopped up. In Stubendorf itself was a large Polish population, but they were mostly poor peasants, whereas the well-to-do and educated people were German; the latter were in position to make most of the noise and did so. They looked upon the Poles as a subhuman race, born to be ruled by the *Herrenvolk*, and now this *Volk* had a Führer who was going to bring it to pass. The unanimity with which he was supported made a great impression upon Irma; but she mustn't mention the fact, because Lanny would say: "It's because all the dissenters have been murdered or put into concentration camps; and what sort of unanimity is that?"

III

They were welcomed to the modernized and comfortable Schloss, which didn't seem so grand to Lanny now as it had at the age of fourteen. Seine Hochgeboren was an old-fashioned Prussian nobleman, very serious and formal, but intelligent within the limits of his training. He considered that he was doing something quite modernistic in receiving two fashionable but untitled Americans into his home. He had done so after he had met them in Berlin and carefully made sure that their money was real; also that they met influential persons, and could be discreetly pumped as to the attitude of Britain, France, and America to events in the Fatherland. The General Graf, a high-ranking officer of the Reichswehr, accepted the new government as it was his duty to do, and if he had any reservations in his mind no foreigner would be permitted a glimpse of them. He had no apologies to make, but took the dignified position that what Germans did became right as soon as they had done it.

Irma was impressed by this German aristocracy, almost as much as by the English. They were age-tested and from this they derived assurance; compared with them she felt herself a *parvenue*—though of course she wouldn't admit it, even to herself. However, she watched what they did and said, and made mental notes. She had learned that when she didn't know what to say, she could keep quiet, and this suited well her placid disposition. Afterward she could ask Lanny about the subject, finding it convenient that her husband knew so many things. His statements could be depended upon when they had to do with music, poetry, painting, or with history—everything except politics and economics. The fact that he was bored by the aristocracy and made fun of them was perhaps another way of being aristocratic; sometimes it impressed his wife and sometimes it annoyed her.

After a proper period of sociability Lanny revealed the purpose of his journey. He showed the telegram from Zoltan and asked if he might be permitted to inspect the Hubert van Eyck which was in the possession of the Baroninwitwe von Wiesenschmetterling. Seine Hochgeboren froze up and said that he doubted very much whether his elderly relative would consider parting with this family treasure; Lanny, who had encountered this attitude many times and accepted it as part of the bargaining process, explained suavely the cultural importance of great collections which were being made in America, their effect in bringing sweetness and light to a well-to-do but spiritually backward people. Such was the European tone toward America, and Lanny had learned from Zaharoff that one must belong to that nation in which one is putting over a deal.

The Baroninwitwe lived in the Neumark, not far off their route returning to Berlin. If it had been in well-to-do but spiritually backward America, the General Graf would have called up his aunt and made sure she was at home and told her about the matter. But this was the spiritual but frugal Fatherland, and so the master of the Schloss contented himself with writing a note and giving it to Lanny. However, the American was fairly certain in his own mind that his host would send a telegram or otherwise give warning to the old lady, so that she would demand a high price or perhaps refuse to put a price until she had taken his advice.

IV

Kurt Meissner still lived in the five-room stone cottage which the lord of the castle had set aside for his use. It was the Nazi party which had paid Kurt enough money to build a studio near by—much like the one Beauty Budd had built for him at Bienvenu. Kurt's gentle blond wife was becoming what the ladies call plump, and had presented him with four children who were perfect models of what the Nazi leaders approved but so rarely exemplified. The eldest was six, a pink-cheeked and solemn-eyed little boy, who already played the piano better than Irma Budd had ever learned to do with the help of the most expensive teachers.

Kurt was the same long-faced, severe-looking man, prematurely aged by war and suffering. Being slightly older than Lanny, he had always patronized him, and now felt gently sorry for him because of the way he was wasting his life. While Irma practiced her German with the admiring *Hausfrau*, Kurt took Lanny to his studio and played his new piano sonata; Lanny listened attentively, and thought: "It is rather dry. Kurt is now imitating Kurt. That is, when he's not imitating Bach. The fountain of his inspiration is drying up. That adagio is almost a plagiarism of Beethoven. Those stormy passages are forced." And so on. It makes a great difference in what mood and with what predisposition one approaches music; this same sonata had just been rendered by its composer to an audience in Breslau, which considered him the new Germany's most promising composer and had listened to the work with rapt attention.

Lanny knew what he was expected to say, and said it. He knew how to deal with Kurt, because for fifteen years or so he had considered him a great man and his spiritual mentor. He knew all the phrases of admiration and devotion, and he must use them now, and tell himself that he was doing it for Kurt's own good. Some day this Nazi nightmare would pass, and a noble soul would awaken and rub

his eyes and be glad that Lanny had stood by those ideals to which
they had pledged themselves in boyhood—of love and service to all
mankind and not merely to blond Aryans.

By tacit agreement they left the subject of politics alone, and did
not once mention a family of Jewish *Schieber*. Kurt was free to assume that since Freddi was buried and the rest were free, that unhappy page might be turned and forgotten. When Irma was alone
with Kurt she took the occasion to tell him that Lanny was conducting himself much more sensibly now; Kurt was glad to hear this, and
said so. Kind and fundamentally good, but weak—this was the composer's judgment of his boyhood playmate, and Lanny let it stand
that way.

Living a double life, had been Rick's phrase; and here it was.
Lanny was a spy in Hitlerland, a secret agent in the enemy's country.
It is supposed to be romantic and exciting, but that is in the imagination of persons who have never experienced it. There may be some
who like to lie and cheat and find pleasure in outwitting other persons, but Lanny was not among them and it hurt him every time he
said something to Kurt which did not represent his true beliefs.

He had to remind himself that Kurt had done this himself, as a
German agent in Paris right after the armistice. Would it occur to
him now that Lanny might be returning the compliment? If so, the
composer would probably not reveal it; he would dig deeper under
Lanny's position, as entrenched troops do in wartime, mining and
countermining. Lanny watched for signs of this; for he feared that
Kurt was deeper than he and would probably outwit him if it came
to a real showdown. They would be two antagonists in darkness,
groping for each other's throat; yet they would still be friends, using
the language of love and, strangely enough, feeling it.

Yes, Lanny decided that no matter how hard he might be fighting
Kurt, he would still be yearning after him, with true old-fashioned
German *Schwärmerei*. All the time they were playing four-hand
piano compositions, Lanny knew this with every fiber of his being:
while they prayed in solemn ecstasy with Bach, while they danced
in gilded ballrooms with Mozart, while they labored in spiritual an-
guish with Beethoven. Brothers have fought against brothers, and

fathers against sons, in all civil wars; and here was a new kind of war, spreading rapidly all over the earth: National Socialism against true Socialism, racialism against the brotherhood of humanity.

V

The widow of the Baron von Wiesenschmetterling lived in a fine old mansion entirely surrounded by potato-fields. At present they were bare and dark, but if you had come in midsummer you would have found them green, and would have seen a hundred or so Polish women, clad in what appeared to be potato-sacks, patiently hoeing the furrows from dawn to dark. They were brought into Eastern Germany by long trainloads, and all Germans agreed that they had been providentially created for two purposes, to produce potatoes and to produce potato-hoers.

The mistress of the estate was a white-haired lady with a large bosom covered with black silk and old-fashioned ruching. Over it she had placed her best string of pearls, saying plainly that if you thought she was hard up and was going to sell any of her art treasures, you were vulgar intruders. She looked upon all Americans as dubious characters, and what business had they ever had to come and kill Germans? She held herself stiffly, and did not unbend even after she had read the note from her nephew. She could find no fault with the appearance of this young couple, or with the German speech of the man; the young woman had sense enough to keep her mouth shut, and that helped. The noble widow, *gnädige Witwe*, consented to let them inspect her picture gallery; and only when Lanny told her that she had real treasures and began to explain their qualities to his wife, did she realize that he was an exceptional person. On the field of the arts even the most implacable of enemies can lift their visors and salute each other.

The Hubert van Eyck was only about sixteen inches wide and twenty inches high, but a great deal had been crowded into that limited space. It represented a stained-glass church window, and so was art within art. It was done with extraordinary finesse and exactness, so that you forgot it was small and thought you were in church.

It portrayed the Blessed Virgin seated upon a throne, clad in a jeweled robe of remarkable splendor, really almost good enough for an archbishop. Above her hovered three cherubim who, presumably because they were young and active, didn't need any robes. Golden sunlight shone upon the varicolored scene, and appeared to be as bright as when it had been painted more than five hundred years ago. It was marvelously contrived to look like glass and at the same time to look real.

Lanny never tried to do business in a cheap way, to depreciate what he was buying; no, indeed, he was an aristocrat among experts, and dealt only in what he could praise. He delivered his "spiel"— oddly enough, the Americans use that German word, while the Germans call it a *"Rolle."* He was trying to help his country to acquire worthy art works which might some day stimulate American painting. His clients were able to pay for the best; but naturally, there being many old masters, Lanny would recommend those which offered the most for the price. He explained that it was his practice never to make an offer for a painting; he invited the owner to state the price at which he or she was willing to sell, and he would cable that price to his client, and if the offer was accepted he would come in a day or two and pay the sum in cash.

The young expert examined several other paintings which the Baroninwitwe didn't say she would be unwilling to sell; he gave her a list of these, and would be pleased if she would quote him a price on each. He wasn't wasting his time or hers, for while he examined them he was busily thinking of persons who might purchase this and that. He left the severe old lady his addresses in Berlin and England; and when they had left the mansion and were driving past the potatofields, Irma said: "Do you think she wishes to sell?"

He answered: "It depends upon the state of her mortgages." He explained that most of these estates had been loaded down with debts in wartime; many of them had come under the shadow of the *Osthilfe* scandal, which had had so much to do with the Nazis' getting into power.

Irma had heard talk of this affair, but had paid no attention to it, so Lanny told how the government of the Republic had paid vast sums to the great Prussian landlords to help them in reconstruction, and most of the money had been wasted. Hindenburg's son had been involved, and that had helped to break down the old President and force him into a deal with the "Bohemian corporal," as he had been accustomed to call the founder and Führer of National Socialism. The question whether this van Eyck would ever be viewed in the United States might depend upon whether the aunt of Seine Hochgeboren had been able to collect her share of this respectable German graft.

VI

They returned to Berlin, arriving late in the evening. Next morning Lanny attended to his mail, and Irma telephoned some of her fashionable friends and was invited to lunch with the Fürstin Donnerstein. Lanny was invited, too, but he said that the ladies were much happier when they were able to gossip alone, so he would go and have a preliminary look at the Salon. It so happened that this was Tuesday, the sixth of November, the day on which, exactly at noon, he was supposed to be standing on a certain street corner in a working-class district of this *Hauptstadt* of Naziland. It happened also to be Election Day in the land of Lanny's forefathers, and Robbie Budd was predicting that the American people would come to their senses and elect a Congress opposed to the lunacies of the New Deal.

If a handsome young *Ausländer*, wearing a neatly trimmed little brown mustache and a fall overcoat to match, goes driving in a sport-car in a part of Berlin given up to six-story tenements inhabited by the poor, he will attract some attention, but not so much as you might suppose. The poor do not go strolling on work days, and they have their problems to think about; at noon they are hurrying to get something to eat and do not linger outdoors on a raw gusty day. If a young *Herrschaft*, as such a stranger is called, parks his car and gets out and strolls, they will glance at him with a moment's curiosity, but no more; some *Strassenjunge* may follow him and beg for a pfennig, but that is all. If he stops on the corner and raises his hat to a slender and frail-looking young woman wearing a worn and

drab coat and a felt hat with no ornaments, that will cause no sensation, for the poor people of all city streets have learned the facts of
life and accept them. If they see the woman acknowledge the greeting and start to walk along with the man, the *Polizei* will not interfere, and everyone else will make allowances, knowing that life has
been terribly hard for the women of Germany for a full two decades.

However, this wasn't the customary sex encounter, but something
which the Geheime Staats-Polizei might have paid a small fortune to
know about. Lanny Budd was saying: "So it's you, Trudi!" And
Trudi Schultz, staring straight before her, was murmuring: "You
may trust Monck. I know him well."

"Are you really sure?" Lanny persisted.

"I would trust him as much as any person I know."

"I ought to be told a little about him, Trudi——"

"Frau Mueller," she corrected, with a swift glance behind them.
"Tell me where I can communicate with you through the next
weeks."

"I expect to be in England until just before Christmas and then to
return to my home in France. My mail will always be forwarded."

"Are you reasonably sure of its not being opened?"

"As much as anyone can be. No one in my home tampers with it."
Trudi had met Irma and knew her attitude.

"Thank you with all my heart, Herr Schmidt. It is very important
to us all. And now I ought to go. We are too conspicuous, walking
together."

"I want very much to have a talk with you, Frau Mueller. I have
come a long way for it. Can't you let me drive you for a while?"

"It is a dreadful risk to take!"

"I cannot see how. You go on walking down this street and I will
get my car, and after I make sure I'm not being followed, I'll come
up behind you and stop. You step in, and we'll be gone out of sight
before anybody has time to give a thought to us."

"I will attract attention in your car; I'm not dressed for anything
so elegant."

"They will think I am taking home a new cook." Lanny could
grin even at such a tense moment; he still hadn't suffered.enough.

"They will think something less polite," replied the young woman. "But—all right, I will go on walking until you come."

VII

They drove, and no one paid any attention to them. Soon they were out in the country, where there was no possibility of being overheard, so they could drop the feeble disguise of "Mueller" and "Schmidt." Trudi could look at him without fear, and he could take a glance at her now and then when driving permitted. As an art lover he had said that her features represented a triumph of some idealistic sculptor; he had never seen a woman's face more expressive of high thinking and fine feeling. When he had first met her four years ago, a student of drawing and a Socialist devotee, he had been struck by her look of alertness, of concentration upon whatever new idea was presented to her; by the way she held her head—high-spirited was the term he had chosen to describe her. She made him think of a pure-bred racehorse; watching her at work and seeing her intense concentration and delight in achievement, he had thought: "Here is a real talent, and I must help it to recognition."

In those far-off happy days it had been possible to believe in ideas, and to discuss them freely, and to feel sure that in the long run the soundest would prevail. In those days before Hitler, Trudi Schultz had had color in her cheeks, color that came and went with the excitement of achieving a good portrait or with the discussion of Socialism versus Communism, democracy versus dictatorship. Ludi and Trudi—Lanny had been amused by the musical combination—had argued as Lanny himself had so often done, that the reason there were so many splits and so little real co-operation among the left-wing groups was not so much conflict of ideas as of personalities; the lack of tolerance and open-mindedness, of the old-fashioned virtues of unselfishness and love. The reason one advocate could see no good in the other's point of view was that both were jealous and greedy for power; the movement was racked and rent because men thought about themselves and not about the masses they professed to serve. Listening to this ardent young couple at a gathering of the intelligentsia in the school which he and Freddi Robin were helping, Lanny had thought: "This is the true German spirit, which Beethoven and Schiller dreamed of spreading over the world. *Alle Menschen werden Brüder!*"

Now Ludi was gone, and his wife was a fear-ridden, grief-tormented soul, who had not had a moment of real peace or happiness for a year and a half. She twisted her hands together as she talked; her finely chiseled nostrils quivered, and now and then tears would start in her eyes and run down her cheeks untouched. These cheeks were colorless, and Lanny could be sure that her work, whatever it was, left her no time and perhaps no money to eat properly. He would have liked to suggest taking her somewhere for a meal, but he knew this would be an intrusion and an error of taste.

She wanted to bring him to the same state of mind as herself, to make it impossible for him also to enjoy peace or happiness. Since she was taking the risk of being seen with him on streets and highways, she would put the occasion to use by impressing upon his mind the tragic need of help under which she and her comrades labored. She would persuade him to lend his powerful aid in saving Ludi if he was still alive, or if he had perished, in saving his comrades and his cause.

VIII

Lanny had never had a chance to tell any of these German friends what he himself had seen and experienced. Now he listened to the familiar tale of cruelties beyond the imagining of decent human beings. Trudi told him about the fate of this person and that whom he had met at the school receptions. Pale and shivering with horror, she declared:

"They seize men and women, old and young—they respect nobody. They carry them off to the woods outside the city and beat them to death and bury them where they lie or leave them for others to find and bury. They drag them into dungeons which they have in the cellars of police stations and party headquarters, where they torture people to make them confess and name their friends and comrades. Things happen, so hideous that you cannot bring yourself to talk about them; nothing worse was ever done by the Spanish Inquisition, or by Chinese torturers, or by savage Indians in America."

"I have heard a lot about it," responded Lanny. He decided not to say more at present.

"Germany has become a land of spies and betrayers; you never know whom you can trust. They teach the children in the schools to spy upon their parents and denounce them; they torture perfectly innocent people because of something some relative has done. No servant can be trusted, no employee, hardly a friend. It is impossible for half a dozen persons to meet, even in a private home; one dares not express an opinion or even ask for news. You never know at what moment of the day or night will come a banging on the door, and it's a band of Stormtroopers, or the Gestapo with one of their vans to carry you away. You live in the shadow of this awful thing and can never get it out of your mind. Because I am a woman, and because they have so many sadists and degenerates among them, I carry a vial of poison, ready to swallow it before they can lay hands upon me."

"Listen, Trudi," he said. "Why don't you let me help you to get out of this country?"

"And desert my husband? Oh, Lanny, you must know I couldn't do that!"

"I hate to say it, but what is the chance of his being alive and not having been able to send word to you for a full year and a half? Surely some of his fellow-prisoners must have been released!"

"You can't tell anything about it, Lanny. Everything happens in the dark. They have people in their solitary dungeons whose names are not known. And even if I knew that Ludi was dead, I would have to stay for the sake of the others. How can I rest while my dearest friends are undergoing these torments and in such dreadful need of help?"

"But can't you perhaps help them better from the outside?"

"I have watched the exiles, from Russia and other countries; they are impotent people, cut off from their roots. They lose all sense of reality. They become strangers to their own people. They live in a little false world all their own."

"But you are an artist. You could put what you know and what you feel into your work. You could be another Käthe Kollwitz."

"Some people have to stay here and keep the spark of freedom alive. There are millions of Germans who need us—all the old party comrades, and those who voted for us, the workers and the intellectuals. Most of the time we do not know who they are, but they are still alive and surely have not forgotten all that we taught them in the old days."

"But how can you reach them, Trudi?"

"That is something you ought not ask. I am under a solemn oath not to give a hint of our methods without the consent of two other comrades; and if I ask their consent and reveal you to them, there is one more chance of a leak. I don't mean that you might talk about us, but somebody else might and cast the burden upon you; we might be betrayed, and someone might decide that you were to blame. You must realize how it is—we may have a Gestapo agent working among us right now, and so your name would become known to them. It is ever so much better as it is, with no one knowing about you but Genosse Monck and myself."

"All right," said Lanny. "You know that I trust your word."

"I give you my assurance that we have a way of reaching the people, and telling them the truth about what is going on in Germany and in the outside world. We have told them the truth about the Reichstag fire, and about the number of those murdered last June and July. The Nazis admit less than one hundred, but we have listed more than twelve hundred and our lists have been circulated. The Nazis know that, and of course they are hunting us day and night; so far I do not think they have any clue. Even if they get some group it will be small; we have built ourselves like the worm, which can be cut into sections and each will go on growing by itself. We are bound to succeed in the end, because a great people will not let themselves be dragged down into such degradation."

IX

Lanny Budd had done some reading in the literature of martyr-dom. He knew that liberty has nowhere been won without blood sacrifice, and now he was learning that it cannot be kept without further payments. Through his mind would come at times a procession of verses which he had read and learned: his Shakespeare, his Milton, his Byron; also *Egmont, Wilhelm Tell, Die Räuber*—there had been lovers of freedom in Germany, too. Kurt Meissner had taught his American friend some verses about the Tirolese innkeeper Andreas Hofer, who had taken Innsbruck by storm from the forces of Napoleon; when the students came in a festival and wanted to sing his hero deeds, he made them a speech, one line of which Lanny had never forgotten: *"Wir sind all des Todes Eigen"*—we are all death's own.

A grown-up American playboy realized that this was an important moment in his personal life. Something inside him was humbled and shamed, and he felt that he wanted to live the second half of his life to better purpose than the first. He said: "Just what is it you wish of me, Trudi?"

"There are many ways you can help us abroad. We may not always be as successful as we are now, and we may need such things as radio tubes or a printing-press or paper, things it would be too dangerous to obtain here at home. For the moment, our great need is money. Monck has told me what you said about your own position——"

"Never mind what I said, Trudi," broke in the grandson of Budd's, in one of those emotional moments to which idealists are liable. "I'll get you some money now and then. I'll take it as my job."

So here he was, pledging himself again; forgetting that he was a married man, that other people had claims upon him, a vested interest in him; taking upon himself that task which Irma considered the height of lunacy, the overthrowing of the National Socialist government of Germany. It would become his job to earn the money, and a handful of social outlaws hiding in tenement rooms were going to print leaflets or something, and perhaps poke them under doors or leave them on park benches, and by this means overcome the power of the Geheime Staats-Polizei, of the Sturmabteilung and the Schutzstaffel and the Wehrmacht, with their enormous armaments, their tens of thousands of highly trained experts, their incessant watchfulness and skill in torturing and killing!

"I ought to have some way of reaching you, Trudi," he said.

"I have racked my brains to think of a safe way. I am a poor workingwoman, living in a tenement, and I would not dare receive letters from abroad. Nor do I want to trust anybody else with the secret about you."

"Can Monck come to England or France now and then?"

"He can arrange it, but it is difficult and risky. How often are you in Germany?"

"I never intended to come at all, until I got your message. However, I can arrange to come occasionally."

"That would be expensive for you, Lanny."

"I travel on my wife's money," he told her, with a smile. "She wishes it that way, and I have long since abandoned my scruples in the matter. I tell myself that hers is capitalist money—she doesn't have to earn it and it is her pleasure to spend it. Most of what I earn I will bring to you."

"Won't your wife wonder what you are doing with so much?"

"Happily, the idea will not occur to her. It is the mark of elegance among the rich that you do not bother your head with money. If the whim takes me, I buy a picture and put it in my storeroom, and I may not remember to mention it to my wife."

"It sounds quite fabulous. People of our sort cannot imagine such a way of life."

"I have had opportunity to observe the effects of inherited wealth, and for the average young person it is a sentence to futility and boredom. It cuts the mainspring of activity; the person no longer has to do anything, and so he doesn't, and if he tries, he fails nine times out of ten. You at this moment are providing the strongest incentive to labor that I have ever had in my life."

She couldn't keep from smiling. "Lanny, you are an angel! If I believed in such, I would be certain that you had been sent from heaven."

"I am planning just now to purchase three of these celestial creatures. They are cherubim, which I believe is a high order in the hierarchy; but they have no overcoats and I cannot imagine them in the climate of Berlin in the month of November."

X

The angel from overseas was moved to tell his friend about his visit to the Baroninwitwe, and by this means succeeded in amusing her for several minutes. He mentioned that the price of the picture could hardly be less than a hundred thousand marks, and so, if he sold it, he would have several thousand for the comrades. The question was, how was he to get it to her?

Trudi could think of no safe way for them to meet except as they had just done. She gave him the name of a street intersection close to her own home, so that she could without great trouble arrange to pass there at noon every day. "I will arrange to do my marketing at that time," she told him. "The only thing that will keep me away is being ill, and in that case I will write you that I cannot send any drawings at present."

Said he: "It would be inconvenient if you were ill on the day when I had a large sum for you. Therefore, you can do a service to the cause by keeping well."

"I will do my best, Lanny——"

"I impose a condition as part of our bargain: that you pledge yourself to use part of the money to purchase one liter of milk per day and drink every drop of it yourself. You show that you need it, and this is to be considered doctor's orders."

"All right," she said, gently; then, after a pause: "When you see me on the street, do not speak to me, but watch in what direction I start to walk; then you may get your car and follow me, and after a couple of blocks you may stop for me. I will walk on the right side of the street and will be carrying a package. If I carry it in my left arm, so that you can see it, you will know that it is all right to stop;

but if I carry it in my right arm, it means there is something wrong, and you will drive on around the block, and not stop until the package is held in the crook of my left arm."

"*Sehr klug!*" he said, amused. "And now one thing more: suppose I am able to get you quite large sums of money, could you put them to use?"

"What do you mean by large?"

"A hundred thousand marks."

"*Herrgott!*" she exclaimed. "I never thought of anything like that!"

"It may not be easy to spend large sums without attracting attention. Do you handle them yourself, or do you pass them on to others?"

"Mostly I pass them on."

"And won't these others be curious as to where you get them?"

"Naturally; but they know they are not free to ask."

"They doubtless remember that you know me. Won't they think of me as the possible source?"

"No, for they have read about you in the Nazi press. They'd be more apt to think of the Robin family."

"How much money can you handle effectively at present?"

"I hadn't expected to meet that question. Two or three thousand marks at a time, I should think."

"And how often?"

"We could spend that every month, if we had it."

"All right," he said; "here is some to start things going." He took from his pocket a package containing a couple of thousand marks and slipped it into her hand. "Don't make the mistake of moving too fast," he warned. "Spending money is a conspicuous thing, and the larger the sum, the greater will be your risk. I'd hate to be the cause of your having to drink the contents of that vial."

XI

During the year and a half that Lanny Budd had been living a double life he had been troubled by the thought of what his friends in Berlin must be thinking about him. There was no help for it—

except for this one comrade, and he wanted to make certain about her. "Listen, Trudi," he said. "It may be a long time before I see you again, and there are some things I want you to have clear in your mind."

He took her back some thirteen years, to the early days of the Nazi movement, when Kurt Meissner had introduced him to a son of the head forester of Stubendorf, a young enthusiast who had loaded him with literature of the movement, and later on had taken him to call on Hitler. He had taken him a second time a year ago; and Trudi said she had read about that visit in the papers; all the comrades knew of it.

"Of course they assume that I'm a renegade," he remarked.

"They don't know what to think," she answered. "They know that you saved Freddi Robin."

"Let them stay in uncertainty. You know how I make my money, and to do that I have to meet persons in power. I took one of the Detaze paintings to Hitler in Munich, and that fact was worth a small fortune to me in sales and in the opportunity to go where I pleased and to meet the right people in Germany. That is the world we live in. All I want to be sure is that you understand, and that no matter what I do, you will not doubt my good faith."

"I promise that, Lanny."

"In the course of my efforts to help the Robin family, I achieved the honor of a personal acquaintance with General Göring. He seemed to take a fancy to me—I admired his prowess, and he found pleasure in displaying it. That might be useful some day."

"It sounds utterly fantastic, Lanny."

"In every revolution and in every war there have been men playing a double role and dealing with both sides. It isn't according to my taste, but I am beginning to see possibilities in it. My father is going in for the manufacture of airplanes, and he will be expecting me to be useful to him; in return I may feel justified in making him useful to me. I don't want to say any more about this, except to be sure that whatever happens, you will not mention your connection with me or your knowledge of my role."

"I'll die before I do it, Lanny."

"I have an idea which may be worth while and about which I would like your advice. You know that the fat General seized the palace of my Jewish friends, and you know the fine paintings which were a part of his loot. It happens that Zoltan Kertezsi and I selected nearly all those paintings, and it would be easy to find a market for them in America; they might bring several million dollars, and there would be a commission of ten per cent. That is one way by which I could get large sums of money for you, and it would amuse me to persuade an old-style Teutonic robber-baron to contribute to his own undoing."

"*Knorke!*" exclaimed the woman.

"There is this drawback, that Göring would be getting nine marks for every one that I got. Thus I might be strengthening the Nazi cause far more than I was hurting it. What if he used the money to buy my father's airplanes?"

Trudi thought before answering. "He will buy the planes with the money of the German people, never with his own. For himself he is building a grand estate on a peninsula up in the North Sea. He is a greedy hog, and I do not believe he would give a pfennig to the government, but rather take away all that he dares."

"Then it wouldn't be a mistake to offer to sell his pictures?"

"If he wishes to sell them he could do it without your help—isn't that true?"

"Yes, no doubt."

"Well, then, let him spend what he pleases upon his own glory, and we will use our share to tell the German people what lives their false leaders are living."

"O.K.," said the American—a phrase which is understood wherever the movies go. "I may have the honor of being invited to that estate, which he is calling Karinhall in honor of his deceased wife. If I succeed in becoming his art adviser, I will appear in the next few days at our rendezvous wearing a feather in my hat!"

"Not too large a feather!" said the anxious woman outlaw.

6

On Top of the World

LANNY went dutifully to the Salon, and then, returning to the hotel, reported to his wife that he had found a new painter who impressed him greatly. She for her part was full of news about the doings of important personalities in Berlin, a lot of it scandalous; but repeating it wasn't regarded as anti-Nazi activity—you did that in whatever world capital you were visiting. Human nature was the same everywhere, only worse the farther you came toward the east; now, somewhat alarmingly, the east appeared to be coming westward.

Lanny said: "A bright idea has hit me: all those pictures that Göring got from Johannes, he probably doesn't care about them and might like to have them sold."

"Do you suppose he would let you?" exclaimed the wife. She realized that this would keep her charge out of mischief for a long while.

"It can't do any harm to offer. I thought I'd call up Furtwaengler."

"Don't mention what you have in mind," said the cautious wife.

He called the official residence of the Minister-Präsident of Prussia, and found the young staff officer disengaged. He and Lanny always outdid each other in politeness, almost like two Japanese, and now they went to it over the telephone. The Oberleutnant said that he had read of Lanny's arrival and intended to call him up; Lanny said: "I have got the better of you." He asked after the officer's family, and about his health, and that of Seine Exzellenz the Minister-Präsident General—he had a long string of titles, but four were enough for ordinary conversation. Furtwaengler replied: "*Er sitzt auf der Spitze der Welt,*" and added: "I believe that is good American." Lanny guessed that this was another case of movie influence.

"If you are free this evening why don't you run over to dinner?" said the subtle intriguer. "Bring your wife, if you think she would enjoy it."

Irma dressed herself in raiment fine but scanty, and Lanny in tails; the staff officer appeared in his black and silver dress uniform with the white skull and crossbones, and his tall and angular country wife in a low-cut gown which revealed her shoulder-bones both front and back. A good *couturier* would not have let her make these disclosures, but she was the daughter of a cheese-manufacturer from Pomerania and didn't yet know her way about *die grosse Welt*. In Prussia wives have to pay for their husbands, and then for the most part they stay at home and devote themselves to their three K's, which in English are three C's: Cooking, Children, Church.

II

In that large and elegant hotel dining-room, with obsequious waiters bowing around them and exposing dishes of steaming-hot foods, Irma presented an expurgated version of the conversation of the Fürstin Donnerstein, while Lanny mentioned casually his intimacy with French financiers and revealed himself living next door to an English castle and dropping in informally upon staff members of the Foreign Office. When the four were alone in the drawing-room of the Budd suite, the two ladies sat in one corner and talked about ladies' affairs, while Lanny expatiated upon the menace of French foreign policy and the untrustworthiness of French political careerists.

The Oberleutnant in his turn talked about the one and only party and its plans and hopes. A strange thing, to which Lanny could never entirely adjust his mind: the young S.S. man knew that his American host had penetrated to the very heart of the party's treachery and cruelty, had witnessed soul-shaking sights and lost one of his dearest friends to the Nazi terror; but the fat General, Furtwaengler's boss, had seen fit to take it all as a joke, and the staff officer had apparently decided that it had been a joke to Lanny as well. A curious quirk in their psychology, which an outsider had to try hard to understand: their collective egotism was such that they were rendered incapable of understanding other people's minds, and in spite of their utmost cunning they remained naïve and vulnerable; as if a man should put on heavy armor for battle, but leave a large opening over his solar plexus.

The National Socialist German Workingmen's party had achieved in the past two years such triumphs as had never before been known in history. They knew they were going on to fresh triumphs; they had it in their hearts and were full of the *élan* which it gave them, the "strength through joy." They sang exultant songs about the future, they dressed themselves in fine uniforms and paraded with banners celebrating it, they organized colossal and magnificent pageants to tell all the world; they were quite literally intoxicated with their own grandeur. "Germany belongs to us today, tomorrow the whole world"—and how can the world fail to enjoy the prospect as much as we?

Here came these two Americans—rich, to be sure, but what is mere wealth compared with titles and honors, fame and glory, vision and *Geist?* Wealth is an incidental, one of the rewards of courage and daring; all the wealth of the world lay exposed before the Nazis, as Pizarro had found it in Peru and Clive in India. This American pair had the wit to see what was coming and to climb onto the Aryan bandwagon. They enjoyed the privilege of meeting Seine Exzellenz the Minister-Präsident of Prussia, Reichsminister of the German Empire, Air Minister, Commander-in-Chief of the German Air Force, Chief Forester of the Reich, Reich Commissioner, and so on and on; they were permitted to address him informally, to joke with him and share some of his confidences. How could they fail to be overwhelmed by the honor, and to march in spirit in his triumphal progress?

Lanny had ordered the best champagne for dinner, and afterward he served brandy and liqueurs, and while sipping them lightly himself he kept his guest's glasses full. So the blond young Aryan's face became rosier than ever and his talk more naïve. He revealed the fact that Germany was going to win the Saar plebiscite; the matter had been arranged with German thoroughness and everything would go through *planmässig*. He didn't go so far as to say that the murder of Barthou had been arranged, but he remarked with a smile that it was certainly most convenient, and that in future French politicians would be more cautious in their policy of *Einkreisung*. He expatiated at length upon the wonders of the last Partyday, and became lyrical in describing the ecstatic state of mind of the rank and file. *Sieg heil! Sieg heil!*

So at last, when Lanny Budd, associate of noble lords and multi-millionaires, thought it safe to remark: "I have some information which might be of interest to Seine Exzellenz," the Oberleutnant did not hesitate for a moment, but said: "*Herrlich, Herr Budd!* I will speak to him the first thing in the morning."

Afterward, when Herr Budd told his fashionable lady about this success, she remarked: "My God, we certainly paid a price for it! Can you imagine anything duller than that poor country gawk he drags along with him?"

III

The old-style Teutonic robber-baron sat in the sumptuous private apartment of his official residence, the room with the large black table and the gold curtains of his own designing; however, the lion cub had been banished, having grown too big for play-acting. The vast bulk of the Minister-Präsident General was covered in one of those gorgeous uniforms, to the designing and construction of which so large a share of the clothing industry of the Reich was now devoted. This one was of pale blue with a darker blue stripe, and insignia of which Lanny did not know the meaning. Whatever the uniform, the wide sash was never omitted, and the large gold star with eight points hanging from two white ribbons.

"*Ja, Lanny!*" bellowed the fat man when he saw his guest. His broad face with heavy jowls, usually sullen, lighted up with pleasure, and he seized the American with a large moist hand—but not flabby —grab it hard to protect yourself! It pleased his whim to be genial in the presence of this favorite of fortune, of whom he had made use in an especially successful coup, the plundering of one of the richest *Judschweine* in Germany. Surely it couldn't be that Hermann Wilhelm Göring laughed loudly in order to conceal embarrassment!

"*Grüss Gott, Hermann!*" responded Lanny, seeing that he had been advanced in social status.

"*Also!*" exclaimed the fat warrior. "You are on the way to becoming a crown prince of the air lanes!"

Lanny was taken aback and showed it. "You have indeed a good secret service," he remarked.

"Did you ever doubt it?" queried the host. Then, more seriously: "Your father should come to see me; it might be to our mutual advantage."

"*Na, na!*" smiled Lanny. "You are not financing any airplane factories outside the Reich."

"*Aber,*" countered the Air Minister, "we buy planes, and would buy more if they were good."

"One for a sample?" retorted the other. He knew he was supposed to be impudent; he was the court jester.

"How can you say such a thing? Who could ever say that I took anything without paying for it?"

"Who could say it if I couldn't?"

At this the stout General turned into a Kris Kringle, whose round belly shook when he laughed like a bowl full of jelly. It was to be doubted if anyone had had the nerve to address him in that fashion for many a long day.

"*Setze dich, Lanny,*" he said, in fatherly fashion. "Seriously, tell Robert Budd that if he gets that thousand-horsepower engine, I will lease his patents and he won't have to argue about the price."

It was quite disconcerting. Lanny felt himself enveloped in a net of espionage, and shuddered inwardly, thinking of Trudi. But then he realized that Robbie had been talking his project all over Paris and London, and of course Göring's agents would have sent him word. But what a contrast in efficiency! Robbie had been to consult the authorities both in England and in his own country, and both had high-hatted him; but here this old German *Raubtier* sent for him and invited him to name his own figure! It boded ill—and especially since Lanny knew that Robbie would be apt to accept the invitation!

IV

This was a stag affair, and Irma had not been invited. They lunched at a table wheeled into the room, a meal consisting of a boiled turbot with thick rich sauce, and then of *Hasenpfeffer*. Apparently the great man didn't give any heed to notions of diet; he stuffed himself in the middle of the day, and pressed quantities of food upon his guest. He talked fast and with his mouth full, so that he was more repellent even than usual; but Lanny laughed at his jokes and admired his capacities and did not let himself be shocked by sexual anecdotes. When the waiters had served the food the General growled: " *'R-r-raus!*" and they vanished and did not return until he pressed a button.

Now was Lanny's opportunity to show that he could and would bring information of value to the military organizer of Naziland. He had given thought to the problem and chosen his course with care. He would never tell Hermann Wilhelm Göring anything that would be of real use to him—unless it was something that Hermann Wilhelm Göring was sure to know already. The visitor would be prodigal of information of this sort, and it would be accurate; so Seine Exzellenz might be kept on the alert, hoping for something new. If he asked directly, Lanny would say he didn't know, but would try to ascertain. How long he could make out with such a program he couldn't guess; Rick had said: "Not very long," and Lanny had answered that any time the General grew tired of his society, he could find some more compliant *Spitzel*.

The host led the talk to France, and Lanny told him about the anti-Nazi fixation of Barthou and how greatly his fellow-plotters had been disconcerted by his death; speaking to the man whom he suspected to be the real murderer, Lanny pictured the plight of a Foreign Minister who had interposed himself in the effort to save his royal guest and had been shot through an artery of the arm;

he might have been saved if any of his staff had had the wit to tie
a handkerchief about the arm and turn it with a stick or a fountain-
pen; but no one had had such wit and he had slowly bled to death.
Lanny went into the gory details, thinking he might be able to spoil
the murderer's appetite for Moselle wine; but no such effect was to
be noted.

The visitor talked about the new Foreign Minister of France,
whom one of his financial supporters had called a *fripon mongol*.
The "rascal" part was true, Lanny said; and as for "Mongolian," the
innkeeper's son had learned to joke about it himself, because of his
swarthy complexion, thick lips, and strangely slanted eyes. Göring
asked if he really had Mongolian blood, and Lanny said: "Who could
guess? The races have been so mixed in that part of the world."
Lanny knew exactly how to please a pure-blooded blond Aryan.

The visitor told what he knew about the character of Laval, and
little of it was good. He talked about the two hundred families who
were reputed to rule France, and expressed the opinion that Laval had
become the two hundred and first and would from now on serve
their interests automatically. "Their own wealth concerns them so
deeply that they have no time to think about their country. It would
not trouble them too greatly if you were to bomb the rest of it, provided you would agree to spare their mines and steel mills and other
valuable properties."

"A good idea," said the wholesale killer. "I will take it up with
them."

Lanny would have been worried if he hadn't felt certain that
Göring had already done it.

V

The luncheon table was wheeled out, and the fat General lighted a
fat cigar and settled back in an overstuffed chair in a pose of con-
tentment. They were alone, and the time had come for a showdown.
"Tell me, Lanny," said he, "have you given any thought to the idea
of helping me now and then?"

"I have given much thought to it, and I find it troubles me, because I lack a sense of competence. I doubt my ability to be worth my keep."

"You might let me be the judge of that, my friend. I have had some experience in judging men."

"In this case you are far too generous. When one has been an idler for thirty-five years it is not so easy to change."

The judge of men fixed his gaze intently upon his guest. "Do you find yourself under any special strain at this moment?" he inquired.

Lanny smiled. "Only that I have eaten enough for two."

"I would ask you to do nothing but what you are doing now. It is your privilege to meet many persons who are of interest to me. I know that you are curious about them and amused to watch their minds work. Could you not find it worth while to come and tell me what you have observed? Suppose, for example, I should suggest that on your next visit to Paris you should cultivate Pierre Laval, study his temperament, and help me to understand what approach to him will be most effective."

"Surely, Hermann, you have plenty of people doing that sort of work for you!"

"I have not tried to conceal the fact from you; but I do not know one of them I would trust so well as you."

Lanny, who hadn't been born yesterday, but something over twelve thousand yesterdays ago, knew exactly how much weight to give to such a remark. "You honor me," he said. "And, as I told you, so long as it is play, I can enjoy doing it. But if I accept compensation from you, at once I feel under pressure; I begin to wonder whether I am earning my salt, and decide that I am a complete *Tau-genichts!*"

"Your New England conscience," said the fat General. "I have never before had an opportunity to observe it in operation."

"It is sometimes inconvenient to its owner," replied the grandson of the Puritans; "but those who deal with him find it useful."

"You must understand that we Prussians also have our code, though perhaps not the same. I should not feel comfortable asking favors of you unless I was in position to make some sort of return. Can you not tell me of anything you would accept?"

VI

So Lanny had what he had been angling for, and it was time for him to jerk the hook. Said he, promptly: "When you put the matter to me that way, Hermann, I will make you a straightforward answer. I have what I suppose is a sort of profession; at any rate, it has enabled me to earn more than I need, and spares me the embarrassment of living on my rich wife. For lack of a shorter name I call myself a *Kunstsachverständiger*."

"I am informed as to your reputation," replied the Minister-Präsident; and it appeared as if he considered himself the one to jerk the hook. "You may perhaps have heard that I am building a rather good hunting-lodge for my friends. I want to furnish the place adequately, and nothing would please me more than to have your advice on the subject. Would you undertake to buy some art works for me?"

"What I had in mind was something different from that. I was thinking of the old masters which were in the palace of Johannes Robin. I don't know whether I ever mentioned it, but my associate and I selected and purchased those paintings."

"I have heard many comments upon the excellence of judgment displayed."

"We gave a great deal of study to the collection, and I think it really is good. My idea was that possibly your tastes might be different from mine, and you might care to turn some of those works into cash. I have prepared a list of what was paid for them, and would be glad to try to find purchasers at the same prices. It will cost you nothing, let me add."

"But I thought you were going to suggest some way by which I could reward you!"

"The purchasers would pay me ten per cent commission. That is the basis on which I work with them."

"But isn't it fair that I also should pay?"

"I have a rule which I have never broken, that I do not take commissions from both parties. I represent one or the other, and try to serve his interest."

"*Aber*—why shouldn't you serve *my* interest and let *me* pay the commission?"

Lanny maintained his winning smile. "You are kind and I am grateful; but it happens that I have a standing arrangement with several clients in America who are building up collections. They expect to add ten per cent to the prices I quote them; so why not let them go on doing so?"

"*Famos!*" exclaimed Göring. "But mightn't I get higher prices with the help of your persuasive skill?"

"I doubt it, for the reason that Johannes did his buying before the depression, and it will not be such an easy matter to find purchasers now. I am only offering to try, and am telling you in advance that I may have to come and confess failure. Johannes was a man who wanted what he wanted, and more than once he insisted upon paying prices higher than I considered wise from the business point of view. On this list which I have prepared from my records I have stated the actual prices paid, and in a few cases I have penciled in a lower figure, which I fear is the most I could advise any of my clients to pay now. It is, of course, for you to say whether or not you care to accept any of my suggestions."

"Tell me how you achieve these feats," said Göring. "Do your magical millionaires always pay whatever you tell them?"

"By no means. They have a habit of setting great value upon their money. They will ask: 'Are you sure it is worth that?' and I will reply: 'There is no fixed price for a work of art; it depends on how badly you want it.' Sometimes I am told to offer a lower figure, and then I take the cash and lay it on the table in front of the picture owner. I have observed that the actual sight of money exercises a kind of hypnotic effect upon many persons, and those who would resist a bank draft collapse in front of a packet of thousand-mark notes."

The Teutonic Falstaff was amused by this portrayal of human frailty. He called Lanny "*ein ganzer Kerl*," and said: "Give me the list and I'll look it over. A number of the paintings don't mean much to me, and maybe I'll turn you loose to plunder those plutocrats of yours."

VII

There was nothing to do now but wait—which wasn't such an ordeal with a suite in a de luxe hotel and every service at command. Smart Berlin society threw open its doors to an American "glamour girl," and after a half-dozen wardrobe trunks had arrived by express, she was ready to go day and night.

The prince consort arrayed himself according to the decrees of the fashion dictators, and accompanied his spouse to luncheons, *thés dansants,* and elaborate long dinners followed by music and dancing. He shook hands with numerous large gentlemen who seemed to have the bulk of whales and approximately their shape, starting with close-cropped heads and perfectly rounded all the way down, except for two or three deep creases at the back of their pink necks; their ladies were built on the same scale and had voices suited to Wagnerian opera—Lanny's irreverent imagination saw them in flowing white robes, galloping to the rocking-horse rhythm of the *Walkürenritt.* Their conversation was serious, and you might give deep affront by mixing a *Hochgeborener* with a *Hochwohlgeborener* or addressing a *Frau Doktor* as an ordinary *Frau.*

The younger set was not so heavy, either in body or in mind; they played golf and tennis, danced with spirit, and motored hither and yon; they admired Americans, used American slang, and bore no grudges because of the war. Like the daughter of J. Paramount Barnes, they made their religion out of having a good time. They were not interested in politics—except for repeating some comical story about the leaders of the fantastic new *Regierung;* when they had done that, they had proved themselves enlightened persons and could go on dancing. The *Regierung* rarely interfered with you if you had money and confined your witticisms to the right sort of people—those who also had money. When Lanny asked the grandson of one of the steel kings what he really thought about it all, the *Grünschnabel* answered: "*Zum Teufel!* It's a problem of getting the votes of millions of morons, and the Nazi way seems to suit them in my country."

The larger magnates and their wives had decided ideas. For them the Hitler invention meant no more strikes or labor-union agitation, no more Reds fighting in the streets; it meant wages fixed and per- manent, resulting in such prosperity as heavy industry had never before known. In short, the Third Reich was the magnate's dream, and Lanny was struck by the curious resemblance of their conversa- tion to that of his father. The only difference was that they had it while Robbie longed for it but didn't know how to get it. The election in his homeland had gone in the opposite direction from what he had predicted, and his hope of putting restraint upon that man in the White House had gone glimmering. Robbie didn't go so far as to ask for an American Hitler, but he took to predicting that one was coming, and if a likely candidate had presented him- self and asked for funds he might not have been sent empty away.

The masters of Germany's immense steel, coal, chemical, and electrical industries said a few formal words of regret over the excesses of their new government, but hastened to point out that such things always happen during any social readjustment. They added that all Germany needed now was to have her lost territories restored, and then Europe might be assured of a long period of peace and prosperity. Lanny wanted to say: "Peace and prosperity based upon the all-out manufacture of armaments?" but those were the things he had to keep locked up in the other half of his per- sonality.

VIII

When an American playboy wearied of Berlin fashionable so- ciety, there were the art galleries and the concert halls. The Nazis had burned most of the worthwhile modern books and censored the art exhibitions, but collections of old masters stood untouched, and you could still hear Bach and Beethoven, Mozart and Brahms— if not Mendelssohn and Mahler and the other Jews. Lanny would turn his wife over to the smart ladies or to one of the eager young dancing men, and lose himself in the contemplation of masterpieces which spoke to him of that Germany he had known and loved as a youth and which, he told himself, survived in a region beyond the range of Nazi "Big Berthas" or the possible flight of General Göring's planes.

He went to a concert in the Philharmonie and heard a fine rendition of the Fifth Symphony. He gave up his soul to that of Beethoven, and felt himself lifted into a kind of divinity, endowed with new perceptions and powers; he shared in the struggle of mankind against those forces which have sought to block the upward progress of the race. He dreamed mighty dreams, and when the last notes of the glorious music had died he came back to the real world refreshed and strengthened for new efforts.

But Lanny was not the same trusting and happy lad who had first heard this classic art work; he had learned more about the world, and his thoughts were more complex. Looking about the concert hall at the men and women, young and old, who had been mystically made one with him, he observed that several of them wore Nazi uniforms, and what could that mean? Was it possible to transform Beethoven's passionate longings into any sort of Hitler ideology? To Lanny that appeared as the sin against the Holy Ghost; but evidently it had been committed, for the young Nazis looked just as inspired as the dreamiest *Mädchen* or the most reverent *Tonkünstler*. "*So pocht das Schicksal an die Pforte*," Beethoven had said; and what did those hammer blows of fate mean to a Stormtrooper? To what door was admission being demanded? Was it the French armies at the bridgeheads of the Rhine, or the Russians at the forts of East Prussia?

Hardly the best of thoughts to take into a concert hall! The alien rebel appealed to the soul of Beethoven on behalf of his cause, and the father of modern music told him that the knocking on the door was that of the Stormtroopers raiding the home of the Schultzes and dragging away Ludi and Freddi to torture and death. The second theme, gently pleading, was the soul of Freddi, which would live on in Lanny Budd's soul for as long as he had one or was one.

The rebel's thoughts wandered and came to rest upon an anecdote which had been told him by a Dutchman with whom he had chatted on the packet-boat from Harwich to the Hook of Holland. A Nazi friend had been extolling to this Dutchman the conditions within the Hitler realm; there was such perfect order, and the streets were so clean; everybody had work and enough to eat; everybody knew his duty and did it gladly—and so on. "Ah, yes," the Dutchman had countered; "but when I hear a step on my front porch at four o'clock in the morning, I know it's the milkman!"

What was this strange duality in the soul of the German which made it possible for him to dream the noblest and holiest of dreams, and then go out and perpetrate the most hideous atrocities? What was it which had made Germany the land of Beethoven, Goethe, and Schiller, and at the same time the land of Bismarck, Hindenburg, and Schicklgruber alias Hitler? Evidently the German did not know how to harness his aspirations and make them work in his everyday life, especially political. He delighted in lofty abstractions expressed in the longest words and used like counters in a game, but without ever turning them into cash. His ideas were like the screws of a steamship during a violent storm; they race frequently in the air, failing to come into contact with the water and produce any motion in the vessel.

IX

One morning the mail brought a letter on old-fashioned stationery, bearing the crest of the Baron von Wiesenschmetterling. It informed Herr Lanning Budd that the Baroninwitwe would be pleased to consider an offer of one hundred and twenty-five thousand marks for the Hubert van Eyck painting. She wouldn't quote in dollars, of course, but at the then rate of exchange it was about fifty thousand. Irma thought it monstrous for such a tiny piece of canvas; but this was a real old master, two centuries older than Rembrandt. Lanny said it might call for dickering; to begin with he wrote a carefully studied note calling the old lady's attention to her phrasing and stating that he could not undertake the negotiations upon the basis of a promise to "consider." Might he have her assurance that if within the next thirty days he brought her the sum of one hundred and twenty-five thousand marks in cash the painting would be his?

While waiting for a reply, he escorted Irma to more entertainments; until one morning he received a ceremonious visit from the Oberleutnant bringing him a note on the impressive stationery of the Minister-Präsident of Prussia, authorizing him to sell a list of paintings at various specified prices. A total of seventeen were listed, and the expert was amused to observe that they included all the Italians, most of the French, and several of the English, but none of the German, Dutch, or Flemish. There were conclusions of a political nature to be drawn from this. The Nazis were hoping to make friends with Holland and Belgium, but were in a state of intense irritation with Mussolini, who was busily intriguing with the Austrian government, seeking control of that near-bankrupt country. The fat Kommandant of the German Air Force had made a couple of trips to Rome, but with ill success according to all reports.

Irma, who knew the paintings, looked over the list and commented from another point of view: "He is keeping all the nudes!" Yes, a psychoanalyst could have told a lot about an old-style robber-baron from that list of rejects. He didn't care anything about the Blessed Virgin or any such neglected females; he didn't care for old people of either sex or for the proletariat of any tribe or color. What he cherished was beautiful young women in scanty garments, and especially when they had large ruddy limbs, after the style of Rubens; also princes, statesmen, and soldiers in gorgeous costumes, with jewels and lace and orders of whatever design. Did he intend putting these to use as fashion-plates?

Anyhow, it was a job, though not an easy one, for all Lanny's suggestions of reduction in price had been overlooked, and a couple of the prices had been hiked. But Lanny had explained that he sometimes came back with counterproposals, and presumably the Minister-Präsident was taking precautions. It could do no harm to bring him a lower offer; his official executioner couldn't chop off the head of a *Kunstsachverständiger* who happened to be an American citizen. The total sum which Lanny was invited to contribute to the great man's exchequer was slightly more than a million marks, and even if he took Zoltan Kertezsi in on some of the deals, he would earn enough money to keep Trudi Schultz and her fellow-conspirators in funds for a year or two.

X

Lanny and his wife had a luncheon engagement, but he begged off in order to write letters and cablegrams. After Irma had departed, he decided upon a respite, and went for a drive into the Moabit district. As his chariot rolled, his thoughts were busy with the second-in-command of the Nazis, trying to probe the mystery of this unusual acquaintanceship. Did Göring really believe that Lanny was friendly to his cause and would be willing to help him? It was hard to imagine. A wholesale murderer, with the guilt of the blood purge and the Reichstag fire and other crimes beyond the reckoning of history, would hardly be apt to take up casual friendships or fall victim to the charms of a dilettante of all the arts, including conversation. Having at command the greatest spying-organization in the world, he will hardly admit any person to his intimacy without knowing that person's record and connections. Could he fail to have learned about the Red uncle and the Pink school in Cannes, and that Lanny had got kicked out of Rome ten years ago; that he was a friend of Blum and Longuet and Steffens and others, and that his best chum was an anti-Nazi playwright? What could Göring be trying to get out of such a person?

A mystery complicated enough to make the plot of a melodrama for Eric Vivian Pomeroy-Nielson, if that fastidious highbrow would condescend to anything so far down in the dramatic scale. Was the Air Kommandant using Lanny as a preliminary to doing business with Lanny's father? Or did he have his eye on Irma's fortune, planning to get Lanny into a serious scrape and then plunder Lanny's wife as he had plundered Johannes Robin? Was he expecting to use him as a decoy, to draw members of the underground movement into the Gestapo's net? Trudi had vouched for Monck; but suppose Monck was fooling Trudi and getting ready to meet Lanny's friends and probe his secrets? All these were possibilities, and seemed more probable than the idea that this vain and cruel man was really enjoying the company of the grandson of Budd's.

Maybe they were following him here in Berlin! That at least was something he could make sure about; he drove his car around a block, and every time he turned a corner he watched in his little mirror to see if any other car made the same turn. None did; so he decided that he wasn't imperiling Trudi at present. He drove up the street which she had named, timing himself to pass the corner exactly at noon. There she was, also on the dot; walking on the right side of the street, and carrying a small package in the crook of her left arm, in plain sight as he drove up behind her. He passed her, going slowly, and in the next block drew up by the curb and waited until she came along and stepped in. They drove on, and again he turned a corner and watched carefully; but there was no pursuit.

XI

"I didn't know where to get a feather," said Lanny; "but I got the job with the General."

He told her about the luncheon in the official residence, and to the woman it was a sort of ogre-story, a visit to Bluebeard's castle. "How could you swallow his food?" she exclaimed.

"I ate too much," he replied. "It was part of the job. If I go there often, you may see me looking like him."

"*Gott behüte!* What on earth do you talk about to such a man?"

"Mostly you listen to him talk. You find that it has to do with himself and his prowess, and of course with the army and especially with the air force he is building. He has a strong ego, and his aim in life is to compel other persons to submit to his will. He is much better company than some of the other Nazis, because he does not bore you with their jargon; he talks like a man of the world who is interested in power and assumes that you are sensible enough to understand that."

"It does not disturb his sleep that he has killed tens of thousands of persons and is having a hundred thousand tortured in prisons?"

"I am sure he sleeps as soundly as any other fat man. You must understand that he does not have our conception of human brotherhood. He is a professional killer of other men; he has been trained for it since youth, and during the World War it became the most exciting of games, in which he staked his life upon his skill. Frau

Magda Goebbels called my attention to the fact that so many of the Nazi leaders have been airmen. It was a school for the making of initiative and daring, and for the eliminating of the scrupulous. I am sure that Göring would hesitate no more over eliminating you than you would over a bedbug."

"I am put in my place," said Trudi, managing a wry smile.

"Now this wholesale killer is conducting a school for young Nazis, teaching them initiative and daring. Incidentally, and indirectly, he is teaching the same thing to young working-class leaders. It is a harsh school."

She thought about that before she spoke again. "Tell me, Lanny, suppose you had a chance to address the workers of Germany—only one chance—just what would you say to them?"

The car rolled on for a block before he answered. "I believe I would point out to them that the increase in employment of which the Nazis boast is based entirely upon the manufacture of armaments; also, it depends upon the piling up of debts, and so it cannot go on indefinitely. It can have but one end, another slaughtering of the workers."

"Suppose you had a chance to bring them some sort of message from the outside world, what would it be?"

"That the workers of France and England and America are of a pacifist disposition; they do not want to rearm their countries and they have succeeded in cutting down military budgets to a great extent. But of course if Germany goes on rearming, that will automatically force the neighboring countries to follow suit. It is obvious that when a nation turns its whole substance into war materials, as Germany is doing now, the time will come when that nation has to go to war—it can do nothing else because it is equipped for nothing else, and it must use its armaments or else be suffocated under their weight."

"We do not get the Socialist papers from abroad any more, Lanny. Can you tell me of some foreign statesman who has said that, and who might be quoted?"

"Léon Blum has been saying it over and over, both in his speeches and in *Le Populaire*."

"Very well," said the woman. "We will attribute it to him. The next time you come into Germany, bring us some clippings like that; they will be useful."

"O.K.," said Lanny, somewhat offhand and without realizing that he was taking one more step toward trouble. Or maybe he knew but didn't wish to admit it to himself. Wide is the gate, and broad is the way, that leadeth to destruction, and it is a common observation that when you have taken the first step through that gate and along that way, it becomes easier to take the second and the third.

XII

When Lanny got back to his hotel there was a cablegram, always an interesting event in the life of an art expert. Among Irma's Long Island acquaintances was a young matron known as "the princess of pickles"; she had inherited a block of stock in a great industry having to do with the canning and processing of foods. Two or three years ago Lanny had cabled her from Vienna about a Blessed Virgin by Jan van Eyck, and she had promptly forwarded the price. In due course she had discovered, as most of his clients did, that it was a beautiful thing and that owning it was a source of rare distinction. So, immediately upon receiving the quotation from the Baroninwitwe, Lanny had cabled this same client that she had an opportunity to obtain a Blessed Virgin by the elder brother of Jan and thus be unique among American collectors so far as Lanny's knowledge went. Now came a reply that a hundred and twenty-five thousand marks had been placed to his account in one of the great banks of Berlin, but that he would be expected to get his commission out of this sum.

That was the kind of thing which made Irma Barnes so furious with the rich; she called it "jewing down," and she said, what was five thousand dollars to Brenda Spratt? Lanny grinned and said that if you counted it in the form of canned pork and beans it might amount to a carload. He was used to all sorts of counter-proposals, and had seen one of his clients give up a priceless painting rather than pay the extra ten per cent; he added one of his father's favorite anecdotes, about a lady in Newcastle who had desired to sell her mansion but had refused because the purchaser insisted upon the curtains' being included in the deal.

It would mean another trip to the Neumark, and one of those bargaining-duels which Lanny had learned to enjoy. He performed a mathematical operation to determine the purchase price with his commission added. It worked out at one hundred and thirteen thousand six hundred and thirty-six marks and thirty-six pfennigs. It would sound better if he renounced his claim to the pfennigs and offered the Prussian lady an extra mark. He phoned to his victim and made an appointment to see her after lunch the following day; also he phoned Zoltan about the deal, and told Irma that he had fixed it up with his colleague, who was supposed to have a client desiring the picture but unwilling to pay so high a price.

XIII

Lanny got a large bundle of crisp new notes from the bank and stowed them in an inside pocket; he didn't have to worry about hold-ups, because in Germany the only kind was official, and if you possessed an American passport you were immune. They drove on a day of rain which turned to light snow before they got to their destination. The potato-fields were a vast magical blanket, suggesting a world where there had never been any suffering; but it was an illusion, for if you had known how many thousands of human bodies had fertilized those fields through the centuries it would have ruined your appetite for "earth-apples," as the Germans call them.

In the drawing-room of the elderly stout aristocrat, overcrowded with things old enough to be valuable even though they were ugly, Lanny played the game which had become his substitute for war. A poet had told the world that the colonel's lady and Judy O'Grady were sisters under the skin; Lanny had never bought pictures from either of this pair, but he had bought them from members of the French, Spanish, German, Austrian, Polish, and Russian ruling classes, and had proved that their manners and morals were not even skin-deep when immense quantities of their country's currency were dangled before their eyes.

The Baroninwitwe von Wiesenschmetterling became indignant when she learned that this young American upstart had presumed to make an appointment and expect her to waste her time haggling over a few marks. She had set her price, and had written him a second note—not yet mailed—granting him an option. Why had he not told her over the telephone that he wished to try to force a reduction in her offer? Lanny said he was sorry. He had not understood that it would be an offense to make a counterproposal; and after all, a hundred and thirteen thousand six hundred and thirty-seven marks was not a sum to be sneezed out of the room. He said it with his amiable grin, and added that he would be glad if he could leave the package behind him, because it was so heavy it had stretched his coat out of shape. He dragged it forth, and saw the Baroninwitwe's eyes grow larger—it was hardly likely that she had ever seen such an amount of cash in all her baronial life.

It was a struggle to the death of the noble lady's temper and very nearly of Lanny's endurance. "This is really an immense sum of money, *gnädige Baronin;* it cost a lot to cable so much to Germany and I'll hate to have to send it back. My client's statement is positive, and I know from previous experience that she will not change. Please be so kind as to read the cablegram." She refused, but when he put it into her hands, her curiosity got the better of her; this showed that she could change her mind and that she was not such a forbidding personality as she endeavored to appear.

There was a table near her chair, and he unwrapped the package on it. "I want you to realize that this is not stage money," he said. "This, as you will see, is the bank's own label—in this bundle are fifty one-thousand-mark notes, and here is another of the same; and this smaller collection makes the complete sum. In my ten years' experience as a *Kunstsachverständiger* it has rarely happened that I have handled so large an amount of money——"

"*Aber*—never before have you had a Hubert van Eyck!" She almost screamed it.

"I have purchased a Blessed Virgin by Jan van Eyck from a relative of yours—and for a much smaller sum."

"I know, I know, but that is not the same! You realize it as well as I do."

They argued the merits of the two Flemish brothers and the comparative rarity of their works. Here was a treasure unknown to the art world, a family possession for three hundred years, and he came and tried to shop for it as if he were buying the old clothes of her major-domo! When she said that, Lanny decided to resort to the last extreme. He put the bundles of money together and said, with dignity: "I am sorry, *gnädige Baronin*, that I have wasted so much of your time." Irma, who had been sitting motionless, a statue of silent contempt, arose, and the two of them started to take their leave. "I shall be leaving for England tomorrow," he said.

Lanny had known men who could stand that, but never a woman whom it had not broken down. "*Gut denn!*" said the noble widow, torn between greed and rage. "I'll meet you half-way. I'll split the commission with you. You may have five per cent and pay me the balance."

"I have brought no more with me than I have shown you, and I am not in a position to change my offer. I have to divide my commission with my associate——"

"But what have I to do with that?"

"If he has assisted me, he has earned his share."

"But what have you yourself done in the matter? You have made two trips here, you have written me one letter and sent one cablegram to your client—that is all!"

"*Verehrte Gnädige*, you overlook the most important detail: I have spent a matter of ten years learning to do these things. I have not merely learned the names and addresses of persons who are willing to take my word for paintings, but I have established a character so that they trust me. Do you think you could find, anywhere on this earth, a person who would cable you one hundred and twenty-five thousand marks to buy a painting which the person had never seen or even heard of until your message arrived?"

They had an argument standing on their feet. Irma was disgusted, and started to go out to the car, and that was good.

"I'll tell you what I'll do—my last offer! I'll allow you ten thousand marks, and you pay a hundred and fifteen thousand. *Einverstanden?*"

This was cheese-paring, and she must have known it. But don't make the mistake of being impolite, for she might become really mad! "*Verehrte Baronin*," said Lanny, in the kindest tone he had in his repertoire, "you have a lovely and rare painting and I have not tried to conceal my admiration for it. I have offered you a very high price, and I think I have done well for you. I also think that I have earned my proper share. I have never in my life cut my own commission, because I know that the work I do is honest and is worth the price. If you accept my offer you will count this large sum of money, and then sign the bill of sale in triplicate, after which I will hand you the money with one hand and you hand me the picture with the other, and we will both be better off than we are now."

He had to walk all the way to the front door of the mansion and had begun to be seriously worried; but finally she said: "*Also gut— kommen Sie zurück!*" She sat down and counted every one of the notes, stopping to wet her fingers for every two or three. She signed the documents, and Lanny wrapped the Blessed Virgin in a piece of oilcloth which he had brought. He was about to take his departure when she became suddenly human and invited the young couple to a *Teegesellschaft*. But Irma had gone out to the car, and he was afraid she would refuse to come back; she wasn't very well, he said, and they desired to get back to Berlin before dark.

XIV

"Oh, that odious woman!" exclaimed the heiress, whose money had come so easily.

"I have met worse," said Lanny, well content.

The wife would have liked to say: "I can't comprehend why you insist upon going through such scenes, for the small sums you get out of it." But Emily Chattersworth had urged her to forgo these criticisms and let Lanny play the game which he had mastered. Instead she remarked: "I really can't see why you should pay anything to Zoltan. He hasn't helped with this deal, has he?"

Lanny didn't wish to tell what Zoltan's help had really been. He said: "I'll offer to pay him, but I know he won't take it."

"Another thing," added Irma. "You've got your money into Germany, and how will you get it out?"

"It can stay for a while," he replied. "Sooner or later I'll see a painting that I want."

There was no need to say more, for Irma would have forgotten about it in a few hours. He drove next morning and drew ten thousand marks from the bank and went to the rendezvous with Trudi Schultz, omitting no precautions. He staggered her when he put this sum into her hands. "It'll save my having to come again so soon."

"But, Lanny, how am I to keep so much money?"

"Find some hiding-place in your room—one where the Gestapo won't think to look."

"But suppose the house should burn down."

"If that happens," he smiled, "be sure you get out, and don't bother about the money. I can get more—but I can't get another Frau Mueller!"

7

Spirits of Just Men

I

CHRISTMAS at Wickthorpe Lodge was a delightful occasion, with friends coming and going, messengers bringing gifts, surprises being planned, a rushing here and there with artificially created excitement. Bright fires blazed in every room and the house was warm, the way Irma liked it. It meant servants coming with full coal-scuttles and going with empty ones; but that was no trouble in this delightful land where prompt cheerful attendants could be had at ridiculous wages. Lanny, the economic determinist, said it was the English land system, which excluded the country people from their birthright; but he had learned not to make "grouchy" remarks in the presence of his wife, and especially not at the season when peace and good will were supposed to prevail.

Beauty came from London with her husband. She and her daughter-in-law got along famously, the older deferring to the younger and doing everything to turn the spotlight upon her; it was according to her code that the world existed for the young, especially of the female sex—they were entitled to their turn. As for Beauty's husband, that gray-haired and rosy cherub wouldn't ever be in the way of anybody; for who can object to being loved, especially in a quiet and non-invasive way? Parsifal Dingle had healed little Frances of a mild cold; at least, he had treated her by his method of prayer and meditation, and the trouble had disappeared. He didn't make any claims, but left it for you to draw your own conclusions. He was just the person to have around the house at Yuletide, a sort of Santa without whiskers. At this season everybody practiced what Parsifal preached—and if only they had been willing to live the rest of the year in the same spirit, what a different world it might have been!

The young people, home from school, were coming and going from one house to the next; they came in with eyes shining and cheeks glowing from the cold; they drank hot punch, laughed and chattered and danced, and then raced off to some other place. Alfy followed "Marcy," as they called her—impossible to say more than two syllables when you were so busy enjoying life. Theirs was a different kind of love from that which Mr. Dingle taught, and apparently it didn't make you so happy. The young couple got into one of their fusses, and it was off again and on again; Christmas Day they weren't speaking, and Marcy was telling her mother about it in tears. Lanny thought it was too bad, but they didn't ask him for help. Beauty said it was part of the process of getting adjusted, but Lanny thought she was too optimistic. "I never had any such troubles with Rosemary," he said; to which his mother answered: "Yes, but you lost out with her!"

II

In one of the attic rooms of this large house lived a stoutish elderly woman whom you would have taken for a retired nurse or housekeeper; she was known to all as "Madame," and spoke English with a Polish accent. Nobody could have been more unobtrusive; she seemed perfectly content to sit in her room and play various games of solitaire, and when Irma's maid, her friend, came to see her, she would tell how the latest batch of games had eventuated. Never would you have guessed that this dull-seeming, slow-moving old person was the repository of one of the oddest and most bewildering gifts with which a prankish Nature or Providence had seen fit to endow humankind.

Some member of the Budd family or their privileged friends would send up to her room and ask if she felt in the mood for a sitting; almost always she would say Yes, and would repair to that person's room, and sit in an easy chair, lay her head back and close her eyes—and then what fantastic events would begin to happen! You would hear the deep bass voice of an Amerindian chieftain, dead a couple of hundred years according to his own account and speaking with a Polish accent! But don't laugh—for before you had got your mouth open he might be telling you something about your great-uncle, whose very name you would have to look up in the family records; or something about yourself that you had thought was a secret from the whole world.

Lanny Budd, free-spoken and too humorous, had managed to get himself "in Dutch" with "Tecumseh" by asking persistent questions of a skeptical nature; so it was rarely that the old creature—whoever or whatever he was—could be persuaded to serve him. "Oh, so you're back again, Mr. Smarty!" the booming voice would say; which certainly didn't sound Iroquois or Polish. It was unfortunate, because Lanny was one who really wanted to understand these mysteries, and had stood for a lot of ridicule on Tecumseh's behalf. People wouldn't make subtle distinctions in matters occult; either you knew it was all tommyrot or else you were a victim of it.

But Lanny kept on trying, because he had witnessed events which were beyond explanation by what the world was pleased at the moment to consider "normal." By and by the world might change its mind and decide to include a lot of new things as normal; but they weren't going to do it at the behest of a playboy, a darling of fortune whom they knew as Mr. Irma Barnes. Lanny held a great respect for science, and it was his hope that some day a really learned man would come along and experiment with Madame Zyszynski and find out how she did these things. He had found scientists who admitted that it was quite remarkable, but that didn't keep them from going back to their everyday routine, disregarding the possibility that there might be unknown universes all around us, or in us, or through us, trying in vain to let us know about themselves.

III

At this time Lanny was persisting, because it seemed to him that if there was a world of spirits, Freddi Robin, newly arrived among them, would certainly be seeking to communicate with his former friends. But Tecumseh had become annoyed by the very idea of "that Jewish fellow" and would have nothing to do with him. A slow, tedious, and for the most part thankless task, probing these dark regions of the subconscious mind! Each of us has his own, and apparently something of other people's; an ocean of mindstuff in which few soundings have been taken and which is full of creatures stranger than any Loch Ness monster. Put your net down in it, and you may bring up a burden of seaweed and a wriggling mess of jellyfish; you may try time after time with no better luck. But then, just as you are about to quit in boredom, up comes something that shines with an unearthly light—or maybe some writing derived from a lost Atlantis!

"Tecumseh," pleaded Lanny, with abject humility, "do be kind to me. I know that my Jewish friend is in the spirit world now, and he would surely talk to me if you would find him."

What was it that brought results after so many failures? The power of some spirit? Or some new train of thought in Lanny's own subconscious mind? Impossible to say; but on the day after Christmas, sitting with Madame in his own study, the investigator got something that jolted him like a mule's kick. "There is no Jew here, but there is a young man who says he is a friend. He is tall and has a sort of yellow hair, rather wavy. He is drawing a picture of you and it is good. He says you will know him that way."

"Does he give any name?"

"He says something that sounds like Lood. Do you know him? Lood-veek?"

"I know him well," said Lanny, promptly. "I am delighted he has come."

"He hears you say that and is happy. He rubs out the mouth in the drawing and makes it smiling."

Here was another of those strange, confused, and confusing manifestations! Gertrud Schultz had identified herself to Lanny by means of a drawing, and now her husband was doing the same! Was that because they were two artists with but a single thought? Or was it because Lanny had got the idea fixed in his mind, and now the subconscious mind of Madame was incorporating it into the fantasy-creation which was called Tecumseh? Very certainly Lanny hadn't mentioned Trudi and her drawing to anybody in this world.

"Tell him I am most anxious to hear whatever he cares to tell me," said Lanny; and added, ingratiatingly: "Also, I am deeply grateful to you, Tecumseh."

"You will really appreciate me some day. This man writes on the drawing-board that to you he is Ludi. Is that right?"

"Quite right. Ask him how he is."

"He says he has escaped from terrible suffering. He says he never believed in the spiritual life. He used to laugh at you and at me, but he will surely never do it again."

"I beg him to come often and tell me about himself. There are reasons why I wish especially to know."

"He says: 'How is my wife?'"

"She is well."

"He asks: 'Have you seen her?'"

Something like a lightning flash took place in the mind of Lanny Budd. One cannot lead a double life and not have suspicions of even the most innocent-seeming events. Could it be that the Gestapo was reaching into the spirit realm? Could it be that some agent had managed to make friends with Madame and was using her, with or without her own knowledge? Either idea seemed fantastic, but Lanny couldn't keep them from his mind—and it was exactly as if he said the words aloud. "You do not trust me!" exclaimed the deep bass voice. "How can I ever help you?"

"I do trust you, Tecumseh!" exclaimed the secret agent. "Don't you know the story of the man who prayed: 'Lord, I believe, help Thou mine unbelief'? Help me now by giving my messages to Ludi. Tell him that I have seen his wife and she thinks only of him."

"I would like to communicate with her, Lanny." It was Ludi himself, speaking directly, something which happened only when a séance went especially well. He used precise English, as he had done in the old days when Lanny had visited the Berlin apartment of the Schultzes to inspect Trudi's art work.

"It would be hard to arrange, Ludi; you know the circumstances. Some day, perhaps, but not now—unless you can reach her where she is."

"I have tried, but I cannot; there is no channel."

"I hope to see her again some day, and I will deliver your messages. Give me some password, something that will convince her it is really you."

"She has a strawberry mark just over her right knee."

A curious "psychic phenomenon" indeed! Lanny was always trying to persuade himself that these revelations were a product of telepathy, or mind-reading, or whatever name you chose to give it. He hadn't told anybody about Monck or what this man had said about Trudi's birthmark; it seemed to him obvious that at this moment the mind of Madame was taking things out of Lanny's

mind and weaving them into her story. Fascinating to watch, and
to a psychologist perhaps as hard to believe as the existence of spirits;
but surely it wouldn't help to convince Trudi that her husband was
actually sending her a message.

IV

The investigator thought as hard as he could. He had to step
warily, knowing that the querulous chieftain might decide to break
off the conversation at any instant. "Ludi," he explained, "you must
realize that your wife goes swimming in summer, and many people
see that mark. Can't you manage to think of something which only
she would know?"

"All right," replied the strange voice—composite of an old Polish
woman, an Iroquois Indian, and a Berlin commercial artist and
Social-Democratic party member. "Tell her: 'Chin-Chin.' "

"Will she know what that means?"

"She will know."

Suddenly there came from the throat of the old woman a burst
of sound, the barking of a little dog; it was so realistic that Lanny
could have imagined the creature within a few inches of his ankles,
leaping at him in a fury and compelling him to kick it away. This
went on for fully a minute, and was followed by silence.

"Was that Chin-Chin?" inquired the investigator.

"That was me," said the spirit voice. Ludi wasn't required to be
perfect in his grammar—and anyhow, there are grammarians who
defend that form. "Trudi will tell you about it," he added. "People
do silly things when they are young, and happy, and very much
in love."

"Of course," said Lanny, who had been all three. "She will want
to know how you came to pass over, Ludi." The phrase is considered good form among spiritualists.

"It would be better not to go into that. I was in Oranienburg. I
couldn't stand it any more, so in the night I chewed my wrists until
I tore the arteries."

"Tell me where you are now, Ludi. You know that will mean a lot to her."

"She will come here some day and then she will know."

"I want to try to convince her," persisted the American. "You can help me by explaining matters. Do you have a body where you are?"

"What would I do with the body I left in Oranienburg and that the Nazis burned in a furnace?"

"You know all the things you knew on earth. Do you know other things also?"

"Very many. I am my own mind, but I am other minds, too."

"Minds of people on this earth or on your side?" It was an ill-chosen question, which had the effect of breaking up the show. "What's the use of all that?" burst out the voice of the old-time warrior. "You aren't going to believe what he tells you; you're just figuring over the old stuff."

"Oh, please, Tecumseh!" pleaded Lanny. "I'm trying so hard to help my friend and his unhappy wife."

"He is a good fellow," announced the chieftain. "For his sake I will tolerate you; but you are no good at all, you just tie yourself up in long words, and you wouldn't believe it if I should smack you one in the eye."

"Try it some day," said the playboy, spunkily. "It might be good for me."

"You sit with Madame in the dark some night, and I'll show you what I can do. Only you'll say it's a teleplasm! Go on about your business now."

And that was the end. Lanny knew it would be useless to plead. A long silence; and then Madame began to sigh. When she came out of her trance she inquired, as always: "Did you get good results?"

"Very good, indeed." Lanny was happy to say it, because it pleased her. She never asked what you had heard; she had the idea that this was bad form, since people often got embarrassing secrets about themselves or others. Instead she lay back and closed her eyes, resting. Finally she remarked: "I won three games of Patience this afternoon."

"You cheated yourself," he replied. It was his customary jest, at which she never failed to titter. She had adopted him in her heart as an imaginary son, replacing one whom she had borne and lost; every moment that he would spare out of his fashionable life to chat with her was one she would cherish and dream over.

V

Robbie Budd was back in Newcastle, but there weren't any Christmas holidays for him; he was working harder than ever in his life before, bent upon showing his world that he was not merely a great salesman and promoter, but also an executive, in every way the equal of his father, who had failed to appreciate him all his life and had died without atoning for the error. Robbie had collected large sums of money and was going to spend them with a speed and efficiency which would astonish the town of his birth. He was going to build a fabricating plant which would be his own to run, whose products would be his own to market, with no father and and no elder brother to hinder or check him. Robbie had made his blunders of overoptimism, but he had learned from them and would not repeat them; there would be no more speculation in Wall Street, only production in Newcastle, and of an article which was in the position of the motor-car thirty years ago. Once more there was a chance to reap fortunes; and in spite of the Bible statement, the race would be to the swift and the battle to the strong.

In Robbie's forward-leaping land it was no uncommon thing for a man to raise several million dollars for a new enterprise and then be in a hurry to get it started. There were men who knew how to design industrial plants, and Robbie was now closeted with them day and night. There were men who knew how to dredge tidelands and make docks and a model harbor; others who knew how to grade land, and had tools which would do it with magical speed. Robbie was now making contracts with these, and with others who would come and pour concrete foundations the moment the frost was out of the ground. Before summer a forest of steel girders would arise where formerly had been marshes and cow pastures. All this was commonplace in the "land of unlimited possibilities."

Robbie threw up his job with Budd Gunmakers, and Johannes Robin, coming home from South America, set to work to help with contracts and purchasing. The firm of "R and R," which had been Lanny's joke in youth, was now a firmly based reality. Hansi and Bess being married, Lanny having risked his life to save Johannes and Freddi, Robbie having helped Johannes to get on his feet again —all these were ties stronger than any law could have devised. A one-time Jewish money magnate would give his friend the benefit of the skill he had acquired in more than forty years of trading, and would never worry about what he was going to get in return. He could be sure it would be generous and, what was more important, it would be out of reach of the Nazis!

Mama and Rahel packed their few belongings and departed from Bienvenu, writing letters full of thanks to Mrs. Dingle and Lanny and Irma for their kindness. Irma said nothing to her husband, but he knew what a relief she found this; for how could anybody enjoy the pleasures of social life in the atmosphere of grief and fear which those poor Jewish people inevitably spread around them? Irma was glad also on account of her little girl, because she didn't want those two children to become too fond of each other; she had no mind to find herself some day in the position of Robbie Budd and his wife, with a Jewish son-in-law and the possibility of a half-Jewish grandchild. All right to have Jewish friends, but mixing your blood was something different.

VI

Right after the holidays the Lanny Budds—or the Irma Barneses, as their friends often said it—were planning to return to the Riviera for the winter. Lanny in the meantime had managed to find purchasers for two of Göring's paintings, and it was a question of how to handle these deals. To Irma it appeared simple to send the money and let the fat General ship the paintings directly to the purchasers;

but Lanny said: "How could I ever know what they got?"

"You mean you think he'd send them the wrong pictures?" There was a note of indignation in Irma's voice, as if the governing classes of the whole world were being insulted.

Lanny explained patiently that there was a great deal of rascality in the art world—he didn't say in the Nazi world. "Paintings are imitated so cleverly that only an expert can tell the difference. Somebody might do it without even Göring's knowing it. My duty is not done unless I personally see the painting shipped. Otherwise, if the customer complains, I have no defense, but have to refund his money and take the loss."

"That's going to be a nuisance, your having to go to Berlin all the time, Lanny."

"I'll let these customers wait till the weather gets warmer," he answered, with a smile. He would have liked to tell Trudi about the séance, but he wanted still more to be fair to his wife and not deceive her any more than necessary.

However, the day before they were leaving England a letter came, having all those signs which he recognized—the German stamp, the writing, and the cheap envelope. He put it into his pocket with some other mail until he was alone. Then he read:

> Dear Mr. Budd:
>   If you should see your friend Schmidt, the art dealer, please tell him that I have some sketches which I should like to show him. They are not the same as the last, but better, I hope, and have to do with interesting personalities. This is important to me. Thanking you for past favors,
>
>   Mueller

That was all; but it was enough to cause Lanny to reconsider his plans. "Irma, I've been thinking about it and I believe I ought to run over to Berlin and get those paintings before I settle down for the winter."

"Oh, how provoking!" she exclaimed. "Why do you want to make yourself a slave like that?"

"It'll only take a couple of days, and you don't have to come. Wait for me in Paris if you prefer."

Paris was always an agreeable place for waiting. You could do shopping, if you had what it took, and there were plays to be seen and fashionable friends to go about with. This young couple had two cars which they were taking to the Riviera, so they arranged that the chauffeur should drive Frances and her governess and maid direct to Bienvenu; Irma found traveling with children a nuisance and always avoided it if she could. Lanny would drive his wife to Paris and then proceed alone to Berlin.

There was but one dubious aspect of this project. "Lanny, can I really trust you in Germany?"

"Darling," he smiled, "how could I be under better auspices than the head of the Prussian state?"

"You know what I mean! You'll be getting mixed up with those friends of Freddi and Hansi again."

He had thought carefully what he would say, and had learned a number of formulas. "My dear, I have important business to transact and I'm not going to let anything interfere with it. If I do this job, the old pirate may give me others. Don't forget that Germany is a treasure-house of great art, and America can use a lot of it."

"Lanny, I tell you I couldn't stand anything like you put me through before. I've got to make that plain to you. I can't stand it and I won't!"

He knew that he had to grant her the right to say it all over again; it is a part of the duty of husbands to hear about their past sins. It is the part of wisdom never to argue, or question any statement, however inexact it may seem; merely utter soothing words, and the fewer the better—Mother Nature having apparently planned women to talk and men to listen. "Yes, dear," he repeated. "I'll take the best of care of myself, and not stay a moment longer than necessary."

VII

Irma wanted him to take a train; but he liked to drive, even in January. He paid no attention to the weather—unless it was a blinding snowstorm, he went right through. He would need only one day in Berlin, and he wanted to bring the paintings out with him, and have them packed and shipped from France—trusting no one in Naziland. If anything delayed him, he would telephone without fail; meanwhile Irma would be gossiping with the Duchesse de Ceci and the Comtesse de Cela, and on the way to Bienvenu she would entertain him with all the latest scandals of the *haut monde de Paris*.

He motored without incident, and saw once more the factory chimneys of Germany, pouring forth smoke day and night; also the patient people, performing whatever hard tasks were assigned them, and winning the sympathy of an American who rarely had to do anything except what his fancy dictated. He arrived late, spent the night at the Adlon, and in the morning telephoned the Oberleutnant, a sort of glorified secretary in military uniform, who met him by appointment at the palace. Up to twenty months ago this marble edifice had belonged to a Jewish *Schieber*, and in it Lanny and his wife had eaten and drunk delight. Now it was the home of the fat General's lady favorite, a darling of the German stage and screen; Lanny's taste was all over it, and he hoped the statuesque blond beauty appreciated what he had done for her.

The two paintings, *Head of St. John*, a fragment of a larger picture by Tiepolo, and *Parliament Buildings on the Thames* by Monet —curious contrast of old and new—had been taken from the walls and set aside for him. He examined them and made sure they were what he wanted; then he put a bank draft into the Oberleutnant's hands and took the bills of sale which had been signed by the Minister-Präsident's personal disbursing officer. Lanny wrapped the precious works in two oilcloths he carried for the purpose, and two uniformed lackeys bore them to his car. "You can show these documents at the border," said the staff officer, "and if there is any question about it, tell them to phone me." Lanny thanked him, asked after his family, answered questions about his own; they smiled, bowed, shook hands, and parted the best of friends.

VIII

Lanny was returning to Paris, but he chose a devious route, not prescribed in any motorist's guidebook. He turned a number of unexpected corners, and ended up in the Moabit district exactly at noon. As he passed a certain corner, there was a young woman in a worn brown coat, with a bundle of sketches in the crook of her left arm. He passed her and stopped as before; she stepped in without a word, and away they went—but not toward Paris.

Lanny watched in his little mirror, while Trudi sank low in her seat to make herself inconspicuous, and turned her face toward him so that it could not be seen by persons passing. "Lanny," she exclaimed, "it is so kind of you to take this trouble!"

"My expenses are being paid," he replied, amiably. "I have two paintings in the back seat, for which I have just paid your Air Kommandant the sum of forty thousand marks. It means that I have four thousand for you, if you can use them."

"I have used most of what you gave me, and to good purpose."

"O.K. Is that why you wrote me?"

"No—something even more important. Are you sure we're not being followed?"

"I'll take another turn," he replied. The car roamed here and there about this old working-class district of the *Hauptstadt*. "All clear!" he said, in American. "Shoot!"

"I have some documents of a most confidential nature which I thought you might be able to put to use. They are photostatic copies of reports to Göring's office, showing production of military planes in violation of the Versailles treaty. You perhaps do not know that we are manufacturing certain types of transport planes in Germany, while in Sweden the same types are being made for our government, but having armament; they bear the same type numbers, but the armored ones have the initial K, that is, *Krieg*. With these documents you can prove that Göring is getting more warplanes than France and Britain combined."

"Holy smoke!" said the art expert. "How do you get such things?"

"That is one question you are not permitted to ask. Suffice it to say that all our friends are not yet dead, or even in concentration camps. Old-time party members come to us; some of them have turned Nazi as a camouflage."

"That is pretty risky business, Trudi."

"They risk their lives, and so do we. Whether you care to help us is for you to decide."

"What do you want me to do with the documents?"

"It is a field altogether strange to me. I should think the information would be of interest to the military authorities of France and England."

"Anyone would suppose it; and if I tell you that they might do nothing about it, you would be shocked. But I know some of them, and they believe what they want to believe and nothing more."

"Even if you put the documents into their hands?"

"They would want to know how I got them, and if I didn't tell them, I'm afraid they'd begin to suggest they mightn't be genuine. All intelligence departments forge documents for their own purposes, and naturally they are sure that others are doing the same. They can't trust any anti-Nazis, because they have the same sort of people in their own country and fear them even more than they do Hitler and Göring."

"I haven't told you everything yet," said Trudi. "I have photostatic copies of Wehrmacht intelligence reports, sent in by agents in Paris and London, giving data as to the situation of military objectives such as oil-depots, gas-tanks, arsenals, and other bombing-targets."

"Oh, my God!" exclaimed the American.

"They are evidently the results of surveyor's work; that is, they tell you, so many meters north-northwest of some prominent object —things like that."

"Are they in code?"

"They consist entirely of names of places, distances, and directions. They are abbreviated, and for place names they give only initials. The person who brought them to us has supplied interpretations which make it all quite clear. One hundred and forty-seven meters due north of such and such a station of the Paris Métro there is an oil-storage depot; so and so many feet southeast of the south entrance to Waterloo Bridge there is a warehouse full of explosives—things like that. Don't you suppose that might be of importance to the English authorities?"

"I've no doubt they'd read them with great interest," replied Lanny, "and doubtless would check them carefully. But would they do anything that made any real difference? You should hear my father talk about the British brass-hats, their dumbness, and their utter, impenetrable complacency. It is beneath their dignity to worry or even to take precautions about anything. They are as solid and as self-satisfied as their own Rock of Gibraltar."

IX

Lanny took his friend for a long drive, discussing every angle of this complicated problem. His final decision was that the documents ought to be published in some paper. The brass-hats wouldn't fail to read them, and the public clamor would stir them up, if anything could.

Trudi had but one objection. "It might be pretty hard on the person who got them for us."

"Does he imagine that you can turn these documents over to the British or the French military authorities and not have Göring get wind of it in a few days? Just as you have spies in his office, so he has equally efficient ones in every army and navy headquarters in the world."

"I suppose so," admitted the woman. "We may have to get our friend out of the country."

"Let me suggest something I thought of while I was figuring out ways to help Freddi. Devise a scheme to cast the suspicion on some good Nazi official. That is a way to confuse them and break them up." When she did not answer, he added: "Tell me this: have you the right to let the documents be published?"

"I was told to make whatever use of them seemed best."

"Very well; I'll take them on that basis."

"Do you think you can get them out safely?"

"It happens that I am in position to do so. There's no use going into details."

"You must be careful, in disposing of them, that there's no trail leading to you; for surely the Gestapo will get busy with all their resources, and if they trace it to you, you'll not be able to come back here again."

"I understand, and I think I know a way." She had told him not to ask questions, and now he showed that he had learned the lesson. "I wasn't bargaining for anything like this, but I see it's important, and you may count on me to do my best. If I fail, it won't be from lack of careful thought."

X

That subject settled, he told her about a stout old woman, widow of a butler in the home of a Warsaw merchant. Trudi had heard all about Lanny's interest in spiritualistic matters; it had been part of the gossip concerning the rich American couple, and had cost him a good part of the respect which the comrades might otherwise have felt for him.

"I have never given any thought to such matters, Lanny," she said, taking no chance of offending him.

"I know, but you're going to give some now. Last week I had a séance, hoping to get Freddi, and instead I got a voice that said he was Ludi."

"*Ach, Gott!*" He felt her start. "Did it sound like him?"

"Not especially; but it usually doesn't. What I did was to ask for a sort of password; something that you would be sure to know."

"And he gave one?"

"He said to tell you 'Chin-Chin.' "

She sat up, forgetting about the traffic and the possibility of being seen. "Oh, Lanny, how amazing!"

"You recognize it, then?"

"It was a little Skye terrier we had."

"He barked with great excitement—short, quick barks—you'd almost think he was crazy."

"Did Ludi say that?"

"He did it. At least there was a lot of barking, and when I asked if it was a dog, he said: 'It was me.' "

The woman sat with her hands pressed together until the knuckles were white. "Lanny, that takes my breath away! Ludi used to play with the dog; he would get down on his hands and knees and bark at him, and the dog would bark back, and you could hardly tell one from the other. It used to terrify me, because the dog became so excited, and I was afraid he might bite Ludi's nose."

"Ludi said: 'People do silly things when they are young, and happy, and very much in love.' "

The woman bowed her head in her hands and began to weep silently. It was too much, hitting her all at once. The fact that Ludi was dead—and the fact that he was alive! But was he? Right away arose those doubts which torment people who begin to consider the possibility of survival; especially when they have built their faith upon the dogma of materialistic interpretation—not merely of history, but of psychology, and of everything else on, under, or above the earth!

The woman began to stammer questions through her tears. Did Lanny really believe it was Ludi? What else had he said? Did he say what had happened to him at the hands of the Stormtroopers? And what was happening to him now? She was ashamed of her tears, because she was certain that it was all nonsense; but even to think about it was more than she could bear. The strangest paradox imaginable: she couldn't believe that Ludi was dead unless she first believed that he was alive, and she couldn't believe that he was alive unless she first believed that he was dead! And which did she want him—dead in this world and alive in a future, or alive in this world and certain to be dead before long? Also, which was more precious to her, love for her husband or love for her Marxist doctrines?

Lanny couldn't solve those problems for her. He could only tell her everything that had happened, every word that had been spoken. They were out in the snowbound country by that time, and he drew up by the roadside and consulted his notebook to verify details. Then she wanted to know about Madame from the beginning, and those strange phenomena the very thought of which had bored her two or three years ago. Zaharoff and his duquesa, Lady Caillard and her husband—"Vinnie, Birdie, and a Kiss!"—and then about Johannes's Uncle Nahum, and all the other shadow figures who had haunted the personality of Madame, like so many bats in the twilight, fluttering past a light and then out into darkness again.

"Lanny, I must meet that woman!"

"We have brought her to Berlin more than once, and it may be possible to do it again. Meanwhile, here is something you might do." He told her how he and his wife had each of them visited a different medium in Berlin at the same time, and had got what was called a "cross-correspondence"; that is, two parts of a message which fitted together, in this case a verse from the Bible. One of these women was fashionable and high-priced, but the other was poor and obscure. Lanny consulted his notebook and wrote down her name and address for Trudi.

"Don't say an unnecessary word," he advised. "Give a false name if she asks. Pay her five marks or whatever she charges, and sit still and listen to what she says."

Immediately the Marxist conscience of Trudi Schultz began to trouble her. "Lanny, it seems wicked to spend money for such things when the cause needs it so badly!"

"I'm interested in this subject," replied the young plutocrat, with a grin. "I make it obligatory—like the liter of milk every day! By the way, I see you have been getting that, for it shows in your face."

XI

Lanny gave his friend the money he had brought, and then deposited her in the vicinity of a station of the Underground from which she could get to her home. Then he set out toward the west, and when he was out in the country he stopped and unwrapped the documents which Trudi had left with him, freight more dangerous than so many cans of nitroglycerin. With tools in his car he took off the cover from the back of a picture frame, spread the documents flat against the back of the canvas, and tacked the cover into place again. It wasn't a perfect job, but he counted on the priceless bill of sale with the letterhead of the Minister-Präsident of Prussia and the official stamps and seals, so overwhelmingly impressive to every German functionary.

He wasn't going to Paris, but to Amsterdam, an orderly and well-conducted capital a safe distance out of Naziland. As he drove he tried to imagine all possible mishaps which could occur at the border, and to rehearse what he would do and say in connection with them. By no means the best thought-companions on a cold January day with flurries of snow in the air making careful driving imperative. He made up his mind to take the most haughty of attitudes; to stand on the prerogative of his expensive car, his impeccable clothing, and above all his almost divine document. Under no circumstance would he permit anyone to lay profane hands upon the precious paintings; he would produce a veritable tornado of *Donnerwetter* and threaten instant loss of office to the underling who dared to defy his commands. He would compel that person to telephone immediately to the Minister-Präsident's staff officer; or, if this was refused, Lanny would insist that they wait until he had had opportunity to do so himself.

But all this worrying proved entirely unnecessary; such mishaps simply do not take place under *deutsche Zucht und Ordnung*. The fine car drew up in front of the painted pole which barred the highway, and the driver descended to meet the officials who came forth from the station. It was dark, and snow was falling; there were dim shadows while he stood in the rays of a flashlight. He swung up a stiff right arm and declaimed: *"Heil Hitler!"* They answered—it was obligatory, also automatic. He dropped his arm again, and in his best German announced: "I am an art expert"—fortunately the Germans have a full-sized and impressive word, *Kunstsachverständiger*, literally, "art-object-understander." He went on: "I have traveled to Berlin at the request of Minister-Präsident General Göring and purchased from him two art works which I have in this car. I am instructed by Oberleutnant Furtwaengler of the Minister-Präsident's personal staff to present to you this bill of sale for the works as evidence that the matter is according to command—" *befehlmässig*, another impressive word. "Here also are my passport and my exit permit, which has been signed by the Minister-Präsident's office."

"*Sehr wohl, mein Herr.*" They fell over themselves. Nothing so momentous had come their way in many a week. "*Will der Herr nicht hinein kommen?*"

"I'll wait and stretch my legs," said Lanny. "*Heil Hitler!*"

"*Heil Hitler! Heil Hitler!*" They didn't even ask if he was taking out money or anything else that was *verboten.* They hurried inside, and never were documents inspected and stamped so promptly. Others came out to have a glimpse of the wonderful car and the wonderful Herr who only a few hours previously had been in the actual presence of the Godhead; not El Shaddai, the Terrible One, but the Teutonic Odin, God of the Furious Host. The documents were returned with bows, and Lanny took them and put them with slow dignity into an inside pocket; he stepped into his car, the barrier was raised, and he rolled into the Koningrijk der Nederlanden.

XII

In a comfortable room in the Hotel Amstel Lanny put in a midnight call for Eric Vivian Pomeroy-Nielson at The Reaches. He felt safe now—if the Gestapo hadn't been interested to follow him in Berlin, they would hardly be doing it here. "Excuse me if I woke you up," he said. "I'm in Amsterdam on picture business, and Irma is waiting in Paris. There's something I need your advice about. Can't you and Nina take the Harwich ferry tomorrow evening? I'll meet you at the Hook in the morning and drive you to Paris and we'll have a lark."

"Well, I'll be damned!" said the baronet's son.

"I can't explain it, but it's important, and you'll understand when I see you. Don't say anything to Nina about it, just call it a holiday and let me pay the bills—it'll be worth it many times over to me. If she can't come, you get somebody to motor you to Harwich and let me pay for that."

"You must have sold some big pictures, old top! It's a date!"

Lanny called his wife and told her of this arrangement. She said:

"Oh, goody!" and felt no surprise because people jumped here and there in search of pleasure. She herself had just got back from a theater party with Denis de Bruyne. Lanny said: "Furtwaengler sent his love—I believe you have made a conquest." He laughed, because he could imagine the *moue* she would be making. She regarded the Nazi staff officer as what the Germans call an *Emporkömmling*, a "little upcomer."

Lanny had the two paintings brought to his room with him and now he took off the back of one and spent a good part of the night studying the photographs—twenty-four sheets, carefully selected. He thought: "If this doesn't wake up the British and French, they'll deserve what is coming to them." He thought of the model airplane factory his father was planning, and had an impulse to go and help. But no, what he was doing was better. Set up a big alarm bell and start it ringing!

He slept with the documents half under him, and in the morning he borrowed a needle and thread from the chambermaid—having a hard time persuading her not to do the work for him! He sewed the documents in several parts of his coat-lining, and then, feeling like a padded Chinese, he had his paintings carried down into the hotel basement and separately crated by the porter. He took them to the express office and shipped them, duly covered by insurance; after which he went for a walk in this fine old city of frozen canals and snow-covered trees.

In the Ryks Museum the kindly authorities had provided comfortable plush-covered benches upon which an art expert could sit for hours and study the fine points of several of the world's great masterpieces. During his lifetime the creator of these works had been treated none too well; he had died bankrupt and miserable, but now he was honored, and his finest works were placed in separate rooms with ample space and perfect lighting. Amid reverent silence Lanny could lose himself in a time three hundred years gone, imagining himself in conversation with the five "Syndics," members of the Clothmakers' Company. This association had made good cloth and from it their tailors had made good clothing; the five gentlemen had put on their best, and their wives had seen to it that all the accessories were right, while an eccentric genius named Rembrandt van Rijn was immortalizing their features and figures. They looked out at Lanny with such life that he was prepared to have them speak, and was sure it would be a worthwhile conversation; for they were obviously cultivated gentlemen, who knew how to make use of their wealth and whose ideas were by no means limited to the quality and prices of cloth.

In an adjoining and much larger room the visitor renewed his acquaintance with a great canvas, covering an entire wall, *The Sortie*, sometimes known as *The Night-Watch* although it appears that the sun is streaming onto some of the accouterments and colored raiment of the watchmen. It is the painting which ruined poor Rembrandt, because the gentlemen who had ordered it wanted a portrait gallery, with each of their faces given equal prominence, whereas the bold painter had presumed to compose a scene. They were marching out to repel invaders; and Lanny had a hard time keeping his attention on the fine points of the art of applying paint to canvas, because he was thinking about the position of a small and civilized country lying alongside a powerful one which was rapidly sliding back into barbarism. He wanted to cry out to all the polite and friendly Dutch people whom he saw in this museum: "Keep your night-watch, and your day-watch, too, because the Nazis are making surveyor's maps of all your bombing objectives! Do not give too much thought to splendid uniforms or other such details, because you may have to dig down into your everlasting mud to hide from bombs and grenades and flame-throwers and poison gas!"

XIII

Nina and Rick arrived, and Lanny bundled them up and drove them to Paris in time for lunch. Afterward the two ladies discussed their affairs in Irma's room, while Lanny took his chum into his own and told him what it was that made his coat fit badly. After Rick had got over his amazement he said: "It's ghastly, Lanny, but I doubt if we British will really do anything about it, because our governing class can't make up their minds whether Hitler is good or bad—in other words, whether he intends to march east or west."

"Good God!" exclaimed the American. "If he's going east what does he want with surveys of London and Paris?"

"Oh, well, they're all getting such data—that is, unless they're too lazy, as I rather think we are just now."

Rick agreed that the only hope was to use the documents to stir up the public. An active journalist didn't have to be told what an explosion they would make, and he offered to take them straight to a liberal editor whom he knew and who would give them ample space and advertising. But Lanny said: "You've contributed to that paper, so you will be one of the first persons the Nazis will set out to trail. They will find out that you came to Amsterdam right after I left Germany; and they may even find us registered at this hotel."

"*Whoo-ee!*" said the Englishman.

"I've given a lot of thought to the job, and it's far from easy. You can't imagine what efforts Göring will make to trace this thing down; he'll stand the whole Gestapo on its head. If anything turns attention to me, they'll watch me the next time I come into Germany, and get every person who meets me."

"Right you are, son."

"These documents have to be published by some paper with which neither of us has ever had anything to do; a paper without any left tendencies, so that Göring will decide that the job was done by respectable government spies."

"That will need some thinking," declared Rick. "The *Times* has gone over to the pro-Hitler clique and the *Daily Mail* is practically a Fascist organ." He went on to canvass the other papers, and finally chose one which he said was completely reactionary, interested in rearmament from the point of view of British Empire security. "Too bad to promote its circulation, but that can't be helped. Hitler's going to make strange bed-fellows in all the nations around him!"

Said Lanny: "The documents ought to be taken to the paper, not by you but by somebody who is pledged never to mention where he got hold of them."

That also called for thinking. They discussed public men whom they knew, whether personally or by reputation, to find one who was honest, at least to the extent of being for England more than for himself. In the end Rick's choice fell upon a member of Parliament whom "the pater" knew slightly; one of those Englishmen who manage to combine Church of England piety with capitalist-class politics and the construction of bigger and better dreadnoughts. Rick would seek a private interview with this statesman, vouch for the genuineness of the documents, and pledge him to deliver them to the newspaper publisher without any hint as to how they had reached England.

"By the way," said Lanny, "I'm not saying anything to Irma about all this, and it might be just as well not to tell Nina."

"More than that," countered his friend, looking him in the eyes. "Neither of us is going to say one word about this—ever. Shake hands on it and mean it!"

8

The Dusky Clouds Ascending

I

THERE were three comfortable dwellings on the Bienvenu estate, the Villa, the Lodge, and the Cottage—the first being the home of the Dingles, the second of Lanny and Irma, and the third of Nina and Rick or other friends when they were free to come. Also there were two small structures known as studios, one having been built for Marcel and one for Kurt in the old days. Marcel's studio was now occupied by Lanny, his books, piano, and music, while the other was for Hansi and Bess when they came, and otherwise for any noisemaker or other eccentric person whom it was thought wise to

segregate. Lanny was always coming upon someone who claimed
to have genius, and Irma had been told that it was a distinguished
thing to have such persons on the place—only she begged that they
wouldn't be Reds or Pinks, because they brought such undesirable
company. Since Lanny was trying to avoid displeasing not merely
his wife but also a fat Nazi general and his secret police, he made a
practice of meeting his off-color friends at some obscure lunching-
place in the city of Cannes.

Bienvenu was an extremely humble affair according to Barnes family standards, but Irma put up with it for the sake of love and the
climate. The main trouble was, there was no room for entertaining
on what she considered an adequate scale, and outdoor affairs were
subject to the whims of the weather. The problem was solved by a
combination with Emily Chattersworth, who had two fine drawing-
rooms at Sept Chênes, her Riviera home, big enough for dancing.
Emily was no longer equal to the task of entertaining, yet she
couldn't bear to give up her friends or to neglect to make use of a
celebrity when one came along. So Irma would come up and act as
hostess, with the older woman to advise her. After some argument
Irma had gained the right to pay for the "talent," also for the food
and drink. Emily's staff of well-trained servants would do the work,
and the utility king's daughter would watch and learn every detail
of the subtle duties of a *salonnière*. That was the career she had
chosen, and the experience would be equally useful whether she decided to apply it in Paris, London, or New York.

So a season passed pleasantly enough. Visitors came back to the
Riviera, and costumes and jewels and titles were flaunted. Prosperity
appeared to be reviving after a long financial drought. Franklin D.
Roosevelt had been President of the United States for two years, and
while the Supreme Court had thrown out some of his schemes, the
general idea of free spending was coming to be accepted, even by
those who scolded at it. The device enabled people to live, and after
the fright they had had, that was enough. The masses got money
from the government and spent it in grocery and clothing stores, and
these in turn bought from the wholesalers, and these from the manufacturers; so it went, all the way down the line, and bonds which

Irma owned began to draw interest and stocks to earn dividends. Each quarter her income was a bit larger, and all this reinforced her own firm conviction that money was made to be spent.

People gathered around, eager to help her spend it, and she was generous because that was so much the easiest way; she didn't want glum or anxious faces anywhere in sight, and would put money in the bank to Beauty's account and to Lanny's, and if she found them trying to economize she would say: "What's the big idea?" Living with or near the daughter of J. Paramount Barnes was like being on board one of those old-fashioned, full-rigged clipper ships with every sail set—a wet sheet and a flowing sea, a wind that follows fast, and fills the white and rustling sails and bends the gallant mast!

II

The Saarland plebiscite was held in January, and resulted in a nine-to-one vote by the inhabitants in favor of a return to Germany. The district had always been German, and doubtless would have voted that way without the colossal propaganda campaign which the Nazis had put on. But the Nazis liked such campaigns, they were the breath of Nazi being, and they were practice for other campaigns which were scheduled for everywhere along the German borders. They included not merely speeches and music and marching, but also the boycotting of merchants and the terrorizing of opponents by brownshirted rowdies of the Deutsche Front, armed with revolvers, daggers, and hard-rubber truncheons.

As soon as the election results were announced, the Nazis prepared their "long knives," and so most of the French population picked up what belongings they could carry and fled. Many came to the Riviera, because it was warmer and therefore a more pleasant place in which to starve. Many were of leftist tendency, and they hadn't been starving for long before they heard about that extraordinary American family with a son and heir who had a tender heart and who was simply rolling in money, being married to one of the greatest heiresses in the world. So came numbers of begging letters in the Bienvenu mail, and many of them were heart-rending. Visitors came to the gates, and when they were told that the young master was not at home they would go away and put their wits to work on some method of getting hold of him.

There had been a sort of amateur secret service at work on the Budd family, and all the Reds and Pinks knew exactly the situation. The mother was a butterfly and a good deal of a fool, while the wife was reactionary, even Fascist in her sympathies; these two guarded the place like dragons and told all the servants not to let strangers past the gates. The time to catch Lanny was when he came to town; then if you pounced on him and told him a hard-luck story, he couldn't say No. Another method of contact was through Raoul Palma, director of the École des Travailleurs du Midi; so it came about that new persons joined the school and asked for jobs as teachers, with salaries however small. Lanny would give money to his Spanish friend, but always under the condition: "Do me the favor to pretend that you got it somewhere else."

III

There came a letter from Rick, saying: "I have seen the gentleman whom I hope to interest in your pictures, and I think the deal will go through." Then a second note: "The picture deal is O.K., and I believe you will be satisfied." A week or so later the documents were published, in installments, day after day, and there was a tremendous sensation; the baronet's son wrote about it freely, as he would have done if he had known nothing about the matter in advance. There were interpellations in Parliament, and vague answers to the effect that the government were taking cognizance—the English government were always plural, and also they were dignified, imperturbable, and slow to anger when they wanted to be. There was a new term coming into use for statesmen and officials who avoided getting angry with the Nazis; they were called "appeasers," and the Nazis quickly found out who they were and made the most of their state of mind. Jesse Blackless had pointed out to his nephew the fact that those who were most afraid of displeasing the Nazis appeared to be least afraid of displeasing the Soviets.

Lanny got copies of the London papers, and clipped them and sent them to his father. "This looks to be genuine," he wrote, "and ought to help sell your products when you get them ready." Robbie replied: "Hot stuff, and if I thought it was genuine I'd send Johannes over now! Send me anything more of the sort that you come upon. Also, ask your fat friend about it the next time you see him!"

Ramsay MacDonald, still holding on as Prime Minister, made a speech protesting against German rearmament. Ramsay made speeches about many evils, and assumed that this was equivalent to abolishing them. Hitler made a speech in reply, telling how pacific were the intentions of his government; and all the appeasers said: "There, now, you see how he is being maligned!" Wickthorpe told Rick that Downing Street—the British Foreign Office—had made strong representations to the Wilhelmstrasse, and the Wilhelmstrasse had promptly denounced the documents as fraudulent. His Lordship added that he was inclined to accept this, and Rick was not in position to dissent. Among other things Rick sent to Lanny was a clipping from a Left paper of London which said that, if the truth ever became known about these revelations, it would be found that aircraft manufacturers outside of Germany had had a hand in the preparation of them. Rick put some exclamation points in the margin of this, and Lanny Budd, son of an embryo aircraft manufacturer, didn't fail to appreciate the humor.

Also, there came one of those plain-looking missives from Berlin. "Mueller" expressed her gratitude for his wise use of her sketches, and promised to make some more. Lanny knew that the circulation of English newspapers was still permitted in Germany, and while those particularly dangerous issues had doubtless been confiscated, the details would be known to both the Nazis and their foes. In the midst of the darkness of intrigue that covered Europe, you cast your bread upon the waters—such small crumbs of truth as you could collect—and wondered if the Preacher had been right and would you ever find them again, and where, and when, and how.

IV

There was a diplomatic chess-game being played, with the continent of Europe as the board; a new and immensely complicated kind of chess in which the pieces, instead of being lined up on opposite sides, had each his own color and played his own game. Each king, queen, knight, castle, even the smallest pawn, had his group of elder statesmen who put their heads together in anxious consultation, and after days and perhaps weeks of arguing they made a move; whereupon the whole aspect of the board was altered, and the statesmen of all the other pieces put their heads together and argued and agonized, until some group made a countermove, and at once the clamor of protest and the buzz of consultation started up afresh in all the other chess-chancelleries.

Britain and France had been playing as partners, but were greedy and suspicious, each of the other, and Britain was willing to let Germany grow stronger in order to keep France from growing too strong. So France turned to Russia, which she hated, trying to work out a deal for common defense against a greater danger. Hitler and Mussolini, two upstarts jealous of each other, were ready to break all the rules of the game in the effort to grab something for themselves. Pierre Laval, fresh from a visit to Moscow, paid one to Rome, in which he cooked up a deal with Mussolini pledging them both to mutual assistance should Germany take what was called "unilateral action" in the matter of rearming. Meanwhile the British Foreign Secretary was angling for an invitation to Munich in order to negotiate with Hitler the terms on which Britain might grant him permission to rearm. Then, of course, it wouldn't be "unilateral action"!

Such was the state of affairs on the sixteenth of March, when Hitler in one of those sudden moves which Europe was learning to know to its terror, upset the continental chessboard by announcing conscription and universal military service in Germany; also that the army, which the Versailles treaty had limited to a hundred thousand men, was to be increased to more than five hundred thousand. At the same time he issued to the German people one of those flamboyant manifestoes, which to Lanny Budd was like hearing his raucous

scolding voice. For the ten-thousandth time "Adi" recited the out-
rages of the Versailles *Diktat;* for the ten-thousandth time he repeated
the tale which he had invented and taught to the German people,
that the Allies had promised at Versailles to disarm themselves; for
the ten-thousandth time he made that declaration of peaceful and
honorable intentions which cost him nothing and was worth several
army corps to him and his party:

"In this hour the German government renews before the German
people, before the entire world, its assurance of its determination
never to proceed beyond the safeguarding of German honor and
freedom of the Reich, and especially does it not intend in rearming
Germany to create any instrument for warlike attack, but, on the
contrary, exclusively for defense and thereby for the maintenance of
peace. In so doing, the German Reich government expresses the confident hope that the German people, having again reverted to their
own honor, may be privileged in independent equality to make their
contribution toward the pacification of the world in free and open
co-operation with other nations and their governments."

V

A great many people thought that Adolf Hitler Schicklgruber was
insane, and they wrote and talked that way concerning him. When
Lanny's friends asked him about this, he replied that it might be a
question of definition. If Adi was a lunatic, he was one of that well-
known kind which possesses and displays the utmost cunning. He
had learned about the British habit of weekends, and so he made it
a rule to announce his bold moves on a Saturday. No British statesman could possibly take action on that day, and every British statesman would have all day Sunday to pray over it, to contemplate the
horrors of war and work himself into a state of conscientiousness.
He would threaten and bluster, of course; he had to do that in order
to be re-elected, but he wouldn't take any action—so Adi figured.

For a while Lanny Budd was fooled, and thought that the Versailles law—the only law that poor Europe had—was going to be
enforced. The French government issued a call for common action,

and French troops moved up to the German border. The British liberal and labor papers, those which Lanny read, all clamored for the ending of this intolerable menace. The statesmen rushed here and there like ants whose nest has been upset; they argued and scolded and issued high-sounding pronouncements. The French appealed to the League of Nations, whose duty it was to enforce the law, and the League summoned its Council to decide upon a course.

Lanny, the optimist, cherished the dream that Nazism was going to be checked at last, and he was disconcerted by the letter which came from his English chum, saying: "What's the use of getting excited about German rearmament when you know that it's been going on for years? And don't make the mistake of expecting any action from the sort of statesmen we have here. The British lion is old and has lost nearly all his teeth."

Lanny couldn't believe it, and waited in a state of tension which threatened to interfere with his health. He composed a long letter to Rick, which caused his friend to protest: "No good convincing me. Convince Ramsay, the world's worst maker of phrases! Convince Simon, the world's worst pettifogging lawyer!"

Sir John Simon, British Foreign Secretary, had spent his long life confusing property-rights, and thought to confuse Hitler in the same way. Or, at any rate, so Rick said of him. The big Tory papers were all for "peace," and they were the papers from which nine-tenths of the British people got their ideas. As for the League, it hadn't stopped Japan from taking Manchuria, and wasn't ever going to stop any greedy power from taking whatever it could. The Nazi tiger was coming out of his cage—one small step at a time, and very softly, on padded feet, purring most beautiful phrases about making his contribution toward the pacification of the jungle in free and open co-operation with other predatory beasts.

Lanny couldn't give up his hope. How could a man go on living in a world such as Rick portrayed—a world governed by knaves or fools, or a combination of both? Something ought to be done, and Lanny was getting unhappy with himself about it. Here he was dressing up and helping to entertain his wife's friends; taking her out to parties whose sole distinction was the amount of money which had been squandered upon them; exchanging words of little consequence with persons who were considered *distingués,* not because they were wise or good, but because they had learned to spend their wealth upon highly conventionalized forms of costume and conduct. Lanny would drink tea, and dance, and bridle his tongue when political subjects were brought up. When he could stand no more of it he would go off to his studio and pound upon the piano—loudly enough to wake the ghosts of Marcel Detaze, who had painted the pictures on the walls of this studio, and of Great-Great-Uncle Eli Budd, who had willed Lanny most of the noble books which lined the rest of the wall-space.

Irma had come to understand that she had drawn an odd card in the marriage lottery. She knew that he had to let off steam, and didn't allow herself to be disturbed by thunderous sounds rolling over the estate. But after an hour or two, when she thought he had had a good "workout," she would appear in the studio door clad in a Chinese silk wrapper with magnificent embroidery, plus a pair of bathing-slippers, and holding by the hand a lovely little daughter who had just celebrated her fifth birthday with a party for all the aristocratic children of Cannes and the Cap d'Antibes. "Come on, Beethoven," she would say—or Chopin or Liszt, as she happened to guess. And of course Lanny couldn't resist such condescension; he would slip into his bathing-suit and they would race down to the blue Mediterranean, the temperature of which was exactly right at this time of the year. So the grandson of Budd's would forget the world's woes and follow the advice offered to Alexander the Great:

> Lovely Thais sits beside thee,
> Take the good the gods provide thee.

VI

Now and then, in some newspaper or magazine—mostly the leftward and wishful-thinking ones—Lanny would come upon some reference to the underground movement of Nazi Germany and the great success it was having; then something would warm up inside him and he would have a few hours of deep inward peace. He dictated letters and mailed out copies of photographs of paintings which he recommended to his clients, and by April he had found purchasers for three more of Göring's works. He was beginning to worry about not hearing from his fellow-conspirator; but at last came a note like the others: "If you see Herr Schmidt, the art dealer, tell him that I have some more sketches, which I hope he will interest himself in. Mueller."

Lanny had been preparing his wife, telling her of the orders he had got and suggesting a trip to Germany in the spring. Irma, for her part, had been preparing a more elaborate program. Her mother in the Long Island palace was clamoring about being neglected and not having seen her adored granddaughter for nearly a year. Irma had been afraid to take the child to America for fear of kidnapers; but now these seemed to have been all caught, and Irma wasn't the sort of person to stay worried about anything very long. Said she: "Let's go and spend at least part of the summer, and see how Robbie's getting along with his job."

They would visit Berlin and then sail from Bremen, or from London in case Lanny wanted to see Rick. They would motor, of course; and just as they were discussing whether to go by way of Paris or Vienna, there came a postcard from Pietro Corsatti, American-born Italian who represented a New York newspaper in Rome. They hadn't heard from him for a long time, but would never forget him because of the part he had played in helping to get them married. Now he wrote on a picture postcard showing an alluringly colored scene, a blue lake, a little island with a huge vine-covered palace having a red roof, and behind it green mountains capped with snow. "Isola Bella" was its name—Beautiful Isle—and underneath it "Pete" had written: "Another gab-fest. Why not come and listen in?"

Irma, who rarely read the newspapers, didn't know what this meant; Lanny explained that at Stresa, on Lago Maggiore in the Italian Alps, the statesmen of Britain, France, and Italy were assembling in the effort to agree upon a program to tie Hitler down and make him behave. Pete's suggestion struck a spark in an amateur publicist's soul. Over a period of many years he had been wont to grace these international gatherings with his airy presence; he knew

most of the correspondents and some of the diplomats, and it was
fun to watch history in process. He said: "Wickthorpe will probably
be with the British staff." Irma replied: "Let's go!"

After their fashion, at half a day's notice, they tossed their things
into their bags: winter things as well as summer, because, while it
would be warm in Italy, there would be heavy snows in the Alpine
passes. No need to make detailed plans; they would go like the wind,
where they listed, and in due time would write or wire instructions
for their packing, and for the twenty-three-million-dollar child and
her staff. Beauty was staying on at Bienvenu, having not yet decided
upon plans for herself and husband; she might be in England visiting
Margy when Irma and Lanny arrived. Such was the delightful way
of the rich. When a hot spell came, they picked up and moved to the
north; when chill winds arose, they fled south again; they were birds
of passage, beautiful and elegant birds of passage for whom the
modern world had been made.

VII

First the route along the Côte d'Azur, to Lanny as familiar as the
letters which composed his name. Then the Italian Riviera, full of
exciting memories. All border passport controllers had little books
with alphabetical lists of undesirable characters; but Lanny's sins
were eleven years old, and he trusted that the list wouldn't go back
that far, and it didn't. Up through the passes to Milan at the loveliest season of the year, with fruit trees in full blossom, turning the
humblest garden into a place of magic, filling the air with delicious
scents. Lanny loved this country and its people—at least the poor
ones, so cheerful and friendly—and he jabbered away with them
whenever he had a chance. If he hated those in authority he kept his
mouth shut—even when alone with his wife, who considered all authority as necessary, or it wouldn't exist.

Lanny knew the beautiful mountain lake, forty or fifty miles
long. Stresa is one of its smaller towns, popular with tourists and
crowded with tile-roofed villas and hotels. They hadn't wired for
accommodations, because Lanny thought his name might attract the

attention of his old enemies, the Fascist *Militi*. There were plenty of other resorts along the shore, and no trouble to drive a few miles. The precaution proved wise, for never had a conference been so thoroughly policed. Perhaps it was the recent killing of King Alexander and Barthou; Mussolini was harboring some of those conspirators and protecting them, but when he himself was on the scene it was quite another matter.

Here in Stresa the *carabinieri* were everywhere, and in hotels and other public places were swarms of men whom no one had trouble in recognizing as detectives. The sessions were held on a tiny island having one great palace and nothing else, so there was no difficulty in protecting its secrets; motor-boats with armed police kept intruders away, and an airplane overhead made certain that no adventurous revolutionist dropped bombs on visiting statesmen. Lanny and his wife arrived after dark, and the first thing they noted was searchlights in the sky and others sweeping the surface of the lake from motor-boats.

Lanny thought it the part of wisdom to establish his social status; so, as soon as they were in their suite, he put in a call to the hotel which had been set aside as headquarters of the delegations. It was evident from the sounds on the telephone line that one or more persons were listening in, and that was what he wanted. He asked for the secretary of Lord Wickthorpe. "Certainly, Mr. Budd, I am sure His Lordship will be glad to speak to you." Then, after a wait: "His Lordship wishes to know if you and Mrs. Budd will come for tea tomorrow afternoon." After that, Lanny could be sure that, however carefully the authorities might watch him, they wouldn't request him to leave.

VIII

At these conferences there was always a press headquarters, a sort of clubhouse for the swarms of correspondents. Thus it was easy to get hold of Pietro Corsatti. Would he have dinner? Indeed he would; but why not come with Pietro and meet some of the bunch? This pleased Lanny more than anything; it had been his function to pay the bill, and his privilege to listen while the men who knew what was going on in the world shared their "tips" with one another. Most of them had known the grandson of Budd's over a period of years; he wouldn't betray any confidences, and if they mentioned him and his plush-lined wife as among the visitors at a diplomatic "gab-fest," that would enhance the prestige of a budding *Salonnière*. The newsmen liked Irma because she was easy-going and informal, having been trained in café society; they cultivated Lanny because he had social contacts which might make him a source of news.

The correspondents were having the devil of a time here at Stresa, they reported. Never had speech-making statesmen been kept so aloof as out on that island, where Napoleon had once entertained an Italian diva. The future of Europe for a hundred years might depend on what they were deciding, but the information you got was contradictory, and the Americans were having to pad their dispatches with accounts of Blackshirt parades and the loveliness of almond blossoms. The journalist with an Italian name and a Brooklyn accent cried desperately: "For Pete's sake, get Wickthorpe to spill some beans!" Lanny replied: "For Pete's sake, I'll do what I can."

Laval and Flandin were representing France; a queer pair, one squat, the other several inches taller than anybody else and that much duller. Pete said they were the calamity twins of France, and MacDonald and Simon were the same for England. Il Duce was here, representing himself; he had just issued decrees doubling his own army, and now France and England were trying to buy him to some program that would at least look like restraining Hitler. What price was Musso demanding, and how much of it was he going to get? These were the questions which tormented the journalists; and the extreme secrecy meant bad luck for somebody. Austria, perhaps? Or was it Abyssinia? "Poor niggers!" exclaimed one of the Americans; he had read Thoreau in his youth, and didn't like killing, but fate had made him into a war correspondent, and his editors had sent him here because they thought that something was "cooking."

A few months ago there had been an "incident" at a place called Ual-Ual, which wasn't in any gazetteer, and which consisted of a

well and some mud-huts in the Ogaden Desert near Italian Somali-
land. Native troops accompanying a border commission had driven
some Italian troops away. This had been an insult to Il Duce's dignity, and his kept press denounced the intolerable conditions of dis-
order existing in this backward land. To watchful editors it meant
that Mussolini was getting ready to start that empire which he had
been promising his young Blackshirts for a matter of twelve or thirteen years. Pete pointed out that the headwaters of the Nile are in
that land, and surely Britain wasn't going to let anybody dam them
and divert them from the cotton-fields of the Sudan!

So they argued, outspokenly, and Il Duce's badly disguised detectives sat at near-by tables and listened, scowling. Lanny, the most
vulnerable person there, said the least. Later in the evening they
heard shouts in the square outside, and they left the *trattoria* and
joined the throngs which were hailing their stuffed-shirt leader.
"*Duce! Duce!*" They made it into a sort of chant, accenting and
spacing the two syllables equally, so that nobody could have been
sure whether they were saying "Doo-chay" or "Chay-doo." The
great empire-builder was in a hotel in front of them, and presently
he appeared on a balcony, clad in breeches and riding-boots. Ap-
pearing on balconies is one of the principal functions of a dictator,
and always a spotlight is ready to make him look grand in his shiny
uniform—even if he is rather short and thick through the middle like
the leader of the Fascisti.

Fifteen years had passed since Lanny had first seen this man of
destiny in San Remo, a thin, pasty-faced fellow with a little black
mustache and a black suit and tie; a renegade Socialist editor, being
cursed in public by one of the men he had betrayed. Now, walking
on the Promenade with Irma and their friend, Lanny told the story
of this encounter, and what he had learned about the "Blessed Little
Pouter Pigeon" from a couple of his former associates. Before the
World War he had appeared in Milan, a wretched half-starved
youth whining about his syphilis, and the Socialists had taken him in,
fed him, and taught him all he knew. Now those Socialists were dead,
or in exile, or slowly dying on barren rocky islands in the Mediter-

ranean; but this new Caesar was grown so great that he appeared on illuminated balconies, and when Americans wished to say what they thought of him they had to refer to him as "Mister Big."

IX

In every town where a conference took place there was always some resident English family of social acceptability, to whose home the wearied statesmen might repair for refreshment. Wickthorpe's secretary phoned to Mr. Budd, saying that he and his wife were invited to such a home on the lakeshore. They were received by an elderly lady and her two unmarried daughters, and introduced to other English residents—the hostess had made friends or enemies for life by extending or withholding invitations to this affair. Members of the diplomatic staff drifted in, including the gray-haired and mustached Prime Minister whom Lanny Budd looked upon as a pathetic renegade; but the renegade didn't know it, of course, and bowed graciously, saying: "Ah, Amer-r-ricans! I am r-r-really fond of your country." Tea was served in lovely Dresden cups, and in addition to little cakes there were scones in honor of a Prime Minister who came from Lossiemouth. They were passed around by means of a wicker table mounted on rubber-tired wheels and called "the curate," because its invention had deprived large numbers of amiable young Englishmen of their principal social function.

Wickthorpe was glad to see them, and was especially attentive to Irma, in a dignified and respectful way. He had always behaved thus, and Lanny's mother had observed it and had hinted at it tactfully to her son; but Lanny wasn't going to worry about any such matter—Irma had always had hosts of friends, both women and men, and how could people help admiring her? "Ceddy," that is, Cedric Masterson, fourteenth Earl of Wickthorpe, introduced her to distinguished persons, including the long and clerical-looking Sir John Simon. Lanny saw the ladies watching and putting their heads together, and knew they were saying: "That's Irma Barnes, the American heiress." They would look at Lanny and add: "That chap is her husband—some sort of art broker, they say." No use expecting people to say kind things behind your back in fashionable society, for they have social positions to guard and would cheapen themselves if they allowed too many to break into the sacred precincts.

It was Saturday afternoon, and everybody seemed to have plenty of time. Two distinguished diplomats played croquet with young ladies on the lawn, and others sat in groups under blossoming magnolia trees and talked about friends at home. Wickthorpe introduced Lanny to a couple of young fellows who were filling the same role of secretary-translator which the American had played in Paris at the age of nineteen. They and His Lordship talked freely about what had been happening on Isola Bella—it had all been settled that morning, it appeared, and the conference was ready to adjourn. The independence of Austria was to be guaranteed, and the three powers pledged themselves to oppose "by all practicable means" an evil thing called "unilateral repudiation of treaties." That meant, of course, Hitler's recent pronouncement about rearming; and Lanny was greatly heartened—until he began thinking about the word "practicable." He had been among diplomats enough to learn how they said something which seemed to mean something but didn't; how they put in weasel words which would sneak away with the substance of any sentence.

"Just what is practicable right now, Ceddy?" he inquired; and the answer was: "Oh, well, you know we don't want to get into a war."

"I hope not," said Lanny. "But suppose Hitler won't stop for anything less?"

"Well, but he's got to, old chap. If we fight Hitler, we're both playing Stalin's game."

"Yes, I know. But if you don't fight, maybe you're both playing Hitler's game."

They had no time for further discussion. As Wickthorpe was turning away he remarked: "I say, Lanny, you understand that what we've been talking about is strictly under your hat."

"Oh, of course," said the other, with a pang for his friend Pete. "But, if it's settled, why don't you give it out?"

"Well, you see, some of our leading papers don't publish on Sunday, so we're holding the announcement for Monday morning."

X

The news was released in due course, and the diplomats entrained for Geneva, where the Council of the League was due to meet, and, it was hoped, take a firm stand against the violators of law. Brass bands played the delegates out of Stresa, and marching throngs of Fascisti sang to them of the future glories of Italy. Lanny and Irma bade farewell to their friends and set out through the Alpine passes on the way to Vienna. It was the season of spring floods and avalanches, which are no respecters of social position; but Lanny was a skilled driver and Irma was not the nervous sort, so they enjoyed some of the world's most celebrated scenery.

In Vienna he had an appointment with one of the old empire's nobility who had at last consented to put a price on some of his art treasures. They were invited to tea in one of those half-abandoned marble palaces on the Ringstrasse, and looked at old masters and argued over what they would bring in the American market. This displayed an elderly aristocratic couple in the worst of lights to Irma Barnes; but they had the titles and manners and there could be no denying that they had once had the "stuff."

Poor souls, they had lost the war, and it was necessary to treat them with great consideration. What seemed small sums to a utility king's daughter were of the utmost importance to them, and they suffered agonies of soul under the process of deflation which Lanny felt obliged to put them through. "If you really want me to make sales, this and this and this is what you will have to accept." They wanted so badly to get an offer; but Lanny was immovable. "I do not make offers. I tell you that at such and such a price I will try to find you a buyer; but you must make the offer." In the end, close to tears, they gave way.

A night at the opera, and next day the motorists were at the Polish border. It wouldn't do to pass so close to the Meissners without stopping, so Lanny telephoned to Kurt and, learning that he was going to Berlin to conduct one of his works, invited him to come along in the car. Driving to Stubendorf, Lanny said: "Let's not say anything about having stopped in Stresa. They will look upon that conference as an anti-German conspiracy."

Irma, a comfortable person, well satisfied with the world's arrangements, wished that people wouldn't quarrel and upset everybody's peace of mind. She was inclined to take the point of view of those she was with; at least to let them think that she did so. She was sure there ought to be some reasonable settlement of Germany's claims, but she hadn't insisted upon it while having tea with the fourteenth Earl of Wickthorpe and his colleagues. She would agree with the Meissners that Stubendorf ought certainly to be allowed to go back to Germany; but if she had been visiting one of the Polish families of the district—well, she hadn't met any Poles, and their case wasn't clear to her. Both sides had factories, and both needed the coal which came from the mines under these hills. "Why can't they buy it from each other?" she wanted to know, and Lanny mentioned that profits go to those who own and not to those who buy. "You ought to know that!" he said.

XI

The arrival of this fashionable American couple always created a stir in Stubendorf. Seine Hochgeboren was away, so they stayed the night at the home of Kurt's father, the Comptroller-General of the great estate. They slept in the rather small room which had been Kurt's, and which Lanny had shared with him on his first Christmas visit more than twenty years ago. The Meissners were warm-hearted people, and they still saw him as the gay and graceful lad who had shown them Dalcroze dancing and amused them with his American accent. He hadn't known that he had one, of course, and they had never told him, but had cherished his quaint phrases after he had gone. Now he was here with his heiress wife, and since the pair had been guests several times at the Schloss, it was doubtful if the family of a mere *Beamter* was good enough to receive them. A lot of fuss had to be made and extra food prepared.

Kurt and Lanny played music out of the treasury of four-hand compositions. The family all sang for a while, and it was so lovely that tears ran down the cheeks of the old couple. The father's health was failing, and he wasn't going to listen to music much longer, at least not played on the old piano in his somewhat crowded living-room. They didn't spoil that sentimental evening with talk about politics or anything in the ugly outside world. Irma thought: "Now I am meeting the real Germans; and oh, dear, why can't they stay like this always?"

But no, indeed; Germany was ringed with enemies—*die Einkreisung*, they called it—and they were getting ready to break that ring. In the morning the travelers shifted their bags so as to make room for Kurt in the back seat and they drove into Germany. First they were held up by not very prompt or courteous Polish border guards, and Kurt said: "You see what we have to go through." Then, on the first level plain they came to, uniformed young Germans were drilling in the yet unmelted snows. None of the travelers commented, but all three were thinking: "It is the big new army the Führer has promised!" Later they passed an airport, and planes flew close overhead, as if inspecting a foreign car and its occupants; all three of them thought: "The new fighter planes of General Göring!"

They talked about music, and the paintings that Lanny had handled, and about Robbie's new business undertaking. Kurt was always glad to hear how Beauty was getting along; he said that she had saved his life after the war, and in the Continental fashion he spoke frankly about the years of happiness she had given him. Once when a sparkplug fouled and they stopped to have it fixed, Irma and Kurt strolled up and down and she told him: "Lanny is behaving much better, and I am really happy about him." She meant it, for like most humans she found it easy to believe what she wanted to. Sometimes it appeared as if life could hardly have gone on in these days of old Europe's trials if it hadn't been for this odd human faculty.

Kurt didn't wish to stay in a fashionable hotel; he had already promised to visit the family of his brother Emil, a colonel in the Reichswehr. He was going to be busy with rehearsals, which his friends might attend if they would be interested. Nothing would have pleased Lanny more, but he had business he must see to. So

they parted for a while, and as Lanny drove on to the Adlon he was
wondering: "Am I really fooling him? And just how much?" He
knew that he was fooling Irma pretty well, and it hurt him; but it
was one of those things which couldn't be cured and must be endured.

XII

Lanny had telegraphed Furtwaengler, announcing that he and his
wife were on the way; now, in the morning, he phoned the Oberleutnant, whose first words were: "*Ach schade, Herr Budd,* you
should have been here for the wedding!"

"Why didn't you let me know in time?" asked the visitor. He
meant it for a joke, but the staff officer took it for a rebuke and was
profuse in apologies. Only after he had received forgiveness did he
feel free to rave over the wonders of that greatest of all German
social events, the marriage of the Führer's second-in-command to
Emmy Sonnemann, the stage and screen star who had been his official mistress for some time. After the ceremony there had been a
reception in the Opera House—the performance had been held up
for more than an hour while Minister-Präsident General Göring and
his bride stood in the great hall at the head of the staircase, shaking
hands with all the eminence of the Third Reich and the diplomatic
world.

Lanny said: "I read a lot about it in the foreign press. I saved some
clippings for you."

"*Danke schön!*" exclaimed the worshipful young Schutzstaffel
man. "We are collecting everything and will prepare scrapbooks for
the National Bibliothek."

"How are the happy couple?" inquired the visitor, gallantly, and
was informed that they were both sitting on top of the world. The
Oberleutnant had become fond of this phrase, which he believed was
the very latest American slang, and Lanny didn't suggest how uncomfortable this position might prove to a man of Seine Exzellenz's
figure.

Lanny specified what pictures he had come to purchase, and mentioned with seeming casualness that he and his wife had been attend-

ing the Stresa Conference. No competent staff officer would fail to get the significance of that. "Seine Exzellenz will wish to see you! Will you hold the wire?" Lanny did so, and presently was told that the Minister-Präsident was due to leave that afternoon and spend a night and a day in the Schorfheide. Would Herr and Frau Budd honor him by coming along? Lanny replied that nothing would give them both more pleasure.

He hung up, and remarked: "So, we are going to see Karinhall!"

"And Emmy, do you suppose?" asked Irma.

9

Shape of Danger

I

IN A WHITE marble palace on the fashionable Königin Augusta-strasse lived Irma's friend the Fürstin Donnerstein, second wife of a Prussian landowner and diplomat some thirty years older than herself. She had first met Irma on the Riviera, before the latter's marriage, and had taken a fancy to her; they had gone about together, gossiping about nothing very much. Now the Fürstin had three children in her nursery and was bored, missing that gay free life on the Coast of Pleasure and finding Berlin society stiff, cold, and dull. Her husband's position required that she go out, so she picked up a great deal of news, of which she desired to make the normal use. When Irma came along they would have a regular spree of gossip, the American having to swear that she wouldn't repeat a word of it in Germany.

So it would be: "*Ach, meine Liebe,*" and: "*Na, na, meine Gute!*" Hilde, a tall blonde, rather thin for a German matron, smoked too many cigarettes, and perhaps as a consequence of this was nervous and intense in manner. She would begin: "*Man sagt—*" and then she would look about, lower her voice, and say: "Perhaps I'd better not"—which was provoking. She would get up and go to the door of her boudoir and open it suddenly and look out. "You never can tell. One's servants have all become *politisch gesinnt*"—she spoke nine-tenths English and one-tenth German. "It is you Americans who are to blame. They have heard of that *fabelhaftes Land* where there are no class distinctions, where anybody can become rich and nearly everybody does. So now we have a *kleinbürgerliche Regierung*—the little man is on top, and we are prisoners in our own homes. Somebody may report on us, and some official may welcome a chance to show himself *eifrig* at our expense."

Irma had seen in some homes a device called a "cozy," a sort of little tent made of quilting, to be set over the teapot and the hot-water kettle to keep them warm. Now Irma learned that it was used by Germans to set over a telephone, because they had the idea that there was some secret device which could be installed in the receiver so that outsiders could listen to conversations even when the phone was disconnected. Hilde wasn't sure if it was so, and didn't know how to make sure; so, when talking to Irma she carefully put the "cozy" over the phone, and when they were leaving the room she took it off, so that no servant might see what she had been doing. "*Wirklich*, it is like living in Turkey in the days of the sultan!"

Hilde Donnerstein was no conspirator, nor was her husband; they were simply two members of the old nobility who were, as she said, out of fashion; they resented the tough crowd who had seized the power and the glory for themselves, and they took revenge in telling personal scandals and funny stories about the absurdities of the *Emporkömmlinge*.

"*Ach, meine Liebe!* I must say I don't envy you your visit to that monstrous Karinhall! But I suppose you are curious about Emmy—no doubt you have seen her on the screen. *Ganz karyatidenhaft—*what is it that you say?—statuesque—but as for acting, *äusserst gewöhnlich;* all people of taste stay away. Of course, I suppose an opera house is the proper place for the wedding-reception of an actress. It is characteristic of our time—*eine Filmkönigin* instead of a real one!"

"Lanny says the film queens do it much better," remarked Irma.

"How can we judge? But really, when you consider what the life of that couple has been—you have heard that their affair has been of long standing?"

"I have heard rumors."

"They were getting along reasonably well; *der dicke Hermann* said: 'You know that I cannot marry you, of course'; and Emmy, who is not so bright, didn't know, but was afraid to say so. But one day the pair were in a motor accident—*schrecklich*—the car into a tree crashes; *der Dicke* is not much hurt, *aber die Geliebte*, she has her skull cracked and is in hospital a long time, and of course it is something that cannot be hidden, *die ganze Welt* talks; Hermann must go every day to see her, and it becomes a scandal. Then just the other day *unser*—" The Fürstin wishes to say "*unser Führer*," but doesn't quite dare, even in her own boudoir. She says: "*Die Nummer Eins* wishes to send his Number Two to the Balkans on a diplomatic mission—you know how it is, we must have allies there, our enemies seek to undermine us in every part of the world; and Hermann proposes to take his woman with him, she must have a rest, and he will make a little holiday of it. But *die Nummer Eins* says: '*Bist du toll?* You will force your mistress upon them? They will take it as an insult; they will say: "What do you think we are— niggers, perhaps?"' *Die Nummer Eins* is furious, and gives the fat man a dressing down. 'Marry her!' he says. 'I have had enough of scandal in my party—make her your wife, or we are *unten durch* in the Balkans!' So that is how we had this grand *Staatshochzeit mit Empfang*, with gifts the like of which have never been seen in all the world. It is what you say in America, *eine Hochzeit vor dem Gewehrlauf!*"

Irma didn't know these words, but the Fürstin explained that it was when the bride's father or her brothers come with guns and fetch the groom. Irma said, greatly amused: "Oh, a shotgun wedding!"

II

While Irma was enjoying this high-class entertainment, her husband was looking at an art show, and afterward driving his car into a Berlin slum. Promptly at the stroke of twelve he passed the agreed-upon corner and picked up his "underground" friend. Spring was here and the day was bright. She had left her heavy coat at home and wore a gray cotton print, the most inconspicuous that could be found; her hair was parted straight back and covered by a black straw hat—in short, she was a poor workingwoman, with no nonsense about her, and in her arms she was carrying a paper bag.

"Is that what you have for me?" he asked, but she said: "No, just groceries. I was afraid to bring what I have until I was sure you were coming."

"What is it?"

They were driving on a little-frequented street, but, even so, Trudi glanced about nervously and lowered her voice. "I have photostatic copies of confidential reports to the Wilhelmstrasse—that is the German Foreign Office—covering the details of our intrigues in various capitals; reports of our ambassadors and instructions to them."

"Good Lord, Trudi!"

"It will not be so easy to make use of them this time, I fear, since they expose the double-dealing of other nations also, and England among them. I cannot imagine any but a Socialist paper being willing to publish them."

"There's one bourgeois paper, the *Manchester Guardian*, which has a reputation for publishing the truth regardless of whom it hurts."

"Well, you will have to be the judge. You might give them to different papers, according to what they contain. For example, dispatches from our ambassador in Rome, telling the inside story of the deal between Mussolini and Laval. You know that Laval went to Rome at the beginning of the year and spent several days with Il Duce. Afterwards he gave the Chamber of Deputies the solemn assurance that he had made no concession imperiling the rights of Abyssinia."

"I made note of his language," said Lanny. "It was most explicit, but even so, I didn't believe him."

"He has made a 'gentleman's' agreement, permitting Il Duce to take the country without the interference of France. What worries Mussolini is that while he's tied up there, Hitler may take Austria; and so they have a mutual guarantee against this."

"If we could prove that, Trudi, we'd blow the lid off the diplomatic teakettle."

"Our ambassador states it categorically. Italy has already shipped thirty thousand troops through the Suez Canal, with complete equipment and supplies for a six months' campaign. Operations will begin in the autumn, when the rainy season there is over."

"What else have you in this magic box?"

"You have read about the decision of the Stresa Conference?"

"I was there five days ago."

"All three of the powers have been secretly negotiating with the German Foreign Office behind one another's backs—that is, they think it's secretly."

"But of course they all find out!"

"The real question is, what is going to be done at Geneva. The Wilhelmstrasse has the assurance that no overt action will be taken. Of course the Nazis don't care about speeches—that gives Hitler a chance to make more speeches and to play upon the persecution complex of our people. A committee of the League will be appointed, but no one of the Big Three is prepared to demand any action to stop German rearmament. Sir John Simon is angling now for another invitation to Berlin to negotiate permission for German naval rearmament up to a fixed percentage of the British."

"One of the newspaper men at Stresa told me that," responded Lanny. "It means a complete sell-out of France!"

"The Nazi argument is that they are not arming against the French fleet, but against the Russian. The Soviets have some new submarines, and it is not in the British interest that they should get command of the Baltic."

"There it is again!" exclaimed the American. "Everything goes back to their fear of the Reds. If they have to choose, they prefer Fascism every time."

"There's an intrigue going on between Mussolini and the British over the lake called Tsana, the source of the Blue Nile. Some day there will be a big dam, and the question is whether the waters shall flow to the Sudan or eastward to where Mussolini is going to settle his Fascist families. The British are willing to let Abyssinia go, provided they can have the lake and its headwaters; but Mussolini won't give them enough, and it looks as if there'd be a showdown before the end of the year. The Wilhelmstrasse is happy over that, because it will mean that we can have the *Anschluss* with Austria, and perhaps close the Polish Corridor also. Göring is planning to travel to the Balkans next month to cement alliances there—our new trade routes lie that way, down the Danube with our machinery and munitions, and returning with wheat and oil and raw materials."

III

So there was a diplomatic map of Europe, drawn by the cartographers of the Nazi Führer. Lanny recalled his friend the young S.A. sports director, Hugo Behr, who had been shot in the face during the blood purge of less than a year ago. Hugo's crime had been that he had taken seriously the second half of the label, National Socialist, and had urged that the party should attempt to carry out its promises to the little people of the Fatherland. In his last days on earth he had explained to Lanny how the course the Führer was following would make him the prisoner of the Reichswehr, or rather of the Junker officers who controlled that highly disciplined fighting-force. "If he bases his program for re-employment entirely upon armaments, it means that sooner or later we shall have to fight, because that's all you can do with guns and tanks."

Here was the prophecy coming true. Anybody who was capable of thinking could see that the little people of the Fatherland were being led into another slaughter-pit. The trouble was, there were so few people anywhere in the world who could think or were willing to take the trouble; and in Germany so many of them had had their faces blown off, or were shut up in concentration camps, being made into physical and nervous wrecks. Lanny recalled a remark he had heard the Führer make on the subject of the spiritual, nature of man: "The greatest of spirits can be liquidated, if its bearer is beaten to death with a rubber truncheon."

"You're right about those documents, Trudi," he said. "They are dynamite, and if they're in a safe place I'd rather wait and get them when I'm ready to leave. My bags are likely to be opened at the hotel; and tonight I'm invited to visit Karinhall, which you must admit is hardly the safest place for them."

"*Unglaublich!*" exclaimed the woman. "How do you manage such things?"

"It is simple. I have a bank draft for a large sum of money, enough to keep the fat General that way for many months to come. Incidentally, his staff officer has offered to show us the wedding-presents, the wonders of which have been broadcast to the world. Don't you wish you could come along?"

"You make me believe in miracles—even if you cannot make me believe in spirits!"

"Oh, by the way, did you go to see that medium?"

"I did, and it was pathetic. She told me I was about to get a letter from a dark man."

"Well, it might happen, in spite of all your doubts. You have decided that what I brought you was not a message from Ludi?"

"I have to give up thinking about it; it makes me too unhappy. I have enough problems in this present unhappy world."

"I have had several more séances; but all I got was my grandfather Samuel Budd telling me to hearken to the Word of the Lord; or else the voice of Marcel, telling me that he is painting pictures of a wonderful new world—but his descriptions lack the clarity which characterized his brushwork on earth."

They came back to the documents which Lanny was to carry out of Germany. He said: "I'll do it once more, but after this we'll have to arrange some other way. The Gestapo will be checking on everybody who comes and goes, and they'd be sure to make note if the publications coincide with my departures. And anyhow, I have to go to America for most of the summer."

Lanny didn't give any hint of how he had handled the former job, nor did he ask Trudi what the repercussions in Berlin had been or whether any of her friends had got into trouble. She came to him out of the darkness, and he retired into another darkness; but where they met was a spotlight, and while they were in it they had to watch every step. They agreed that on the day after the morrow Trudi would come to the usual corner at three in the afternoon; that hour was better for Lanny, because by then he could have got his wife tired of looking at paintings and ready to keep some engagement. When the two conspirators saw each other they would not stop or speak; Trudi would go and get the documents, and half an hour later would meet him at a different corner and hand them to him; both of them would make sure they were not being followed, and Lanny would watch both times for the "all clear" signal. This having been agreed upon, he gave her the money he had brought for her, and then set her down in the neighborhood of an entrance to the Underground. It was the same place where he had once set Freddi Robin down for the last time and the recollection gave him a shiver of dread.

IV

Toward the latter part of the afternoon the huge baby-blue Mercédès limousine of the Minister-Präsident General called at the Hotel Adlon for the American couple and their bags. Wherever this vehicle came, the awe-stricken flunkies bowed low, and the reputation of the foreign guests was made forever after. The two favored ones were taken to the ministerial palace, where the Oberleutnant escorted them for the ceremony of viewing the gifts. Three large rooms had been set aside for the exhibition, and a dozen S.S. men in their black uniforms with silver braid and the skull and crossbones had been set to watch the treasures laid out on dozens of long tables. It was like a visit to Tiffany's or Gorham's, only more so. Every sort of jewelry known to man, or to woman, and every design of gold and silver plate and utensil. Der Führer had presented to his loyal friend one of the three existing portraits of Bismarck by Lenbach. The bridegroom had presented to his lady a transparent blue zircon of enormous proportions—everything in the way of jewels that one woman could carry, diadem, earrings, a bracelet, a ring, a necklace; the staff officer said it had cost thirty-six thousand marks, and he didn't consider it necessary to lower his voice.

This was glory, this was success; a long way up the ladder of fame for a man who had started as a humble Reichswehr lieutenant with no special influence, and who had got stuck in the trenches at the outbreak of the World War. But even now the General was only at the beginning of his dizzy ascent—his whole manner told that to his guests; his step was firm and quick, his laughter exuberant, his handclasp somewhat crushing. He was clad in a white uniform with a pale-blue stripe that matched his car, and his orders and decorations made Lanny think of Tiffany's again.

The bags had been moved into a second car, and with the General and his guests rode two of the older staff officers. Furtwaengler and another youngster followed in a second car, and the bags of all of them in a third. At Lanny's feet was an object covered with a rug, and on the way he kept moving his feet over it; his expert knowledge told him that it was a submachine gun. He couldn't be sure whether it was a Budd, but he knew that the firm had sold thousands of them to the Nazis for the street fighting with the Communists. *Der dicke Hermann* was taking no chances!

All the way the great man talked about airplanes, and aviation as the science of the future. He talked technicalities, because Lanny was an insider. He wanted to know how Budd-Erling was coming along, and Lanny, who had had a letter just before leaving, had no reason for withholding the fact that the frost was out of the ground in New England and the foundations due to be completed. In his boyhood he had learned the technical terms of ballistics, and in his recent talks with his father he had learned about wing loading and supercharging, increased compression ratios, anti-knock ratings, controllable pitch propellers. When he mentioned casually that Robbie had actually got an engine with a thousand horsepower, the General demanded to see one right away. Lanny grinned and said: "It will please Robbie greatly to have you make the first approach."

The head of the Prussian state had apparently not learned fear from his recent auto accident. They drove at high speed, with a long mournful horn warning other cars out of the way. It was dark when they arrived in the Schorfheide forests and all the visitors saw was a blaze of lights in the new palace, called a "hunting-lodge." Lanny had seen a number of these constructions, in both the New World and the Old, so there was nothing novel to him in a great hall with a huge fireplace, a long banquet table, bearskins on the floor and heads of many kinds of antlered creatures on the walls. All you needed was a quarter of a million in any currency, and architects and interior decorators would turn you out such a job complete in three or four months; a good steward would get you a trained staff of servants in forester's livery, or military or medieval or *opéra bouffe* as preferred.

But not a *Filmkönigin*—no, that was something you had to go out and find for yourself, and it would cost you more. Emmy Sonnemann was built on generous lines, equipped to play Brünnehilde or any of the other Choosers of the Slain; in fact she had about reached the point where if she became any plumper it would be *bouffe*. But it would no longer matter, for it had been announced that she was going to make only one more stage appearance, and then would do her duty to the Fatherland and set an example to other German brides. She had abundant blond hair, bright blue eyes, placid features, and color which you couldn't be sure about, since she might have brought her makeup artist with the rest of her wedding-cortege. Her manners were those of the stage, rather than of the aristocracy; she welcomed her guests with effusiveness, pressed food and drink upon them, called them by their first names, and afterward sat on the arm of her bridegroom's chair and kissed him affectionately. Her first husband had been a leading Communist, and Lanny wondered what impression, if any, that had left upon her mind. He would have liked to be alone with her and try to find out.

She was obviously a kindly and somewhat naïve person, and Irma liked her. Easy to see why audiences came to look at her on both stage and screen; also, why directors avoided giving her roles which called for the manifestation of intense passion. When the two guests were in their own room they carefully avoided expressing opinions, for the architect of Karinhall would hardly have failed to include wiring for espionage. However, when the two were lying in bed, Irma whispered, softly: "Oh, Lanny, that poor woman!"

"She seems to have got what she wants," ventured the husband; to which the wife replied, still in whispers: "What do you suppose *der Dicke* weighs?"

V

In the course of two years of power the Minister-Präsident General had added a number of new titles to his list; besides being Reichsminister without Portfolio and Minister of Aviation and Chief of the German Air Force, Field Marshal and General of the Gestapo and President of the Reichstag and of the Prussian State Council, he was also Minister of Forestry and Master of the Hunt; which meant that it was a part of his role to be a country gentleman and have fine horses even though he rarely hoisted himself on top of one. Now he wanted to show his splendid estate to his guests, and it was a bore to them both, because Irma had been brought up on an estate and didn't care a hang about it, and Lanny had had to entertain country gentlemen by looking at their estates ever since he had been a small boy and had really enjoyed it. Emmy went along, because she was a bride and it was her duty to follow her man and tell him that his possessions were the most wonderful in the world. Lanny and Irma assented meekly and didn't dare look at each other for fear of revealing what was really in their minds. One feature of the place was a shrine to Karin, the owner's former wife, and before this a candle was always kept burning.

Afterward the General governed Prussia over the telephone; as always when angry, he shouted as if he expected to be heard without a wire. Then he summoned Lanny to his study for a talk, and the playboy felt the cold blue eyes of the wholesale killer boring into him. For a matter of four or five years Lanny had been speculating about the possibility of telepathy, and now he was thinking: "*Ach, du lieber Gott,* suppose it should start working now!"

But it didn't. This Hermann the Great was neither medium nor conjurer, but had to get his information by the ordinary objective method—hiring agents of very little competence, so he complained. If he could get valuable tips by social blandishments and a few smiles from his *Filmkönigin,* it would be a bargain. Apparently what he wanted was to be told about Stresa, and about the prospects at Geneva, where the League was now carrying on its solemn procedure of condemnation. Had Göring's agents in Italy reported to him that Irma Barnes and her husband had been socially received by the English residents of Stresa, and introduced at a tea party to MacDonald and Simon? Anyhow, *der Dicke* would only have to listen for a while, and he would hear his art broker refer familiarly to the leading statesmen of all three of the Stresa allies.

Lanny had lain awake in the small hours of the morning, reflecting upon the peculiar problem confronting him. As before, he had to assume a pose of omniscience before the fat General and yet tell him nothing he didn't already know. Also he had to use care not to employ too many of the facts which Trudi had told him. Some of them he couldn't leave out, because they were the salient facts of the hour and had been told to him by others, also. But he must be careful not to assemble them in such a way that if the documents were ever published it would flash over Göring's mind: "The very things that Lanny Budd revealed!"

VI

The art expert began with a summary of the situation which the cynical Pete had allowed him to read before it was put on the wire to New York. "My general impression is that you and the Führer haven't much to worry about in this case; you have got away with it, as we say in America. You got a slap on the wrist at Stresa, and you may get several more in the course of the year, but nobody is coming after you with a gun."

"We are sitting in at a poker game," responded the General, "and playing for very high stakes."

"Your hand is not a strong one; but the same is true of your opponents. It happens that this game is different from poker in that nerve counts for even more. Also, it is possible to change the rules in the middle of the game—which cannot be done at cards."

The General smiled; he was continually being impressed by the intelligence of this seeming-idle young man, and that was why he desired so greatly to put him to work. "Then you don't believe our opponents will try to put 'sanctions' on us?"

"What I believe, Hermann, would be of no use to you. What I am telling you is the general impression among insiders, both the diplomats and the newspaper men, of whom I happen to know a number. On Isola Bella most of the time was spent figuring out how they could appear to do something while really doing nothing. Large elements of the public in both France and Britain clamor for action, and so it is necessary to appear determined, even menacing; but no one of the countries is willing to move, because no one can trust any other. Take Britain and Italy—what agreement can there be between them, now that Mussolini has definitely committed himself to the raid on Abyssinia? Is Britain going to let him have Lake Tsana and get his foot into the door of Suez? Of course not!"

"You think he has really committed himself?"

"With all those troops in Eritrea and more on the way? Are they going for that hellish climate? And why does Mussolini go to such trouble to make a bargain with Laval? Il Duce was staggered by what he was able to get—he hadn't believed there was a man in all France who was fool enough to make such a deal."

"What deal do you mean?"

"*Na, na, Hermann!* You know much more about it than I!"

"I have heard rumors, naturally; but I am interested to see if your information confirms mine."

"Well, they have a hard and fast understanding that France will not interfere with Mussolini's adventure and that Laval will co-operate with Mussolini in making sure that you do not move into any of your lost territories."

"Is that generally known in the diplomatic world?"

"It is known to those who have a right to know. I got all the details in Paris as soon as the deal was made. It happens that my father and I know men who were Laval's paymasters before he made so much money of his own. He still consults them."

"Precisely what does Laval think he is getting out of such an arrangement?"

"He is fool enough to imagine that he is getting an ally. I could tell him otherwise, because it happens that I have known Mussolini from of old; I heard him orating when I was a youth, and my father was a friend of the American ambassador to Italy at the time that Mussolini made his famous march to the Eternal City in a Pullman car. Richard Washburn Child was what his last name implies; he thought he was saving civilization by getting the House of Morgan to lend Mussolini two hundred million dollars to start his empire. Just so Laval now thinks he is saving France by becoming a friend of the man who is teaching the children of his Balilla that Nice and Savoy and Corsica and Tunis are all parts of the new Roman empire."

"How long will the French public be content with that course?"

"It does not depend upon the public, but upon the Comité des Forges. My father and I visited Zaharoff not long ago and I listened while they canvassed the situation thoroughly; the attitude of these men is precisely that which you know in Germany—I have heard Thyssen and Hugenberg explain it in the days when they were backing you: they want law and order, and the putting down of the Communists. In France now there is a strong movement for a Front Populaire among Reds of all shades, and the big business men are looking for any leader, any movement, any alliance that will counteract it. They would be perfectly willing to do business with you if you would allow them their share of Eastern European markets."

"Would you be willing to take a message to these men from me?"

"It would not be to your advantage if I did so. I would be putting a label on myself, and from then on they would be careful what they said in my hearing. As it is, I am an American, and therefore a neutral; a gentleman idler, and my questions are naïve. They talk even more freely to my father, since he is one of their sort, and in return he tells them what they wish to know about America. You should understand my relation to my father. He expected me to become his assistant; he educated me for that from boyhood and taught me to keep all his business secrets. As a munitions salesman he dealt with persons high up in the different countries; to me a general was somebody to take sailing and an ambassador was somebody I could beat at tennis because he was apt to be out of condition."

VII

So an American playboy prattled away, tossing the names of the world's greatest as if they had been so many brightly colored balls for a juggler. Was he telling Hermann Wilhelm Göring anything Göring didn't know? He hoped not. But everything he said was right, and in each case Lanny provided several different sources from which he might have got the particular item. He didn't say that he was an intimate friend of Ramsay MacDonald and Sir John Simon and Anthony Eden and the rest; he merely told anecdotes about their personal peculiarities, and quoted them as having said the things which they would and must have said. It was hard to name anybody he hadn't listened to.

He talked about the negotiations over naval limitations between England and Germany, which were supposed to be the most precious of state secrets at the moment; he mentioned offhand and as a matter of course the twelve sea-going submarines which Germany was building at Wilhelmshaven—in spite of the Versailles prohibition and the *démentis* of the Wilhelmstrasse; also the tonnage of the battleships in process. Of course Germany was building against Russia and not against France—at least that was what Laval and his friends wanted to believe. "It may be different when you are ready to move into the Rhineland," said the playboy, with a smile, and the fat General didn't attempt to deny or to contradict any of these brash and undiplomatic assumptions. The General must have been wondering whether he himself had been talking in his sleep; or perhaps whether the American had been consulting that Polish medium whom they kept in their home and about whom Lanny's wife had been telling Hermann's wife!

The upshot of it all was that Göring realized he had a valuable friend, and at an absurdly low price; it occurred to him that it might be the part of wisdom to raise the price at once. He said: "*Sagen Sie mal*, Lanny; you're having trouble with the rest of those paintings, I imagine. Are the prices too high?"

"I'm rather afraid they are. You will remember I warned you; nobody has as much money as they had ten years ago—save only yourself, Hermann."

The fat man tossed back his head. It was really impudent, and tickled him greatly. He was experiencing that which caused the kings of old days to have a court jester: boredom with sycophancy, the cloying effect of flattery, the need of the human system for some new flavor, some pungency or tang in social intercourse.

"I have offered to divide with you," said the master of all Prussia, "and I put no limit on your demands."

"I am an art expert," replied the American, "and I like to find purchasers for beautiful masterpieces."

"Well, since you must have it that way, I'll reduce the price of mine. Would that help?"

"It might, if you wish to dispose of them."

"*Jawohl*, suppose I make a cut of ten per cent all along the line. Or would twenty be better?"

"It would be wiser not to ask me about that, since I am representing my clients, and it is my duty to get them the lowest prices I can."

"I'm willing to take my chances. You sell the rest of the paintings or what you think fair. I want to show my confidence in you."

"That is very kind," said Lanny. "I can't recall that any owner of a painting has ever taken that attitude to me."

"Art is not my principal interest in life just now," replied the fat commander. There was a twinkle in the cold blue eyes, and for the moment he seemed human; Lanny had to keep saying to himself: "Don't forget, he's the killer!"

VIII

Late in the afternoon one of the staff cars took the guests back to
Berlin, and in the morning Lanny went to the former Johannes
Robin palace and presented his bank draft, inspected the three paintings, and saw them carried to his car. He received another of the
invaluable bills of sale, also the exit permits for himself and wife.
Irma had proposed that they start at once, but Lanny had pleaded
that there were art shows he really should take in. Irma had made
a luncheon engagement, to be followed by a session of a game called
bridge, whose rules are international and are not changed while the
game is in progress.

So, at a quarter to three o'clock Lanny was driving in the Moabit
district, turning many corners and watching in his little front mirror
to make certain that no other car followed the same eccentric course.
He rolled through one stone canyon after another, endless vistas of
those six-story tenements which have become standard for wage-
slaves in Megalopolis throughout the world. Here they were cleaner
and less dingy than in any other city Lanny had visited, and now in
bright spring weather the flowers in window boxes made the scene
almost cheerful. Nobody except a few children paid any attention
to a car rolling quietly, and there was no need to come through the
same block twice, for there was an oversupply of blocks, and except for the names at the corners a stranger could not have told
one from another. It was the same with the people of the neighborhood; subdued and standardized creatures, prisoners of the machine,
cliff-dwellers of capitalism.

With his watch on the seat beside him Lanny came to the familiar
corner on the stroke of fifteen o'clock, as they called it on the Continent. He looked for the figure in the gray print dress and the little
black hat, but he did not see it, and slowed up his car to look down
the intersecting street from which on previous occasions she had
appeared. But she wasn't there, nor was she on the street down
which he drove. They had set their watches together, but of course
one of them might have got wrong, so after driving a couple of
blocks he made a right turn, coming around two blocks and back

to the appointed corner. Again he watched in every direction; but
no Trudi.

He was beginning to be worried. She had always been prompt on
the minute, and he knew that nothing would keep her from this appointment except sheer physical disability. They had repeated the details of their understanding so carefully as to preclude the possibility
of mistake. If she had come too early, she would surely not have
gone away without waiting or coming back on her tracks to look
for him. Perhaps she had done so while he was making his encircle-
ment; so he drove down the street again, this time making a left
turn, so as to take him around two different blocks and avoid making
his car conspicuous. He studied the street signs to make sure there
was no mistake; this was the corner, and the time was now fifteen
minutes past the hour.

He kept up this procedure for quite a while, driving this way and
that, circling all the four blocks which made the intersection and
coming back again and again. He decided that one of them must
have misunderstood; Trudi must be at the other corner agreed upon,
the one where he was to have received the documents. He drove
to that corner, and repeated his procedure of driving around one
block and then another; but in vain. He came back to the first place,
and did more circling, keeping a look-out in every direction—not
merely for Trudi, but for Stormtrooper or other Nazi uniforms,
policemen, or loiterers who might betray interest in a de luxe
motor-car.

IX

At last the sickening conviction settled itself in Lanny's mind:
Trudi Schultz wasn't keeping this appointment, and there was nothing
to be gained by waiting any longer. He gave up and drove at random
on one of the boulevards, so as to think without interruption. Something had happened to his fellow-conspirator, out in that darkness
into which she disappeared; something serious, for nothing less
would have stopped her. She might have been struck in the traffic,
or have met with some other serious accident; but far more probable

was the thing from which Lanny's mind shrank in agonized dread—
that the Gestapo had got her!

It might be, of course, that they were looking for her; she had
received a warning and had fled; she was "sleeping out"—the phrase
used by these "underground" people to describe the condition when
they did not dare come to their homes or to stay in any one place
for two consecutive nights. If that was so with Trudi she would
surely drop him a note to the Adlon; she would find some phrase
to convey to him the idea of danger. They had talked about this,
and she would be careful to write so that the shrewdest police agent
would find nothing suspicious.

Of course, if the Gestapo had actually got her, they would be
torturing her, trying to wring her secrets out of her. They might
have had her for the past two days, and if so, that graceful and
active figure would be a cringing and shuddering wreck. The
thought of it made cold sweat come out on the forehead of Lanny
Budd; made him dizzy, so that he had to stop his car at the side of
the Potsdamer Platz and turn his face from the passers-by. He
thought only of Trudi, and not of possible danger to himself—for
he was certain that this woman would die as many deaths as need
be before breathing the name of one of her friends. But then he
thought: "They may have Monck, too!" He thought: "Monck may
be their agent!" At no time since their first meeting had Trudi mentioned this man, and Lanny had no idea where he was or what he
was doing. If he was a spy, or if he gave way and talked, then
Lanny himself was in serious danger, and instead of wandering dis-
tractedly about the streets of Berlin he ought to be getting his wife
and his belongings and streaking it for the border.

X

Once more a lover of *die schönen Künste* came face to face with
the tragedy which had befallen Germany. One of the world's most
civilized peoples had got into the clutches of this monstrous thing,
this lunatic's dream turned into reality and setting out to uproot
and destroy every humane and decent influence among sixty

millions of people! If you were a citizen of this land you had to submit and become its slave; to sweat and toil and bleed for it, to share all its vileness and its crimes, to let it take your children and distort their minds and make them into little monsters in its own image. Either that or else sacrifice forever your safety and peace of mind; become a hunted creature, with a hunted soul; know that the evil thing was stalking you, dogging your footsteps day and night, lurking in your home, bribing your servants, teaching your own little ones to report you and bring you to destruction! You had to live in the knowledge that the slightest misstep, a single betraying word or even look—or for that matter the lie of an enemy, a discharged employee, a disgruntled servant, a rival in love or in business—might serve to throw you into an underground dungeon and subject you to such tortures that you would cry out for death!

Lanny was back in the days of Freddi Robin, when he had waited and feared and imagined dreadful things—none of them worse than the reality. Hoping for a telephone call or a message; waiting hour after hour, day after day, for something which wasn't going to come. Then at least he had had Irma to whisper to; they could go out in the car and indulge in the privilege of normal human beings, to say what they thought. But now he had nobody; he had to carry this burden alone, and have it increased by the necessity of acting a part and keeping his wife from guessing that he had trouble on his mind.

At first he thought he couldn't stand it. He would take Irma in the car, tell the truth, and throw himself on her mercy. But he knew that she wouldn't have any mercy; she had told him the state of her mind and given him fair warning. She had suffered the Freddi affair because she had to; because Freddi had been the brother of Lanny's brother-in-law, and Irma had been a guest in the home and on the yacht of Freddi's father. Those were ties which you couldn't refuse to acknowledge, much as you might hate and resent them. But what did Irma owe to Trudi Schultz?

She had met Trudi two or three times, rather casually; once at an evening reception at the school, where she had disliked everybody; again when the young artist couple had been invited to a gathering in the Robin palace, where they had felt out of place and looked it. To Irma all shades of Pink were Red, and if the Schultzes weren't that, they were dupes like Lanny himself. They had brought on this Nazi terror, they had "asked for it," in the current American slang; now, if they wanted to overthrow the German government that was their business, and if Lanny wanted to help them it was Lanny's business, but in neither case was it going to be the business of Irma Barnes.

No, Lanny must go back to the hotel and talk about the pictures he had seen; he must invent some excuse for remaining in Berlin, for he was determined to come once more to the appointed corner both at twelve and at fifteen o'clock. Something might have happened; Trudi might have had a fainting-spell owing to lack of nourishment; she might have fallen and broken her ankle. He must get hold of an afternoon paper, to see if there was any story about an unidentified young woman being knocked senseless by a taxicab or a bandit. Also, he must look in the amusement section for an entertainment that he could persuade Irma to be interested in. When he got back to the hotel he must call up somebody and make a date to see an old master and try to get a price on it.

These activities would help to keep his mind off the idea that the General's bloodhounds might be hot on his trail; that the General's torturers might be sharpening their knives and practicing the shrill whistling sounds of their whipping-rods. Lanny Budd, who had made an effort to enjoy the hospitality of Karinhall and had succeeded reasonably well, now thought: "That fat slob may be looking over those stolen reports and Trudi's confession!" He thought: "I ought to have shot the son-of-a-bitch while I had a chance." But no, that wouldn't have changed anything, really. Some other capable Nazi would have carried on, and the system would have become yet more ruthless and determined. What was needed was truth-telling about it, the shouting of its crimes from all the housetops of the world; and after that—Lanny tried to peer into the future, but it was like trying to see to the bottom of a volcano in eruption.

XI

Irma hadn't arrived when he reached the hotel, so he had more time to get himself together. He consulted his lists and found a picture on which he could possibly get a price; if he did so, he would send a few cablegrams and have an excuse to wait for replies. He would take Irma to a movie in the evening, to keep her from getting impatient. Movies are run in the dark, and that would be good, because he could shut his eyes and think about Trudi in the hands of the Gestapo without Irma's seeing his fear-stricken face. If he shivered at the thought of what might happen to himself, Irma would attribute it to events on the screen.

No messages came; nothing happened; and to Lanny it was like one of those nightmares in which you know that you have been there before. But in the case of Freddi Robin he had been able to get some information because he happened to know one disloyal Nazi. Now that Nazi was dead, and where should he look for another? There wasn't a person in Germany to whom he could mention the name of Trudi Schultz without risk of destroying not merely Trudi and her associates, but his own chances of being able to do anything for Trudi's cause.

Irma proved to be unexpectedly compliant about the extra day's stay. She was trying hard to be considerate and fair. She went with him to look at the painting, and agreed that it was fine, though the price was high. It was so high that he couldn't offer it to his clients; but he didn't tell her that, he said he would send a couple of cablegrams. It would take but a day or two more, he remarked, casually; and only then did his wife begin to make a fuss. Really, there had to be some limit to delays; she had made promises to her mother, and also an engagement in London. "I want you to do what you enjoy, Lanny, but it's not fair to turn us both into slaves to this picture business!"

He had made the mistake of choosing a picture which was owned by a person of good repute, no Nazi; so Irma could argue that in case a sale was made, they could surely count upon having the right picture shipped. "Good Lord, I'd be willing to guarantee it;

I'll put up the money if the man cheats you!" And what could he say? He pleaded for one day extra, promising to leave the morning after next; and so she gave way.

After all, what sense was there in staying? If there was a question of the documents, Trudi could find some other way to smuggle them out; Monck might bring them to England and send them to Lanny by registered mail; Lanny could forward them to Rick by the same means. As for fretting and eating his heart out with anxiety, he could do that just as well in London or on Long Island; more easily, in fact, because he wouldn't have the extra tension of lying to his wife. If ever he did get a letter from Trudi, if ever he could think of a way to save her, there would still be steamers crossing the Atlantic, and it would be nearly as easy to think up an excuse for returning to Berlin as for staying now.

XII

Was it cowardly of a Socialist to go off and leave his comrade in her plight? This was Trudi's job, he told himself; she had chosen it for herself, knowing clearly its risks. She had refused to give him any means of communicating with her, so surely she couldn't blame him for not doing it. Nevertheless, he would go on being dissatisfied with his job, of playing prince consort to an heiress, taking her to picture shows, and lying to her because she wouldn't permit him to have a social conscience. He had told Trudi that he could get money for the cause in that money world and nowhere else; and Trudi had been glad to have that sort of assistance. But it had worked out to this: that while she lay in the dungeons of the Gestapo, Lanny would drive off in a fancy car, cross the ocean in a luxury liner, and spend the summer in a Long Island show-place with two- or threescore servants to wait on him. No amount of arguing could make that seem a satisfactory division of labor!

No message of any sort; and on the morning set for their departure Lanny packed his things with a heavy heart. He purposely took a long time, for there was a second mail before noon, and something might come by that. No need for hurry, he told his wife; it was a clear day and they would drive fast, and catch the Hook of Holland ferry in the evening. He talked about the news from Geneva; the first mail had brought a card from Pete, and now Lanny was reading aloud an item from the morning paper which showed how correct Pete had been. The League committee had appointed subcommittees, a time-worn device for postponing action. Lanny beguiled his wife into talking about a journalist, born in Naples and raised in Brooklyn, who took a disparaging attitude toward all "wops." Irma, interested in people, let herself be beguiled.

At last, however, the husband could think of no more devices. Their bags were locked up and carried away. He went down and paid his bill at the cashier's window. He asked at the desk for a message, and there was none. The car was at the door, the bags stowed, and Irma appeared in her quiet but elegant traveling-costume, conscious of her ripe brunette beauty, gazed at by all men and women, and knowing it. A splendid tall personage in uniform opened the door for her and then hastened to open her car door; the bellboys bowed, and Lanny followed, scattering largess, one of his functions.

Irma took her seat, and Lanny had gone around to the other side to get in, when there came a bellboy running with a letter in his hand. Lanny thought: "Oh, God!" His heart hit him a blow under the throat. It was one of those cheap envelopes that Trudi used, and the handwriting was hers. He opened it hastily and read:

Dear Mr. Budd:
Very urgent circumstances made it impossible for me to complete the sketches as I hoped. Please accept my apologies. *Glückliche Überfahrt!*
Kornmahler

He got into the car, a bit dizzy. "What is that?" asked Irma, and he had an answer thought up in advance: "Young artist whose work I took a fancy to. Promised to send me some sketches, but something went wrong." He handed the note to his wife, so that she wouldn't be looking at him for a few moments.

"Is this why you wanted to wait?" she inquired.

"No, no," he replied; "they can come by mail just as well."

"Kornmahler," she remarked. "An odd name!"

"Probably Jewish," he said, starting the car. "Graingrinder" instead of "Miller"! Trudi had known that he would get the point; she was in hiding somewhere, and had to change her name in a hurry! Also, she was telling him that there was nothing he could do about it. Happy crossing! *Bon voyage!*

BOOK THREE

The Worst Is Yet to Come

10

The Head That Wears a Crown

I

IT IS the nature of the human creature to have desires, and part of the process of civilization to devise new ones. The creature forms ideals, he sets himself goals, and then labors to attain them. When he has got there he looks about, and finds that it isn't so satisfying as he had imagined; already he is in process of forming a new ideal, of setting himself a new goal. The unfortunate creatures are of two sorts: those who are so low in the social scale that they have no hope of attaining their desires, and those at the other end of the scale, so well provided with everything that they have nothing to strive for, and thus fail to make the efforts whereby their capacities are developed.

Lanny Budd was one of these latter unfortunates; or so, at any rate, he felt himself while playing his role of prince consort on the Long Island estate. He was the young lord of Shore Acres, the only male there having authority; and while the females owned the place and ran it, they deliberately deferred to him and abrogated their rights in his favor. They did this because they wanted him to stay; they wanted the place to serve his pleasure, and they were puzzled when it failed to do so. They watched him anxiously for signs of discontent, and their attitude was communicated to the servants, who never fail to know the circumstances of those families upon which their lives are centered. Mr. Lanny doesn't like this place, Mr. Lanny wants to go back to Europe and take his wife and daughter with him. If he goes, the staff will be cut down, a lot of us will lose our agreeable jobs; so let us find out what it is that Mr. Lanny lacks, and let us bring it to him on a silver platter, or perhaps the gold service which is kept locked in the safe built into the wall of the master's bedroom. He is of a friendly disposition, so let us smile and say a cheery "Good morning." He appears to be preoccupied right now, so let us steal about our duties on tiptoe. Now he is frowning—have we done anything to displease him?

There is something peculiar about this young master—really quite unprecedented. Mr. Binks, the second footman, declares that he is a Socialist. He takes several papers full of that sort of stuff, and when he throws them into the trash Mr. Binks read them, and now he is talking like a Socialist, too; he says that the rich are a lot of parasites and ought to be put to work like everybody else. For God's sake, how does one please a young master like that? By being a bad servant instead of a good one? Mr. Binks reads aloud a sentence which Mr. Lanny himself has marked in the paper, quoting a party named Walt Whitman, who says: "Give me neither masters nor servants; give me comrades and friends." And what does that mean? Would Mr. Lanny like us to come and sit down in his study and be comradely? And what would Miss Irma make of it? The older servants still call her Miss Irma; it is a privilege which marks their rank.

II

The executive head of this estate is Mrs. Fanny Barnes, *née* Vandringham, and she is one of the old sort, with no nonsense about her; the servants have no difficulty in knowing their place when she is around, and that is most of the time. They know everything about her and her family, because in one of the many cottages of the estate there live aged pensioners, one of whom was Mrs. Barnes's nurse and is now a fountainhead of ancient lore. She can tell how bitterly Mr. J. Paramount Barnes, the utilities king, used to quarrel with his wife, and so he didn't leave the estate to her but to Miss Irma, or rather to a trusteeship, so that his daughter won't come into full possession until she is thirty. Meantime, she is away most of the time, and doesn't care very much about the place, so Mrs. Barnes has everything her own way, and a hard taskmistress she is.

The real center of the demesne has come to be little Frances, the twenty-three-million-dollar baby, as the newspapers still call her, though the value of the fortune has been cut in half by the depression. But things are coming back, and dividends are being paid again. That ought to please the well-to-do, but it appears that taxes take most of it—the ladies and gentlemen all worry about them, finding fault with the President and calling him bad names. Mr. Lanny grins, teases them, and sometimes gets into an argument. Evidently that is a part of being a Socialist; you are glad to see the rich taxed, even though you are one of them. A hard thing to imagine!

Mrs. Barnes holds her little granddaughter as the most precious treasure and guards her like an old dragon; has her sleeping in her room, and doesn't mind being waked up by her; watches her food, sends for the doctor if she sneezes once, and doesn't like to see her taken off the estate. She is jealous of Mr. Lanny's mother, who lives in France and has the child the greater part of the time. But Mrs. Barnes does not let Mr. Lanny see this; she humbles her pride, trying her best to please him and make him feel that Shore Acres is his real home. She is all the time taking her brother off and scolding him because he talks too much and bores Mr. Lanny with his opinions, especially about politics and the stock market and that sort of thing. "Shut your fool mouth!" she says, loud enough for her maid to hear, and of course the story is all over the servants' quarters before the day is done. Poor Mr. Horace Vandringham, nobody feels very sorry, for he is a big domineering fellow who makes a lot of noise and trouble for the help, giving orders when he has no right to; he cannot bring himself to realize that he is a down-and-outer, a charity boarder, and the pride of his sister will not permit her to put him definitely among the pensioners.

Lanny and Irma are the privileged ones, the reigning queen and prince consort, whom all serve gladly. Free and easy-going, laughing a lot, good to look at, and always dressed at the peak of fashion— surely there are no people in the world more to be envied than these two! And yet they aren't always happy, you can see it if you watch them closely. There are stories going the rounds of impatient words and irritated looks. They go out a great deal, and servants don't always find out what happens, but they can guess, because the friends come to Shore Acres and one gets to know them and sees how they behave. They play cards a lot, and some of them lose money which they can't afford. You can tell that by their looks, and sometimes you hear husbands and wives fussing as they go out to their cars— oh, yes, there isn't much kept hidden from servants. A big place like this is a world of its own, and while it doesn't have a newspaper it has many busy tongues.

These playboys and girls—they are getting to be middle-aged but they don't want to admit it—are many of them unhappy and they drink too much. Mr. Lanny drinks very little, and he doesn't like to see Miss Irma take more than a couple of cocktails. The servants know that and don't take the trays to her, at least not while her husband is near. That is one of the things they have fusses about now and then; not long ago he had to help her up to bed, and next morning they had a real row. Her eyes were red with weeping, and she must have promised, because now she drinks much less; she tries hard to keep him with her, and not have him go off to the city and meet the queer sort of people he likes. Once he took her to some radical meeting, and they had an argument in their room. Her maid heard snatches of it and told it in the upper servants' dining-room: he said and she said—always when they tell such stories it is "he" and "she," and they will go on for an hour without mentioning a name. There can be only one he and one she in a feudal community.

III

Across Long Island Sound lies the small city of Newcastle, known as the home of Budd Gunmakers and soon to be better known as the home of Budd-Erling Aircraft. Budd's still made machine guns and automatic carbines and pistols, but most of it was now a hardware plant, which meant that it had lost its social status in the eyes of the old-timers. Lawford Budd, Robbie's eldest brother, was still vice-president in charge of production, but the president now was a Wall Street man, and the board of directors consisted for the most part of dummies representing a syndicate of financial men. Robbie looked upon it with contempt, and his two sons had withdrawn, and so had several of the executives and plant managers. All had come into the new institution, which was going to be a one-purpose plant, with everything new and shiny, designed and operated according to the latest wrinkles of the scientific management people.

As little as a generation ago, if a man had announced that he was going to build a great factory to produce airplanes that would fly faster than two hundred miles an hour, everybody would have known that he was crazy. Indeed, it had been possible for the Wright brothers to stay up in the air over the sand-dunes of North Carolina in their flimsy wood-and-canvas "crate" for many minutes at a time over a period of several months without having the press of the country pay the slightest attention to them. What they were doing was impossible and therefore the stories couldn't be true. But now it had been possible for Robbie Budd to sell five million dollars' worth of stock, and to have some of the best engineers in the country design and erect a building where planes and nothing else were to be turned out on an assembly line, and he wasn't called crazy, but, on the contrary, one of the town's most progressive citizens. All looked up to him and said they had always known that he had it in him; he walked with new dignity, gave orders with quiet assurance, and saw that they were carried out promptly.

Lanny and his wife motored to Newcastle, by way of the ferry to New London, and paid a visit at the Robbie Budd home. Esther, Lanny's stepmother, welcomed them cordially. His early sins had been forgiven and perhaps forgotten; he, too, was a success, quite apart from his rich wife—so his relatives and old-time friends tried to make him understand. His profession of art expert was impressive, his musical talents were considerable, he was a linguist and a traveler, almost an ex-diplomat and certainly a friend of the great. The members of the country-club set hastened to honor both husband and wife. If he voiced pinkish opinions—well, it was in the Budd tradition to be eccentric and tell the world to go to the devil, and this appeared to be the newest way.

The sales offices of the new concern were in New York, and here Johannes Robin was in charge. He had got a home for his family half-way between the city and the plant, so that he could commute to either. It was Irma's duty to go with Lanny for a call, and they chose a Sunday afternoon. Papa and Mama, Rahel and the little one were all together again; they had bought a comfortable old-fashioned New England house of two stories and a dozen rooms, and said they expected to spend the rest of their lives here. Irma thought it was the right way for people of their sort to live—far more sensible than an elaborate marble palace and a yacht. She received graciously their thanks for her kindness in the past, and no great lady could have been less condescending to those who had been reduced in social status. Johannes's hair had turned gray and there were more lines in his face, but he was the same urbane and subtle person with the flavor of old-worldliness about him.

IV

Robbie escorted the couple to see the new plant, now magically approaching completion. Rows of piling had been driven into the marshes, and great dredges had lifted the mud out of one side and dropped it into the other, so as to make steamship berths and docks. The cow pastures had been covered with concrete, and a skeleton of steel had risen over them, and now it had walls of glass and a roof of some patent material. Out of its floors sprouted innumerable bolts, to which machines large and small were to be attached; the concrete was covered with cabalistic signs in various colored crayons. Overhead were trolleys on which airplane parts would be carried, swinging from steel chains. Everything had been planned to the fraction of an inch, and the blueprints were numerous enough to have covered the floor of the building.

Part of it was a great foundry, and a power plant was already belching black smoke, making electricity for the construction work and the lighting at night. Already some of the machines were arriving, mysterious in their waterproof wrappings. "Come back in another month," Robbie said, "and you won't know the place; in six months we'll be rolling out our first plane, and you can take a ride in it." He was doing the honors personally, because Irma was his largest single stockholder and was entitled to know just what her money was buying. She was greatly impressed and asked many questions, showing that she was thinking not merely about her money but about the work it was going to do.

Lanny was content to look and let the others talk. He believed in machinery and the power it gave to humankind, but he was ill satisfied with the uses to which it was being put. He dreamed of seeing it collectively owned and serving collective purposes; but there was no use saying a word about this to either his father or his wife. These two belonged together, for they understood and supplemented each other. Irma had the "stuff," and Robbie put it to use for her; they would share the profits, and expect the rest of the world to work for them and do what it was told. For those who were dissatisfied with the arrangement there would be a company police force—already it was being organized and taught its duties by that dependable ex-cowboy Bub Smith, who had taught Lanny how to shoot guns, and had pretended to be a Socialist while acting as bodyguard to Baby Frances at Bienvenu.

V

The consequences of Robbie's social theories became apparent to Lanny while passing through the district surrounding the plant. Robbie expected to have a thousand skilled men at work in a month or two, but it hadn't occurred to him to make arrangements to get them here or provide them with places to live. All that, according to the master's philosophy, was a matter for private enterprise. The men would be skilled workers, getting good pay and having their own cars, and Robbie did his part by setting aside a tract of the company's land on which their cars could be parked. Where the men were going to have their homes was up to them, and the matter was being settled by a swarm of speculators who had got wind of the new project and had come rushing to buy up the adjoining land. Now there were "subdivisions," and busy salesmen marking out lots with little colored flags, and bringing people in busses from the cities to look at the land and eat free lunches of hot dogs and coffee. Already scores of workers' homes were arising; they would be jerry-built, with silly little pretenses at elegance but nothing substantial, and as a result the workers would soon be putting in their spare time mending leaky roofs and cracked plaster and windows and doors that got stuck. But all that was their look-out, not the company's.

It was the thought of starry-eyed New Dealers that housing-projects might be constructed at the same time as new factories; that parks and schools and playgrounds might be provided for workers' families from the very outset. That was done as a matter of course in the Soviet Union, and that fact was enough to damn it for the rugged individualists of New England. Lanny knew there wouldn't be any use mentioning the idea now; he had been mentioning it for the past eighteen years—ever since he had met the first Pink while a pupil at St. Thomas's Academy in Connecticut.

He knew in advance every word his father would say; Robbie intended to institute what was called "welfare work" in the new plant, as soon as things got going and he had time to think about it; but he didn't ask Lanny to help, and Lanny knew why—because from the first moment the question of labor unions would come up, and Robbie was going to run an open-shop plant or die in the effort. "Free labor," he called it, and meant by the phrase that the men were free to do what he told them or move elsewhere and do the same for some other hard-headed industrialist. The men who had charge of the providing of rest places and recreation for the workers wouldn't be "cranks" picked out by Lanny, but sensible fellows who knew where their salaries came from. They would organize baseball teams and bowling-tournaments and run a company organ full of pep talks and production slogans.

So Robbie Budd was in triumphant course of producing another center of industrial feudalism in a land which preached democracy and government by popular consent. Robbie's new town wouldn't be called a company town, and it wouldn't be company-owned, but would be company-run by devices which Robbie didn't have to invent, for they were standard practice in this sweet land of liberty. The workers had come swarming from nobody knew or cared where; they wouldn't know one another and would have no ties or loyalties. They would be free to vote for political candidates every year or two, and they would assume that these candidates were crooks, and for the most part they would be right. Robbie or one of his agents would appoint a political boss to run the town, and at election time would put up campaign funds to elect the candidates whom the boss had chosen. If any men were active in opposing the company's wishes, whether as to policies, unionism, or anything else, those men would be "let out" and would move elsewhere. Such was the system, and Lanny knew that he wanted no part in it. If he was planning to denounce it, good taste required him to begin somewhere else but the place where his wife's money and his father's time, energy, and reputation were being thrown into the pot.

VI

From a safe distance of three thousand miles the amateur publicist watched events in the unhappy Continent on which he had been born. He saw them through the medium of newspaper dispatches written by men whom he knew; also of letters from Rick, and Raoul Palma, and one to his father from Denis de Bruyne. At the beginning of May the French signed a treaty of mutual defense with the Soviet Union, and Denis said that it represented an effort to bluff Germany. But in order to bluff successfully you have to look as if you meant it, and France didn't mean it. Hitler knew it well, and took the treaty as a basis of propaganda attacks. Pierre Laval meant the treaty so little that it wasn't even presented to the Chamber for ratification, nor was it implemented by any military arrangements. Marianne wouldn't trust her new ally with any of her defense secrets—and what sort of ally was that?

At the end of the month the *fripon mongol* became Premier—a sort of booby prize, Rick said, for having proved himself the most inept of living French statesmen. Early in June, Ramsay MacDonald was replaced as Prime Minister of Britain; poor old packhorse for the Tories, he had carried them as far as he could, and now they set him down to rest and dream in a pasture called the Lord Presidency of the Council. His place was taken by a steel manufacturer named

Baldwin, whose specialties were pipe-smoking and pig-raising. "England also has her two hundred families," wrote Rick, "and they don't have to hide themselves behind the mask of an innkeeper's son." The first act of this new "jumped-up blacksmith" was the treaty for naval parity with Germany, which had been so incredible that insiders had laughed at Lanny when he talked about it. Now John Bull kindly gave the Germans permission to build up to thirty-five per cent of his own sea-power and actually included the right to parity in submarine building. The tiger that had been let out of his cage was now invited into the family dining-room—though of course seated near the foot of the table.

Benito Mussolini, Blessed Little Pouter Pigeon, was bound by no less than nine treaties to respect the independence and territorial integrity of that ancient land called Abyssinia and sometimes Ethiopia; but he was going right ahead with his propaganda against it, and shipping soldiers and supplies to his Red Sea bases. This was an excellent thing for the British, who owned most of the stock of the Suez Canal Company and collected goodly sums for every ton of shipping and every soldier traveling through that long sandy ditch. It was also excellent for the New England-Arabian Oil Company which Robbie Budd had founded and recently sold out to Zaharoff and his associates; they were right there with the fuel which Mussolini couldn't do without, and in return they would take the food and wine and oil of the Italian people.

Lord Wickthorpe went with a British mission to negotiate with "the blighter," and when he came back he told Rick about it, and Rick wrote it to Lanny on his old battered typewriter. Bit by bit, like careful traders, the British had offered Il Duce everything he could hope to get, asking only that he should proceed under the forms of legality and let the League hand it to him on a golden platter; but no, he was determined to take it by force, for the sake of the effect on his domestic situation. Some forty years ago these black fighting-men—a mysterious race supposed to be descended from wandering Jews—had given invading Italian troops an awful licking, and Il Duce wanted the glory of wiping out that disgrace. He saw himself going out there and receiving the submission of the "Lion of Judah," then coming home in a triumphal procession and building a monument to himself in the Forum.

The only real obstacle in his path was British public opinion. Four years previously the Tories had got into power in a snap election, in which, polling fifty-five per cent of the vote, they had got ninety-one per cent of the House of Commons. Now the British people had proceeded to organize independently and take a poll of eleven and a half millions of themselves, and they had voted something like thirty to one in favor of staying in the League. They had voted thirteen to one in favor of prohibiting the manufacture and sale of armaments for private profit—imagine the feelings of Robbie Budd when he opened his paper and read that item of news! With Mussolini's African adventure before them, these amateur voters had been asked if a nation which insisted upon attacking another nation should be stopped by economic and non-military measures, and they had answered Yes by fifteen to one. Asked whether such an aggressor nation should be stopped by military measures, they had answered Yes by nearly three to one. In the face of such a vote Mussolini brought to completion his plans to march into Abyssinia; and what was the League of Nations going to do about it? What was the Tory government of Britain going to do about it?

VII

Soon after his arrival at Shore Acres, Lanny had received a note from Trudi Schultz, forwarded from Bienvenu; a duplicate of the one he had so nearly missed in Berlin. After that, nothing for a couple of months; he had to accustom himself to thinking in a special way about these people who were "death's own." Their owner might have claimed them or they might be on the way to him by the route of dungeons and concentration camps. A letter might come, or it might not; and there was no good fearing or worrying in the meantime.

One came in the middle of July; a real letter, the longest he had ever received from Trudi: "I am very busy, illustrating a work of fiction dealing with the time of the Emperor Diocletian. The heroine is a persecuted Christian who has to flee; there are several scenes of vigorous action, and these are difficult for me, because, as you know, my drawings have so far dealt with still life. I should value your opinion of my work highly, and hope you will be visiting Berlin. I am expecting to move and not sure of my address but will get in touch with you when I hear of your arrival. It is convenient that you are a famous person whose comings and goings are reported in the press. By the way, my clerical friend has been ill for some time and is confined to his bed. I do not know just what is the matter with him; he does not talk about his ailments. Hoping that this finds you and your family well and the picture business thriving, I am, respectfully, Kornmahler."

Lanny didn't need to spend much effort interpreting this elaborate parable. Trudi was being sought by the Gestapo and was in hiding; she couldn't give an address, but wished him to come to Berlin and find some way to get himself and his picture business into the newspapers; then she would get word to him. The clerical friend, of course, was Monck, and she was telling the tragic news that he was in a concentration camp but was not betraying his friends.

Serious news indeed for the grandson of Budd's. Maybe the man hadn't talked yet, but he might talk tomorrow, and his first statement would be that the money for the criminal activities of his group was being put up by an American playboy who posed as a friend of the Gestapo General, and, indeed, was getting his money by acting as an art broker for the Nazi second-in-command. That would be of genuine interest to the Secret State Police; and what would they do about it? The question called for no little guessing. An art lover of imaginative temperament could spend hours, especially the wee small ones in the morning, picturing scenes with the fat General, and with the acting head of his Gestapo, a former schoolteacher named Himmler who had managed to make himself the most dreaded individual on the continent of Europe. Lanny's first thought was: "That settles me for Germany!"

But very soon he began having second thoughts. Trudi hadn't been obliged to tell him about Monck; she had taken a risk doing it

—and why? Obviously, in order to be fair. She was saying: "The danger is greater; perhaps you won't want to come." And what was his answer to be? Should he say: "The danger is too great, and I give up"? If he said that, what would Trudi think of him? What would he think of himself? For more than half a year he had been maintaining his self-respect on the basis that now he was really doing something worth while. He had won new regard from Rick on the basis of being no longer an idler and parasite. Should he now say: "The job was too risky, and I had to quit"? Or should he merely keep quiet, and let Rick go on thinking of him as something he didn't dare to be?

A gnawing began in his conscience and did not stop. He had been justifying his life of luxury by the fact that he met his clients that way, kept up his prestige, and so made his picture deals. Clients would repose confidence in a social equal, but hardly in a subordinate, a professional no matter how truly qualified: such was the world of snobbery. So Lanny made money easily and abundantly; but what did he want it for? So that he could buy new suits of clothes whenever his wife or his mother cast a critical glance at one he was wearing? Or whenever those public enemies, the fashion creators, decided that coats must have three buttons instead of two, or that lapels should be an inch longer and have an angle somewhat more acute?

VIII

Lanny's thoughts were continually occupied with those comrades in Germany; not only Trudi, but all who were helping her. They were not vague abstractions to him; he had met a score of them, and their names, faces, and personalities haunted him. In the happy days before Hitler they had sat in one another's homes, or in the reception room of the school, drinking coffee and eating *Leibnitz Keks*—a modest proletarian form of celebration—and talking about their cause, what it meant to them and how they hoped to make it prevail. They had used large and noble words: *Freiheit* and *Gerechtigkeit*, *Brüderlichkeit* and *Kameradschaft*. They had quarreled over points of doctrine and tactics, they had been irritated with one another, they had displayed petty jealousies; but it had always been understood that deeper than all such things was the powerful bond between them. They were comrades in a sacred cause, human beings in a world of wolves, civilized men surrounded by barbarians, producers in a society of exploiters, plunderers, and parasites.

And now, did all that mean anything? Was it a real moral force, or had it been only fine phrases, a form of self-indulgence, a system of pretenses, a means of self-advancement for the intellectuals and a whim or diversion for the idle rich? Lanny couldn't get out of it by saying that he had gone among them as an investigator, that he had wished to understand their movement among many others. No, he had told them that he was a "comrade"; he had encouraged them to fight Nazism, assuring them of his own democratic sentiments and of the moral support of all decent and right-thinking men. They had acted on those promises and those hopes. They had done what they could—not all of them, of course, for no movement is perfect. For their weaknesses of character and errors of judgment they had paid frightful penalties and would pay more. The weaklings had dropped out, and a little group, perhaps a mere handful, was carrying on the fight, trying to keep the spark alive, to save the soul of the future.

Trudi hadn't told Lanny what they were doing. She had assumed that there was no need to do so. Lanny had been in the movement for years and had known some of its great leaders. She and Ludi had poured out their hearts to him and Freddi; they had set forth their ideas in detail, and Lanny had agreed with them. He had said to himself: "Here are two people who understand not merely the economic forces which move society, but the moral forces which move the souls of men." That combination of understanding was rare, and these four young idealists, three men and one woman, had merged their souls and their labors. They had forged weapons for the future —and now it appeared that only two of them were left alive to put the weapons to use.

Lanny didn't have to guess what was going on, for the underground movement against Hitler had been pretty well written up in the neighboring lands; even the capitalist press had now and then printed news of it. There was a "flash-sender," as the Germans call it, a secret radio transmitter, hidden somewhere in the country, and every now and then it would start up, revealing forbidden news, exposing official falsehoods, tormenting the Nazis with jeering comments. If it had stayed in one place, it could have been quickly located, but it kept moving; it must be carried in a van or covered car, and the powers of the Gestapo had been set to hunting it—so far without success.

Also there were secret printing-presses; leaflets were printed or mimeographed, and would be found on the benches of workers when they came in the morning, or perhaps in their dinner-pails at noon. Very often it would be the Socialists attacking the Communists, or vice versa—they still kept up their factional disputes, even in the concentration camps. But Lanny could be sure that Trudi was not taking any part in that, because she had agreed with him in deploring the blunder. She would be exposing the fraudulent Socialism of the Nazis and pointing out to the workers how they were being led into the path of war.

These heroic people were depending upon Lanny for their funds. He knew enough about left-wing movements to understand that they would have dropped efforts to get funds elsewhere and be devoting themselves to spending what he sent them. And now their supply would stop. There would be no way for him to notify them not to expect more; they would wait and go on waiting—in the same unhappy state of mind which he had known in Berlin, waiting for word from Trudi. The flash-sender would fall silent because they had no money for new batteries or gasoline for the car; the leaflets would no longer be distributed because there was no paper. Trudi might write to him—or more likely, she would give him up in disgust, and he would never hear from her again, never know whether she was alive or dead. But he, the young lord of Shore Acres, would be safe and comfortable, and if there was anything in the world that money could buy, he could have it for the asking. Everything save his peace of mind!

IX

He had managed to find purchasers for a couple more of Göring's paintings; and after a week or two of wrestling within himself he said to his wife: "How would you like to take another run over to Berlin?" He would have preferred to go alone, but tact required that he invite her.

As it happened, Irma had just received a letter from Margy, the very sporty Dowager Lady Eversham-Watson. Being nearly sixty, she ought to have known that she was "on the shelf," but she refused to. With the proceeds of the rapidly reviving business of whisky-distilling she had got herself a yacht, and instead of being content to invite Beauty and Sophie and other ladies of her own age she craved the society of the young. So, wouldn't Irma and Lanny be her guests for the regatta week at Cowes? It was a great show, which Lanny had seen but Irma hadn't. Irma said: "Poor old Margy's a bore, but I imagine it will be rather swank—what do you think?"

What Lanny thought was: "O.K., let's go!" And so began one of those periods of agreeable confusion in which you make plans and decisions. They would leave Frances here with her grandmother, for they were coming back, having accepted an invitation for a couple of weeks' hunting on one of the estates of the South Carolina tidelands. Irma would take her maid, because you couldn't participate in regatta festivities without a personal maid. But not too many clothes, because they would have several days in London to get yachting-togs. Lanny would look kind of cute in such an outfit; his wife would order one and order him to have it fitted. As a reward for his being so sweet, she would accompany him to Berlin and let him look at pictures for as long as he needed.

They had to choose a steamer, and engage accommodations, and send cablegrams to friends. Lanny called his father and told him; he called Johannes, and found that he had just had a cablegram from Hansi and Bess. The two musicians had left South America for a tour around the world and had got as far as Japan. Now they had learned of a Congress of the Comintern to be held in Moscow, the first in seven years, and they were leaving by way of Vladivostok to take in this show.

Lanny, too, had heard about this coming event. The Third International had summoned its parties all over the world to send delegates, to consult concerning the new emergency which confronted them in the upsurge of Fascism-Nazism. Rumor had it that a change in the party line was contemplated; some sort of united front was to be set up with the Socialists and other liberal forces. This was what Lanny had been urging for many years; he could say that the Comintern was about to adopt his party line! Having attended a dozen conferences of "bourgeois" statesmen, he would have greatly enjoyed attending one of revolutionists. But, alas, nobody could go from the Kremlin to Karinhall, or from Karinhall to the Kremlin! He said to Irma: "We'll meet Hansi and Bess when they come out, and hear all about it."

Irma said: "*You* can!"

X

Early one morning a procession set out from Shore Acres: two cars and a station-wagon, the first with Irma, driven by her husband, with their five-year-old darling between them, and Miss Addington, the elderly English governess, in the back seat; in the second car, Mrs. Barnes and Uncle Horace, driven by their chauffeur, and with one of their favored pensioners beside him. In the station-wagon rode Céleste, Irma's Breton maid, and a load of trunks. They drove to the pier where the great Cunard liner was already rumbling her whistle. Lanny's car had steel chains put under it and was lifted into the hold; the trunks were piled into a heavy rope net and thus let down into another hold; the three passengers and their guests went up by the gangplank, preceded by stewards carrying armfuls of their bags. Moving the rich about the world is a task involving a lot of labor for other people, but the rich themselves maintain a calm and unhurried aspect. "The sons of Mary seldom bother, for they have inherited that good part."

To go away is to die a little, the French say; but the sons and daughters of Mary do their dying in private, and in this case only little Frances shed any tears. She liked steamships and wanted to go along. When the call came: "All ashore that's going ashore!" she wanted violently to remain, and it wasn't complimentary to her grandmother and her great-uncle. Irma had to promise to throw her a red paper ribbon, and for that she went eagerly.

This pleasant custom had grown up in recent years. The steamship people furnished rolls of thin paper ribbon of bright colors; the passenger held one end and tossed the roll to a friend on the pier, and he or she caught it, and so they were connected by symbolical bonds until the vessel began to move and all ties were severed. Irma tossed a red one, and it was caught and handed to the twenty-three-million-dollar child. Lanny tossed a blue one, and she wanted that also, and stood with a ribbon in each fist, carrying on with both parents a conversation of which they heard no word. However, she heard her father's voice: "I'll be back soon!"

Lanny said this because it was the proper thing; but inside him a voice whispered: "*Oh, yeah?*" This voice had taken to speaking at intervals by day and night, and was pretty well spoiling Lanny's enjoyment of the agreeable life which fate had assigned him. Irma noticed it, and would say: "What makes you so glum, Lanny?" He would answer: "I'm just thinking." Irma was thinking, too, and guessing that her strange husband wasn't entirely cured of his Pink vice, and was brooding because the world didn't behave according to his formulas.

Pressing against Lanny's chest on his right side was a wad which he had wrapped in a handkerchief and kept pinned in his inside coat pocket. It contained a large number of hundred-mark notes, which he had acquired by visiting different money-changing agencies in New York, using care to attract no attention. One of the results of his meditations on the problem of what might be happening in Berlin: he had decided that he had taken a serious chance by going to his regular bank, drawing out a large sum, and passing it on to Trudi Schultz. Doubtless the bank had kept a record of the serial numbers of those notes. In Naziland, a record was kept of everything; the hairs of your head were numbered, and if too many sparrows fell to the ground in your garden the fact would be reported to the *Polizei*. Suppose one or more of those notes had been found on Comrade Monck or some other arrested person and the source of the funds had been traced! This was just one of a great number of imaginations which were trying to ruin a yachting-regatta for Lanny Budd.

11

Farewell to Every Fear

I

IN THE month of August the weather man is apt to be less unfriendly to the English, which is perhaps why the Cowes regatta is held at the beginning of that month. Yachtsmen and yacht lovers assemble from all the shores of Britain and indeed of the Atlantic; the Solent is crowded with vessels large and small, both steam and sail. Everything is new and shiny; white sails, white paint, and spit-and-polish brass; the sea green, or blue-green, with whitecaps when it breaks; the sky a light blue, and the clouds like wind-filled sails. Everybody puts on nautical clothes and a holiday air, and nowhere on the scene is there the slightest sign of what the English hymnbook refers to as sorrow, toil, and woe.

This was the jubilee year of the event, so there were jubilee cups offered by King George for the best records for yachts of various classes. There were several races each day, of various lengths, around certain buoys and lights outside the harbor; sight-seeing vessels trooped out in the morning to follow the contenders, keeping politely off the course, shepherded by guard vessels with little flags to mark their authority and officials with megaphones to warn the careless. You stood by the rail, conscious of your sea-costume and also of your sea-legs, and watched the contenders through binoculars which made it almost as if you were on board. If you were an old-timer you displayed knowledge of the vessels and their owners, and the records which they and their predecessors had established. You knew the "corrected times," and even knew who had designed the various boats. It was a classic example of what Veblen calls "the conspicuous consumption of goods"; the frail craft were built for one purpose, to carry the utmost amount of sail and slide through the water at the utmost speed; they cost thumping sums and in a couple of years were obsolete because some other designer had gone them one or two better. Therefore, when you joined a yachting crowd you were telling the world that you were tops financially and had been for some time.

Late in the day you came back into the harbor of your boat club, sunburned and with salt in your eyebrows. You bathed and dressed in evening clothes and perhaps went ashore for dinner and dancing, or were invited to some other yacht, or had friends invited to yours. All talked about the day's events, paid off their bets, and made new ones. In the first three days of this regatta the winds were featherlight, and that favored the English yachts; in the last three days there were "spanking" breezes, which favored the American, which had to be a shade more substantial in order to cross the ocean. So there was plenty about which to wager and to work up patriotic excitement. Margy Petries, proprietor of "Petries' Peerless," wasn't sure whether she favored the vessel called *Yankee;* remembering she was also a dowager countess, she would consider "hedging" on her bets.

There are always some bridge fiends who cannot pass an evening without their rubber or two, and these would retire to the saloon. The young people would bring out phonographs and dance on deck. The vessels were closely crowded in their yacht-basins, and motorboats were chugging this way and that; but English decorum prevailed even over the waters, and you danced to your own music, and enjoyed knowing that you were socially impeccable. King George went on board the *Yankee* for dinner, the second time that had happened in the history of Cowes, and it was "Hands across the Sea," an admission that Britain was preparing to share her rule. Irma was so impressed that she said: "Lanny, don't you think it would be fun to build one of these yachts and learn to sail it?" She was always thinking about some gadget that might capture her husband's fancy, and the more expensive it was the better, because, after all, if you could do things that nobody else could, weren't they the things to do?

II

Among the guests was what Margy called the "old crowd," including Beauty and her husband, and Sophie and her new husband —she might, according to the European custom, have kept her title though divorced and remarried, but she said that America was good enough for her, and this was considered a radical, almost revolutionary action. Also there came an old friend, Edna Fitz-Laing, of whose marital scandal Lanny had been an eye-witness in his boyhood. Now her lame English officer was dead, and she was a widow, rather poor, so Margy was being kind to invite her as well as a couple of elderly bachelors who might be attracted by her remnants of beauty. Two of them, with the idea that each might be jealous of the other!

There were enough bridge-players, and Lanny could sit on deck in the evening and chat with Rick. The baronet's son and his wife were here because Margy knew this would please Lanny and cause him to bring his heiress to Margy's affairs. That is the way to keep in the swim and build yourself into a social personality; by understanding your fellow-humans, their prejudices and desires; by learning how to mix them and make them have a good time.

Lanny and Rick, a pair of social philosophers mature beyond their years, reclined on deck chairs and gazed at the golden stars in the clear sky, thinking of their distance, and how insignificant were the two-legged creatures dressing themselves up and strutting on a very small planet. How long the stars had been there, and how short a time was allotted to the creatures—and what were they doing with it? The newspapers came from the city, and you could study the details of their activities, at least those which the press lords considered fit for your perusal. Both the art expert and the lame ex-aviator were students of this press, and had learned to read between the lines and draw conclusions different from what the vendors intended.

Mussolini was admitting having sent more than a quarter of a million troops to Eritrea, his jumping-off place into the land of the Negus, known also as the Lion of Judah and King of Kings; the ardent young Fascists were singing a song—you could get the lilt of it even in English: "Of the whiskers of the Negus we will make a little brush to polish off the boots of Mussolini!" Their hero now had a million of them under arms, and while the lovely yachts were gliding over the blue waters of the Solent he mobilized three more divisions. The League was continuing the farce of pretending to mediate between the black whiskers and the prognathous jaw, but they couldn't get anywhere because the two Italian members of the arbitration board refused to join the two Abyssinian members in naming a fifth. It was plain to all the world that Mussolini was merely stalling until the end of the rainy season, a couple of months off.

In the Geneva debates the Italians were having the ardent support of their friend the innkeeper's son from Auvergne who was now Premier of France. In that land of revolutionary traditions the class war was being waged merrily; there were strikes in the arsenals, accompanied by violence; with the secret backing of Pierre Laval the Croix de Feu was practicing what it called "lightning mobilizations," also the conversion to military purposes of the airplanes owned by its wealthy members. "I no longer care a hang for legality," said Colonel de la Roque, its founder, and Lanny had been to their meetings and could imagine the yells with which his followers would greet this declaration.

The American could tell about conditions in New York; how rapidly the Nazis were organizing, with many large camps where they drilled. Just before his sailing they had held a meeting in Yorkville, the German quarter of the city, in which their uniformed guards had worn revolvers. The steamers of the German lines which came to the port brought loads of Nazi propaganda which·was mailed out to their "Bund" headquarters all over the land. This had provoked a fury of indignation among the anti-Nazis, and they had mobbed the steamer *Bremen* at its sailing a week before Lanny's own departure.

III

Over in Moscow the sessions of the Comintern were under way, and on the third day of the Cowes regatta, while the wind was light and the *Enterprise* was winning the forty-mile race for the big Class J yachts, the Bulgarian delegate Dimitroff made a fiery speech announcing plans for the "united front" against Fascism all over the world. This was the man whom Lanny had heard defending his life against the fat General Göring at the Reichstag fire trials less than two years ago. He had sought refuge in the Soviet Union, and now the Nazis agreed that they had made a mistake, and that in future such men would be silenced at once and forever.

On the day when the wind freshened and the *Yankee* won, the co-ordinated press of Naziland burst forth in furious onslaughts against the Comintern, calling upon the friends of order throughout the world to join with the Führer in destroying this vipers' nest. On the last day of the regatta the American Earl Browder called upon the Communists to broaden their appeal, so as to win the farmers and workers and middle-class elements of his country. From the American press came indignant protests to the effect that Moscow was breaking the promise it had made as the price of American recognition, not to make Communist propaganda in the United States. To this Moscow had its answer: Moscow had nothing to do with what the Comintern did, the Comintern was an independent assemblage of delegates from all the countries of the world.

When you confronted a diplomatic evasion such as that, what were you going to call it, a lie or a fib? And was it your program to repudiate and expose all lies and fibs? If so, you would have a busy life, for the world was lining up on opposite sides of a revolutionary struggle, and who in all history had ever waged war without falsehoods? Certainly not anyone who had won his war! Didn't every nation try to deceive its enemies as to its plans? Didn't every nation send spies into the enemy nations and wasn't deception the essence of their job? Above all, who was Lanny Budd to raise this issue, being now on his way into Germany to do a fancy job of lying?

The gravest of moral problems confronted a social being in these unhappy times. For when you let down the bars and admitted the right to lie and to cheat, you were undermining the very bases upon which human societies are built. Particularly when you admitted the right of political parties to lie and cheat, for how, then, could anybody have faith in them? How could their own followers know what they were or what they would become? And yet, here in old Europe you didn't have any ideal government to pin your hopes to; you had a number of far from perfect governments and had to choose the least objectionable. If you took your stand on what you called fundamental moral principles, it was like retiring to a mountain top, away from all human affairs; you could live there like a hermit, or a Hindu mystic, gazing at your own navel—until the guns started shelling your mountain top, and the bombing-planes took it for an objective!

IV

On Sunday morning the American couple motored to Wickthorpe Castle to spend the day and night. This was important for Lanny, because he met Gerald Albany and others of the government set and heard them discussing the problems of that very dangerous hour; if he met Göring he would be able to repeat what they had said, of course withholding anything that was really confidential. He played no favorites, but told his English friends about his last meeting with the fat Commander of the German Air Force and what that loquacious personage had revealed about the wonderful new fighter planes he was building, the many skilled pilots he was training, and how they were going to knock all enemy planes out of the air in the first hours of a war. Alas, this didn't do much harm to Göring, because Ceddy and his friends were serenely certain that the fat General was bluffing, trying to plant fear in their hearts against the day when Hitler would be ready to militarize the Rhineland, or whatever his next move might be.

Irma knew no reason for being in a hurry, so on Monday they drove to London and she did some shopping and had her hair waved and enjoyed a leisurely tea with one of her women friends, while

Lanny did his professional duty by looking at the offerings of the various picture dealers. In the evening they went to see a comedy which had been running all summer, called *Tovarisch*. It had to do with a Russian grand duke and his wife who were refugees in Paris, living in destitution because they wouldn't touch a huge sum which the duke held in trust in a Paris bank for his no-longer-existent government. It was reported that Herr Hitler had greatly enjoyed this play—after having taken the precaution to ascertain that its author was a pure Aryan!

Among great numbers of refugee "Whites" in Paris and on the Riviera, Lanny Budd had never met any who resembled these romantic figures. When at the end the grand duke's patriotic feelings caused him to turn the money over to the Soviet government, Lanny enjoyed the "happy ending" to a fairy tale. In the next morning's papers, he read news of the Comintern Congress, also editorials of embittered loathing in the London press—but nothing either humorous or romantic. Old Europe was a kettle full of seething hatreds, and the only question was, at what moment would it boil over and in which direction would the scalding stream flow?

There came a letter from Irma's friend the Fürstin Donnerstein, who was spending the hot season in a chalet on the Obersalzberg, near the Austrian border. She called it "little," but you could be sure there would be a number of guest rooms. "Do come and see it," she pleaded. "Berlin is absolutely impossible in August. From our upstairs veranda you can see the Berghof, the eagle's eyrie where our great Führer hides, and perhaps Lanny will take you to visit him." She had heard of the playboy's having had this great honor, one which neither she nor her husband had ever enjoyed.

"How about it?" asked Irma; and Lanny responded: "Would you really like to meet Hitler?" She said it might be amusing, and certainly it would be an adventure to tell her friends about. Lanny thought: "Whatever I can get Adi to reveal about his plans will be of use to Rick, and to Blum and Longuet, and Raoul Palma, perhaps even to Trudi. Certainly they'll take it more seriously if I get it from the horse's mouth."

To his wife he said: "I'll ask Heinrich Jung about it when we get to Berlin." He hadn't been to see his oldest Nazi friend on recent trips, partly because Lanny himself had been too busy, and partly because Irma found Heinrich and his wife such bores. That was the one thing which the daughter of J. Paramount Barnes refused to endure, and Lanny planned to take advantage of that trait in Berlin. He would have to get away from Irma in order to see Trudi, and it might not be so easy when all her friends were out of town. But if he went to see Heinrich at the latter's office, and if this fanatical enthusiast took him to see some Hitler Youth demonstration, or school, or recreation center—those were things which would move Irma to remark: "I'll go to a picture show by myself!"

V

There wasn't any need to telegraph reservations to the Adlon in the midst of summer heat, but Lanny did so and specified the hour of his arrival. He didn't have to mention that he wanted the reporters to be on hand, for every leisure-class hotel seeks publicity and takes it for granted that all patrons do the same. So when the American party arrived, the press was in the lobby, watching respectfully a procession composed of one heiress, one prince consort, one maid, and three bellboys loaded with four suitcases apiece.

Seated in the drawing-room of their suite, Lanny ordered drinks for the reporters and told them about the Cowes regatta, the art treasures he meant to purchase, and the visit he purposed in the neighborhood of the Führer's retreat. Every Berlin newspaper had accounts of Lanny's last interview with the nation's idol, and this made it certain that he would get space in the morning. "Kornmahler" would see these items, and there should be a letter very soon.

Lanny figured that it might arrive by mid-afternoon; and meanwhile he would be the most attentive of husbands, so as to excuse himself for later neglect. The weather was warm and sultry, and he said: "How would you like to drive to one of the lakes and have a swim?" In that flat province of Brandenburg, once a swampy forest inhabited by aurochs, bears, and barbarians, were lakes enough for all the population of a metropolis to sail on and swim in. But on a weekday morning nearly all that population was at work, and visiting Americans could have boat-houses and bathing-pavilions to themselves. The hotel porter would tell them where to find the most exclusive, and they could pass a pleasant morning and afterward have lunch. Irma wouldn't stop to wonder what they were waiting for, because she had all the time there was in her life.

When they got back to the hotel, there was the expected note, the briefest possible: "I have some sketches which I hope you will like. I would be pleased if you come at twenty-two o'clock any evening that is convenient to you." That was all. Trudi had never before asked him to come at night, and he guessed that it was because she no longer dared to appear on the streets by daylight.

Lanny's first thought was how to get away from Irma at ten o'clock in the evening. But the fates were more than kind to him; there came a telephone call from the Frau Ritter von Fiebewitz, who happened to be in town, on her way from the mountains to the seashore; wouldn't they come and have supper with her—an impromptu affair, since she had only one servant with her? Irma wanted to go, and Lanny said: "I'll tell you what: I'll take you there and leave you, and then I'll take Heinrich to dinner and save you the boredom. If you're not present, he won't expect his wife to be invited. I'll drive him home afterwards, and your friend can bring you to the hotel, no doubt."

"Or I can take a taxi," said the young wife, amiably. It had worked out like a bit of magic.

VI

The son of the head forester of Stubendorf had risen to high rank in that branch of the party machine which had charge of the education and training of the Führer's youth; but Heinrich Jung still saw Lanny Budd as the darling of fortune who had come visiting, spreading an aura of elegance, chatting airily about the great ones of Europe's capitals. The National Socialists considered themselves revolutionists and destroyers of Europe's old culture, but only the crudest and most fanatical had freed themselves entirely from its spell; thus to his Nazi friend Lanny was still a romantic figure, received as a guest at Schloss Stubendorf and recognized by the *gleichgeschaltete Presse* of Berlin. Before Heinrich came to the Adlon to dine, he took the trouble to hurry home and put on his dress-uniform, much too warm and smelling strongly of moth-balls. When he met his brilliant friend his blue Nordic eyes shone with happiness and his rosy Nordic cheeks which had grown plumper with the years acquired two naïve and quite charming dimples.

"*Ach, Lanny!*" he exclaimed. "When are you going to come out for us?"

"What do you want me to do?" smiled the host. "Put on a uniform?"

"*Warum nicht?* It would become you, and you would have a distinguished career. In no time at all you could become the *Gauleiter* of New England. Our people over there are not doing so very well."

"All my friends in New England think I am a foreigner," replied Lanny. "They would not follow my lead."

He asked what Heinrich was doing at present, and, as always, this started a flood. The Nazi official had been on the point of calling up, to beg Lanny to come with him on the morrow to Nürnberg. There was a National Socialist school for selected young men who had been brought from all the nations of the earth—fifteen hundred students chosen for their special aptitudes from fifty-one different lands; they were the future national Führers and world masters. Heinrich had been chosen to lecture them about the *Hitlerjugend* and how this marvelous organization had been built during the past decade. The term of the school was closing, and there would be impressive ceremonies, including memorial services in front of the War Monument: flags and banners, drums and trumpets, martial hymns, all that ritual which thrilled the soul of a pure Nordic *Herrenmensch*. "Lanny, you wouldn't be able to resist it!"

"Perhaps that is why I don't go," replied the irreverent American. "I couldn't settle down and work as hard as you, Heinrich; but I admire you for it, all the same." The cheeks of the head forester's son glowed with pleasure, and Lanny signed to the waiter to fill up his glass. The lavish host had ordered a liter of the best French champagne and would see that his friend drank the greater part of it.

"As a matter of fact I'm really busy right now," the host continued. "I am selling some of Minister-Präsident General Göring's paintings for him. He has rather extraordinary taste, you know, and I find it instructive as well as profitable to co-operate with him." Lanny talked with easy familiarity about Karinhall, and Emmy, and the wonderful wedding-gifts, and the fat General's skill as a hunter of wild boars—taking the hunter's word for it. Since Lanny's visit to the preserve, official announcement had been made of the film star's intention to retire and present the German people with an heir, and this stirred in Heinrich that philoprogenitive instinct which characterizes a *Herrenvolk* on its way to power and glory.

All through dinner the American listened to good Nazi propaganda; then he took his friend up to the suite, where they had coffee and brandy, and Heinrich talked about the sad fate of his one-time friend Hugo Behr and others who had been so tragically misled as to oppose the Führer's will. The international situation now showed how right the Führer had been; how Germany's freedom could be won by boldness and in no other way. Heinrich quoted a speech recently made by General Göring to the effect that he wanted and would have "no dishwater internationalism" in the Fatherland. Lanny, who had pleaded at the Paris Peace Conference against the cutting off of Stubendorf from the German Republic, was taken by the young official to be in complete sympathy with anything the Führer saw fit to do; so the listener had only to go on listening.

VII

Presently there was a chance to change the subject. Lanny remarked: "Irma and I are planning to drive to Salzburg tomorrow, to visit a friend in the mountains there. I wish we could drive you as far as Nürnberg, Heinrich, but Irma has her maid along, and with all the bags she's about buried."

"Oh, that's all right," replied the other. "There's a party car going with three of us."

"This occurred to me," continued the other. "It might be good form for us to drop in and pay our respects to the Führer, if you think he would like it."

"Oh, Lanny, I'm sure he would! I wish I could go, too; but you know how it is—I cannot neglect an important duty to our youth."

"Of course not. What would you advise me to do? Would you like to phone and find out if he would care to receive us?"

"*Gewiss*, if you wish it."

"Well, why not put in a call from here?" Heinrich was greatly excited by this honor, and Lanny knew the hotel staff would be the same; he guessed that before the call had been completed the whole of the immense establishment would know what was going on.

Heinrich spoke the portentous words with proud distinctness: "*Hallo. Heil Hitler! Bitte, des Führers Heim, Der Berghof, in Berchtesgaden, Obersalzberg.*" After that he could hardly sit still in his chair, and could talk about nothing but, should he ask to speak to the greatest of men personally, and would the greatest come? Lanny, who had had much to do with the great, advised that the proper procedure was to ask for the Führer's secretary; there was pretty sure to be one on duty at all times. Avoid attempting to give an important message to butlers or maids, who lack familiarity with the outside world and may get names wrong, especially foreign names. Lanny knew that Heinrich's own name was one of power, because in his youth he had twice visited Adi in prison and that was something the ex-painter of picture postcards would never forget.

The phone rang and Heinrich picked up the receiver with a trembling hand. Lanny listened to the conversation: "*Hallo. Ist dort Der Berghof? Heil Hitler. Hier Heinrich Jung. Wollen Sie mich bitte mit dem Sekretär des Führers verbinden? Ja? Danke schön.*" A wait, and then: "*Sekretär des Führers? Heil Hitler. Hier spricht Heinrich Jung, Gruppenführerstellvertreter des fünften Gaus der Reichsjugendführung und ein alter Freund des Führers. Heil Hitler.*"

So much for preliminaries, and Heinrich went on to explain that the American Lanny Budd and his multimillionaire wife—Heinrich hadn't had to be told to mention this—were motoring to the vicinity of the Berghof, and Herr Budd, who had already twice met the Führer, desired to call with his wife and pay their respects. Again there was a wait, longer this time, and at last a beaming smile exploded upon the round Aryan features of the Hitler Youth official. "*Ja, ja! Bitte, einen Augenblick.*"

He turned to Lanny. "The Führer will see you tomorrow evening at twenty-two o'clock. Can you be there?"

"Sure, I'll be there." Since Lanny didn't intend to load himself up with the pictures until he was ready to leave Germany, he had nothing to do but see Trudi this evening, and could start early next morning. He wasn't surprised by the lateness of the appointment, knowing that Adi suffered from insomnia and kept late hours.

Of course he didn't fail to thank his old friend for this honor. Few persons in the Fatherland could have done this, he said, and added that he and his wife would be careful not to say a word which would trouble the great man, who sought this retreat in the high mountains to commune with his soul and escape from the cares of state.

It was then a little after nine o'clock, or twenty-one continental. Lanny said he had an engagement to meet his wife, and hoped that Heinrich wouldn't mind being sent home in a taxicab. The head forester's son said he hadn't got that important yet, so Lanny escorted him downstairs—flushed in the cheeks and extremely talkative with mixed liquors—and put him into a car, paying the driver twice what the fare could amount to. "*Heil Hitler für dich und grüss Gott für die Frau!*" said Lanny, knowing that his friend's plump little spouse came from Bavaria.

VIII

Lanny got his car and drove, and promptly on the stroke of twenty-two—a great many strokes to count—he was at the corner where for the past eight months or so he had been meeting his fellow-conspirator. His heart was in his throat; for suppose she didn't come, or—just supposing!—there should come in her stead one of the armored cars of the Gestapo, accompanied by a couple of fast-driving motor-cyclists with side-arms!

But no, here she was! Wearing a hat with a wide brim, which shaded her features from the street lights and the moon; walking fast, and looking neither to right nor to left. Lanny drew up to the curb not far ahead, and she sprang in quickly, saying: "Drive!" His high-powered car started away, and he asked: "Is anybody following you?"

Her answer was: "They have been following me everywhere." He turned a corner, and watched for car lights behind him or for a car without lights. After several turns he was sure they were safe for the time being, and said: "You can rest for a while; nobody is going to pay any attention to you in this car."

"Oh, Lanny!" she exclaimed. "I have been having the most dreadful time ever since I saw you last. I've hardly had a day of peace. The police got on our trail, and they have taken most of my friends. It is too horrible to talk about or even to think about."

"You had better tell me a little," he said, gently. "After all, I am in it too, you know."

"That is one of the things that have made me sick. I waited a couple of months, trying to make up my mind whether I ought to bring you back into Germany again."

"All the Nazis appear glad to see me. I have an appointment to call on the Führer at Berchtesgaden tomorrow evening."

"*Herrgott, Lanny!* You might kill him!"

"Would you advise me to?" He thought it worth while to make sure.

"I didn't mean that. I mean, they wouldn't let you near him if they had any suspicion of you."

"I have been consoling myself with that idea. I don't suppose he wants the pleasure of torturing me personally. Tell me what you have been doing, so that I can advise you."

"We were getting out an underground paper—fifty thousand copies of a tiny four-page weekly, with the real news. They got our press and our printer, and two of our key men who were doing the distributing."

"So you've had to quit?"

"For the present. I am afraid to go about, because they have my picture on a sheet which they distribute. Twice they have arrested the people with whom I have been staying, and that is the most awful thing to me; I don't know what to do—I give the kiss of death wherever I go."

"Trudi," he said, gravely, "how much do you really know about Monck?"

"Oh, Lanny, you mean that you suspect him? He has been one of our most devoted comrades; he's a marine engineer, a skilled man, and he has worked in the party since he was a youth."

"How did it happen that the Nazis spared him until just recently?"

"He went underground, as we all have done. Believe me, I thought long and hard over the right man to send to you. It is easier for a seaman to go abroad than for a woman. I am sure he would have betrayed you at once if he had meant to. The Gestapo doesn't wait to strike, and they would never have let you come into Germany and distribute large sums of money if they had any hint of it."

"Do you know anybody known to Monck who is still at large and working for the cause?"

She thought for a while. "Yes, I do; at least I think I do. You can never be sure from hour to hour. That is the most trying thing about the life we live. You go to a friend's room, thinking to find shelter for the night, and you are afraid to tap on the door, because it may be opened by a man in uniform. No use trying to run; he will shoot you in the feet. That leaves you still able to talk."

"Well, Trudi," he said, "I don't know what to advise. If you can't function any longer, I'm ready to help you get out."

"Oh, I can't desert the comrades! So many of them, in such dreadful trouble! We all pledged ourselves to carry on."

"Yes; but it's possible to edit and print a paper in France or in Holland and to smuggle copies in. I might be able to help you with that and still keep my part a secret, so that I could continue to earn money."

"It is something to think about; but I am staying with a family now whose head is an old printer, and he thinks he can find a way to buy a hand-press, so that we can go on."

"All right," he answered; "if that is what you want, here's five thousand marks. I took the precaution to buy them in New York, and some in London, so I don't think they can be traced." He had hidden the precious wad in his car while entering Germany, and on the way to this rendezvous he had dug it out. Now he put it into her hands.

"I don't know if I ought to take it," she countered. "I'm not sure if I can use it to advantage, the way I'm having to live now."

"Forget it," he replied. "You have to live in any case, and so do your friends. What can I do better with Göring's money?"

IX

Meetings with Trudi Schultz were few and costly. Lanny didn't expect to see her again on this trip, so he had tried to think of all the questions he had to ask and the arrangements he had to make. He didn't ask for details of her work or the names of those who had been seized by the Nazis. He remembered many whom he had met in the old days, and was curious as to their fates, but he left them in the shadows. She asked whether his wife had any idea of his activities, and he said he didn't think so. He defended Irma as well as he could; she was what her environment had made her, and she was still young. He told his fellow-conspirator that he was expecting to return to New York, and gave her his address there. Also they agreed upon certain code words, the names of painters, so that she could tell him if she needed a printing-press, or paper, or whatever it might be. Lanny had once brought a van-load of Marcel's works into Germany for exhibition, and he could repeat that stunt if necessary, concealing quite a quantity of goods under a hundred paintings!

Finally she said: "I'm afraid to travel in the subway, and I had to walk a long distance here, so I'll let you set me down in the Schöneberg district, where I am living now."

He drove according to her directions, and when she was ready to be set down, he said: "You know, I'm not curious about where you're living, but I hate to put you down at random, not knowing how things may be. Can't I drive you through your block and let you have a look? Then I'll drive around the block a couple of times so that if you find anything has gone wrong you can come out and join me."

She told him the block, one of scores all alike, as in modern capitals. Scarcely had they driven into it when she caught his arm and whispered: "There are two cars in front of the house! Turn around!"

He saw the cars, facing his way, and knew they could start and catch up with him while he was backing and turning in a not very wide street. "Sit still!" he commanded. "Sink down in the seat! Lay your head on my shoulder!" He sat forward slightly, so as to hide her face but not the fact that she was there.

In this position they drove past the two cars. At the wheel of each Lanny saw that most dreadful of sights, the Schutzstaffel uniform, steel helmet and black shirt with armband containing the skull and crossbones. One glimpse was enough, and after that he drove with eyes straight ahead, not altering his speed. It was his guess that a man with a fancy foreign-made car, driving a young woman on a summer's night, would not arouse special interest in the Gestapo. When he got farther down the street and saw in his little mirror the cars remaining where they were, he hit it up and turned the next corner, and got quickly out of the Schöneberg district of Berlin.

X

Trudi Schultz had sunk into a heap, shaken with sobs. At first he thought it was the reaction from her terror, but then he realized that she was not thinking about herself. "Oh, Lanny, those poor people! They will be dragged away to some cellar by those devils and torn to pieces, to make them tell where I've gone."

"Do they know?" asked the man, thinking about himself for once.

"*Nein, ausgeschlossen!* I told them I was going to interview a man who can get us some paper without the police tracing it. But, Lanny, if you knew them! The most devoted comrades, workers who have toiled all their lives and put their pfennigs into party dues and literature! The man's face lined and hair turned gray too early, and the woman thin and harassed, with work-worn hands and forearms that seem to be nothing but whipcords. And two children—a half-grown boy and a girl—the S.S. will torture them, too. It does no good to say you don't know anything; they don't believe you, they go on whipping you senseless, they make your whole body one mass of raw wounds."

"I know," Lanny said. "I have seen it with my own eyes." He let her have another spell of weeping; after which he thought it was time to put her mind to work. "Listen, my dear. You know I have a date with Irma, and I can't go on driving all night."

"Yes, yes, I understand. I am imposing on you cruelly. Put me down any place." ·

"But where do you mean to go?"

"I haven't an idea. I can't think of another family that would dare to take me in—or that I would have the right to impose upon."

"Can't I take you somewhere out of town?"

"What good would it do? If I go to a hotel, or take lodgings, I have to register with the police within twenty-four hours, and I have to show my identification card, which I destroyed long ago. I am an outlaw."

"Well, my dear, you can't just go on walking about the streets; and you certainly must know that I wouldn't be happy driving off and leaving you."

She didn't know what to say; and after an interval he decided that the time for action had come. "Listen, Trudi," he said, "we have an old saying, that he who fights and runs away may live to fight another day. I'm going to take you out of Germany."

"How can you do it?" she asked.

"That is something that will require thinking. But first I want to know, will you come?"

There was a pause. "All right," she said, at last, her voice low, as if it hurt.

"*Gut!*" he exclaimed. "The first thing, I have to tell my wife, because we shall need her help."

"Will she give it, Lanny?"

"She won't like it, of course; but it will not be possible for her to refuse."

"I don't want to come between you and her, Lanny."

"I don't think it will be as serious as that. She is a sensible person, also kind-hearted. When she realizes the situation, she will not wish to throw you to the wolves."

"Will you tell her the whole story?"

"I must think about that. The first thing is to get you into the hotel."

"*Aber, Lanny!* You are dreaming of taking me into the Adlon?"

"You will be surprised what a difference it will make when you get some of Irma's clothes on. They'll be a bit large, but she will walk on one side of you and I on the other and I don't think anyone will pay any special attention."

"But if I'm to spend the night there, I'll have to register."

"You'll go in late, and you'll be leaving in the morning, and I doubt if they'll realize the situation before that."

"Lanny, I could get you into horrible trouble!"

"I doubt it, really. We're Americans, and we're well known, and I don't believe the Nazis would want a scandal. I have a perfectly good story if it comes to a showdown: you are an artist and I am a *Kunstsachverständiger;* I helped to get your drawings published in France, and I gave you financial aid because I expected to sell your work and make money out of it. I had no idea of your illegal doings. By the way, you had better give me back that money until we get out of Germany. It'll be more natural for me to have it than you."

XI

Lanny parked the car boldly in front of the hotel. He had put Trudi in the rear seat, and told her to lie back so that her face was out of sight. If anyone spoke to her she would say that she was waiting for Herr Budd; but he doubted if anyone would speak, unless he left the car too long.

The keys to his suite were still at the desk, so Irma had not returned. That was convenient; he went to her room and threw into an empty suitcase a dress of dark-blue silk, not too conspicuous, a hat to match, and shoes and stockings. Whatever Trudi wore had to be complete; a pair of brown cotton stockings would have been · as much a giveaway as a red Socialist badge. He took the precaution to phone to Céleste, Irma's maid, who was in the hotel, telling her to go to bed, as her services would not be required that evening. Then he hurried down to the car and drove away. Trudi pulled down the side and rear curtains, and changed her clothes quickly. What to do with the old ones was a problem, suggestive of a murder mystery. It wouldn't do to have them found in the hotel or in the car. After she had assured him that there were no marks of identification on her clothing, no papers in pockets and no laundry marks, he told her to tie the whole lot into a tight ball, and when he was crossing the River Spree on one of the numerous bridges he tossed the bundle over the parapet.

Now Trudi Schultz was a lady, and a perfect one; but Lanny didn't want to escort her into the suite alone, nor did he wish her to witness the interview between himself and his wife. He parked near the hotel and left her as before. Irma still hadn't arrived, though it was after midnight; he assumed that she was enjoying a good gossip with the Frau Ritter von Fiebewitz, and he used the time to make a thorough search of her bedroom, under the rugs, inside the window curtains, under the bed, to make sure there was nothing resembling a wire or metal disk which might be part of a sound-transmitting device. He took the additional precaution to get a heavy bath towel and wrap the telephone in it. After that he was ready for the "big scene."

Irma had been having a good time, including, no doubt, a couple of cocktails; her cheeks were flushed and she was full of things to talk about. "Oh, Lanny, I'm sorry to be late, but I had such a curious adventure! Did you ever see a *Thingspiel?*"

"I have heard of them," he said.

"Fiebewitz's cousin came and took us out into the country somewhere, and we saw one, in a big open-air theater. There must have been a thousand people, peasants and villagers, and really I felt I was in Germany for the first time in my life. The play was unbelievably crude, but they ate it up—the women were sobbing all around me. It made me think of an *Uncle Tom's Cabin* show I saw once when I was a girl—up in the Adirondacks. Fiebewitz says it is like the old miracle and mystery plays in England."

"What was it about?" Lanny had to be polite now, of all times.

"About Hitler and his saving the German people. It was called *German Passion 1933*, and it showed how Hitler took up the cross —really it was quite blasphemous, because it showed him instead of Christ being crucified by the Jews, and then he had a resurrection and ascended to heaven, and got instructions from an angel, and came back to earth in shining armor to save a lovely blue-eyed maiden with two long braids of flaxen hair; she was Germany, of course, and it sounds silly to tell it, but you can't imagine how deeply moved the audience was. I'm sure those country women all really believed the Führer had had exactly those experiences."

"Listen, dear," said Lanny, quickly. "You'd better come in here if you want to talk about things like that." He drew her into the bedroom and shut the door, led her to a chair, drew up his own, and said: "Something serious has happened. Listen carefully, and please, whatever you think, don't raise your voice."

XII

So began the story of how Lanny had received a note from a young woman artist of talent, telling of her need for help, and how he had gone to meet her; what she had told him about her activities and the fate of her associates, and how he had driven her past her tenement home and what they had seen. It was the truth and nothing but the truth, but of course not the whole truth. He found that Irma didn't remember Trudi; the woman artist had been one of some twoscore persons she had met at a reception of the school, and had disapproved of. It was a perfectly consistent story, and while telling it he thought that he was getting away with it.

But when he quit, he soon discovered that he wasn't! His young wife sat with her hands clenched tightly and her lips pressed together. "You see!" she exclaimed. "I can't trust you! You have got mixed up with that Red business again!"

"No, dear——"

"Don't try to fool me any longer, Lanny! You have been meeting that woman! Tell me the truth and stop treating me like a child."

"I have met her two or three times, and gave her some money—I couldn't very well refuse to help her, when I consider her a real artist——"

"Artist my eye! You helped her because she's a Socialist, and you can't refuse anything those people ask of you. You've been coming into Germany on her account, and not for pictures. And now you've got yourself into another mess, the very thing you swore to me you wouldn't. You got me into Germany on that promise, and you were breaking it and meant to go on breaking it. What is that woman to you that you have to wreck our happiness for her sake?"

"Darling," he said, "let me make one thing clear at the start—there hasn't been the faintest hint of love between Trudi Schultz and me. I haven't so much as touched her hand. She is all wrapped up in the fate of her husband. She clings to the faith that he is still alive in some concentration camp, and that she is helping him by the work she is doing. Please be sure of that, Irma."

There were tears in her eyes. "How little you understand me, Lanny! If you came to me and said you loved this woman, I'd be heart-broken, of course, but I wouldn't stand in the way of your happiness. If you told me that you had been making love to her, and that you realized it was a mistake and that you really loved me, I'd forgive you and try again to make you happy. That would be something I could understand, and if you said you were sorry I could believe you. But this Socialism business is something you aren't sorry about; you consider that it's right, and you mean to go on with it!" She paused; and when he was silent, she insisted: "Isn't that true?"

"Yes," he admitted, in a voice which implied that he was sorry about that. He was surprised by her point of view; impressed by its logic and at the same time shocked by the fierceness of prejudice it revealed.

"That's why I know I can never be happy with you again!" exclaimed the outraged wife.

"Listen, dear," he pleaded; "there is so much to be said on this subject——"

"No, Lanny, you are mistaken. It can all be said in a very few words."

"Don't say them now—please! Try to understand the situation. Trudi has no place in the world to go. The Nazis have seized the working people she was staying with—an elderly printer, a frail mother, and two half-grown children. The chances are a hundred to one that they have them in their dungeons at this moment and are torturing them to make them tell where Trudi is."

"Do they know where she is?"

"They do not."

"But *you* know?"

"She is sitting in our car in front of the hotel; and she can't sit there much longer without attracting attention. The entire police force of Berlin, the Brownshirts, the Schutzstaffel—the whole Nazi machine—have her picture and will be on the look-out for her."

"What is it you want me to do?"

"I want you to help her get out of Germany."

"Just a little simple thing like that!"

"You must remember, dear, this isn't a new problem to me. I faced it when I thought of getting Freddi out. I worked out many different plans."

"None of which was good enough!"

"I didn't have your help then."

"Suppose I refuse to help?"

"I'll have to do the best I can by myself. I'm surely not going to turn this woman out of our car and leave her on the streets to be picked up by those savages."

"And suppose I want the car to go home in?"

"Well, then, I'll have the problem of buying another. Somehow I have to get her to the border. There are people who make money smuggling refugees out, and perhaps I can find them."

There was a long silence. He understood that a struggle was going on in her soul, and thought that she had better settle it for herself. Finally she said: "You have done something quite horrible to me, and something I can never forgive. But I don't want to see you killed, and I'm put in the position where I have to help this woman or run the risk of causing your death. If you can show me any chance of getting her out, I will do my part; but don't for a moment take it to mean that I am condoning what you have done."

"I am on my knees with gratitude, darling, and I will do all that a man can do to make it up to you."

"There is no way you can ever make it up to me, so don't deceive yourself with the idea. I have deceived myself long enough, and this time it's never again. I want to have it understood—I'm going to help, and publicly I'll do and say whatever is necessary; but apart from that I don't want to hear one word from her, and as few from you as possible. I don't mean to be disagreeable—I just want to avoid arguments, and to keep my thoughts to myself, and solve my own problems while you solve hers."

He thought it the part of wisdom to let matters rest right there.

12

Perilous Edge of Battle

I

SERENE and self-possessed, according to the code of the aloof classes, Irma Barnes and her prince consort strolled through the lobby of the Hotel Adlon and out to their parked car. Within sight of the august doorman the wife was introduced to her husband's friend and shook hands with her, and then the three strolled back into the hotel, Lanny giving the car keys to the functionary so that one of the bellboys might take the car to the garage. The guests went up in the elevator to their suite, and when they were in Irma's bedroom, with the muffled telephone receiver, she delivered herself as follows:

"Miss Schultz, my husband has explained to me the unfortunate circumstances, and I have agreed to try to help you. We have decided to postpone conversation on all other subjects until that has been done. You will understand that I am doing it for my husband's sake, and not for that of a stranger; so do not waste any words in thanking me, but let us get down at once to the practical questions of how to proceed."

Trudi gulped once, and replied: "Frau Budd, your husband has not told me his plans, so all I can say is that I am prepared to do whatever you and he tell me. I am deeply sorry to have put you in this position."

"We cannot go backward, so there is no use discussing that." Irma turned to Lanny, who looked at her grimly set face and remembered the large and determined mother in Shore Acres who had tried so hard to prevent this unfortunate marriage; also the buccaneer of Wall Street whose black-mustached and frowning portrait confronted the household at the head of the grand staircase and still had power to intimidate. On Lanny's recent visit, rummaging in unexplored drawers of his deceased father-in-law's library, he had come upon a stack of handsomely printed pamphlets containing a speech which the manufacturer of public-utility pyramids had delivered to the United States Chamber of Commerce in banquet assembled. In it the man of great affairs had stated his opinion of "Socialist crackpots and dreamers"—thus putting a prince consort in his place, just as Irma was now doing!

II

"We cannot leave tonight," declared the husband, in a low voice, "because we have no exit permits; also it would seem phony if we left Germany without putting through the picture deal for which we came. The first thing in the morning I will phone Oberleutnant Furtwaengler and explain that I have an appointment to call on the Führer in the evening; he will recognize the urgency, and will no doubt bring the paintings and the necessary papers at once. If we have our bill of sale with the signature of General Göring's office, it may solve problems at the border—I proved that the last time I went out."

"You mean that you expect to get through without either a passport or exit permit for Miss Schultz?"

"This is what I have in mind. We leave Céleste here at the hotel, stating that we are going to visit the Führer and then return. We take Trudi out with Céleste's exit permit, and we take her into Austria on Céleste's passport."

"But there is Céleste's picture on the passport, and Miss Schultz does not look in the least like a Breton peasant."

"It will be late at night, and Miss Schultz will be lying back in the rear seat, pretty well surrounded by paintings and bags. If any question is raised, I will say that she has been ill and has lost twenty pounds or so. I will also say that I am a friend of the Minister-Präsident General, and am handling these paintings for him; also that we have just come from a visit to the Führer, and that they may call the Berghof, which is only a couple of miles inside the border. I am sure those statements will turn the officials to jelly."

"And then what do you expect to do about Céleste? Leave her in Germany the rest of her life?"

Lanny had worked over a problem like that more than two years ago, when he had been scheming to carry Freddi Robin out of Germany on the passport of a truck driver. He had told that story to Irma, but he didn't remind her of it now. He explained:

"Céleste will be staying safely in this hotel, going to picture shows and flirting with one of the male employees. She gets a letter from you saying that you were called home unexpectedly and that you forgot her papers and carried them out with you, and are now mailing them to her. You enclose money and tell her to join you in London or wherever you wish. Céleste waits, but the papers do not come, and when she telegraphs you to that effect you reply that they must have got lost in the mail. You tell her to go to the French consul and have the matter straightened out; you telegraph the French consul explaining the error and he will give her a new passport. All this may mean that you will have to have a substitute maid for a month or so."

"You overlook one detail: there will be a record at the border where we go out, showing that Céleste's passport and exit permit were used there and that three persons went out."

"In the first place, in wiring Céleste and the French consul you will not say when or where you went out, but will state that we left Berlin hurriedly because we had an invitation to visit the Führer, and you afterward decided to come home at once. The consul will show that letter to the authorities, when he presents the new passport and gets the new exit permit. The authorities will hardly do much investigating in a case of the Führer's guests; at the worst it could not be a serious matter for Céleste, for it will be obvious that she is an ignorant person, a victim of her employers, and that she has no idea what has been done to her. Most probably she will never know just what happened to her; if she does, a small sum of money will salve her feelings. If possible, think up some errand for her to do tomorrow morning, so that she will not see Trudi and will have no idea that we have anyone with us."

Said Irma: "This may mean that you will never be able to come back into Germany."

"We can see how that works out," was the reply. "It is my guess that I can come into Germany any time I have a bank draft for a large sum payable to a certain fat gentleman."

III

Lanny gave up his bedroom to his guest, and slept on a couch in the drawing-room—since Irma did not invite him into her room. Lanny slept, because he knew he had to drive hard on the morrow, and he had grown to some extent accustomed to mixups with the Gestapo. Whether either of the ladies slept they did not tell him and he did not ask. In the morning his first act was to call the worshipful Oberleutnant, who, being a member of the fat General's household, was available early. As Lanny had foreseen, the young officer was overwhelmed by the news about the invitation to the

Berghof, and undertook to get the paintings and the necessary papers and bring them personally to the Adlon.

Lanny removed all traces of his having slept in the drawing-room, and locked Trudi in the bedroom while breakfast was set on a couple of folding-tables; also while Irma summoned Céleste, who slept in the servants' quarters of the hotel. She came, a sturdy peasant woman, always smiling, and of course having no idea of the shabby trick being planned. She looked embarrassingly unlike Trudi Schultz; it was evident that no amount of illness or starvation would ever reduce those broad cheekbones, or cause those features to assume the delicacy and fineness of a woman saint's. But Lanny was planning to blind the eyes of border officials, and he was interested to observe how even a Frenchwoman was thrilled by the news of the visit to the Führer.

The mistress explained that they were taking only two bags and had already put their things into these. She mentioned that her mother's birthday was approaching, and she had meant to send a gift; now she commissioned Céleste to visit the department stores and select something that was completely German and that Mrs. Barnes would appreciate, and send it by mail or express. Irma gave her a hundred-mark note, worth about forty dollars at this time, and sent her off contented and with no suspicion of anything wrong in the Budd family.

Lanny ordered his car and hurried to the Austrian consulate, where a modest *douceur* got him without delay the necessary visas upon the passports of himself, wife, and maid. When he got back to the hotel, the efficient Oberleutnant was on hand, and in one of the parlors of the hotel Lanny examined the two paintings, paid the money, and took the bill of sale with the magical stamp of the fat General's office; also the exit permits. He exchanged the usual courtesies with his S.S. friend, and forbore to ask whether he had recently been down in any cellars, whipping the editors and printers of a Socialist paper.

The paintings were carried to the car and placed in the back seat —fortunately they were not very large. Lanny bade the doorman keep his eye on them, and returned to the hotel and phoned Irma that all was ready. He paid the bill, incidentally mentioning to the clerk that he was driving to Berchtesgaden to pay a call upon the Führer that evening. In the midst of the interest aroused by this conversation, Irma and a well-dressed woman friend emerged from the elevator and went out to the car, followed by a bellboy with a couple of bags. Lanny performed his customary function of distributor of tips; and if it should happen that any of the day staff would compare notes with any of the night staff and realize that a strange lady had passed the night in the Budd suite, Lanny felt sure they would not bother to report it to the *Polizei*.

IV

The strangest ride this habitual motorist had yet taken over the old continent of Europe! Irma had not a word to say, and Trudi respected her wishes; so Lanny conducted himself as a well-trained chauffeur. He had something more than four hundred miles to cover and no time to waste; he kept his eyes fixed on the excellent *Reichsautobahn* before him and his right foot on the accelerator. If any traffic officer on the route Berlin–Leipzig–Regensburg–Munich ventured to stop him, he had the most perfect of answers; if the authority presumed to doubt his word, he had the document from the office of the second-in-command. Seeing this, any traffic officer would volunteer to ride ahead and clear the way.

It was a road over which Lanny and his wife had traveled more than once. The level plains of Prussia, now green with potatoes and sugar-beets—unless they had been taken over by higher authority and were dusty with the tramp of drilling recruits or with great tanks thundering like herds of stampeding elephants. Lanny thought he had seen military preparations before, but never anything like this. There was hardly a large field without a group of youths wearing sandals and khaki shorts and shirts open at the throat, launching one of their number into the air on a glider. Great planes curved and swooped overhead, and time and again the travelers heard sounds of gunfire. Tourists were free to come into the Fatherland and witness these spectacles, and so for that matter were the agents of

Britain, France, and other nations which had signed the Versailles
treaty; but apparently no statesman of any nation could think of
anything to do but make fussy speeches about it.

The hotel had put a lunch into the car, and after they were past
Leipzig Lanny ventured to suggest that Irma should open it up and
pass it about. He munched a sandwich while he drove; then, since
dead silence seemed hardly polite at mealtimes, he bethought him
of a new gadget which Irma had had installed in the car—a radio set
with which to beguile the tedium of motoring. He ventured to
turn it on, softly and diffidently. She made no comment, and so,
reaching in front of her knees, he turned the dial: a Nazi orator
bellowing; a Nazi newsman denouncing a recent British statement
on the subject of German affairs, then, magically, a lovely melody
floating out upon the air, an orchestra playing the first movement of
the *Pastoral Symphony*. "*Allegro ma non molto.* The pleasant feelings aroused in the heart on arriving in the country"—so Beethoven
had written upon the score. It had been the gracious countryside
about Vienna which the master had had in mind, and there had been
fewer soldiers tramping and not a single armored tank rumbling, not
a single fighter plane roaring in the sky.

It might be doubted if ever in the range of musical history there
has been produced a more sustained expression of "pleasant feelings."
Lanny had hopes of the effect these sounds might have upon the
abnormally silent woman by his side. If music be the food of love,
play on! Perhaps it was a live orchestra, perhaps a "canned" one;
anyhow, it played, and presently: "*Andante con moto.* Scene at the
Brook." Call it that if it pleased your fancy, but to Lanny it was one
of those glider-planes floating over hill and dale; the youth in it
thinking not about dropping a bomb upon some of his fellow-
humans, but about the mastery of nature, the widening of vision and
enhancement of the joy·of living. Something like this magical car,
which enabled one to speed from one landscape to the next, lending
to space an element of time, making geography into history and
scenery into panorama.

"*Scherzo.* Jovial assembly of country folk." Lanny knew all about
that, for he had shared the festivities of the peasants of Provence,

and had learned to dance the farandole as a boy. So many innocent pleasures life offered, if only men could be persuaded not to rob and kill! If only they would let Beethoven teach them how to make more joy for themselves, instead of stealing the joy of others! Here the country folk were interrupted by nothing more dangerous than a thunderstorm; and Lanny, who as a rule did not care for program music, found these musical sheets of rain so vivid that he had an impulse to start his windshield wiper. He did not at any time take his eyes off the road ahead, so he couldn't guess whether his moods were being shared by the woman at his side.

"*Allegro*. Pleasurable feelings after the storm, mixed with gratitude to God." Surely no woman could go on quarreling in her mind while that most heavenly melody laid siege to her ears! Surely she, too, must have gratitude—merely to be alive in a world where such beauty had been imagined and recorded! Surely she must cry out: "Oh, Lanny, let us be kind to each other! Let us be happy, and not miss any more of the holy rapture of being!" But if she had such thoughts she crushed them down, and kept that implacable silence, broken only by practical remarks, as when she pointed out that the gas-gauge was low or offered to take his place at the wheel.

V

The forests of Thuringia, and then the pleasant valley of the River Naab, tributary to the Danube. The last time Lanny had been driven over this route was at night; the S.S. had been taking him to Berlin, for reasons about which they had left him to guess. He much preferred it to be daytime, even if the view was the rather unlovely Oberpfalz, sometimes referred to as the Bavarian Siberia. They came into the city of Munich a little before seven, still having a hundred miles to go and no time to waste. Lanny insisted that he wasn't tired; he knew the route, having studied it while planning schemes for Freddi Robin.

A gentle climb into the foothills of the Bavarian Alps; the road became more winding, and there were streams, and here and there little lakes which make the district popular with tourists and vacationers. The sun was down behind the mountains, and twilight was gathering. The campers were at supper, or singing their Nazi songs; the young people all wore military insignia now, and all hikes were drills, practice in hiding from enemies or creeping up on them. Lanny knew that he and Irma saw these things through different eyes; to her it was "Strength through Joy," while to him it was demoralization and cruelty, the breaking to pieces of the Germany he knew and loved in music, literature, and philosophy.

At last the village of Berchtesgaden, named for a witch, Berchta, with whom Bavarian children are frightened into behaving themselves. To Lanny it seemed appropriate that Adi Schicklgruber should have chosen this place for his hideout while plotting the bewitchment of Europe. It was still eight miles to the Führer's retreat; far ahead and high up was a revolving light, like that of a lighthouse, and Lanny knew this to be his destination. "Here's where we have our trouble, if any," he said; and sure enough, at the entrance of the Führer's road there was a barrier painted with blue and white stripes, and a guard-building with several armed sentries in the black and silver S.S. uniform.

Lanny stopped within a few feet of the obstacle, and when the captain of the guard emerged and flashed an electric torch upon him he extended his arm. "*Heil Hitler!*" All the Nazis as one returned the salute. "*Heil Hitler! Heil Hitler!*"

"I have an appointment with the Führer," said Lanny.

"*Ihr Name, mein Herr?*"

"Lanny Budd."

"*Und die Dame?*"

"*Meine Frau.*"

The man flashed the torch upon Irma and then into the back of the car, full into Trudi's face. "You have another passenger," he said, his tone indicating surprise.

"My wife's maid."

"*Aber, Herr Budd,* we have no instructions concerning a third person."

"One does not make appointments for servants, surely!"

"*Aber, mein Herr,* it must be specified. It is strictly forbidden—

*strengstens verboten—*that anyone shall enter unless we have been notified."

"What do you expect me to do?"

"The maid will please to wait here until after your visit."

"*Aber,*" said Lanny, "we are going out by way of Salzburg. Surely it is not to be expected that we shall drive all the way back here for a maid?"

"*Leider, mein Herr.*"

Lanny had learned that with subordinates in the Fatherland you take a high tone; they expect it and also respect it. "That is ridiculous," he said; "it is contrary to good sense."

"*Leider, Herr Budd. Es ist der Befehl.*"

"Well, in that case, the visit is off. *Wir gehen nicht hinein.* What road do we take to Salzburg?"

Horror revealed itself on the countenance of the officer and of the bystanding S.S. men. To have an appointment with the Führer and refuse to keep it on account of anything on earth! *Undenkbar! Echt Amerikanisch!*

Lanny started to back the car and to turn. "*Bitte, Herr Budd, einen Augenblick!*" exclaimed the officer. "I will telephone." A man might be demoted—a man might be decapitated—for permitting such a calamity as this!

"Speak to the Führer's secretary," commanded the haughty one. "Tell him to tell the Führer that Frau Budd has her maid with her, and wishes to go out by way of Salzburg after the visit, and naturally does not wish to drive eight miles back and then make a detour to get to the border."

"*Zu Befehl, Herr Budd!*"

The officer hastened into the guard-house, and Lanny waited. He hoped that Trudi hadn't fainted from the shock of that torch in her face. He didn't turn round to see.

The officer came out again. "*Ihnen ist's gestattet,*" he said, with relief in his voice. "It must be understood that the maid shall remain in the car during the visit."

"Of course," was the reply. "Why should she wish to get out?" The barrier was raised and the car sped on.

VI

The road wound along the side of the Obersalzberg; it had been cut out of solid rock and was quite an engineering job. Lanny drove fast but with vigilance, sounding his horn on all the blind turns. The streaming lights of his car moved swiftly over the sides of the mountain, clothed with pine trees and cut with small streams, each of which had been bridged. There was no better engineer in the world than that General Todt whom the Führer had set to constructing his military highways.

Lanny knew the story of this mountain chalet which had been the Führer's retreat for more than ten years. Originally it had been called Haus Wachenfels, or Watch Rock, and had belonged to a Munich merchant. Hitler had rented it immediately after his release from the brief and amiable term of imprisonment he had served after the Beerhall Putsch. Here he had written, or had had Rudolf Hess write for him, the second part of *Mein Kampf*, and later he had purchased the place and changed its name to Der Berghof—*Berg* meaning mountain and *Hof* meaning yard, farm, manor, mansion, court, or hotel, whichever you chose! The Fürstin Donnerstein had reported that a lot of improvements were being made. Adi Schicklgruber, down-and-out painter of picture postcards, had yearned all his youth to be an architect, and now he had Germany for a building site and the budget of the Third Reich for expenses. He was remaking Munich and planning to remake Berlin, and here in these remote mountains he was listening to the music of the *Waldweben* and the *Feuerzauber*, and building a hideout for himself and the wild witch Berchta.

Approaching the house they came upon another barrier and another guard-building with S.S. men. Lanny stopped, they saluted, and he returned the salute and gave his name. They asked: "Who is with you?" and he replied: "My wife and my wife's maid." They peered in with torches and then told him to proceed.

Lanny had always made it a matter of prestige to arrive on time for an appointment; in spite of delays it lacked three minutes of twenty-two o'clock when his car came in sight of the chalet. The drive widened, and there was plenty of space, so he parked discreetly a short distance away. Trudi was resting in the back seat, and he had told her to keep her eyes closed, sleep if she could and in any case pretend to. Strange things must have been going on in the soul of a Social-Democratic outlaw, transported to the very door of the man whom she considered as Satan incarnate. But this was no time to ask her thoughts.

There was a sentry with a high-powered rifle pacing up and down the drive, and in front of the house a machine gun on a tripod, with two S.S. men sitting beside it. The house was of whitewashed stucco, and in the dim twilight, reinforced by the moon, Lanny could see signs of new construction but could not make out the details. When he and Irma neared the building one of the guards switched on a floodlight which shone blindingly in their faces; apparently the inspection was satisfactory, for the light disappeared as suddenly as it had come, and before they had a chance to knock or to ring a bell the door was opened by a man in livery.

The inside of the chalet was modest. The woodwork was stained dark brown, and the furniture was of the modern, tubular metal sort. There was a spacious drawing-room, with wide windows looking over the mountains, significantly toward Austria, only two miles away. There was a grand piano in the room, and a radio cabinet, and in the center a sort of council table with a dozen or so chairs around it. Here the destinies of Germany were debated and decided; Lanny knew that if Adi could have his way, it would some day be true for the destinies of Europe.

The master of the chalet came forward, wearing the smile which made him attractive in his good moods. He had grown rather stouter, Lanny thought; presumably he was getting plenty of those vegetable plates with butter and a poached egg on top. But his cheeks still had their pasty color, and the little dark mustache seemed stuck on, like that of the comedian who had set the fashion. "*Willkommen, Herr Budd!*" he said, greeting the man first, according to the continental custom. Then he welcomed the wife and held her hand a few seconds too long—he was fond of ladies' hands, it was rumored. "I was wondering if you had allowed yourself time enough," he added; when Lanny told him the hour at which they had left Berlin, he exclaimed: "*Ach, Ihr Amerikaner!* I should put you in jail for an outlaw!"

Lanny said: "If you would keep me in a place like this, I wouldn't mind." That pleased the host, and without heeding the other persons in the room he led his guests to the front window and let them see the moonlight on the mountains and valleys. "I am going to build something wonderful here!" he declared. "I mean to have the biggest window in all the world, and in a second story, so that you can see everything. The statesmen will come from all over to admire this view."

"My guess is the statesmen will be coming for something else," remarked Lanny, and this brought a chuckle. Having read the Führer's book, and many of his speeches over a period of years, Lanny knew his mind and could play upon it, just as he could have played upon the piano which stood invitingly open.

VII

Present in the room were a general, two colonels, and a major; Lanny assumed that a military conference must have been held, but it turned out that they were permanent members of the household. Also two professors, though he did not learn what they professed; he was sure it included the doctrines of National Socialism and the glory of a one-time "Bohemian corporal." In addition there was a dour grim fellow only slightly older than Lanny, with bushy black hair and eyebrows, a square stern jaw and silent manner. Having heard him speak at a *Versammlung*, Lanny knew him for Reichsminister Hess, the Führer's deputy in charge of party affairs and one of two or three Nazis who addressed the great man as "*du*."

Had this company assembled out of curiosity concerning a New York "glamour girl"? It seemed most unlikely. Their Führer in introducing them did not refer to Irma's wealth, but said: "Herr Budd is a boyhood friend of our Kurt Meissner, and Kurt tells me that if it had not been for the Budd family, his musical career might not have been possible."

"Kurt is too generous, Exzellenz," replied Lanny. "A man of genius does not give up so easily. Our family was many times repaid by what he taught us, not merely of German music, but of German *Charakterstärke und Seelengrösse.*"

The visitor meant to continue along this line, but was interrupted by the entrance of a woman known to both him and Irma; the Frau Reichsminister Goebbels, wearing a low-cut gown of pale-blue Chinese silk crepe, seeming to accentuate the paleness of her delicate features, also the fact that she had lost weight in the two years since they had met her. Lanny and Irma waited for her to recognize them, and she apparently waited upon the Führer. "Magda tells me you are old acquaintances," he said; and Lanny answered, quickly: "The Frau Reichsminister was kind enough to take an interest in our exhibition of Detaze paintings." He didn't want her to mention that he had asked her help in rescuing a Jewish family from prison, for he knew that if that topic was broached their host might spend the rest of the evening denouncing the accursed race.

Magda greeted them cordially, and then seated herself and listened in silence. The Führer had noted the name of Detaze, and remarked: "I remember the portrait you brought me at the Braune Haus; a notable piece of work."

"Your critics both in Munich and Berlin were kind to the exhibition," replied Lanny. "Marcel Detaze is the sort of painter to whom you have given approval."

"I would be glad to have a specimen of his work here in this house when I have completed the rebuilding. I understand that his work is mostly landscapes, *nicht wahr?*"

"Land and sea, Exzellenz."

"Well, suppose the next time you come you bring me what you consider a representative work, and charge me what you consider a fair price."

"I would be embarrassed to charge you for it, Herr Reichskanzler."

"*Nanu,* what talk is that? If the works are for sale, why not to me? I will give out the fact that I have made the purchase, and it will not merely promote the reputation of a worthy artist, but will be a step toward the reconciliation of Germany and France, which is one of my cherished dreams."

"If you put it that way, I cannot resist."

The word Führer means leader, and means that, among other things, he is privileged to lead a conversation; so Lanny waited. "You still make your home in France, Herr Budd?"

"Most of the time."

"Perhaps you can help me by telling me about the French people: what is it they desire of me, and how can I persuade them of my good intentions toward them?"

"That is not an easy undertaking, Exzellénz. The French are less homogeneous than the Germans—especially as you have made them. You have to think of the French as several different factions, very much at odds with one another."

"And yet, they would all unite against my *Regierung*, would they not?"

"Most of them hope very earnestly that they will not have to. The French desire peace above everything else."

"Then why can I not persuade them to come to reasonable arrangements with me, who also desire peace first of all? You may have read my speech of last May to my Reichstag——"

"I studied it carefully, and so did all my friends in France and England."

"In that I made a special effort to explain myself to both countries, point by point. Yet it would appear that I have not had much success. Can you tell me any reasons?"

"Do you wish me to answer frankly, Herr Reichskanzler?"

"*Vollständig offen!*"

"*Also!* It happens unfortunately that you have written in *Mein Kampf* that the annihilation of France is one of Germany's aims."

"*Ach, der Unsinn!* We are not talking about literature, but about politics."

"The French note that the book is still being sold, and that you have never repudiated it."

"*Aber!*—that book was written while I was in prison, and very bitter in soul. If I had the time, I would rewrite it; but now I am in the midst of events—I am not longer *ein verhungerter Schriftsteller,* but a man of affairs, and I reveal my ideas in action. If I make a just and enduring treaty with the French, is not that what really counts?"

Lanny could have made reply to this statement: "Herr Reichskanzler, I am embarrassed to know your literary work better than yourself. It happens that the statement about the *Vernichtung* of France appears in the second part of *Mein Kampf,* which was written, not in prison, but in this very chalet where we now sit, and after you had had a year to recuperate from your eight months' incarceration—for which, in any case, the Germans and not the French were responsible." But where in the world was the head of a government to whom one could speak like that? Lanny well knew that to Adolf Hitler facts had no meaning except as they served his purpose. You might as well try to put a large and lively eel into your coat pocket as to hold him to any reality which didn't happen to fit in with his purposes and desires.

VIII

Lanny didn't have to make any further comments, and neither did anyone else; for the Führer had got started at his führing. He didn't want to learn anything, he wanted to tell things; and Lanny knew from experience both public and private that once he had got started nothing could stop him, and that an audience of two was as good as one of two thousand in the Bürgerbräukeller of Munich, or twenty thousand in the Sportpalast of Berlin, or a million on the Zeppelin field during the Partyday at Nürnberg—due now in a couple of weeks. Lanny had heard Adi speak for two hours and a half, and he knew there were speeches of five hours on the record.

Here was an audience of eleven: four military men, two professors, and a party chieftain; the wife of the Reichsminister of Popular Enlightenment and Propaganda; a Franco-American *Kunstsachverständiger;* an heiress member of international café society; and last but not least, the Reichskanzler and Führer of the Third German Reich. He was the one who most enjoyed the oratory and was most deeply moved by it; the longer he spoke, the greater became his earnestness and fervor, the harder he struck with his fists, the louder he raised his voice, and the more alarming became his aspect.

He informed this small select company what would be the verdict of posterity: that in concluding a compact with Bolshevik Russia, the statesmen of France had committed one of the major crimes as well as one of the major blunders of history. He said that this alliance with bloody-handed class war could have only one effect and one meaning, as all the world must know; it was directed against Germany, and was an alliance for aggression, since National Socialist Germany had no power to attack France and no idea of doing so. National Socialist Germany desired only to build up its own economy and to solve the dreadful problem of unemployment, as its Führer had pledged himself to his people to do; but here was a barbarian despotism on the Fatherland's eastern border, ruthless and cruel Asiatic hordes actuated by diabolical Jewish-Marxist theories——

So it went. When Adi added the prefix *Juden* to any good thing it immediately became bad, and when he added the prefix to something bad it became a thousand times worse. Look at the spectacle they were now offering in Moscow! Could any man in his senses doubt that the *Juden-Roten* planned to conquer not merely Germany, but the whole civilized world? They gathered their agents from the four quarters of the globe and set them up on a public platform to boast of the crimes they meant to commit. They were using all the border states of Germany as centers of intrigue and secret warfare against the National Socialist Reich; they printed literature advocating sabotage and terrorism, and smuggled it wholesale into Germany; they had hundreds of agents, both native and foreign, working inside the Fatherland to undermine and destroy it. "There can be no safety for any man or woman in our country against the conspiracies and intrigues of these diabolical foes!" shouted the Führer, and Lanny felt shivers running up and down his spine, thinking how at any moment one of the S.S. men might appear in the doorway and announce: "*Mein Führer*, we have discovered a Social-Democratic underground conspirator hiding in the car of your American guests!"

IX

"We are the implacable opponents of this cannibal band," proclaimed the master of all Germany. "And we call upon decent people of all lands to help us hold them down. We and we alone have the means—I do not mean the material weapons, for in that we have been rendered helpless by the wicked Versailles *Diktat*. The *Juden-Bolschewisten* have fleets of tanks enormously outweighing ours, and they have the greatest armada of planes in the world, ready to pounce upon our cities and destroy them without warning. Against all that, we Germans have the pattern of the new society, and we have the courage and the faith in our own destiny. It is one of the falsehoods of history that the Germans were overcome by arms in the last war—our defeat was due solely to the fact that our moral forces failed us, we fell victims to the stab in the back from these Jewish-Bolshevik vipers we had nourished in our midst."

It took Adi a full hour to run through the gamut of his ideas. He exposed the treachery of France and Britain in failing to disarm—in accordance with the legend which he himself had originated, that they had promised at Versailles to do this. He repeated his assertion that National Socialist Germany was the one truly democratic land, and that he was a deputy elected by thirty-eight million votes. He repudiated every war to subjugate alien peoples, declaring that Germany wanted only Germans, and for this reason her defense forces were the world's best guarantee of peace. *"Friede und Freiheit für alle, das ist National Sozialismus!"* proclaimed the world's champion endurance orator.

Lanny Budd, who had learned all this by heart many years ago, permitted his eyes to stray to the faces of the audience. The military men sat rigidly at attention, that being the discipline they had learned. The professors, now turned pupils, displayed that respect in which German pupils are never known to fail. Black-browed Rudolf Hess, most devoted of disciples, sat like a statue of adoration, his lips slightly parted, as if he were drinking in wisdom by mouth as well as by ear. But most interesting to Lanny was the face of Magda Goebbels; her rather sweet features had worn a melancholy expression

two years ago, and now he thought: "Here is the saddest of women!"
He knew that her crooked little husband had all the beautiful young
actresses of the Third Reich at his command, and the uses he was
making of them might well cause his wife to wear an expression of
martyrdom. Lanny wondered, what was she doing here? He knew
that before her marriage she had been a devoted party worker and
contributor to the campaign chest. Had she now taken up some
duties which brought her here for conferences? And was she the
only woman in this haunt of more than dubious men? No information was offered and of course neither Lanny nor his wife would ask.

X

Did the Führer happen to observe his auditor's eyes wandering?
Or had he learned by painful experience that even the most reverent
audience can stand only so much? He turned suddenly toward the
Americans and said: "It is a shame to weary one's guests with political speech-making."

Lanny was about to utter some polite nothing, when, to her husband's surprise, Irma took the cue. "Not at all, Herr Hitler! What
you have said has interested me greatly. I have heard so many
charges made against you and your ideas, and now I have had a
chance to hear your answers. I want you to know that I agree with
every word you have said."

The Führer of the Germans beamed with pleasure. "I am truly
pleased to hear you say that, Frau Budd. A person of your influence
might do a great deal to correct misunderstandings in America."

"No, Herr Hitler, I have no influence that I know of; but you may
be sure that whenever I have a chance I will tell people what you
have told me."

A most gratifying outcome of a propaganda effort! Only one thing
more was needed, and that was for the husband to speak. "And you,
Herr Budd?" inquired the orator.

Lanny got himself together quickly and forced a laugh. "I am a
devoted husband," he declared, "and you must know that I wouldn't
permit myself to disagree in public with anything my wife says." It

was enough to get by with; the great man smiled, and his court circle followed suit.

Having been good pupils, they were now entitled to a reward. The master of the household clapped his hands, one of the military gentlemen pressed a button in the wall, and there came running into the room the most perfectly round human creature that Lanny had ever beheld; body like a hogshead and face like a full moon, or jack-o'-lantern with its grin. "Herr Kannenberg," said Hitler, introducing him with a sweep of the arm. Lanny had heard of him; a *Restaurateur* of Berlin who had become a court favorite and been placed in charge of the Führer's households—the Berghof, the Munich apartment, and the Chancellery in Berlin. He managed the servants, saw to the preparation of the vegetable plates and the non-alcoholic beer, and whenever Putzi Hanfstaengl wasn't on hand he played the clown.

"*Musik!*" commanded the master, and the rolypoly picked up a highly ornamented accordion and seated himself on the piano stool, presenting a truly comical figure, for his flesh was draped over all sides of the frail support and his legs couldn't quite reach the floor. He began to play and sing: "*Tiroler sind lustig, so lustig und froh!*" He hadn't much of a voice, but was jolly, and had made his place in life that way. While he sang, two servingmen brought refreshments, with a special tray for Hitler, who passed as a saint among his followers because of his habits in eating and drinking.

"*Hab' oft die ganze Nacht an ihrer Hütten g'wacht,*" sang the minstrel; and then it was: "*Z' Lauterbach hab' i' mein' Strumpf ver-lor'n.*" He yodeled mournfully about this tragedy of the lost stocking; and Lanny wondered what Trudi Schultz would be making of the sounds. The day had been warm, and the windows of the drawing-room were open to the cool night breezes laden with the scent of pine and fir. She would hardly be asleep in such a crisis, and the revelry wouldn't seem to her to have any saintly quality; rather it would be that of ghouls dancing over the suffering bodies of her comrades. True Socialism had been murdered, and this base counterfeit was dancing on its grave!

XI

The fun grew faster, and the fat clown's face lighted up with glee, as he began one of those chants in which all over the world country folk mock at the smart people of the cities: "*In Berlin, sagt er, muss du fein, sagt er, und gescheit, sagt er, immer sein, sagt er, denn da haben's, sagt er, viel Verstand, sagt er, ich bin dort, sagt er, viel bekannt!*"

While pretending to listen, Lanny thought about the words which had come from his wife's lips. Did she really mean them, or was it simply part of the quarrel with her husband and with the strange woman who disputed the possession of her husband's mind? To Lanny the words had been like a blow in the face, revealing to him what Irma had been thinking during the past night and day and what he might expect when they were again by themselves. The *Pastoral Symphony* had been altogether without charm to soothe the savage breast.

There came a pause in the revelry, and Hitler said: "A friend of Kurt Meissner should be a musician, Herr Budd."

"On a very modest scale, Exzellenz; but Kurt and I have practiced together all the four-hand piano compositions we could find. Would you like me to play for you?"

"*Bitte sehr*," said the Führer; and Lanny seated himself at the very fine piano. He wasn't going to enter into rivalry with any court favorite; he didn't feel gay at that moment, but on the contrary grief-stricken at the spectacle of the world's woe. He had just seen Loki, god of lies, performing his tricks and winning his triumph; and since Lanny couldn't say in words what he thought and felt about it he would let Beethoven speak. Beethoven was Lanny's friend and refuge in all conflicts with the Nazi Loki; and now Lanny struck the opening chords of the sonata which has been ineptly called *Moonlight*, but which is an utterance of the most profound and poignant grief. "Come and listen, O mighty Führer, and learn what the great soul of Germany thinks of you and your glory! Come and weep for the ten million little monsters whom you are rearing up to torment and poison all Europe!"

But no, it wouldn't work! Beethoven was dead, and this usurper would take his music and turn it to his own ends. Adi Schicklgruber would be hearing these mournful notes as a lament for his dead Nazi heroes, a tribute to his "blood-flags" and his whole ritual of Moloch! Woe, woe, unending woe, and blood all over the weeping world!

One movement was enough. "*Ausgezeichnet!*" exclaimed the Führer. "I see that you not merely know how to play, but what to play."

"I will be happy to come and help celebrate your house-warming," replied the guest. He wasn't sure whether this household was conducted according to the protocol of royalty and whether he should wait to be dismissed. He guessed it couldn't do much harm if he offered to take himself away before he had worn out his welcome, so he said: "I am afraid we have had more than our share of your time, Herr Reichskanzler."

"We have enjoyed your visit," responded the host, "and hope that you will both come again." It was a dismissal, and the visitors rose. "I regret that I cannot ask you to spend the night," added Hitler. "We have been so crowded here that our guests have to sleep in tents."

"We have friends waiting for us near Salzburg," replied Lanny. "They will be more than ever glad to welcome us when they learn of this honor we have enjoyed." If you can make such speeches at the proper moment you may be assured of enjoying honors in all the courts of the earth.

They shook hands with the company, and Irma exchanged a few words with the Frau Reichsminister. As the Führer was escorting them to the door Lanny said: "One thing, Exzellenz: I am wondering if the border is open this late."

"The border is open all night," was the reply. "If you have any difficulty, phone here and we will straighten it out."

No words could have been more welcome. They went to their car, stepped in, and drove away quickly. When they were out of hearing, Lanny whispered: "Are you all right?" Trudi answered: "Yes!" "Did anyone look into the car?" She answered: "A man walked up and down the whole time, but he didn't look in."

XII

It was only about fifteen minutes' drive to the border. Before they reached it Lanny stopped and said to Trudi: "I want you to sink down in your seat out of sight and pretend to be asleep. I have authority from Hitler to pass through, and I don't believe they will look into the car at all; so we may get by without mentioning you."

"But suppose they do look and find her?" objected Irma.

"I will say that I didn't suppose they were interested in a servant. Trudi will have her passport and exit permit if they demand it." He handed them to her.

"It sounds risky to me," declared the wife; "but it's your funeral."

"I think I know them," he replied. "Watch my smoke!"

He drove to the border post, stopped quickly, and stepped out of his car before the officials emerged with their flashlights. "*Heil Hitler!*" he said, and gave the snappy salute which it was obligatory for every German to return. "*Heil Hitler!*" "*Heil Hitler!*"

Straightway Lanny started his *Rolle*. "We have just come from a visit to the Berghof, and the Führer assured me that the border would be open."

"*Natürlich, mein Herr. Die ganze Nacht.*"

"He has just instructed me, if there is any delay, to have you call the Berghof and he will personally straighten the matter out."

"*Sehr wohl, Herrschaften! Was wünschen die Herrschaften?*"

"I am an art expert and have just come from Berlin, where I have arranged to dispose of some pictures for the Minister-Präsident General Göring. I have here the bill of sale with the stamp of his office. Here also are the passports and the exit permits of myself and wife."

"*Gewiss, gewiss. Wollen die Herrschaften eintreten?*"

"*Nein, ich warte hier. Bitte beeilen Sie sich, es wird spät.*" Lanny's German was good enough so they wouldn't know he was a foreigner, and his car was one of the sort which confers authority. The officials hastened inside, and in a minute or two emerged with the passport properly stamped. Lanny stepped into his car and started the engine; the barrier was lifted, and the car rolled into Austria.

13

A Brand from Heaven

I

SALZBURG has an "Old Town" which is just the way it was when it was a Prince-Bishopric of the Holy Roman Empire, some eight hundred years ago. It has a cathedral, a castle on a height, and other medieval features; also, nearly two hundred years ago, an infant called Wolfgang Amadeus Mozart was born in one of its old houses. To some wide-awake hotel-owners of recent times had come the bright idea of a Mozart festival, and this had grown into an elaborate music event lasting the whole month of August; eminent conductors and stage directors were engaged, and crowds came from all over Europe and America. If you wished to have a real holiday you put on Alpine costume, which for the men consisted of dark-gray or brown leather pants, held up by highly ornamental suspenders. The pants stopped above the knees, and made you feel queer, but it was fine for the mosquitoes. You stuck some sort of trophy in your hat, a *Gemsbart* or a *Spielhahnfeder*. Perhaps you carried a *Bergstock*, and climbed the mountains and hunted the wary chamois.

In the excitement of getting Trudi Schultz out of Germany Lanny had forgotten this festival. But when they came into the new town they found all the smart shops lighted up and crowds coming out from a concert hall; he said: "We may have trouble getting rooms."

Trudi had been weeping softly in the back seat. Now she spoke: 'I must not go to a hotel with you; there are bound to be Nazi agents here, and if I am recognized the information will go back to Germany and compromise you hopelessly."

No doubt Irma had been weeping into her pillow the previous night, and might do more of it this night; but Trudi Schultz wasn't going to see it, nor was Lanny. In a voice of studied calm, she inquired: "Just where do you plan to go, Miss Schultz?"

"I will go to Paris. I ought to separate from you at once, and not have you or Lanny associated with me in the public mind."

"As to Lanny," replied Irma, coldly, "I have nothing to say. It is my own intention to take the first train to some port where I can sail for America. You may wish to change your plans when you learn that I shall be traveling alone."

"No, Mrs. Budd," replied Trudi, "that will not alter my plans. I will positively not interfere with Lanny's life, and I am terribly sorry if I have been the means of making unhappiness between you and him." She might have gone on, but the more she said, the worse she would have made it.

II

Lanny suggested that their first problem was to find out if there was a room for any of them in Salzburg. He drove to the Hotel Austria, and was informed that they had no vacant rooms and no suggestion as to where such might be found. There were ten thousand visitors in town. Resorting to the telephone, Lanny got the same information at other places. When he came back to the car, Trudi said: "Let me get out here and take care of myself."

"Where will you go?"

"I will get a cab to the railroad station. There might be a train at any hour, and I want to take myself out of your way." She handed him Céleste's papers and got out of the car.

Irma might have said: "You are not in my way," but she didn't. Lanny said: "You may not find it so easy. You will have to get a certificate of identity from the Austrian authorities. And you will need money." He took the wad of bills from his pocket and tried to give it to her.

"I surely won't need so much," she declared; "only enough to get me to Paris and keep me there for a week or two. I will get work and take care of myself after that."

"It may not be so easy as you think," he countered. He divided the wad in halves, and put one half into her hand, giving a sharp push, as much as to say: "Shut up and don't be silly." Trudi obeyed.

"Mrs. Budd," said she, "I cannot go without saying that I am deeply grateful for your help, and with all my heart I regret the trouble I have caused you."

"You can comfort yourself," replied Irma, grimly. "If it had not been you it would have been someone else. The trouble has been gathering for a long time."

"Good-by, Lanny," said the artist. She turned to go, but he followed her down the street. "Just a word, please. When you have a permanent address you must send it to me."

"I ought not to see you again—" she began.

"I'm not going to let you out of my sight until you give me that promise."

"It is a mistake, Lanny; it will break up your marriage."

"That is for me to decide."

"I cannot bear to be the cause——"

"It is something that you cannot help, and it is foolish to try. I refuse to lose track of you."

"Lanny, go back to the car. You will be making your wife furious."

"She has the car and she knows how to drive it. I will follow you now, and to Paris, if necessary, unless you promise to write me."

"I will write," she said; and then burst out: "Oh, Lanny, how dreadful that I should have done this!"

III

Irma had moved into the driver's seat. He wondered if she had been about to leave without him; but all she said was: "Let me drive. We must go to a near-by town, which will not be so crowded."

"All right," he answered. Perhaps it was an overture; and when they were started on the road to Hallein, he began: "There is a lot that I want to say to you, Irma."

"You may say anything you wish; I don't want to be rude and I don't want to quarrel—but you must know in advance that your words will be wasted, because my mind is made up."

"You are going to break with me?"

"I am going to my home, where I belong. I have tried to persuade myself that I could live in Europe, but I know that I hate it."

"You don't want me to come with you?"

"Not while you think and feel as you do."

"Just what do you mean, dear?"

"You know, and it's a waste of breath talking about it."

"Tell me, in plain words, just what are your terms."

"All right, if you insist. You can be my husband and you can have my love if you are willing to say one sentence: that never again while you live will you have anything to do with Communism or Communists, or with Socialism or Socialists, or anything resembling them, regardless of what name they give themselves."

He closed his eyes as if from a blow. "You know I can't say that, Irma. There are Hansi and Bess, and Uncle Jesse, and Rick and Raoul——"

"I know them all; and so I know that our happiness is at an end. Believe me, I have taken a lot of time to think it over—about two years and a half, ever since the Nazis came into power and we went into Germany to meet Hansi and Bess. My common sense told me then, as it's told me every day since: Lanny may be willing to serve as a tail to the Red kite or the Pink one, but such a career is not for me."

A strange thing: he, too, had been hearing a voice of what claimed to be common sense. The suppressed half of his personality leaped suddenly into life, and he was startled by the realization that it would be pleasant not to have to lie; it would be a relief to be able to say what he really thought and do what he really pleased. Be a man and not a mouse!

There was a long silence; at last Irma said: "Let us talk about practical questions. In the morning I shall return to Salzburg and consult a travel bureau and find the quickest way to get to a steamer. If you will give me Céleste's papers I will take them to her, or air-mail them and instruct her where to meet me. Shall I ship your bags to Bienvenu, or in care of Beauty in London?"

"I will think it over and let you know," he replied, in a low voice.

"I hope we do not have to quarrel, Lanny. I have had times of bitterness, when I hated what you believed and was tempted to hate you for believing it. But I am prepared to respect your right to your own opinions, and I hope you will do the same."

"Certainly," he replied. "I still love you, you know."

"I have thought about it a great deal. I do not believe there can be love where there is a fundamental disagreement in ideas; certainly, at any rate, there cannot be any happiness in such love. I do not believe in being unhappy, and I know you don't, either."

"No," he assented. One half of him grieved to say it, while the other half was glad.

"There are matters to be settled about Frances. If we can keep bitterness out of our hearts, we won't have to pull her this way and that, or teach her to distrust either of her parents."

"Oh, surely we mustn't do that, Irma!"

"Before we left the Adlon, I was tempted to make it my condition for helping that woman, that I was to have the right to keep Frances at Shore Acres. But I decided to rely upon your good sense in the matter. You will always be free to come there and to be with her. If you will try not to force your ideas upon her, I will not have to teach her to fear those ideas."

He saw how she had been spending the hours of that long drive through Germany; he hated to admit, even to himself, that he had been spending some of his hours in the same way. He had thought: "If it were a boy, I would put up a fight for his mind; but a daughter —no, she will have to be Irma's daughter!" The twenty-three-million-dollar baby would be ruled by her twenty-three million dollars! Lanny had tried to have some effect upon the upbringing of Marceline, and had learned how fixed the ladies are in their ways, how complete is their solidarity and how powerful their discipline.

"There's one serious problem," he said. "Beauty is going to feel herself robbed."

"Beauty has always been kind to me, and all this is not her fault. I will do everything in my power to keep from making her unhappy. She can come to Shore Acres whenever she pleases; I will give her a house on my estate, just as she gave me one on hers. And that goes for you, too—anything, so long as we don't quarrel, or intrigue against each other for the child's affections. You have seen cases like that, and it is the worst thing that can happen to a young mind; it can wreck her entire life."

"We must permit nothing of that sort," he replied. "As a matter of fact, Beauty is going to blame me for this mess."

"She will tell you that," said Irma; "but of course it won't be true." The utility king's daughter had acquired considerable understanding of psychology during six years' association with a munition salesman's ex-mistress!

IV

Hallein is an old and poor town, but they managed to get two connecting rooms in a hotel, and Irma retired to her room with a polite "Good night." As a matter of courtesy she refrained from locking her door, and Lanny, equally courteous, refrained from going near it. Perhaps if he had stolen in and sat on the edge of her bed and wooed her, he might have won her back and persuaded her to give him another trial. He was tempted sorely; he loved her, and his heart ached with anticipatory loneliness. Was she tempted, too? His door was not locked, and she might have stolen in and said: "Oh, Lanny, I love you! Believe what you please, do what you please, I still love you!" They might have gone on, living a sort of cat-and-dog life, like many other couples they knew.

But no, she had laid down her terms and she would stick by them. Lanny thought: "Can I make promises like that? Can I make promises in any way resembling them?" His answer was "No." At least, that was the answer part of the time; but then he would think of that lovely body, lying there waiting for him, perhaps aching for him; then there would be in his soul a duel like that between fiend and conscience which had gone on in the soul of Launcelot Gobbo. " 'Budge,' says the fiend. 'Budge not,' says my conscience." In this particular case the casuists might have had a hard time deciding which was fiend and which was conscience; it would depend upon the rank you assigned to a man's marital vows and the affection he owed to the mother of his child, as against whatever he might owe to the exploited proletariat, whose ill-requited toil had provided his leisure, his culture—all those things which set him apart from the aforesaid proletariat.

They met politely in the morning. A quick glance at her face showed him that she had been weeping; also that she had done her best with powder and rouge to hide the fact. Was she hurt because he had not come to her? Had her pride been wounded by his pride? He would never know; he had been pushed out of her heart and would not be taken back. When a surgeon cuts living flesh he does not do it by slow degrees; he makes his knife sharp and cuts quickly; and at once the severed stump begins to heal over, forming its own skin and excluding the excised tissues. Lanny recalled some words from *King Lear:* "He that parts us shall bring a brand from heaven, and fire us hence like foxes." Here was the brand, and its heat was fierce, and the pain of it.

Irma didn't want any breakfast, she said; just a cup of coffee; she wanted to drive to Salzburg at once, so as to get a morning train. All right, he would take her, omitting no final courtesy. At the travel bureau she learned that, as she had guessed, the quickest route was by Berlin and Bremen. She would take a German steamer—why not? She had always liked the Germans, always got along with them; and there was no reason in the world why she should not proceed through Germany. Was she not a friend of the Führer, having made her personal declaration of support only the previous evening?

It gave Lanny a fresh realization of what the brand from heaven was doing to them. She was going her own way; she had her own life to live, just as he had. She would choose her own friends, think her own thoughts, and speak them—doubtless with the same sense of relief which he felt, but which as yet he hardly dared acknowledge to himself. Was it that way with her? Apparently not. He was surprised by her decisiveness of words and manner. She had a job to put through and she was doing it. Could it be that she was a harder person than he; more selfish, or at any rate less sentimental? How could it be otherwise, if she was going to be a Nazi or to tolerate the Nazis?

He had a sudden vision of what it would mean to give up his little daughter. Poor kid! She would be brought up in that world; and when she was forty would she look like Magda Goebbels? Thinking such thoughts, Lanny discovered that he might have a hard time not coming to hate the mother of his child. It was a hateful world in which she lived, and she would become one of the pillars of it, one of the makers of it. She hadn't been interested in politics so far; but Lanny had made that change in her. She would understand what politics meant from now on—the defense of her fortune and her privileges. She would know who was threatening to take them away and what measures to use against those enemies.

Quite a train of thought to have been started by watching a woman pay for train and steamer accommodations and order her reservations telegraphed ahead! Then waiting while she wrote a telegram to her maid and a cablegram to her mother—and not telling him what she was saying in either!

V

There was just time to catch the train. He drove her to the station, and they stood together on the platform, waiting for the noisy monster which was to separate their lives. Lanny had got himself together; they had too many memories of happiness, and must not spoil them entirely. "If we must part forever, give me but one kind word to think upon"—so an English poet had written. Irma said: "Don't be too unhappy, Lanny; and don't throw yourself away. We mustn't either of us have the other on our conscience."

"No, indeed," he replied. "You have been very good to me, per·
haps too good, and I shall always be grateful."

"I feel the same way, Lanny. You have taught me a lot—even
hough you may not believe it."

What did she mean by "throwing himself away"? Was she refer-
:ing to Trudi Schultz? She had seen Lanny walk away with the
woman. Had he told her to wait for him here in Salzburg or elsewhere? Nothing was more likely. Irma wouldn't take much stock
in the idea that Trudi would go on pining for Ludi. No, Lanny
Budd was a "catch," and any woman who could get him would
take him. But it wasn't Irma's affair, and she had no right to refer
to it. One couldn't suppose that either of them would live the rest
of their lives alone. When she left him, she gave him the right to go
and find some other woman.

"One thing more, Irma," he said; "a matter of real importance
to me."

"Yes, Lanny?"

"You know that I have been playing a double game in Germany.
I could not do what I wish to do if the Nazis knew my real feelings."

"I understand that."

"I would like to have an agreement that we will not talk about
the reason for our parting. It is really nobody's business."

"That is fair."

"Your family and your friends will not be too deeply grieved
because you have left me. It will suffice if you say that our tastes
do not agree, and that we prefer different company and different.
parts of the world to live in."

"You are right."

"You understand," he persisted, "I might some day get into seri-·
ous trouble if the story got about that you had left me because I[
was working against the Nazis."

"I have no desire to get you into any trouble," she assured him..
"You may count upon me not to discuss your affairs or your beliefs;
with anyone."

The train came in. Lanny put his wife in her compartment and[
set her solitary bag beside her. "Good-by, dear, and God bless;

you!" There were tears in the eyes of both; it was a tragic moment. But the world was full of many kinds of tragedy. What people think about it and what they want to do about it makes them into different sorts of persons, and they cannot live in the same house or even in the same land. The parting between Irma Barnes and Lanny Budd was like the parting between Germany and Czechoslovakia, for example, or that between the Soviet Union and Finland, or that between the New Dealers and the old-line Republicans in Washington. It was a world-wide phenomenon, and if Lanny and Rick and their friends were right, it wasn't going to end until it had split the whole world down the middle.

He stood on the platform and saw the train depart, with such a sense of desolation as he had never before known in his life. A part of his body, his mind, and his soul had been torn from him; and all of him was one ache. Was he ever going to see her again? And what was going to take her place in his life? His very automobile seemed different, like an empty house. The seat where she had sat would be haunted; when he sat at table to eat a meal, the seat beside him would be haunted; when he lay in bed it would be the same.

He wished he had insisted that Trudi Schultz should wait for him. It would have been fun to motor her to Paris, a polite brother-and-sister jaunt. He thought of looking up the trains, and perhaps meeting her at the station. But no, he realized that they must not be seen together; if he was to go on helping her work, it would have to be in secret. Easy enough to arrange that in Paris, but not on the road, for one who had as many friends as Lanny Budd. Gossips would get busy quickly—he must prepare his mind for that, among other unpleasantness. Beauty would hear about it soon—and, oh, God, what tears, what agonies of soul! Lanny decided hurriedly that wherever he went for a while, it would be some place where his mother wasn't!

VI

He was free; free as the wind; he could go in any direction—even back into Germany, if he so desired. He had several thousand marks in cash in his pockets, and a fine car; not many men would have wasted away with grief under the circumstances. True, he no longer had the Barnes millions at command, but he had his profession and his valuable card-file—presumably not all the rich would drop him because his wife had done so. Also, he owned a third interest in about a hundred Detaze paintings, and could sell one whenever he needed the price of a meal!

He thought it would be pleasant to meet Zoltan Kertezsi and talk about pictures. Zoltan had been in Paris, but he was a flea, and you might meet him walking down the street in Salzburg; if Lanny sent him a wire he would step into a plane and come. It would have been pleasant punting on the River Thames and talking to Rick, he being one of the few to whom Lanny could tell his troubles. Just to think of him was to be braced in soul; to hear his voice saying: "It's a damn good thing! It'll make a man out of you!" But Rick was some distance away, and if Lanny went to him, how could he keep from running into Beauty?

Then he thought of Hansi and Bess. They, too, were persons to whom he had a right to pour out his heart. He hadn't seen them for more than a year, and what a lot they would have to tell him—South America, Hawaii, Japan, and now this Comintern Congress! How long was the thing likely to last? He decided that his half-sister and her husband were the persons he wanted with him at this unhappy moment; they would be glad, perhaps even gladder than Rick. They had come to dislike Irma—he knew it, in spite of the fact that they tried to hide it. They would welcome him with open arms and let him drive them wherever he wished. They would go back to Bienvenu and play violin and piano duets for a year and a day!

Hansi's comings and goings were usually determined by concert dates. But now the couple had bolted across Siberia in a hurry, on account of the Congress, so it might be a time when they were footloose and could have a real holiday. They would labor to make a Communist out of him, of course; but he wouldn't mind—he might even let them succeed for a while. It would be a good way to make sure he had got loose from Irma Barnes!

He had no address for them, but he knew that distinguished artists were demigods in the Soviet Union—that was one of the fine things you could say about the place. He sent a telegram, addressed to "Hansi Robin, American violinist, care of Intourist, Moscow," and reading: "Attending festival Irma returned to New York incompatibility what are your plans suggest returning via Vienna waiting here have car reply Salzburg care American Express Lanny." He guessed that the word "incompatibility" would tell them a bookful, and he wouldn't have to add "lonesome" or anything like that. "Have car" would help. Bessie Budd, who had also been brought up in a motor-car, would say: "Oh, the poor fellow! We ought to go right away, Hansi." Lanny, knowing them so well, could hear the violinist answer: "In Salzburg, with so much music day and night, anybody can be happy. Let us see the Congress out."

And sure enough, when the reply came it said:

"Concert engagement prevents immediate leaving will arrive approximately one week cheerio conclusion inevitable new horizons beckon you magnificent celebrations here constructive decisions following your party line never say die oceans love Hansibess."

All that was clear, too, and Lanny was pleased to see that his sister's revolutionary zeal had not entirely stifled her Yankee sense of humor. For many years Lanny had been lamenting the factional disputes of the left-wingers, which exposed them all to the menace of advancing Fascism; so now, when the Comintern had formally declared for the united front with all anti-Fascist elements, it was a masterpiece of family tact to say that the representatives of fifty nations in convention assembled were following the party line of Lanny Budd! And when the mountain so politely came to Mahomet, surely he couldn't reject its advances!

VII

Lanny didn't bother about hunting a room, because he wouldn't mind driving twice a day through lovely mountain scenery. He strolled from the Residenzplatz to the Platzl, and from there to the Café Bazar, watching the picturesque crowds; the ladies from Hyde Park and Park Avenue wearing *Dirndl* costumes, the garb of Tirolese peasant girls, consisting of elaborately embroidered aprons over flowered skirts coming up to a low-cut bodice with broad bands at the shoulders. The men who accompanied them, sometimes bald or gray-whiskered, each hoped to be mistaken for a *Bua*, a peasant lad, and failed to realize how their bare white knees gave them away. "*Salontiroler*," they were called by the natives.

Lanny Budd, who had met the members of smart society in a dozen capitals, greeted several persons and might at once have been "in the swim," but it suited his mood to go alone and brood. He stood by the parapet of a bridge and watched the noisy River Salzach cutting the town in half. He inspected the Magic Flute House. He wandered into the Getreidegasse and climbed three flights of stairs to the little four-room apartment where the Mozart family had lived. He inspected the porcelain stove at which the tiny mite of genius had warmed his fingers; and then in the Mozart museum he looked at the clavichord on which the child had learned his delicate and gracious art.

Realizing that he was hungry, a footloose and fancy-free bachelor strolled to the Traube and ordered a *Wienerschnitzel* and a *Gösser-Bier*. Meanwhile he studied the program of the *Festspiele*. Tickets were scarce, but if you were willing to pay an extra sum you could find what you wanted, and Lanny proceeded to schedule for himself a week of exalted delights—broken only by occasional pangs when he thought of Irma traveling alone and weeping into strange pillows. However, she had little Frances waiting for her; also Mother Fanny Barnes and Uncle Horace Vandringham, to both of whom Lanny was prepared to give her a quitclaim deed.

With the background of a great fortress on a high rock was a lovely spot known as the Mirabell gardens. A casino had been installed there and you might play all the gambling-games and think you were at Monte Carlo. Also there was a modest bandstand, and in the afternoon you might listen to music. As Lanny strolled through, a gypsy orchestra was playing Liszt's *Waldesrauschen*, which is worth anybody's time to hear, so he seated himself on one of the shaded benches of which many rows had been provided. He sat with closed eyes, accepting a great soul's invitation to forget the pomps and vanities of this wicked world.

He was only partly aware of the fact that somebody came and sat on the bench beside him. But presently he began to experience a peculiar feeling; the bench was shaking slightly, as if the other person was breathing hard, or perhaps was afflicted with palsy. People have different ways of responding to the incitements of music, and after this piece was concluded Lanny stole a glance out of the corner of his eye at the middle-aged, rather stoutish gentleman at his side, and realized that he was sobbing softly to himself; carefully repressing every sound, but there were tears streaming down his cheeks and he was making no effort to check or remove them.

This wasn't a place of Anglo-Saxon formality, but of Austrian *Gemütlichkeit;* so Lanny remarked, politely: *"Schöne Musik!"*

"Ach, Gott!" exclaimed the stranger. *"Ein Meister der nicht genug gewürdigt ist!"* It happened that Lanny reciprocated this sentiment, so while waiting for the next number they discussed the Abbé Franz Liszt, the sorrows which had dogged him and the dreams which had inspired him. Apparently it was a Liszt program, for the orchestra played a *Liebestraum,* which proved to be another provocation to tears. Lanny wondered if the gentleman manifested all his musical feelings in this embarrassing way. From his accent, and also from the fact that there was nothing Austrian about his costume, Lanny guessed that he was an Austrian. From the fact that his light summer suit was so clean, he guessed that he was a man of means.

After they had heard and discussed the rest of the program, they were friends according to festival custom, and Lanny invited him to some refreshment. They strolled to the nearest *Restauration,* and after they had exchanged names, Herr Gensmann broke down, wept into his stein of cold *Münchener,* and told Lanny that he had the most dreadful of sorrows that could overwhelm a man at a *Musikfest*—he had brought his wife for a delightful holiday, and she had moved herself into the quarters of an actor who was playing a minor role in Hofmannsthal's *Jedermann!* Just leaving him a note, saying that she was no longer happy with him and hoping he would find his *Glück* elsewhere.

"And what can I do?" lamented the suffering stranger. "We are no longer in the Middle Ages, and I cannot go and drag her back by the hair of her head—and anyhow, she is a large woman. Alas, she has money of her own, and unless this actor fellow should lose it all at the gaming-table I can have no hope that she will ever return to me. Oh, such a lovely woman, Herr Budd—a cascade of golden hair, limbs like alabaster, eyes as blue as sapphires"—Herr Gensmann was speaking as an expert, being in the jewelry business in Vienna. He went into details concerning the charms of his lost *Schatz* which left nothing to another married man's imagination.

VIII

It might have been a relief to Lanny Budd to have said: "A strange coincidence, *lieber Freund; auch ich hab' meine Frau verloren!*" But Anglo-Saxon reticence made it impossible—and besides, it would have set the gossips to work. Herr Gensmann might know any or all of those Viennese *Hochgeborenen* whose art treasures Lanny Budd had purchased. No; lock your own heart tight, and let the foreigner provide the flow of sentimentality! Lanny was graciously sympathetic, and the result was important to him, for his new friend asked where he was staying; learning that he had no room, but was intending to motor back and forth, the economical Austrian soul was shocked, and he said:

"My friend, let me offer you hospitality. My wife and I had each a room, and now—*ach leider!*—one is empty! Why should you not occupy it?"

"But," objected Lanny, "suppose your wife should return?"

"I have no hope; she is a woman of dominating passions. But if she should come, you will be no worse off than at present. Let me explain that we are paying guests in the home of a very fine Salzburg family, Herr Pergler, an official of the city administration. I have engaged room and board for two through the duration of the festival."

"But would these people be willing to accept an entire stranger?"

"You perhaps do not understand the customs of this event, Herr Budd; everybody makes room for as many *Pensionär* as possible.

You must know that since the dreadful war everybody in our muti-
lated country is poor, and in Salzburg many families live the other
eleven months of the year out of what they receive for taking care
of guests during the month of August. You will meet an interesting
family, and unless you have been a paying guest in the past you may
find it an amusing experience."

"That is kind of you indeed, Herr Gensmann, and if you will
permit me to pay my half of the expenses for the time I am with
you, I shall be pleased to accept."

IX

Certainly Lanny did find the Pergler family interesting. They
lived in one of those large apartment buildings which are prominent
in the city, having a chimney-pot for every other tier of windows;
the streets are narrow, and at night the district buzzed like a bee-
hive. Lanny assumed that the members of the family must be sleeping on the kitchen floor; for the jeweler had the living-room and
Lanny the room just behind it, separated by a curtain which it was
necessary to push aside on account of the heat. All shared the bathroom, and crowded about the small table in the dining-room. Lanny
had never before lived in such close proximity to other human beings; but it was made easy by the charming good humor and naïveté
of this family.

They were all young, or acted that way. Mutter Pergler was
sprightly and gay, with a mass of black hair, sparkling eyes, and
well-rouged cheeks. Vater Pergler was small and lively, wearing
pincenez and a sharp little dark mustache. There were two daughters, Julie and Auguste, one sixteen and the other fourteen; they
had been named for the months they were born in, but "Gusti" had
come first. Also there was little Hansel, the kid brother, who like
all such brothers would have told the family secrets, only this family left nothing to tell. They were tremendously thrilled to have an
American movie star—for so Lanny seemed to them—walk into their
house; they had all been to the movies and were fully informed
about that miraculous land where poor workinggirls live in rooms

the size of ballrooms and always have their hair perfectly waved. Lanny owned a car, which made him many times over a millionaire, and when he took the family for a ride he conferred delight beyond imagining.

Not only were they getting twenty-five Austrian schillings a day from him, but they were going to get English lessons as well. They made a family compact—nobody was allowed to speak a word of German, and it produced amazing phenomena, because they all wanted to talk, sometimes more than one at a time, and they pronounced English the way it looked to Germans and ordered the words as in German. They didn't mind if Lanny laughed—the nicest thing about them was that they laughed at themselves as well as at each other and all the rest of the world. They were the oddest combination of sophistication and simplicity; they were certain that they were the world's most artistic people, but also its most unfortunate. Pretenses were impossible; only art, beauty, and laughter were left to an Austrian.

The third supper that Lanny enjoyed in this home—plain country food, with delicacies embarrassingly served for the guests while all the others pretended they didn't care for them—Lanny saw tears running down the cheeks of the slender pale lily named Gusti. He thought it was the *Schlagobers* he was putting on his fruit, and he offered her some, whereupon she burst into tears and fled from the room. "*Na, na,*" said Mutter Pergler, "don't give her attentions, *bitte*, it is just that she has in love with you fallen."

"Oh, no!" exclaimed the shocked *Pensionär*.

"Do not yourself trouble," said the mother, comfortingly. "It is just the age that she comes to."

"She believes that they are a prince," added Julie, addressing Lanny in the plural as she would have done in German.

"She is getting a camera—what is it?" put in the kid brother. "To picture, to have for *Andacht verrichten*——"

"To say her prayers to," explained the mother, forgetting that Lanny knew German better than he knew the Pergler English. "It will all be well when you are going, Herr Budd. She will love-

memories cherish when there is music. *Aber, bitte,* do not allow
that she shall run away with you."

"Oh, surely not, Frau Pergler!"

"Of course, unless you please would like to marry her," suggested
Julie, politely.

"How could he marry her," argued the *Mutter,* "when he already
in America a wife has?"

Said the head of the family, who spoke fairly good English:
"There is a place called Reno that they can go to."

He pronounced it as if it were German: Rain-o. "Is it then so
wet as we have it here?" inquired Julie, not making a pun, but seeking information.

X

With these family scenes as comedy interludes in the Shake-
spearean tradition Lanny went from one to another of the great
events of the festival. He saw *Faust* as a Reinhardt spectacle, also
the morality play called *Everyman*—giving special attention to that
actor who had extended his hospitality to Herr Gensmann's wife!
He heard the Vienna Philharmonic perform Mendelssohn's *Reformation Symphony,* also Bruckner's *Fourth.* He heard *Don Giovanni*
conducted by Bruno Walter, and *Fidelio* conducted by Toscanini.
In a chamber concert hall he listened to a very fine rendition of the
Hammerklavier Sonata, and learned how he might have played the
piano if he had ever really had to work. The great adagio movement
began with Lanny's grief because Irma had left him, and ended, as
always with the major works of Beethoven, as a lament for all the
sorrows which tyranny and greed had inflicted upon the human
race.

Sometimes he took his newly made friends with him. They sat in
the summer courtyard of the Residenz on a lovely warm evening
and listened to a string orchestra playing Mozart's *Serenades.* It was
dark, except for dim lights at the desks of the musicians; the love-
smitten Gusti sat as close to Lanny as it was possible to get and shivered with bliss. There wasn't anything he could do about it, except

to take it as her parents did, a biological phenomenon; girls were that way when they got that way, and all any *Mutter* or *Vater* could do was to urge her to eat her meals, so that she wouldn't fade away entirely. Lanny escorted them all to a café and ordered her to eat one cheese and one salami sandwich, and she obeyed, gazing at him with adoring sheep's eyes in the meantime.

The town was crawling with celebrities, and autograph-hunters flitted here and there. The gossip-collectors cocked their ears; so many people were misbehaving in one way or another that it was really delightful. What chuckles when the tempestuous Toscanini was scheduled to open a concert with the overture to Rossini's *Ladder of Silk,* but the score and parts had been lost; he had taken them home to mark certain nuances, and they had vanished. He played all the other numbers on the program while a frantic search was made —two separate trips to his villa, and finally the missing papers were found in the bottom of his laundry-basket; his chauffeur had carried them into the kitchen, and the maid had found what she thought was a safe resting-place.

Even upon the shrine of the Muses rude politics forced its way. Salzburg stood for the freedom of art, which meant that without intending it, indeed while terrified by it, the town had come in contact with the Nazi steam-roller. First of all, the Jewish question. This was the twelfth season in which Max Reinhardt had produced those spectacles which had won fame throughout the world and brought visitors by the thousands. One of the favorite conductors, Bruno Walter, was a Jew; also, Toscanini had refused to conduct at Bayreuth as a protest against Nazi interference in the affairs of art. Since the music of Mendelssohn was banned from Germany, the maestro revived a long-neglected symphony, the *Reformation,* and gave it here several times with *éclat.* As a result, Hitler had imposed a thousand-mark fee for visas, making it impossible for German artists and tourists to attend the festival. The rest of Europe had responded by making it impossible to find hotel accommodations in the town.

It was war, and the Salzburgers shivered with dread every time they thought about it. Up there in the mountains dwelt the ogre, glaring down upon them. Last summer he had murdered their Chancellor Dollfuss, and what would he do this summer? There had been serious talk of calling off the festival; but, *in Gottes Namen,* how would the Perglers and thousands of other families have had anything to eat during the winter? And without art, what would they have had to live for? Every time the thunder rumbled they shivered in their beds, wondering if the ogre had hauled guns up the new road he had built and was starting to pound their tiny historic city into rubble and ashes.

An hour's drive to the north of here, in the valley of the River Inn, lay the town of Braunau, where this ogre had been born, or perhaps hatched; and Papa Pergler interpreted him according to geophysical principles. There were, he insisted, chemical substances in the heavy fogs which arose from the Innviertel which affected its residents with strange forms of madness. A gently rolling and beautiful country, all the more dangerous to its inhabitants and to the outside world because it lulled suspicions by its peaceful appearance. From it had come an immense German epic known as *Meier Helmbrecht,* which tells about a peasant boy who leaves the home of his fathers and acquires enormous wealth as a brigand knight; he comes back, riding a fine horse and followed by a train of lovely ladies, and astounds the people of his native valley by the splendor of his gifts. "Is that not a direct prophecy of Adi?" asked the Salzburg public servant.

And that was only one of many instances. In that same Innviertel had lived a man who called himself a doctor, and took his patients into a dark chamber, rubbed them with a little electrical stick, and cured them of their diseases. He had prospered so greatly that the government had preferred to collect taxes from him instead of putting him in jail. Also a man who had made gold out of salt water; he had succeeded in interesting the last Kaiser in the enterprise, and had become so rich that he bought the Braunau castle which contained the tomb of Attila. "Get yourself one idea, the crazier the better, and say it a million times," said Herr Pergler, and added that the coat of arms of the Innviertel portrayed the so-called *Stierwascher,* the "Bullwashers." At the fair held in the district a prize had been offered for the best white bull, and one group of growers had no white one, but had taken a fine black one and set out to make it white with soap and water. They had persisted to the very end and had entered the black bull as white. Said Lanny's host: "You may be certain that at least one of those *Stierwascher* was named Schickl-gruber."

XI

Lanny had telegraphed his address to "Hansibess," and in due course received a wire telling him that they were leaving Moscow, and then another stating on what morning they would arrive. He was on hand to meet them, and drove them down into the lovely Salzkammergut, summer playground of Austria. They could talk freely in the car without fear of eavesdroppers; also while sitting on a mossy bed by the side of a tumbling mountain stream. Lanny had had a lunch put up, so they had the whole day undisturbed. They had not met for more than two years, and had no end of things to talk about. To Lanny their arrival was a blessing; they helped to heal the wounds of his spirit, and gave him courage to maintain his own integrity of mind and purpose.

Lanny and Irma had made an agreement that neither would mention Trudi Schultz in connection with their separation. It would inevitably mean a sex-story, for who would believe denials by either of them? They were going to say that they were parting because of "incompatibility"; seven syllables from the Latin which can be made to cover a multitude of sins! Now Lanny thought it enough to say that he had wanted to help the underground movement against Hitler, and Irma had become angry and had decided to go home. Everything her husband believed annoyed her, and it had got so they could no longer talk about the events of the world or tolerate each other's friends.

Said Bess: "You can't imagine what a relief that telegram was, Lanny. It had seemed to us that you were disintegrating; submitting yourself to that woman and being dragged around at her apron-strings. An utterly impossible situation, and we both hope it is over for good."

The granddaughter of the Puritans had matured into a clear-sighted and determined woman. She was twenty-seven, and a decade of continual piano practice had developed a sturdy physique. Her features were regular, though the nose was a trifle long and thin; she greatly resembled her mother, who was shocked by her ideas and the company she kept, but was able to recognize the functioning of the New England conscience. Bess wore her straight brown hair in a bob, and had devised for herself a simple dress for all purposes. It was in one piece, opening at the shoulder and slipping over the head. She had it made of different materials, but always dark brown, with a little gold braid at the shoulders and a belt of the same; no other ornaments. When she came onto the platform, following her husband, she went straight to the piano and seated herself, and her aspect and manner said: "Do not look at me, but listen to the music of great men." When she finished an accompaniment, she sat still, unless Hansi came and brought her forward to make a bow.

All her life was lived on the same plane; she labored to perfect her art, and likewise her mind and character. She would tolerate no frivolity or cynicism, and when she heard such sentiments expressed she would rebuke them by silence. She had just been having a great experience and was flushed with enthusiasm concerning it. She had found the Russians to be kindred spirits; *seriosniye ludi*, that is to say, "serious people," interested in remaking their world in accordance with rational principles. Corrupt and self-indulgent individuals there were, of course, and self-seeking politicians; but the mass of the young people had grown up with the idea of making a free workers' commonwealth. All of them were laboring diligently, studying and thinking. They were pioneers, not so different from those forefathers of Bess who had landed on a stern and rockbound coast and had toiled and suffered for the right to follow their own consciences.

The youth whom Lanny had once called the shepherd boy out of ancient Judea was now a man of thirty; tall and slender, with large dark eyes, wavy black hair, and an expression of great sweetness. But not without sternness, for he was a child of the Prophets, and his forefathers had taught those of Bess. It had been with the old Hebrew

Testament in their hands that the Puritans had found courage to brave the stormy ocean and risk starvation and massacre by savages. So these two were one in their faith as in their art, and they had found confirmation of all they believed in that Comintern assembly of four hundred men and women from fifty nations of the earth. What speeches, what parades and celebrations—and, above all, what music! To the Jewish violinist and the American accompanist it had been worth many years of hard work to come out upon a platform and play the Tchaikovsky concerto for audiences so eager and appreciative.

XII

Lanny listened to their stories and wished he had that sort of mind and could enjoy that firm clear faith. But at any rate he was free to hear them without having any sense of guilt! He could talk to any sort of people he liked, and not feel that he was displeasing his wife! He told about his interview with Hitler; what the Führer had said about the Comintern Congress, and then what Irma had said to the Führer. Lanny had been asking himself over and over: "Did she really mean that, or was it just a burst of rage?" He put the question to Hansi and Bess, and the latter said: "Those Nazis will be swarming to Shore Acres, and she'll be running the most elegant salon for Jew-baiters!"

Lanny mentioned the queer regime under which he was now living. The Perglers had heard of the Hansi Robins and clamored to meet them; so, toward sundown, the *Pensionär* drove his relatives back to Salzburg. He packed his bag and paid his debts, and then treated the family to a grand farewell supper, also to a song recital of a unique sort—the American Negro contralto, Marian Anderson, setting a sophisticated European audience on fire with her singing of spirituals. A perfect evening—except that at the parting the lovelorn Gusti fell into a dead swoon, and Lanny had to take her and her mother home in the car. He carried the girl upstairs to the apartment and she fainted again in his arms. It certainly made a dramatic climax to a festival week.

After midnight the three travelers set out on their journey, and spent the night at a roadside inn. Next morning they rolled southward through the Brenner Pass with its steep pine-tree-covered mountainsides, its roaring streams and small green lake. Here is the main gateway into Italy, by which the Teutonic invaders came; later, over a period of six hundred years, the historians are able to count sixty-six emperors who traversed these twenty-five miles upon one errand or another. To Lanny Budd the most real was an empress by the name of Irma Barnes, whom he had driven down these slopes several times—the last time less than two years ago, after their futile attempt to get Freddi Robin released from the Dachau concentration camp. Lanny didn't mention it to the stern granddaughter of the Puritans, but one half his being was an ache of longing for Irma, and he kept thinking: "*Can* I let her go?"

BOOK FOUR

Truth Forever on the Scaffold

14

When We Two Parted

BIENVENU was vacant except for the servants, who had been well content to own the place for a while and be paid for it. The pale-blue paint was beginning to look dingy on the wood trim of the stucco buildings, and ordinarily Lanny would have set workmen to sprucing things up before the season began. But now Irma was gone, and perhaps they were going to be poor; he ignored the suggestions in his mother's letters and saved her money. He and his guests took possession of the Villa for sleeping and meals; the rest of the time they spent in Lanny's studio, waking the Cap d'Antibes with music, and afterward swimming off the rocks in the Golfe Juan.

Hansi and Bess had been doing a lot of traveling, and were glad of this respite, the pleasantest they could have imagined. Nobody to bother them; no company save the greatest and best. "A good book is the precious life-blood of a master-spirit, embalmed and treasured up on purpose to a life beyond life"—so John Milton had written; and here were books, including Milton's, lining the walls, and in the vacant spaces paintings of Marcel Detaze, and several cabinets with stacks of music for both violin and piano, Lanny's accumulation from boyhood. These master-spirits did not intrude themselves, but awaited your convenience; when you took them from the shelves they poured out treasures more precious than all the wealth of Ormuz and of Ind, or where the gorgeous East with richest hand show'rs on her kings barbaric pearl and gold.

It was unfortunate that Lanny and his relatives couldn't have lived with the poets and composers, and left the evil problems of the time to solve themselves. But Bess was full of the propagandist spirit acquired in Moscow, and was hoping to convert her half-brother once for all and dedicate him to righteousness as a member of the Communist party of France. It all seemed so obvious and simple to her; she had a set of formulas as carefully worked out as any proposition of Euclid—and to her mind as compelling. All that one had to do was to understand and accept them, and further thought on the subject became superfluous.

It was a military view of society. The great mass of the world's workers were in chains, the invisible chains of the competitive wage system; there were only two things to be done: first, make them aware of the chains and, second, guide them in throwing them off. This double job required a discipline known as the dictatorship of the proletariat; then, when both jobs were done, the evil state machine would wither away and the workers would rule themselves in a free society. All this was elementary, and after the demonstration in the Soviet Union there was no longer any possibility of doubting it; the Russians had set the pattern, and workers of other lands had only to follow in their footsteps.

But to Lanny it seemed more complicated. Old Russia had had virtually no middle class, and the governing class had been paralyzed by defeat in war. But other countries had a large middle class, self-conscious and powerful, and when you tried to jam through your proletarian revolution, what you got was Mussolini or Hitler! So then came arguments: Who was to blame for the wrong kind of dictators? How had they come? Lanny thought he ought to know, for he had been there and seen. Grant that Mussolini and Hitler were agents of the capitalist class, subsidized to put down the Communists; that didn't change the fact that they had succeeded, or the fact that success was based upon their posing as members of the lower middle class, saving it from being ground between the millstones of capital and labor.

Lanny argued: "In the English-speaking countries we have at least partial democracy in political affairs, and why not use it to get more and to extend it into the economic sphere? Wouldn't that be wiser than risking everything, and perhaps losing it as you have seen the workers do in Italy and Germany?"

But that meant the parliamentary system; it meant going into bourgeois politics—and so cáme a vehement debate. Look at Ramsay MacDonald, look at boondoggling and the N.R.A. and the other messes of the New Deal! Look at what had happened in Spain in the last four or five years! The people had made a revolution, they had driven out the wretched Alfonso and put in a jurist and man of letters named Azaña, who had believed so completely in moving gradually that he had stood entirely still, and the starving workers and peasants had been so discouraged that two years later the so-called Anti-Marxist Coalition had been able to carry the elections.

"You will see the same thing here in France if you elect a parlor aesthete for your Premier!" exclaimed Bess. "A Socialist lawyer who makes elegant speeches, but wouldn't dream of doing anything to hurt the feelings of your two hundred families!"

"Is that the way you look upon Blum?" asked Lanny, surprised—or pretending to be. "I thought your Comintern Congress had just ordered a *front populaire?*"

"We're willing to do our part," replied the granddaughter of the Puritans. "But that doesn't obligate us to fool ourselves as to the outcome."

Said Lanny: "I doubt very much if anybody can give effective co-operation in a cause that he feels is bound to fail. It will be humanly impossible not to show your real attitude, and you'll be helping to bring about the very failure you expect."

II

So went the controversy; and after a few days and nights of it they had to agree that they disagreed, and would not talk about current problems any more. The same truce that Lanny had had to make with Irma! The fact was, these issues had become so urgent and feelings ran so high that tolerance was too difficult. All over France the various groups isolated themselves, and didn't go where they would meet their political rivals. The task of a *salonnière* such as Emily Chattersworth now exceeded her powers. In the old days she had been able to act as moderator, and when arguments became too hot to turn them off with a witticism; but now the contending intellectuals would almost come to blows, and the more dignified and less noisy would refuse to return unless they were assured that only their sort was to be present.

It was the same also in the École des Travailleurs du Midi; the Socialist and the Communist students had been arguing for years, and while Lanny was overseas they had come to a break. The Communists were accused of trying to sabotage the institution and were expelled in a body. Raoul had written Lanny a long letter about it, which Lanny hadn't known how to answer. Now, as the first effect of the *front populaire* program, the Communists wanted to be taken back and have another chance. But the moderates insisted that the Communists had shown themselves incapable of co-operation; they wouldn't and couldn't be sincere about anything except the promotion of their party, and, no matter what promises they made, they would always be "boring from within."

Raoul Palma of course had to know what Lanny advised. Irma being gone and Beauty not yet come, Lanny could invite him over to Bienvenu to lunch—cautioning him not to bring up the question in the presence of two Red musicians! No, said Raoul, it was his hope that Hansi and Bess would come over and play at an evening affair, which might serve as a kind of ceremony of reconciliation. At least both Reds and Pinks could listen to the same music!

Lanny went for a walk with his friend, enjoying the opportunity to exchange ideas with somebody who didn't consider him an idler and a weakling. What was this about Spain? he asked, knowing that refugees were coming and going and that Raoul was in touch with most of them. A terrible situation, the school director replied; in a so-called republic the workers and peasants were being ground under the heel of the army and the church forces, and thirty thousand were starving and dying in the foul prisons of that unhappy land. Elections were to take place early in the new year, and already the campaign was under way. All the workers' groups throughout France were being asked to contribute funds. If Comrade Lanny could make a donation—and Comrade Lanny of course said that he would.

Conditions were disturbing here in the Midi, also. The Fascist groups were becoming more and more active, and were resorting to gangsterism, as in all the countries bordering on Italy and Germany. They were provided with funds not only from French capitalist sources, but also from abroad. Italian agents were working openly, boasting that they meant to bring all the Mediterranean shores under their system. Some fourteen years ago Lanny had heard Mussolini declare: "*Fascismo* is not for export." He had accepted the statement then, but now he understood that what *Fascismo* said and what *Fascismo* did bore no necessary relationship.

What were the workers going to do in the face of such a situation? Arm themselves? But that gave the enemy a basis for charging that the workers were planning civil war. The reactionaries had nine-tenths of the money, also nine-tenths of the press with which to spread confusion and fear. Said Raoul: "The extreme Left has Russia for a pattern and the Right has Italy and Germany, but where is the pattern for those who believe in the democratic process?"

"We have to make our own pattern," was the reply. "We have to educate the people and organize them into our new united front. We must oust Laval and his gang, and put in Léon Blum."

What was Lanny himself going to do? Merely give advice, which is so cheap all over the world? No, there was something expected of those few among the Socialists who had money. The grandson of Budd's must give until it hurt; he must give not merely the cost of a new coat of paint for the wood trim of the Bienvenu houses, but also what he would have to spend for new clothes in order to please his mother and her fashionable friends. He must get a stenographer, and study his card-file, and write more letters so as to find customers for paintings.

III

There had been two letters awaiting him at Bienvenu. One from Irma, mailed in Bremen, telling him that she was sailing, and wishing him happiness and success. Not a word about her own feelings; she was going to let the wound heal by first intention, as the surgeons say; not reopening or disturbing it. Lanny had lost his wife. He was startled and dismayed every time he realized the fact. And right

away he would begin thinking: Could he get her back? And did he
want to? He would think: "I have affronted her mortally." He
would ask himself: "Am I sorry? Or would I do it again?"

The answer was sometimes "Yes," and sometimes "No," sometimes
both. It was confusing, and he could think of overwhelming arguments on both sides. Could he have refused to help Trudi with
money? Of course not! Could he have left her to wander about the
streets all night and finally jump into one of the canals? No, again!
On the other hand, perhaps the error had been in not telling Irma.
Frankly and honestly, like a man, not playing the sneak and the
cheat. He could hear her saying that, weeping into her pillow on a
German steamer. He argued it with her in his mind: "Suppose I had
told you, what difference would it have made? You'd have refused
to go into Germany; but you'd have felt wronged, you'd have been
angry. Sooner or later you'd have realized that you were being made
to serve as the tail to the Pink kite, and you'd have told me not to
come home. Isn't that so?"

Irma would have to admit that it was; and so what difference did it
make, really? What harm had he done by taking her into Germany?
What harm *could* he have done? The Nazis would certainly not
have arrested her. They might have asked her questions, but she
would quickly have made plain that she had been imposed upon. Far
from doing her harm, Lanny had got her an interview with Hitler—
something that would be a feather in her cap for the rest of her life.
Especially if she really felt as she had stated in the Berghof; if she
was going to let herself serve as the tail to the Nazi kite!

"It's the indignity of the thing that I object to"—so she would
answer in these imaginary debates. He would say: "Tell me this: if
I had left you in Shore Acres and gone into Germany, would you
have told your mother what I had gone for? And would your
mother have told your uncles? And how do you know how far it
might have gone? Can you say it couldn't have got into the gossip
columns? Or that it couldn't have reached some Bund member in
New York? 'The prince consort of a glamour girl is in Germany,
giving money to the underground movement, trying to help undermine the Führer of the Nazis!' How many hours would it have taken

to reach Berlin? How many minutes before the Gestapo got on the job?

"No, no, Irma! You have to admit that if your husband is going to be a secret agent, he has to be secret." "But I don't want that kind of husband," Irma replies; "and so good-by and best wishes." That is going to be her phrase: "I wish you all success." But will she mean it? Will she say it also to Hitler and to his agents in New York? Certainly she cannot mean both; for if the Führer of the Nazis gets what he wants, the grandson of Budd's loses everything that he wants; and vice versa! The utility king's daughter may wish to be polite to both sides in this war, but the time will come when even she will have to choose!

IV

The other letter was from "Kornmahler," and it, too, was brief and formal. "Just a line to tell you that I am in Paris, and to say once more how grateful I am for your kindness. I will let you know when I have some sketches to show you, and when I have a permanent address."

To this note also he gave no little thought. Trudi was going to keep her alias, even though she was safe in France; and what did that mean? She was going to do some sort of work which German agents in Paris were not to find out about. To manage that, she would have to keep away from other refugees; at any rate, from all but one or two whom she might trust. Perhaps she would have Lanny as her contact with Germany. Or perhaps she wanted to be free to go back now and then. She might even want him to take her back. Lanny shivered when he thought about it, but he knew he would have to stick by her. Whatever Trudi demanded of him, his uncomfortable conscience would compel him to do.

She gave him no address. That meant she didn't want him to come until she was ready; until she had some "sketches"—that is, some plan worked out, requiring money or other help. Well, that was what he wanted, wasn't it? Surely he didn't expect to go to Paris and drink coffee with her, or take her to a show, or driving in the Bois! He wasn't expecting to get her some presentable clothes and introduce her to his mother's smart friends! What had bound him to her was precisely the fact that she was different from the other women he knew. She was that stern daughter of the voice of God whom Wordsworth had sung. She and her friends—Lanny thought once more of the line from an old German poem which made him quail: *"Wir sind all des Todes Eigen."* We are all death's own.

There came a cablegram from New York: "Arrived safely after pleasant trip Frances well and happy good luck to you Irma." So she was doing the polite thing, as they had agreed. It was her duty to let him know about the child; but to say that the child was "happy" when her father was absent might be taken as a hint for the father to remain absent. How easy to have said: "Frances is well but misses you"! If she had said that, what would he have done? Bought a steamer ticket? Or sent a cablegram asking: "Would Frances like me to come and see her?"

They were neither of them accustomed to saving cable-tolls, and this message to her husband was perhaps the shortest that Irma Barnes had ever sent. "Pleasant trip," she remarked; it wasn't economy which kept her from saying: "Pleasant but lonely." Lanny thought: "She's really going to end matters!" He thought: "I wonder if she's debating the problem as I am. I wonder what are the thoughts she doesn't write." Not wishing to be outdone in politeness, he answered: "Hansi and Bess here making music best love to daughter affectionate regards sorry." He might have said less and he might have said more. He desired to meet her approximately half-way.

V

The musical couple took their departure by steamer from Marseille. They were going to find a home somewhere on the Connecticut shore, near the rest of the family; also, they were going to have a baby. Mama had written to Bess, pleading for this greatest of all favors; not the first letter of the sort, but the most importunate. They had been married nine years, and surely, if ever—! Mama pointed out that Freddi was gone, and mentioned that Rahel was interested in a young man who was Papa's capable assistant. What a good Jewish mother wanted was for her firstborn to have a son, and the most perfect piano accompaniments could not take the place of this duty which Bess owed to the God who was her forefathers' God as well as Hansi's. Swear now therefore unto me by the Lord, that thou wilt not cut off my seed after me, and that thou wilt not destroy my name out of my father's house!

Lanny, left alone, had too much time for brooding over his loss; so he hunted up his old friend and tutor, Jerry Pendleton, who didn't worry overmuch about the state of the world, but played a fast game of tennis and liked to swim and go fishing. His little French wife was running the Pension Flavin in Cannes, and the boarders could as always be depended upon to eat the fish. Lanny entertained his friend by telling about being a boarder in Salzburg; Jerry in turn told his troubles—his wife's mother had died, and an aunt owned half of the pension and didn't get along very well with her niece. "Hang all women!" was the ex-tutor's comment, and Lanny would have assented, only this might have been taken as a hint concerning Irma.

It was his duty to let his mother and father know about his marital situation. But just how much? Robbie would be grieved, but probably not greatly surprised. Robbie knew that he had an erratic son, and wouldn't expect permanent rationality from him. Lanny was Robbie's wild oat, and the sins of the fathers were being visited upon the children; Robbie had paid a lot, and must be prepared to pay more.

But Beauty was different. Beauty didn't want to pay for her sin; Beauty hated to pay any sort of bill whatever. Beauty wanted what she wanted and couldn't bear to have it snatched away from her. In short, Beauty was going to raise the very devil, and Lanny kept thinking how he could evade payment of that debt. Should he take a trip around the world, as Hansi and Bess had done? Or should he go and see Russia, as they had urged? Perhaps he might suddenly be called to London, the very day that Beauty set out for Bienvenu!

He wrote a note to both parents, telling of his successful business deals in Germany, his meeting with Hansi and Bess, and their visit; he added: "Irma got lonesome for Frances and decided to sail to New York from Germany. I had to come here on account of some of the problems of the school." He guessed that this wouldn't fool either the shrewd man or the shrewd woman of the world. Robbie would phone Irma and, learning that the trouble was serious, would go to Shore Acres and get the story. Beauty would begin having fits; and sure enough, here came a letter by airmail: "Lanny, what does this mean? Is there something wrong between you and Irma? Do for God's sake write me the truth right away, for I am deeply troubled."

The truth, the whole truth, and nothing but the truth, so help you God! Lanny would tell the first and the last, but surely not the middle section. He wrote: "Irma and I disagree, as you know, about our friends and about our purposes. We thought it might be wiser if we stopped arguing for a while. There is nothing for you to worry about, and please don't."

Nothing to worry about! Lanny could imagine his darling mother reading that sentence and bursting into a hysterical laugh. Nothing to worry about in the prospect of losing the brightest star that ever shone in the diadem of a mother-in-law! Nothing to worry about in losing a hold on twenty-three million dollars—to say nothing of a twenty-three-million-dollar child in which Beauty certainly had a share! All that prestige, that glory! All those beautiful dresses that Irma turned over to her after wearing them only two or three times —and that required only some letting out! All that security against panics and debts—look at how Irma had saved Robbie from ruin during the Wall Street crash and how she had helped to set Robbie up in the airplane business! Nothing to worry about!

Beauty and Marceline were guests of Margy at her country place. They were meeting the smartest people, riding horses, dancing, having a lovely time; but all that was nothing in the face of impending calamity. Beauty sat down and wrote a telegram: "Must see you at once will come Bienvenu unless you are coming north please wire your plans."

Lanny replied by airmail: "It is foolish of you to try to interfere between Irma and me. Believe me, dear, there is absolutely nothing you can do. I expect to be in Paris soon on business with Zoltan, and after that I'll run up to see you unless you are soon coming south.

In the meantime I beg you not to excite yourself. Irma and I are not going to quarrel or make any scandal. She especially charged me to tell you that she would welcome you to Shore Acres at any time, and would give you a house there, as you gave her one. We agreed that we are positively not going to discuss our personal affairs with any-one, so you must forgive me if I do not go into details. Suffice it to say that we differ as to the things we like to do and the company we like to keep. Unfortunately neither you nor I nor anyone else can change that fact."

So it went, back and forth. Beauty, of course, took not the least stock in the notion that a husband and wife were parting over questions of philosophy. If that had ever happened it was in some part of the earth which Beauty Budd had never visited. She wrote: "Lanny, for God's sake tell me, is there another man, or is it another woman?" To this her forever incomprehensible son replied: "There is neither man nor woman—unless you count Hitler as a man or the Statue of Liberty as a woman!" What was a tormented mother to make out of a remark like that?

VI

One morning while Hansi had been practicing in one studio and Lanny and Bess in the other, the British home fleet had been steaming past the Cap d'Antibes on its way to the Suez Canal. It was too far out to be seen, but the newspapers told about it, and a British neighbor on the Cap was so excited that he chartered a motor-boat and took his family out to watch the spectacle. Afterward he described it, thrilling with patriotic pride. "The British lion never bluffs!" he announced, proudly; and Lanny, thrilled in turn, believed him and was happier than he had been for a long time. It really did seem unlikely that a huge naval machine would expend all that fuel and human energy for nothing; and so—one of the mad dictators was going to be halted!

Mussolini had begun his glory raid upon Abyssinia, and all through the summer the diplomats had been scurrying from one capital to another, arguing, pleading, threatening, intriguing. The League of

Nations had issued its solemn decrees, its committees of mediation and arbitration had labored, but all in vain. Il Duce was determined to have his pound of dark meat, and to have the fun of slicing it himself. He had gone right on shipping his Blackshirts to Eritrea; children whom he had trained in his Balilla to sing songs in praise of hatred and violence. In a couple of weeks more the rainy season would be over in Northeast Africa, and then *il giorno di gloria* would arrive.

Lanny Budd would have had a hard time answering the question which of the two dictators he liked least; but he had known Mussolini somewhat longer and perhaps that was enough. For a decade and a half this wretched braggart had been murdering or driving into exile the liberty-loving people of his country; all this year he had been poisoning the air of Europe with his mouthings, so that Lanny had come to feel for him a deep and personal loathing. Stop him! Stop him now, before it was too late! If he could get away with this defiance of decency it would turn loose the furies of greed and hate all over Europe; there would be no more civilization, only a pit in which wild beasts fought and tore one another to pieces. All that was needed was for Britain to take a stand; to close the Suez Canal to the usurper, bar him from getting oil, and he was helpless, his blatherings would die in his throat.

That would mean war, Il Duce, declared; he stuck out his jaw and his bemedaled chest—the Blessed Little Pouter Pigeon, Lanny had named him—defying all the world to come and stop him. He boasted of his thousands of planes, whereby he could and would overwhelm the British fleet. Could he do it? Would he dare try? Or was it simply another of his bluffs? Men argued about it wherever they met around the shore of that sea which the dictator called the Fascists' own; they discussed it in every chancellery and war and navy office. The air weapons were new, and who could be sure what they could do? Sooner or later the trial would be made and the answer given— but each nation rather preferred that some other should afford the test.

On the third of October the invasion began. And so there was one question answered; Il Duce meant it. And now, what did Britain mean? What did Geneva mean? The latter gave its reply four days later; the League Council unanimously denounced Italy as the aggressor. Fine! That looked like business! The American observer became so excited that he couldn't stay at home and play music and read books; he wanted to be in Paris, where there would be several editions of the newspapers every day, and parades and speeches, and shouts and perhaps riots in the smoke-filled cafés. He wanted to hear what Uncle Jesse would say about the situation; and Blum and Longuet, and the de Bruynes, and all his other friends. He arranged for his mail to be forwarded, and stepped into his car on a bright autumn morning; in the evening he arrived in Paris and, in accord with his program of economy, put up at a hotel of moderate price: the same where sixteen years ago his mother had hidden Kurt Meissner from the Sûreté Générale and so had got herself involved in an eight-year love affair.

VII

Lanny had seen Paris in a tumult many a time, but he thought he had never seen political passions running so high, never such confusion in people's thinking. To him it was a clear-cut issue between Right and Left, but he found that his Pink and Red friends couldn't see it that way. They hated Fascism, but also they hated war, and here their two enemies were lined up on opposite sides. Few Leftists were able to share Lanny's enthusiasm for the British Home Fleet, and they even questioned the motives of Anthony Eden. Of such hesitations the pro-Italian press took full advantage. "Do you want to die for the Negus?" was their slogan; and the French worker asked himself: Did he? Also, if France let Britain drag her into a war to save the water of Lake Tsana for the British Sudan, what would Hitler be doing in the meantime? They imagined the Führer grinning and rubbing his hands with delight over the prospect of moving into the Rhineland while French armies were busy in the Maritime Alps.

The bulk of the press of Paris and indeed of all France was on the side of Premier Laval and the other pro-Italian politicians. There was one reason, all-important but rarely mentioned: outright purchase.

Here was the tragedy of France, the corruption of those organs upon which the public depended for news and ideas. If you came with enough cash in your hands you could hire the insertion not merely of news stories but of editorial opinion in nearly all the papers of Paris, and now the Italian embassy was said to have sixty million francs for the splitting of the Franco-British alliance in this crisis. Utterly sickening to read the slanders and lies in these papers, descending even to the vilest obscenities. The price of it enabled editors and proprietors to buy jewels and furs for their mistresses to display at the opera and in the cabarets.

Lanny discovered that whatever people believed they believed with fury; so it became necessary for him to take himself off and decide once more about his own role. Which way was he going to serve his cause, as a political propagandist or as a secret agent and source of funds? Certainly if he followed his present impulses and spoke out to everyone he knew, it wouldn't be long before the canine press would be snapping at his heels; also, he would make himself *persona non grata* to most of his wealthy clients. He had been so happy in the thought of being able to say what he pleased, but now a very short trial convinced him that it would prove a costly luxury for an art expert.

Zoltan Kertezsi was in Paris, ready to set a useful example to his younger associate. The genial Hungarian hated violence and tyranny, as every artist and art lover must; but he kept a bridle upon his tongue. When people expressed political opinions he listened politely, and made some mild remark to the effect that it was too bad that such questions could not be settled without passion and clamor. Somebody had to keep the altar-fires of culture alight, and he chose that role and hoped it might not be entirely futile. The passionate ones would look into that gray-mustached face with the candid blue eyes and feel themselves gently rebuked; they wished that they too might dwell upon those heights and breathe that cold pure air.

Lanny, always impressible, was impressed; but when he went off by himself and thought it over, he couldn't see how love of art was going to change the fanaticism of Mussolini and Hitler, or of the Balilla and the Jugend they were training. He went out to Les Forêts, as always when he came to Paris, and in discussing the existing crisis he made the remark that these two dictators were raising up ten million little demons all of whom would have to be killed. His old friend Emily was horrified, and begged him never to let such words pass his lips again. Lanny thought it over and decided that his words were scientifically exact, but that their utterance was hardly compatible with the role of secret agent.

VIII

The long-expected letter from Trudi Schultz was forwarded from Bienvenu. She told her patron that she now had some sketches which were worthy of his consideration, and asked him to drop her a line telling her where she could meet him, as previously. The address she gave was a postoffice box in *"le treizième,"* a working-class quarter of Paris. He wrote at once, naming a street corner in that neighborhood, and an afternoon two days off, to give her time. He drove there, and it was just as in Berlin—except that the mild-looking gendarme who watched her get into the car had no swastika armband and his interest in the episode was purely sexual.

She was wearing the dark-blue dress which Lanny had taken from Irma's wardrobe, and it was somewhat large for her. She was pale and apparently thinner, and he said: "Look here, Trudi, you haven't been keeping your bargain about the milk."

"I've been working very hard," she answered.

"The job of fighting Hitler is a long-range one, I'm afraid. It's no good wearing yourself out and dying before he does. I took a lot of trouble getting you out of Germany, and I ought to have a claim on you."

"Yes, Lanny." She was a serious person, and didn't always get his playful American style. "I have something important to show you. Take me to a place where it will be safe for you to stop and read."

"It's safe anywhere," he replied. "You're out of Hitlerland, you know."

"I thought there might be somebody who knew you."

"Hardly in this part of Paris." They were passing a dingy factory building with dust-covered windows, and he drew up by the curb. "This looks all right," he said, and she put into his hands a tiny pamphlet about four inches tall and three inches wide, containing some twenty pages of very light paper with no cover. He read the front page:

ABRAHAM LINCOLN: *Sein Leben und Seine Ideen*

and then, at the bottom of the page:

Leipzig: Deutscher Nationalsocialistischer Kulturbund

He turned to the first page of the text and began reading, in German:

"Abraham Lincoln was one of the great men of history, and his life and teachings might be of interest and service to the German people if they were truly reported and understood. Known as the Great Emancipator, he gave his life to deliver the Negro people of the North American continent from chattel slavery, and to break the political control of the landlord plutocracy over the southern states; but the party which he founded has been taken over by the finance-capital elements in that land, which use his name and influence to maintain their pseudo-republican rule. Few realize that it was German leaders and sturdy German immigrant soldiers who won the victories of the northern armies in the American Civil War, and that the emancipation of the black slaves of that land is one of the contributions of the Teutonic-Aryan race which have been seized upon and perverted by the banker-Bolshevik dictatorship entrenched in New York and Washington."

"Holy smoke!" said Lanny. "Where did you get this rubbish?"

"Go on," commanded the other.

He obeyed; and in the middle of the second page found himself reading as follows:

"The North American plutocratic empire is of course not the only government which pretends to serve the popular will while actually serving the interests of a wealthy clique. The Republican party of the United States is not the only case of a party which promises emancipation to the plain people whom Abraham Lincoln loved, and then proceeds to embark upon a course of militant imperialism. This is a danger which has confronted the masses throughout history, and against which they have to be continually alert. Militarism has always been the enemy of culture and true prosperity; for wealth which is expended to make killing machinery cannot be used for constructive purposes. If a man should spend all his resources and labor to make a bicycle, he would some day be able to ride on the roads, but would not be able to sail upon the sea. In the same way, if a nation converts all its iron and steel into rifles, guns, shells, tanks, submarines, and fighting-planes, that nation will be lacking in food, clothing, and houses. Moreover, such a nation will be driven automatically to war, because it must use what it has and cannot use what it has not. The day will come when its production is at the peak, and then the nation must act or else admit the futility of all its efforts.

"Thus it appears that a great gun, a submarine, a fighting-plane is a despot as powerful as any southern slave-owner or overseer with his whip. A staff of highly trained men is required to operate such a weapon, and others to replace them when they are killed; others to transport it, and to supply it with munitions and fuel; laborers to supply replacements for damaged parts; men to build the factories, and yet others to grow the food and make the clothing and boots for all these kinds of workers. Thus for every great implement of modern war you condemn thousands of men to unproductive labor all their lives, and you condemn their children and grandchildren to that interest slavery which the National Socialist German Working-men's party pledged itself in its earliest days to abolish.

"Abraham Lincoln was the friend of the common man, and in his debate over the issue of slavery he said:

" 'That is the issue that will continue in this country when these poor tongues of Judge Douglas and myself shall be silent. It is the eternal struggle between these two principles, right and wrong, throughout the world. They are the two principles which have stood face to face from the beginning of time. The one is the common right of humanity, the other the divine right of kings. It is the same principle in whatever shape it develops itself. It is the same spirit that says: "You toil and work and earn bread and I'll eat it." '

"The man who spoke thus founded the Republican party of the United States of America; but today that party is in the hands of great bankers, industrialists, and landlords. So it is that political parties degenerate; so the common people give their devotion to a cause, and discover too late how they have been betrayed. In many countries today are political leaders who have solemnly pledged themselves to the abolishing of monopoly and interest slavery, but those leaders now ride on the backs of the workers, eat their bread, dwell in palaces, dress themselves in fancy uniforms, and ride about in costly motor-cars. Do you not know of such countries and such leaders?"

IX

"I begin to get the idea," said Lanny. "Very clever!"

"Read it all, if you don't mind," replied Trudi. "It is important to me."

She sat in silence while he read a detailed and well-documented indictment of the Nazi program of ending unemployment by the piling up of national debt and spending of national surplus upon rearmament. Germany no longer made public its military budget; but other nations had ways of finding out how it had grown, and automatically they were driven to increase their armaments proportionately. So in the end you had a whole continent, in fact a whole world, engaged in a mad race, whose end must be the most frightful explosion of war in history. Abraham Lincoln had denounced militarism; and what a loss to human culture that his party should have been betrayed and should be serving as an agency of the North American plutocracy! What a tragedy that this great man of the people, this great cause to which the Germans had contributed their labor and their blood, should not be recognized as a German achievement and thus serve the glory of the Teutonic-Aryan race!

At this point Lanny perceived that he was nearing the end of the pamphlet, and that it was finishing in the orthodox Nazi tone, so that anyone glancing at the last page would get no idea of the dangerous thoughts concealed in the middle section.

"Well, what do you think of it?" asked Trudi, anxiously.

"It's built like a bear-trap. Who got it up?"

"I did." He glanced at her and saw a bit more color in her cheeks.

"It seems to me a very neat idea, and it ought to set a lot of Germans to thinking. I agree with every bit of it—except the beginning and the end, of course."

"What I did was to try to remember all the things you had said on the subject of militarism and its consequences."

"Thanks for the compliment. They are none of them original ideas, but they are sound, and you have put them in simple language which a plain man can understand."

"It's my first effort at writing, and I tried hard to produce something that you would find worth while."

Lanny started his car. Safer to talk while driving. "Tell me, what have you done with this pamphlet?"

"I had a few copies printed, so that you and others could see the idea. I can change it if you find anything wrong."

"I haven't a single improvement to suggest."

"Well, then, I can have twenty thousand copies printed with the money I managed to save out of what you gave me in Salzburg."

"Including what you saved by not eating enough?" he inquired. She didn't answer, so he put that question off until later. "Have you any plan to get these distributed in Germany?"

"I have several plans. There are thousands of workers who cross the border into Germany every day, and all sorts of goods are being imported. These will be among them."

"It won't take the Gestapo long to find out where they came from, Trudi."

"They will come from different places, provided we can raise the money."

"I'll do my share," he said. "Tell me, is there such a concern as the Deutscher Nationalsocialistischer Kulturbund?"

"The concern was born and will die with this pamphlet. The next will be of different appearance, and will be printed in Amsterdam or Geneva."

"I see you have cut out a job for yourself. Do you expect to keep from being known as the source?"

"For as long as I can. So far, I have only two contacts here in Paris, and I feel sure that neither will betray me. Unfortunately, I have to expect that the French police will be helping the Germans."

"Surely so long as Laval is Premier of France," he commented.

"Even longer, Lanny. The police do not change when a government changes. The police serve the two hundred families."

X

Lanny was driving toward Versailles, and he commented: "This is the road where the market women marched out on a rainy day and dragged the King and Queen back to Paris. It wasn't so well paved in those days, or so lined with houses, and Marie Antoinette would hardly know it. Did you ever read the story of Count Fersen, the young Swedish nobleman who was her lover and who accompanied her on this march of doom?"

"I only know what was in the school-books," she replied. "They don't mention lovers."

"For my memory this route is lined with *cuirassiers* in brass helmets and plumes, guarding elderly gentlemen in top-hats and frock-coats. They used to travel back and forth to conferences, and we subordinates speculated eagerly as to what was going on underneath the hats. Most of us were disappointed, for it turned out that President Wilson had been studying theology when he should have studied economics."

"The treaty was bad," assented Trudi, "but not half so bad as Hitler represents."

"On the day when it was signed," Lanny continued, "I was under custody in the old Conciergerie in Paris, and I heard the guns and knew what they meant. Afterwards my friends described the scene. Did you ever see the great Salle des Glaces?"

"I have never been here before."

"It's a sight that no tourist misses. May I take you?"

"Oh, Lanny! We must not dare!"

"I assure you, no one will pay the least attention to us. Hundreds of Americans go out there on bright sunny days like this."

"But some of them may know you!"

"If so, what? I am with a respectable-looking young lady, showing her the sights. She might be the daughter of one of my mother's sisters whom she left behind her in New England, close to forty years ago."

"It would start the gossips, Lanny!"

"There is no way to stop them, since my wife has removed to New York."

"She really went?"

"She did, and has sent me a polite cablegram wishing me success in life."

"Oh, Lanny, I am so bitterly sorry to have been the cause of that misfortune!"

"Let me tell you a little story—what happened in the Berghof while you were sitting out in the car and no doubt finding it a long wait."

"The time did seem long, I admit."

"It was somewhat less than two hours; and for a full hour Hitler made us a speech—just such a speech as millions of Germans have been forced to listen to over the radio, under penalty of being sent to a concentration camp. He gave us the whole story that he told first in 1919 and has stuck to ever since: the wicked Versailles *Diktat* and the treachery of the Allies under the inspiration of the Jewish-Bolshevik plutocrats. You know it only too well, I am sure."

"*Ach leider!*"

"Well, Irma listened to it for a solid hour; and when he had finished she stepped forward and told him: 'I want you to know that I agree with every word you have said.'"

"Oh, Lanny, how dreadful!"

"You understand, she didn't *have* to say that. Nobody asked her. It was her own spontaneous act."

"But wasn't it because of her anger with us?"

"No doubt that caused her to speak, but it didn't determine what she said. The reason I gave up and let her go was that later, in Salzburg, she gave me her terms for the future: that I would agree to have nothing more to do with Communists and Communism, or with Socialists and Socialism. Considering that my half-sister and her husband and also my uncle are Communists, and that several of my oldest friends are Socialists, she would hardly have expected me to say yes."

"You're not going back to her, then?"

"I'm going to see my little daughter, and I suppose I'll meet Irma; but I don't expect to reopen the subject, and I doubt if she would let me. We've agreed not to make a scandal. What concerns you especially, she has promised not to talk about you."

"Do you think she will keep the promise?"

"She is getting all that she asked for, and she isn't a vindictive person. She offered me money, provided I wouldn't spend it on Socialism; but of course that's the only thing I would take it for, and she knows that."

"Don't you feel rather desolate?"

"At times; but no more so than you and many people we know. There just isn't any use expecting one's life to be perfect in a time like this."

XI

They wandered through the beautiful park of Versailles, once the playground of the Grand Monarque and his successors, and for a long time one of the world's tourist attractions. In the Petit Trianon they inspected the chapel in which Marie Antoinette had prayed and the harpsichord upon which she had played accompaniments for Fersen's flute. They strolled about the grounds, observing the Belvidere and the Orangerie, the Jeu de Bague and the Temple d'Amour. At the garden front Lanny remarked: "There is a report widely current that if you come here on the tenth of August, and happen to be what is called psychic, you may see Marie Antoinette sitting outside here, wearing a wide flapping hat and a pink dress; also you will see many of the people of her time, moving about the place in costume."

Trudi smiled and replied: "Perhaps there was once a motion-picture company here on that date."

"The tenth of August is the date of the sacking of the Tuileries in Paris, which was, of course, a dreadful experience for poor Toinette. Perhaps she comes here to escape the painful memories."

Farther on was the little lake and stream, and at one of the rustic bridges Lanny stopped. "Here is a spot which played a part in an experience which you may take as a ghost story, not trying to believe it. In my library is a volume called *An Adventure*, written by two respectable English ladies, college-teachers and daughters of clergymen, who came here at the beginning of the century and strolled about these grounds, moved by idle curiosity like you and me. It happened to be the tenth of August, though that date meant nothing to them. They had never been interested in psychic matters and had no idea of what was coming. They had what I suppose one might call a collective hallucination; they saw the people of the *ancien régime* and were spoken to by several of them. Everything seemed strange, but they didn't know what it meant; only afterwards, when they began to compare notes, they realized that one had seen things which the other was certain had not been there. They began looking up old data and discovered that they had seen the grounds as they had been a century and a half earlier, but were not at the time of their visit."

"You take that sort of thing seriously, don't you, Lanny?"

"Much against my inclinations, I have been forced to. It has occurred to me as a possibility that time may not be the fixed and permanent system which it seems to us, but may be a product of our own minds, a form which we impose upon our experiences."

Trudi had no comment, and they strolled on. Presently Lanny remarked: "You asked me if I could manage to get you a séance with our Polish medium."

"Oh, yes," she replied. "Is she still with you?"

"She is visiting Zaharoff at his château near here. It wouldn't do to take you there, but I could bring Madame to some hotel and have her take a room, and then bring you to her. It would be better if I were not present, because I have managed to get her 'spirit control' irritated with me because of my skeptical questions. You see, I please neither side; the Marxists think I am a fool and a dupe and the spirits think I am irreverent."

"I'll try to be open-minded," said this Marxist; "but I can't promise to be convinced."

"I would be foolish indeed to ask such a promise. All that you must agree to is to accept my word that I shall not give Madame the faintest hint about your identity."

"I'll certainly believe that, Lanny."

"Also," he added, "I'm hoping that you'll let me see something of you when I happen to be in Paris. I'm quite sure I'm not being followed, and you can easily make sure about yourself. We can meet at that corner as we did today, and I can drive you to some different part of France where nobody will have the slightest interest in us. You can't work all the time, and if you try to, your work will suffer. At least I can do what I'm hoping to do this evening, find some quiet *auberge* and see that you get one substantial meal. Will your conscience permit that much self-indulgence?"

"Lanny," she said, "I'm not an ascetic; it's just that when I think of what is happening to our comrades, my food chokes me."

"I know, my dear; I've had the feeling many a time. But here we are, in this old tormented Europe, and there's never been an hour since I was born when I couldn't have starved myself for that reason. I suddenly became aware of it at the end of July 1914. That early in my life I had to work out a philosophy that would permit me to eat and sleep and even play music. Cruelty and suffering aren't going to be ended in our lifetime, and it's the part of wisdom to make a rule never to expend more energy in one day than you can restore in one night. So now let us go and find our *auberge*, and I'll tell you how you have to behave with Madame Zyszynski if you hope to get any significant results."

15

Need a Body Cry?

I

BEAUTY BUDD couldn't stand the suspense any longer. She telegraphed that she was coming, and next morning here she was; putting up at her son's hotel, full of strange memories for her, and hardly stopping to take off hat and coat before going to work on him. "Now, Lanny, do for God's sake tell me what has happened!"

He had rehearsed this scene in his mind; knowing her so thoroughly, he had been able to say everything for her as well as for himself. Now, patiently and kindly, he told her that he and Irma had been discovering how they were irritated by each other's opinions and bored by each other's friends; they had finally decided there was no sense standing it.

"Tell me this," she persisted, "just what did you do to Irma in Germany?"

"Nothing different from anywhere else. It's the same old story. I wanted to meet my friends there——"

"Men friends or women?"

He had anticipated this, and prepared a humorous reply. "There have to be both, in order that there may be more."

"Don't be silly. I can't believe that Irma is interested in any other man; I know it must be some woman, somewhere. Tell me, is it that young German artist whose work you were so interested in?"

He was surprised by this; he hadn't imagined that she was keeping a notebook on his doings. But Beauty Budd was like that. Nobody was going to persuade her that any man was interested in any woman's sketches, any more than in any woman's poetry or music or ideas or whatever it might be. Women existed for one

312

purpose so far as men were concerned, and every woman knew it in her heart, no matter how hard she might try to fool herself.

Lanny had to make up his mind in a small fraction of a second. He said, rather severely: "I'm sorry, dear. If you want to take that line, I'm not going to discuss it. I think you might leave it to somebody else to start the scandals on us."

Tears began creeping into her eyes, as he knew they would sooner or later. She would have to have a good cry before this was over, and it was better while they were alone and she didn't have to worry about her makeup.

"I know how bitterly disappointing it must be to you," he continued, more gently. "You just have to make up your mind that this is one of the things you can't help. Irma and I know our own minds, and we've taken the trouble to think it out thoroughly. She is going to live at Shore Acres, and I'm going to live here and there, as in the past. We've agreed that we're not going to have any sort of fuss, and in this I expect to receive the co-operation of my mother. When people ask about it, just say that she seems to like Long Island and I seem to like Europe, and that's that."

"Lanny, there'll be some other man, and you'll lose her."

"I hope that whoever he is, he'll be able to make her happy. I have made up my mind that there is small possibility of happiness in love where people differ in their fundamental beliefs as completely as Irma and I do."

"You're definitely giving her up, then?"

"It was she who gave me up, and I'm accepting her decision because I have to."

"And you don't mean to see her again?"

"I shall probably see her, because she is the mother of my child, and I certainly don't intend to give up the child."

"And what about my grandchild?"

"Irma has been your friend and there is no reason why she should cease to be. Go there whenever you want to, and she will treat you as you treated her when she was your guest. The place is huge, and nobody need be in any other's way. Play bridge with Fanny Barnes, and don't object if she cheats you a little; Irma will make it up with a handsome check now and then, and everything will be jake."

II

Poor soul! She tried to lecture her son on the holy bonds of matrimony, but it was rather late in both their lives; he soon kidded her out of it and forced her to talk about facts. It would be, she argued, a perfectly frightful blow to the family prestige—his, hers, and especially Marceline's. Right now, of all times; such a cruel thing to do to a young girl just ready for the marriage market! Beauty had been planning, with the abettal of Emily and her other smart friends, to give her a grand début at Bienvenu at the beginning of the season in January. But now, of course, it would be a farce. Nothing could save them socially; they would be plunged from the top of the scale to third-rate or lower.

"Listen, old girl," he said, "be sensible and write Irma a nice letter. Tell her how sorry you are and that you want to be friends. Explain how a scandal will hurt Marceline's chances, and suggest that she give her a party at Shore Acres to show that everything is all right. Irma will understand without your dotting the *i*'s and crossing the *t*'s, and I'm sure she'll be glad to do it."

"But, Lanny, I don't want to have Marceline marry in America. I want her to marry here and live at Bienvenu, so that I won't be so lonely."

"Has she definitely broken with Alfy?"

"They quarrel half the time, and spend the other half making up. It seems to me it would be a very silly match, because Alfy has to spend the next four years in college, and he has no income. Marceline will be eighteen this month, and she ought to marry some older man who can give her what she needs now."

"What you have taught her to need," he was tempted to say; but that would have been unkind—and useless, since he couldn't change his half-sister. "Listen, Beauty," he said, "we have to take what we can get in this world and no good crying for the moon. It seems to me your husband is the person to give you advice at this stage in your life. You have talked about spirituality, and what's the matter with your applying a little of it right now?"

"Oh, Lanny," she wept, "what's the good of your telling me such things? You know you don't believe a word of them."

"That shows how little you understand your son," he replied. "Parsifal knows better, I am sure. He has his faith and I have mine and each of us works at it. I don't think that to stop wage-slavery and war, to stop human beings from robbing and killing one another, is exactly a trivial ideal, either in your sight or in that of your Creator. Incidentally, I think my mother has been a very well-preserved lady all her life. You have a lot to be grateful for, and it's the part of wisdom to learn to be happy with it instead of tormenting yourself because you're losing things that you really haven't any use for."

That stern talk frightened her a little, and she tried to dry her eyes. "Lanny, I'm only thinking about my children's happiness!"

"Well, if that is so, understand where my happiness lies. I'm not entirely joyful over losing the wife I love; but I have my faith that I live by, and I don't intend to give it up in order to be kept in a palace and be stared at as a Prince Fortunatus."

"Lanny, you do such dreadful things, and frighten us women half out of our wits."

"I'm sorry about that, dear; but I didn't make the profit system and I didn't make war."

She was staring at him through her tears, which wouldn't stop coming. "Lanny," she burst out, suddenly, "you haven't really been making love to any other woman, have you?"

"Indeed I have not."

"And Irma knows that you haven't?"

"She knows it well."

"Then I'll tell you what I really think. She's a cold-hearted and selfish woman, and what she's doing is shocking and inexcusable!"

He couldn't help laughing. "Well, darling, don't take it as your duty to tell her. It is no part of my plan to turn you into a social uplifter. Just remember that Irma is the mother of your granddaughter, and that, right or wrong, she's the boss. So, whatever happens, keep on friendly terms with her."

"When are you going to see her?"

"I haven't any definite plans."

"You're not going to ask her to come back to you?"

"Not on her terms. How can I?"

"Remember her pride, Lanny, and give her a little the best of it. Women nearly always get the worst, you know."

"I'll tell her I'm sorry, of course. I said it in a cable, but she didn't see fit to take note of it."

"Don't wait too long, dear. Remember what swarms of men will be after her money!"

III

He drove his mother out to Les Forêts, so that she might talk things over with Emily, and find out if Emily had managed to worm any more out of him than his mother had. (She hadn't.)

When Lanny got back to his hotel there was a cablegram from Robbie, saying that he was sailing that night for Cherbourg, and Lanny wondered if that was a conspiracy with his mother, or an overture from his wife, or both, or neither. It was possible, of course, that Robbie was coming on business; he had got his factory going, and his planes were diving and swooping over the field he had built by the banks of the Newcastle River. They were equaling the promised performances, and Robbie was exulting, but also fuming because of the red tape of the bureaucrats and the dumbness of the brass-hats. What did they imagine a fabricating-plant was going to do with its time and labor while they were fussing over commas in contracts and insisting that demonstrations already made should be repeated for some new board? Robbie had been fussing about things like that ever since Lanny had known him. And now it was to be expected that he would be coming to try the French markets, making use of his personal influence and that of his stockholders in France. Especially in view of the new crisis, and the possibility that Mussolini might really have the air superiority of which he was boasting.

Meeting Robbie wouldn't be such a strain as meeting Beauty, for

Robbie was a sensible man and ideas counted with him as they never could with his one-time *amie*. Moreover, Robbie would have had a talk with Irma, and Lanny was curious to hear about that. While waiting, he talked picture business with Zoltan, and they looked at masters old and new and wrote letters to clients. Lanny decided to go shares with Zoltan on the rest of the Göring collection, for Zoltan had many clients of his own and could work at art while Lanny was working at changing the world.

He decided to get the meeting with Zyszynski out of the way, so he phoned the Château de Balincourt and arranged to call for her in the mid-morning two days later. Then he wrote a note to "Kornmahler," telling her that the medium would be at a certain cheap hotel in "*le treizième*" at a certain hour. Lanny would wait in his car across the street from the hotel and would instruct Madame that after the séance she was to go and get her lunch and attend a cinema, thus giving Trudi time to join Lanny and report results.

So Lanny motored into Seine-et-Oise on a rainy and chilly November morning and picked up the old woman—incidentally being told by the butler that the master would be pleased to see him on his return. Poor old Knight Commander, sitting there in his castle waiting for the grim reaper to come and cut him down, and dreaming meanwhile of the woman he had loved and trusted; yearning for any word about her, any faintest perfume of her presence! Come and tell me what happens at the séance, Lanny!

On the way into Paris that dull old woman had her hour of happiness with the adopted son of her fancy. With other people she was content to be silent, but to him she talked about the Hindu servants and what strange men they were and how hard to talk to. She told about her childhood in Poland, where she had lived in a peasant hut and had once raised a calf which her parents had given to her; she had called it Kooba, and everything about it was as real and dear to her as Zaharoff's duquesa to him. If somebody had told her that Tecumseh had brought a message from the spirit Kooba, nothing would have brought the old woman more happiness.

Lanny told her how she was to spend her day, and gave her money to pay for her hotel room, also a pack of cards so that she could play Patience in case the visitor might be late. The visitor's name was Mademoiselle Kornmahler, and Lanny had already instructed her how to behave: to speak no unnecessary word until the medium was in her trance, and after that to treat the Amerindian chieftain with the greatest respect, answer his questions promptly and truthfully, but tell him no more than necessary; to wait until Madame was out of her trance before moving, and then to thank her politely, tell her that all had gone well, and leave without unnecessary conversation.

IV

He deposited his charge and parked across the street a little way down the block. He sat and read some of Richet's *Thirty Years of Psychical Research*, which he was going to lend to Trudi. He never minded waiting, because he always had something to read in his car. After an hour or more, Trudi appeared suddenly and slid into the seat beside him; he dropped the book, started the engine, and said: "Well, how was it?"

"I didn't hear from Ludi," were her first words.

"Too bad!" he replied. "That's the way it goes."

"But I heard many other things. Lanny, it is a most uncanny experience!"

"You bet it is! Tell me everything."

"Well, first he said there was my mother. She was tall, had gray hair, and wore black; that is all true, because my father was killed in the war. But you see, Lanny, I am fairly tall, and so it is reasonable to guess that my mother might have been."

"Did she give her name?"

"Tecumseh said it sounded like Greta. She was called Gretchen."

"A very common name," commented Lanny, who knew how to deal with newcomers to this strange field; "so you might call that a guess, too. Did she give any message?"

"She wanted me to know that she was well and happy. Of course I'd be much pleased to know that my mother is well and happy anywhere—if I knew it was my mother."

"And then what?"

"Then a strange thing: I was told that there was a large, heavy-set man who said his name was Gregor. I said I had once had a teacher by that name; but it wasn't he. He said he had a message for Otto, but I didn't know any Otto."

"What was the message?"

"I was to tell him that Gregor was working with him, and that the despot would be overthrown in time—but a long time."

"That didn't mean anything to you?"

"I thought of Gregor Strasser and his brother, who founded the Black Front against Hitler. You know about them, no doubt."

"I once came very close to Gregor. I was in the room with him when Hitler gave him a fearful dressing down in Hitler's apartment in Berlin. I had such a good chance to study him that I've always felt I knew him. Also I heard him make a speech at a *Versammlung* in Stuttgart. When he was murdered in the blood purge I was in Stadelheim Prison, and afterwards I got a message about it—but that was in a normal way. Since Gregor Strasser occupies a prominent place in my mind, perhaps the message was meant for me."

"Do you know where Otto is?"

"I haven't an idea, though I've heard he is somewhere in Europe, working against the Nazis. For my part I wouldn't be interested, for I wouldn't trust any man who had ever been one of them."

"I agree with you," said Trudi. "But it is extraordinary that this old woman should know about the Strassers."

"She doesn't," declared Lanny. "I'd wager all I own on that. She has no mind for any political affairs. While I was driving her here she told me all about a calf she raised as a child; what the calf ate, the noises it made, and the strange feeling she had when she dipped her fingers in a pail of milk and let the calf suck them. . . . Go on; what else?"

"There was an old man who said he was your grandfather."

"He haunts all my séances. He was very angry now, I suppose."

"He was; he said he wished you to know that you are breaking the laws of man as well as of God. He commands you to return to your wife."

"I don't know any law that obliges me to live with my wife when she won't have me. You see, the old gentleman wanted Irma and me to have babies, and he cross-examined us about it in plain biblical language before he died."

"Do you think it is really your grandfather now, Lanny?"

"I don't know what the devil it is. I know that Zyszynski doesn't know anything about my grandfather, and nothing about my being parted from Irma, because she's been at Balincourt for several months. Anybody else?"

"There was a Lady somebody—Ladybird?"

"That is quite cute," said Lanny. "I'm sorry I never thought of it while she was alive. That is Lady Caillard, called Birdie."

"That is the name."

"She comes frequently. She talks to Zaharoff, and tells him she is in heaven."

"There was a message for Zaharoff, from his wife. She is watching and waiting for him, and he will come soon. That is not such a pleasant message, is it?"

"It will be for him. He would go gladly if he were sure that she was there. He has little reason to love this world, so far as I know his life."

V

That completed the list of the spirit visitors—a strange assortment. Lanny took his friend back over the various episodes and she added details under his questioning. He wished he might have been there, taking notes. "Madame knows that you are associated with me," he said; "so that might account for the messages to me and about me. But it doesn't account for her knowing that Irma and I are separated, or about my special interest in the Strassers."

"On the other hand," countered Trudi, "suppose we call it spirits, did Gregor Strasser know who you were when he got his scolding from Hitler?"

"It is possible that he may have asked someone of the household about the strange young man who had witnessed his humiliation; or again, it might be that spirits know more than they knew when they were people. But what my mind always comes back to is the idea of telepathy. There was nothing in any of these communications which wasn't in either your mind or mine."

She reflected. "It might be hard to say how there could be a communication which mightn't have been known to somebody."

"Quite so. Take the famous case of Glastonbury Abbey, which is in the psychic research books; the communicators were supposed to be long-dead monks, and they told secrets about the architecture of the long-buried ruins. Excavations proved the statements correct. But who can be sure there may not exist some records of those old days, and that some scholar might not have happened to be studying them at the time?"

"Has anybody ever succeeded in working out an answer to that?"

"It can be done with what you might call artificial facts. Suppose, for example, I cut a small slot in a piece of paper, and thrust that paper between the pages of a book at random. It is obvious that when I open the book, certain words or letters will be visible through the slot; but until the book is opened, nobody knows what those words or letters are. Now seal up the book and lock it in a safe, and let people in New York and Australia consult mediums and see if they can find out what will show through the slot."

"Has anything like that ever been done?"

"The records of the British Society for Psychical Research are full of all kinds of experiments along that line; but the trouble is, nobody except members of the society ever reads them. The average scientist just knows it couldn't happen, and therefore it didn't, and that settles it. If you find that it does happen, right away you become a crank like the others, and your testimony has no value."

VI

He turned Trudi loose on the street with the Richet book under her arm, and drove to the hotel and took Madame back to the château. It wasn't often that Zaharoff asked to see anyone, but he had asked for Lanny Budd, and so the art expert went into the library with the big blazing fire and told the retired munitions king of

Europe that another message had come from the duquesa, given to a woman friend whom Lanny did not name. He could have made a hit with the old man by bringing or sending such messages frequently; but he played the game honestly, and wondered if Sir Basil appreciated the fact. Probably he trusted Lanny as much as he trusted anybody in the world. He could never get away from the thought that this agile-minded young American was the son of a business man, and must be expected to be helping his father play the game. Nobody knew this game better than the Knight Commander, and when others tried it on him he watched with a sad heart.

There he sat, warming his aching old bones by a fire of wood from his grand old forests; keeping his false teeth clamped firmly together, so that the visitor might not see or hear the shaking of his jaw; keeping his hands firmly upon his knees so that the visitor might not see their trembling. In those old hands he still held a vast fortune, the extent of it known only to himself. Dominant in his mind was the certainty that these hands were soon going to fall lifeless, and the fortune be left for others to dissipate.

This castle had once belonged to a very old king with a white beard like Zaharoff's; then it had belonged to the king's mistress, whom he had followed on the street and bought through an agent like any other objet d'art. Who would live in it next, and sit before the fire and tell tales about a shrewd Greek ex-fireman and guide to brothels who had acquired the mastery of most of the great munitions plants of Europe and had sold impartially to all nations the means of mutual suicide? Would the Greek know what they were saying about him? Lies, mostly—but the truth had been worse, if they had known it! Would it trouble him what they said? Would he tremble inside, and feel his blood pressure mount, as happened now whenever he came upon the most harmless item about himself in that press of Paris which he had bought so freely in the past? Or would he be sitting in some lovely garden, looking at the duquesa's tulips, knowing the different varieties and observing nature's odd incalculable whims?

Here came this smooth-spoken young man who had known the

duquesa and admired her, spoke of her kindly, and brought rare messages from her; what did that mean? Impossible to believe that he really cared for a slowly dying old man! Was he really interested in psychic research? Or was he merely helping his father to get contracts? He had a rich wife himself; but then, who ever has enough money? Was he perchance wondering if an old friend would remember him in his will? That. is the supreme tragedy of the aged rich. Who ever comes near them that is not thinking that ghoulish thought? Who could tolerate their infirmities, their inde-cencies, except that he or she is taking a gambler's chance at a for-tune—the cheapest and easiest chance? To hell with you, hyenas all, you shan't have a sou of it!

VII

The march into Abyssinia continued, and the diplomatic duel went on in the secret chambers. Lanny had been buoyed up with hope, but not for long after he got to Paris, for all the "insiders" agreed that nobody was going to call Il Duce's bluff. The League had im-posed "sanctions" of a very mild character—not enough to stop the Italians, just enough to infuriate them and cause them to burn Anthony Eden in effigy. The British tried to lay the blame on the French refusal to. support a policy of action; this infuriated the French, who had known as early as September that the British were unwilling to close the Suez Canal or to shut off the oil supplies, the only two measures which might have been effective. So Denis de Bruyne told Lanny, having got it direct from Pierre Laval.

Recriminations everywhere the diplomats met; Rick called it a thieves' kitchen. They were all imperialists, he declared, all in a squabble over dividing the loot. British general elections were due in a few days, and Rick was campaigning against the government can-didates, so he could only write briefly. "The Tories have to pretend to support the League; and the day after the elections they will cut the League's throat. They are even allowing the Italians to carry poison gas through the Suez; gas so declared for transit fees, mind you!"

There was that magnificent fleet waiting at Alexandria; two, in fact, the home fleet and the Mediterranean. In Lanny's ears rang the proud boast: "The British lion never bluffs!" But Rick said the statesmen were shivering at the thought of a mad dictator sending his bombing-planes, his submarines and swarms of tiny sea-sledges on some dark night, and next morning there would be no British lion. There were even rumors that the fleet had been sent without sufficient ammunition—and how could you know what to believe?

In the midst of this long-drawn-out crisis Robbie Budd and his right hand, Johannes Robin, arrived in Paris. It was harvest time for them; Robbie, having foreseen it, had his harvesting-machinery well greased and its engines warmed. He had shipped one of his new fighter planes, the Budd-Erling P7, on board a freighter, and with it came a crew ready to uncrate and assemble it; also a test-pilot who was going to put the marvel through its paces for the French government, and fly it to England and repeat the performance. The French were a penurious people, Robbie said, and would hate like sin to pay cash for planes which they might hope to reproduce in a year or two; but in this game of air-fighting you didn't use what you might have next year, but what you had today. Robbie carried a threat to every war office, that if they didn't get the Budd-Erling P7 the next country would.

A man of great affairs couldn't afford to put up at the second-class hotel where Lanny and Beauty were staying. He and his man Friday had to be at the Crillon, and the mother and son came over to lunch with them and found them so full of business that they hardly had time to tell the news from home. Robbie wasn't going to waste time with subordinates, but ask de Bruyne to bring him together with the French Premier. Beauty said: "I think I could arrange it so that you would meet him socially." She explained that at one of Irma's receptions she had met a titled French lady who was the mistress of one of Laval's closest associates; she offered to see this lady and arrange to have her give a dinner at her home, where Robbie might meet two or three of the key men of the French government and have a chance to talk to them while they were feeling mellow.

"What will she expect?" Robbie asked, and Beauty said: "Not very much, I should think; say, five thousand francs."

"All right," said the man of affairs. "See what you can do; but I'll have to know today, because this crisis may soon be over."

VIII

It was like the old days which Lanny remembered so vividly, when the World War had hit them and he had to become his father's secretary at the age of fourteen. Now Robbie had brought a secretary with him, one who knew French well. Lanny sat and watched the master of affairs read cablegrams, dictate answers, and talk over the phone with important persons. It was late in the afternoon before he said: "Now, son, we'll have time for ourselves. How about a bit of fresh air?"

"Fine!" replied the son. "Walk or drive?"

"Walk, if you're equal to it," said the father—joking, for he was trying to. take off weight and not succeeding any too well. They strolled on the great Place de la Concorde, where Lanny had seen the soldiers bivouacked in war days, the captured German cannon parked in peace-making days, and mobs, Communist or Fascist, combating the gendarmes on several occasions. The hotel suite which had been assigned to his father was the one on whose balcony a maidservant had been shot while watching the rioting less than two years ago. The bitterness of that night of battle was still poisoning the public life of France.

"Well, son," began Robbie, "I've had several talks with Irma, and I needn't say what a sad affair it seems to me."

"She told you the whole story?"

"She says she did; but of course I want to hear your side."

"I really haven't much of a side, Robbie. Irma and I disagree in our ideas, and it makes her unhappy; she wants me to give up my ideas, and I can't. That's about all there is to it."

"Your ideas mean more to you than your wife and child?"

"They mean more to me than anything else, including life."

"That's serious talk, Lanny. You must realize that going up against a bunch of people like the Nazis is no child's play, and it doesn't leave a man's wife much chance of happiness."

"I realize that fully, and I'm not blaming Irma, either publicly or in my heart. It's just her hard luck that she didn't realize what she was taking on. I explained it to her before I asked her to marry me, but she was young and it just didn't register."

"Do you still love her?"

"Of course I love her; but how can there be love when there is no harmony of mind? I know I've made her unhappy in the past and will make her still more unhappy in the future. So what's the use of fooling with it?"

"You're not going to make any attempt at a reconciliation?"

"How can I, when she laid down the law to me that I had to break with all my friends?"

"She was angry when she said that, and I don't think she would expect to stand by it literally."

"Did she tell you that?"

"She said as much."

"Well, why doesn't she say it to me?"

"She told me she had written to you."

"Yes, but nothing like that. She wrote the news about Frances and assured me that she wished me all happiness."

"I think you ought to go and see her, Lanny, and talk the thing out fairly and frankly."

"I know, that sounds reasonable, but it's because you don't realize how much talking we've already done. We just don't agree about any of the things that I really care about. You know how it is with you and me—we argue, but you have a sense of humor, and we kid each other and manage to get along. But Irma has no humor, at least not where her intellectual prestige is concerned; she thinks I think she's dumb about politics and economics, and I do, and so she gets her feelings hurt, and I can't help it. It's just a damn bore, not being able to say what you think and have the other fellow stand the gaff. Take Uncle Jesse; I can fight with him and he gives me as good as he gets and that's the end of it. But with Irma—good Lord, it's like running a newspaper under censorship. I have to accumulate a long list of topics I must never mention in her presence; I have to bite my tongue off a dozen times a day. I can't tell you what a relief it's been to be able to go anywhere and meet anybody and not feel that I've committed a crime."

Robbie was a tactful man, and had known this unusual son for a long time. "I think you ought to go, Lanny," he said. "You don't want Frances to forget you entirely."

"Of course not. I'm planning to see Frances before long; but I don't see what Irma and I can say that we haven't said too many times already."

IX

Robbie wanted to know about the international situation, so urgently important to him, and Lanny told him what he had been able to pick up in Paris. The barefooted black soldiers of the Negus were putting up a tough fight for their freedom, and some of Lanny's Leftist friends were cherishing the hope that in their wild mountainous country they might be able to wear down the invaders. Robbie said: "Poor niggers, they don't realize what has happened since the time of Adowa. Believe me, son, the airplane has changed the world, and a nation or people that loses command of the air might just as well quit and save what it can."

Lanny had heard his father make confident assertions about public events, and his score was far from perfect. "You have something to sell!" he answered, with a grin, and the father replied: "You bet your bottom dollar!"

Robbie was still more confident after he had had his dinner with the *fripon mongol* and other key Frenchmen. He told his son that the Abyssinian goose was already cooked and ready for carving. "Britain and France are going to compromise," he declared. "They understand clearly that they can't afford to see Mussolini licked. It would be a defeat for the white race; there'd be a revolution in Italy, and the Communists would take over the country."

There it was again: Fascism as a bulwark against the Reds! A Communist revolution would be a calamity, while a Fascist counter-revolution might be a necessity! Robbie said that the French army generals would refuse to fight Italy; they would rather turn the politicians out. Lanny had heard it before and knew it was the regular Fascist talk. Who could say if it was true?

He didn't want to argue with his father any more than with his wife. It was his role to ask questions and get information to be passed on to his Pink friends. So now he learned that while the League members in Geneva were being stalled in their program of applying sanctions to oil, the French Premier and the British Foreign Secretary were working out a plan to give Mussolini most of what he was out to grab. The prospect disturbed an American merchant of death and he remarked: "I have to get busy and get some contracts signed before this whole thing blows over!"

They went out to the Villacoublay flying-field just south of Paris to witness the tests of the Budd-Erling P7. Robbie went in a fancy staff car with magnificoes wearing loads of gold braid, and Lanny drove his mother, also the titled French lady who had been paid five thousand francs (about two hundred dollars) for a dinner. A fascinating and at the same time a terrifying thing to watch that man-made bird wheeling and darting in the sky, more rapidly than any creature had ever moved on land, sea, or air up to that moment. To see it mount out of sight, and then come rushing down with the throttle wide open and the motor roaring—down, down, until you caught your breath, certain that it must be too late and that the man inside must be dead; leveling off at the very last instant and sweeping like a hurricane across the field. The test-pilot was helped out of the plane with blood running from his mouth and nose, and it was rather horrible, but it was war. The American Navy had invented this new method of attack, and it was said that the Germans and Italians had both taken it up and were going to win wars with it. "Is France going to lose wars without it?" asked the president of Budd-Erling, addressing officers of the French Air Force.

X

Robbie left Johannes in Paris and set out for London; Beauty went along to help with her social arts, and Lanny motored them—it was like a family reunion. Lanny wanted to see Rick and tell him about Irma, also to consult with him as to what a grown-up playboy might do to keep the Nazi-Fascists from getting control of Europe.

He stayed a weekend at The Reaches, and it was like being at home. He had spent so many of his happiest hours here, and this leftist writer represented the wisest and sanest influence in his life. Rick had just been through a hard spell of electioneering; it had meant traveling here and there addressing audiences, for the most part of workingpeople in obscure halls. Rick had poured his soul into the task of making them realize the need of scotching the Fascist serpent before it had grown to man-killing size. It had been an unpaid, and as the event proved, a futile labor. Because of the division among the opposition forces, the Tories had got nearly two-thirds of the seats with less than half the total votes, and so the betrayal of the people's hopes would go on. Rick's face was lined, and his hair was showing traces of premature gray at the sides; he took the election results as a personal tragedy, and suffered calamities which had not yet befallen but which his clear mind saw on the way.

They strolled outside in the garden, and Lanny told the news he had gathered in Paris, of the secret negotiations between Laval and the British Foreign Secretary, Sir Samuel Hoare. Rick said his father had heard rumors of the deal, supposed to be the gravest of state secrets; now he learned just which provinces the "poor niggers" were going to surrender to Il Duce, and how the rest were to be governed by an Italian "adviser." Rick said: "That's the damnedest sell-out of public opinion in the history of this country!" When he learned how sure Lanny was of having it right, he added: "How would it do for me to tip off some news chaps about it?"

"Exactly what I was hoping," replied the American. The playboy thought for a while and said: "I met a New York journalist the other day; if the story came from there it could never be traced to you.

Suppose I ride up to town with you in the morning and attend to it?"

Lanny told about his domestic problem. The advice he got wouldn't have pleased his father and mother, for Rick had never liked the match and had been afraid that it would cost him a friend. He said that a fortune such as Irma Barnes's represented an accumulation of social crimes and was a corrupting force which very few could withstand, certainly not an amiable and pliable art lover. He said: "Stay away from Irma till the wound has healed; let her find another man, or you find another woman, somebody who believes what you believe and will encourage what you want to do." Lanny's mind told him that this was wise advice; but there was something in him that winced when his friend added: "I wouldn't be surprised if she hit it off with Ceddy Wickthorpe. It would be an admirable match from the point of view of both of them."

The code of the smart intellectuals required Lanny to take this lightly. "My mother has been trying to hint that to me for a year or two," he remarked. "Have you seen any signs of it?"

"They wouldn't let you see any signs," declared Rick; "but you can trust Beauty's insight in matters of that sort. Ceddy is having the devil's own time to keep going in the face of rising taxes, and the Barnes fortune would be a windfall to him. Irma would modernize the castle and make the grandest countess in the realm. Your job might be to persuade Augustus John or Gerald Brockhurst to paint her portrait."

"I have thought of both," said Lanny, with a smile. "But are they quite up to it?"

"They might rise to the occasion. And as for her ennoblement, just keep out of the way and leave it to economic determinism!"

The anti-Nazi conspirator wasn't at liberty to give any hint concerning his associate in Paris. All he said was: "I am doing something for the cause which I'm pledged not to mention; but I want you to know that I'm not just playing round."

"Good for you, old top!" replied the Englishman. He put his arm about Lanny and gave him a squeeze, a form of demonstration he did not often permit himself.

XI

Lanny went back to London and appeared in the smart world with his smart mother. This return to the period of apron-strings of course did not fail to excite comment. Three months had passed since the parting of the heiress and her prince consort, and the event had been noticed in those newspaper columns which occupy themselves with the doings of the rich. The brilliant young ladies and gentlemen whose business it was to flit from flower to flower and collect the honey of gossip came to Lanny with sly and insinuating questions; they expected him to answer in the same tone, and he did so. "My wife has her reasons for wishing to be at home for the present. I am here on picture business, and am planning to leave for New York before long." He would say it with a grin, and add: "Nothing more." Cablegrams would be shot to New York, asking about storks on the extensive red-tiled roofs of Shore Acres. Telephone calls would come to the estate, and Irma would be furious. Lanny, who hadn't said a word but the truth, thought he was entitled to have a few smiles out of his misfortunes.

There was going to be a grand evening reception and dance at the town house of Margy Petries, to mark the coming out of Marceline Detaze, just eighteen, and one of the loveliest young creatures your eyes ever fell upon. Her mother had decided that a London début would be distinguished, and it had better come before the scandal broke. Here Beauty was in her element, working two rackets at the same time, selling airplanes and a daughter; there was no conflict between the efforts, for the same man might elect to buy both, and it would all be in the family.

From the mother's aspect, manner, and conversation you would never have guessed that there was anything "spiritual" about her; but upstairs in a room of this ample dwelling, full of historic memories, a retired real-estate salesman from a small town in Iowa sat for hours at a time in front of his fireplace with his eyes closed. He was doing what he called praying, a form of mental exercise which consisted in fixing his mind upon images of the good, the true, and the beautiful, to the exclusion of a world ·full of the bad, the false, and the ugly. The method must be working, for whenever Beauty entered that room she came out with a light of hope in her eyes and feelings of love in her heart. Was it not love of Marceline which prompted her to find the child a proper husband? Was it not love of Robbie and the other stockholders, including Margy, her hostess, which prompted her to try to sell fighter planes to the British who apparently needed them so badly? Truly, it would be terrible if the British home and Mediterranean fleets were to be destroyed; what then would protect this beautiful old town house, and the spreading country estate, and all the other charming places where Beauty Budd had been having good times for more than thirty years—ever since Petries' Peerless had become Eversham-Watson and had brought her here and introduced her as the ex-wife of Budd Gunmakers?

A touching and pathetic thing to see Marcel's daughter at this great moment of her life; a lovely frail butterfly just emerged from her chrysalis, waving her wings in ·the sun and preparing to take flight into the wide world. A wonderful rose-pink toilet had been got ready and Lanny was privileged to see it in advance. No use trying for the serious talk which he had been preparing in his mind; he could get time for only a few words: "Are you going to break off with Alfy, dear?"

"Oh, Lanny, he's so fussy! He quarrels with everything I do. He thinks I'm nothing but a silly."

"Well, are you?" he wanted to say; but it might have spoiled the party. "Have you invited him?"

"Of course. I wrote him a nice note, even though he was an old bear the last time I saw him. I suppose he'll come, if his very important studies permit; but I don't believe he'll enjoy it, because he thinks that parties are frivolous and that I ought to be learning nursing or something."

"Well," said Lanny, "he thinks there'll be another war, and he expects to be an aviator, so he may need to be nursed."

"Oh, Lanny, you think of such depressing things! I believe you taught them to him!"

XII

Beauty found time for a word of warning to this wayward son of hers. One of the persons he might meet at this affair was Rosemary Codwilliger, pronounced Culliver, only you didn't have to pronounce it since she had become the Countess of Sandhaven. Lanny said: "Rick told me she was in town."

"Tell me honestly, are you going to take up with that horrid woman again?"

"Unless she has changed greatly, she's not in the least horrid, Beauty. She was gentle and kind, and taught me no end."

"She seduced you, and then turned you down twice," declared this stern moralist. "That's enough for any man's mother."

"If she had married me," countered the man, "she'd have been just as unhappy as Irma, and what good would that have done either of us?"

"Tell me, are you going to let it happen again?"

"If it will comfort you to know, I am going to live in poverty and chastity and devote myself to improving mankind."

However, he didn't talk that way to Rosemary when he met her in the ballroom. Seven or eight years had passed, and he was prepared to see the ravages of time, but there was none to be observed. She was a year older than he, but that doesn't mean so much in the mid-thirties as it does in the mid-teens. She had been in the Argentine and then in the Far East; evidently she had taken care of herself wherever she was. She was of that sort, serene, unhurried and unworried; the best of everything came to her, for she had inherited that good part. Her heavy flaxen hair had lost none of its luster and her shoulders and back none of their smooth whiteness. She wore a cream satin gown with one deep-purple orchid at the V in front. Had she put that on for him?

"Oh, Lanny!" she exclaimed. "It's so good to see you! I came just on your account."

"I had to come anyhow," he replied; "but I'm glad you're here. You haven't changed a bit. Where is Bertie?"

"He's in the Canadian Rockies, trying to shoot a wild sheep. How is Irma?"

"She's quite well. She's in New York."

"Are you happy, Lanny?"

"Who is, entirely?"

"We all hope to be; and you deserve it, because you're so kind."

"Happiness doesn't always go with kindness. It's as wild as a Rocky Mountain sheep."

They danced, and it was just like the old days; they moved together, they felt themselves one, they were wrapped in a garment made of a thousand agreeable memories: the nights on the banks of the Thames, looking at the stars on the water and listening to Kurt playing the piano; the nights on the shore of the Golfe Juan, listening to a distant orchestra playing the barcarole from the *Tales of Hoffmann. Belle nuit, O nuit d'amour, souris à nos ivresses; nuit plus douce que les jours, O belle nuit d'amour!* Nights much later, ten years or more, when they had sat before the fire in her villa and he had recited to her all the poetry he knew.

She was one of the most adorable of women, and if he wanted to be consoled, her bosom would be soft and warm. She said: "Bertie has quit the diplomatic service, you know; they worked him too hard and wouldn't give him any real promotion; and anyhow, he wanted to be free and play round." Lanny knew what that meant: "My husband prefers shooting sheep to taking care of his wife." "Playing round" meant some other woman, as it had meant in the old days. She might as well have said: "I am free, Lanny, if you want me."

Did he want her? He did and he didn't; such problems are less simple at thirty-six than at sixteen. He had time to think it over, for of course they couldn't dance together the whole evening; that would have made a scandal. He strolled out on the terrace, it being a still evening and not too cold. There was young Alfred Pomeroy-Nielson pacing up and down, very ill-contented; he had had one dance with his beloved and couldn't expect more at her début party.

"Hello, Alfy!" said the old friend of his family. "How do you find Magdalen?"

"Oh, it's all right," said the youth, English fashion; then, in a sudden burst: "Tell me something, will you, Lanny?"

"Anything I know, old man."

"Does Marcy really love me?"

"Well, that's not for yes or no. She's a very different person from you, and what she means by love may be different from what you mean."

"She keeps me in a dither all the time. Sometimes I think it's my fault, and sometimes I think she means to. I imagined that love would mean peace and understanding, but I discover it's a struggle of wills. Is that right?"

"What something is and what it ought to be are often quite different." Lanny took the arm of the tall slender young man, who at this time happened to have exactly half as many months on earth as Lanny himself had. With his dark hair and keen intellectual features he seemed a return to life of Rick as Lanny had seen him when he had volunteered as a flier and come to Paris for a two-day furlough.

Moved by sudden pity, the older said: "Alfy, I'll tell you something that your father and mother know, but otherwise it's a secret. My own marriage happens to be on the rocks right now."

"Oh, Lanny, I'm so sorry!" Alfy was quite overcome, partly because he had believed this a really happy union and partly because of the honor his father's friend was doing him by his confidence.

"That may account for my being pessimistic," Lanny went on. "But this is what I've been thinking about love and marriage for many years: that the most indispensable thing is intellectual harmony. Nietzsche says somewhere that the most important question for a man to consider is whether he's going to be bored by what the woman says to him at breakfast every morning; for that is what marriage comes down to."

"That's a new thought to me, I admit, Lanny."

"It is something to think about beforehand, rather than afterwards, and save yourself a lot of regrets."

"Then you don't think I ought to try to marry Marcy?"

Lanny smiled. "Don't put that responsibility on me! I'm telling you what has caused my unhappiness, and you decide whether it means anything to you."

They went inside, because Lanny had promised to give an exhibition dance with his half-sister; they did the maxixe, a society dance which had been popular when Lanny was a boy, but which was judged too strenuous for modern taste. They took the ballroom floor, and the fashionable company sat in the chairs which lined the walls. Half-brother and sister made a lovely couple, and knew each other so well they hadn't had to rehearse. Robbie Budd was there; he watched and thought that his one wild oat had produced two very fine flowers. (He took Marceline for his, because he had set Beauty up in Bienvenu and had supported both the painter and the child.) Beauty watched, bursting with pride, for these flowers were hers beyond dispute—and who now would say they were not worth the price they had cost? Apparently no one, for there was vigorous applause, and the couple had to do an encore.

A most effective way to show off a débutante; the mothers of eligible sons sat gazing through their jeweled lorgnettes and weighed the problem of a French painter's daughter who could hardly be as good as she looked. The grandson of a baronet watched and weighed, and so did his mother. Rosemary watched, knowing nothing about Alfy and his problems, but thinking about Lanny: "Should I have married him? Or would I rather be a countess?"

She danced with him again; after which they sat in one of the side rooms and he brought her food and drink, and they chatted. Having given sound advice, Lanny now decided to apply it. The news about the Hoare-Laval Pact, as it was called, had appeared in New York that morning and had been in the London papers of the afternoon. Addressing an ex-diplomatist's wife, Lanny remarked: "What's this, Rosemary, about a deal with France over Abyssinia?"

"I've been told about it," she replied. "Too bad it had to break into the newspapers ahead of time. It will stir up a lot of fuss."

"I suppose so," he admitted.

"What can we do?" she went on. "We certainly don't want to get into a war over a place like that. If we have vital interests there, we ought to be able to make some reasonable arrangement."

"I imagine you could put Mussolini out without too much trouble," he remarked; "but you might get something worse in his place."

"Exactly!" exclaimed his old sweetheart. "Most probably some wild-eyed Red."

So Lanny decided it was up to him to take his own advice. When Rosemary said: "Will you come to see me?" he answered: "I'm afraid I won't have time, old darling. I'm working hard for my father, and then I have to go back to New York. I'm not free like you, alas!"

16

Survival of the Fittest

I

LANNY thought he had never seen such a show of public anger as resulted from the publication of the Hoare-Laval Pact to surrender Abyssinia to Mussolini. Rick spoke at a huge mass meeting in Trafalgar Square and at another in Albert Hall, and at both places the audience roared its indignation over this betrayal of a public trust. The intensity of feeling was due to the recentness of the elections; there hadn't been time for anybody to forget the promises made by the government. One feature of the campaign had been a poster showing Baldwin's fist hammered down on the Covenant of the League of Nations, with the proclamation: "OUR WORD IS OUR BOND." And now, before three weeks had passed, they were selling the League out and turning its procedure into a farce!

Lanny thought: "Well, I helped a little." He said it to his chum, who replied: "Stay right where you are, my lad, and bring us all the news you can pick up." This was pleasant for Lanny in a way, because it spared him the pain of breaking with his environment; it was hard in another way, because his feelings were becoming so intense. He had to keep repeating Zoltan's formula: "I am an art lover, and do not take sides on political questions." To himself he said: "It's exactly like living with Irma!"

He took his father and mother back to Paris. Marceline went along, for she and Beauty were going to Bienvenu for the season's doings. As for Robbie, he expected orders from both British and French governments, but they were smaller than he had looked for and he was more than ever disgusted with bureaucratic sluggards. He owed it as a matter of courtesy to report to Zaharoff, and Lanny drove him out there, and watched again how this old man's being came to life while listening to talk about marketing instruments of death. He chuckled and said: "I remember my first sale of the Nordenfeldt submarine, which in those days was as hard for the officials to believe in as planes are now. I sold one to my own Greek government, and then I went to the Turks, whom I hated, and said: 'The Greeks have one of these, and so your whole fleet is in direst peril. You must have two if you wish to feel safe.' So they bought two; and after that no government in Europe could withstand me."

Robbie knew that story, and told the old spider that it was a classic of their industry; whereat the spider was pleased. "The man you ought to visit right now is Mussolini," he said; but the American replied: "Unfortunately my hands are tied, because my government has issued an imbecile neutrality proclamation, forbidding the sale of munitions to any belligerent."

"Well, then, go to Göring," suggested the Knight Commander. "That will surely stir them out of their sleep."

"I have been invited by him," was Robbie's answer. "I've been waiting until I had something definite to tell him about what the others are doing."

"Tell him anyhow," said Sir Basil. "In my day I made it a rule to tell people that things were so, and then I went ahead and made them so. When I found that the Maxim machine gun was better than the Nordenfeldt, I told the world that it was my gun that had done the work. It wasn't long before I had bought Maxim out, so what difference did it make?" Few people had ever seen the munitions king of Europe laugh, and now, when Lanny saw it, he thought it an unlovely spectacle.

II

Lanny had guessed that his father wouldn't be overlooking the German market, and had been prepared to be asked for an introduction to the German Air Commander. Now, however, he learned that Göring had sent an agent to see Robbie in Paris and that Robbie was going to Berlin in the next few days. As it happened, Zoltan had got an order for one of the General's pictures; and Lanny received a letter from a merchant in Berlin, one of Johannes's old associates, saying that hard times and increased taxes had decided him to follow Lanny's suggestion and put a price on several old masters. So, on the way back from Zaharoff's, Lanny said: "Would you like me to drive you to Berlin?"

"I don't think I ought to take the time, son; I ought to fly. Why don't you come with me?" It was mid-December, but aviation technique had been so perfected that passenger planes were rarely off schedule. Lanny said: "All right," for he mustn't forget that it was his father who had given him the tip about the Hoare-Laval deal, and possibly the fat General would talk more frankly to a man of large affairs than he had ever talked to an art lover. Certainly, if you were going to be an anti-Nazi spy, you couldn't have picked a better father than the president of Budd-Erling.

Robbie had told Zaharoff that Göring would probably want to lease the American patents; but Robbie wouldn't consider that, he was going to keep the business in his own hands, and the old munitioneer had agreed that this was the part of wisdom. "Make him pay, plane by plane," he said.

Neither of them appeared to have considered the possibility that the fat General might steal Robbie's designs. On the drive back to Paris, Lanny brought up this question, and the father replied: "Business men don't do things like that. It wouldn't pay them in the long run, because nobody would have anything more to do with them."

"You think of Göring as a business man, Robbie?"

"He's rapidly becoming one of the biggest. I'm told he's building the greatest steel plant in Germany, and it's privately owned."

"Yes, Robbie; any pirate or bandit might go into business after he's got enough money. I suppose Al Capone might have, if the government had let him alone."

"Well, when he did, he'd be a business man; he'd learn that the way to make profits is to do business on a big scale, and in order to do that you have to make your word count with the people from whom you buy and to whom you sell. What you call capitalism pays a lot better than any piracy or banditry ever did."

"Oh, I know that," replied the errant son, and smiled to himself, thinking how naïve his father was—as naïve as any Nazi!

Lanny knew that it wouldn't do any good to pursue the subject, because this man of great affairs would pay no attention to what a Pink might say. Robbie was just like Irma, he refused to believe that the Nazis were as bad as they advertised themselves, and he found excuses for each and every evil deed that was brought to his attention. They had plundered Johannes Robin—yes, of course, but then Johannes had been an unconscionable *Schieber,* and as such he should have taken the precaution to get out of Germany at once and not try to sail on a yacht.

Robbie wouldn't say that to Johannes, naturally—he rarely mentioned the Nazis to his associate. But both of them had been business men all their lives and would take it for granted that their duty to the stockholders of Budd-Erling outweighed any duty they might owe to truth, justice, humanity, or any other glittering generality. Robbie would handle the German market himself, and no Jewish names would appear in connection with the concern; after the profits had been made—well, *pecunia non olet,* money has no smell, and Johannes, a stockholder on a small scale, would put the dividend checks to his bank account and not to his nose.

"And besides," said Robbie, pursuing the argument, "how could I keep Göring from stealing my designs if he wants to? He can buy one of my newest models through an intermediary, and when he has one he has everything."

"What would you do if he stole them?"

"I'd threaten to sue him, and he'd know I have a case. I mightn't get justice in his courts, but I'd put my case before the business world in Britain and France and America, and it would cost him many times as much as he'd stand to gain. You see, son, our business men are trading with the Germans all the time, regardless of politics. Standard Oil has a big deal regarding patent rights with I. G. Farben, the German dye trust, and so have the du Ponts. The A.E.G., the electrical trust, is in the same position, and I don't doubt that the Hermann Göring Stahlwerke have many such understandings in America. Anyhow, the men who run those big German trusts are Göring's bosses, don't you ever forget it; they'd soon make him see that he's no longer a bandit but a captain of industry."

"I suppose so," said Lanny, meekly. He, too, must play his game according to the rules.

III

Father and son had an early breakfast in Paris and a late lunch in Berlin, after which a staff car called for Robbie to bring him to the fat General, while Lanny went to see his client, inspected his art works, and agreed upon a list of prices. When he got back to the hotel, there was a call from Kurt Meissner; Lanny had telegraphed to Stubendorf and the message had been forwarded to Berlin, Kurt being here to see his music publisher. Lanny said: "*Herrlich!* Come to dinner!" He called Heinrich Jung, who was no less pleased, and began telling Lanny over the telephone all the wonders of a new illustrated textbook which his organization was distributing to German-speaking youth all over the world. Lanny had to remind himself that he was a Nazi neophyte, and that the achievements of the New Order were his own.

Twenty-two years ago this Christmas the three boys had romped in the snow at Stubendorf, and listened to the old Graf speaking to his people about *deutsche Treue und Würde*. How Lanny had loved the Germans in those days! It seemed to him it was the Germans who had changed and that he was the true disciple of Beethoven and

Goethe; but he could never make them see it, and if they could read his thoughts they would call him a viper whom they had nourished in their bosom. Did Kurt guess? Lanny couldn't be sure; he watched for signs of it in Heinrich, feeling sure that Kurt would not fail to warn the young official. But Heinrich appeared his usual naïve and enthusiastic self, and talked as if Lanny were a swimmer poised upon the bank and needing only the slightest push to get him into the water.

Lanny had a story to tell about his visit to Berchtesgaden, and who had been there, and everything that had come from the mouth of the adored Adolf. Lanny gave the credit for this honor to Heinrich, and the Hauptförster's son was so pleased and so absorbed in the narrative that he almost forgot the large fat pheasant which his host had caused to be placed before him. Lanny told what his father was here for, and about the achievements of the new Budd-Erling fighter. Good news for the Fatherland, and Lanny neglected to mention that Robbie had also been marketing the plane in Britain and France. Heinrich told of the elaborate program whereby hundreds of thousands of the youths of Germany were being taught to soar in glider planes, so that their future training as aviators would be easy; Lanny said that he had seen this in the course of his motoring during the summer, and Heinrich added that his organization had issued much literature about it, and he would furnish Lanny with a set.

Kurt revealed that he was planning to come to Paris before the winter was over. He didn't want to become provincial in his tastes, and had decided to make a study of French music, also to give recitals in Paris; that might be a way of building up friendship between the two peoples, as the Führer so greatly desired. This sounded like the old Kurt talking, and Lanny was pleased. He had never given up the dream he had acquired at Hellerau, that the arts might become a means of international unification; the art lovers, the good Europeans, would teach brotherhood and humanity to all the peoples. *Einen Kuss der ganzen Welt!*

Lanny described his visit to Salzburg, which seemed to him another Hellerau; but he found his two friends unwilling to accept this festival as a manifestation of the German *Geist.* To them it was a somewhat pathetic effort of dissident elements to maintain a resistance to German solidarity. Kurt and Heinrich wanted, not merely political and economic *Anschluss* with Austria, but intellectual and artistic as well, and they heard without joy about the crowds which had made it impossible for Lanny and his wife to find hotel accommodations in the town.

Lanny didn't mention the break with Irma; he said that she was at Shore Acres, and he was planning to go there before long. He might be back in Paris later, and would be glad to see Kurt and do what he could to promote his musical efforts. Emily Chattersworth would help, also; Kurt asked how she was, and expressed admiration for her. How much of it did he mean? Lanny wasn't going to forget how Kurt had come to Paris as a German agent and had exploited Emily's interest in music. Was he coming now as an agent of the Nazis? Of course he must know that Lanny would be thinking of this; their relationship would be complicated.

IV

Robbie Budd came in toward the end of the evening, well pleased with himself, having apparently made a hit with the fat General. He had been invited to stay for dinner in the ministerial residence, and with several staff officers had talked aviation and what the various nations were doing with it. Robbie had collected a lot of information, and didn't mind revealing the fact to his son's old friends. He didn't have to do any play-acting, for his point of view was clearcut and elementary—he believed in the survival of the fittest, and just at present fitness was proved by ability to appreciate and willingness to purchase the Budd-Erling P7. Since Germany apparently stood first in possession of these qualifications, the criterion was satisfactory to Kurt Meissner and Heinrich Jung.

The American of large affairs thought that he had seen some big things in the course of his life, but he admitted that he had learned something when he was escorted through the new building in Berlin which was to house the offices of the German Air Force. Three thousand rooms, if you could imagine such a thing—and instantaneous connection with every airport and military establishment in Germany. Imagine the size of the force which was going to require all that administering! Robbie talked technicalities, and the German pair listened with a glow in their cheeks, even while they didn't understand the details. Lanny watched and thought to himself: "No, Kurt, you're not going to Paris to learn about French music, or yet because you want to help the spread of an all-European culture!"

After the guests had left, Robbie talked about his business affairs. As he had foreseen, the fat General had wanted to lease his patents; if the Budd-Erling stood up to the tests which were scheduled for tomorrow morning, the General would offer him an annual cash subsidy, with a twenty per cent increase year after year for as long as the patents were used. That was to take the place of a royalty on each plane—since the number of planes manufactured would have to be a military secret. Robbie said that this cash payment would be velvet for the company, the investors having taken stock for their rights. It would put the concern on easy street, and Lanny could see that his father was strongly tempted. He gave no thought to the moral questions involved; if British and French planes were ever machine-gunned and driven out of the sky by Budd-Erling planes, it would teach something to those bureaucrats and brass-hats whom Robbie Budd had been fighting ever since the last war. What but a machine-gun bullet could penetrate their armor-plated skulls?

"Strictly between you and me," remarked the manufacturer, "I believe that Göring is making a serious mistake; what he really needs is bombing-planes, for how else will he be able to get at Britain? It's the British who will need the fighters for defense. But you see, Göring was a flier in the last war and his mind is obsessed by those memories. He talked for an hour or more about his own exploits, and made plain that what he expects is a series of individual dogfights. He has visions of swarms of young Germans winning glory like himself, and the qualities he wants in his planes are speed and maneuverability. He doesn't foresee the coming of heavier planes, with armor and doubled firepower. But of course it's not up to me to teach him his business; I haven't any bombers to sell!"

"Make him pay!" exclaimed the son; and the father replied: "Oh, boy, trust me!"

V

Lanny might have gone to witness the tests, but once had been enough for him; he was sick of images of wholesale slaughter, and conversation about it, and especially about the profits to be derived from it. It seemed to him that he had been born into a most unlovely time and place and section of society; he yearned for some remote and peaceful isle in the South Seas. That being impossible, he made an appointment with Oberleutnant Furtwaengler—now promoted to be Hauptmann—to meet him and get the painting; he would have it crated and turn it over to the care of the American Express Company. Also he was sending cablegrams concerning his other client's paintings; it might be possible that he would have orders for some of these before Robbie was ready to leave. There would be some money to turn over to Trudi Schultz, and a lot of data which Rick might make into a series of articles.

He was sorry he hadn't gone along with his father, who came back late in the day with a wonderful story. The plane had stood the most exacting tests, and the fat General had been so pleased that he had shown the plane's creator some of the closely guarded secrets of the new German Air Force. Robbie had been taken to Kladow, a village near Berlin which had been turned into a center of aviation research. It was now a tract eight miles in circumference, with four thousand men at work day and night on the buildings and grounds. It was like an immense university, in fact two of them, an Academy of Air War and a Technical School of Aviation. There were models of every airplane known—to Robbie's consternation the fat General had shown him copies of all the seven Budd-Erling models, and stood shaking with laughter as he watched the American's face.

Also there were models of every sort of military target, and students practicing at bombing them. There was one of the most powerful radio stations in the world, and even a yacht club on a lakeshore. The goggle-eyed visitor had been escorted into one of the underground hangars, so deep that no bomb could reach them and with the entrances so camouflaged with nets and other devices that no air photographs would reveal them. Everything complete under there, including living-quarters for the operating and maintenance staffs; a reading-room with the latest technical magazines, and writing-pads so that the men could make notes of anything important. "By God!" added the awe-stricken business man. "They even had a freshly sharpened pencil alongside each pad!"

What was it that caused the master of this magic thus to reveal his secrets to a stranger? What had induced him to boast that Germany was now spending upon military preparations five times as much as Britain and more than two and a half times as much as Britain and France together? Was it the sudden impulse of a braggart? Robbie guessed that it was a considered policy; the Nazis wished to frighten their opponents and to spread a legend of invincibility, against the time when the Führer might be ready to make his next move. "You can see it working in the case of Italy," he remarked. "The British are afraid to fire a gun at Suez, because they can't really be sure that Il Duce is lying about his new air force."

"Is he?" asked Lanny; and the father replied: "How can I be sure?"

Of course Kladow was "just the nuts" for Robbie Budd. He could go back to Paris and London and tell harrowing stories about what he had seen. They would think he was exaggerating, naturally; but they couldn't know, and vague anxiety would creep in under their brass hats. "This war," Robbie would tell them, speaking of it as if it had already begun, "this war is going to be different from the last; it's going to be right over your own heads, and all you diplomats, bureaucrats, and office-rats will have to dig deep holes." They didn't appreciate his crude American humor.

VI

For once Lanny was in agreement with his father, in the desire that Britain and France should have fighting-planes. It distressed him that the Nazis should be getting any; but Robbie had his answer all pat: "If I didn't get Göring's orders I mightn't be able to keep going, and America wouldn't have my fine fabricating-plant. With the ocean between us and our enemies, what we need is not great numbers of planes, but the means of building them quickly. If I sell a batch to Göring, I'll go home and put the cash into building a better one; already I've got the 'mock-up' started, and a year from now I'll have that better plane and Göring will have nothing."

"Unless Göring uses your planes to get something in the meantime, Robbie."

"Well, he can't get anything from America, and that's all you and I have to worry about."

Robbie had turned down the offer to lease his patents; he was here to sell planes, he said, and the next day he sold twenty of them, at $21,500 each. A contract was prepared, with Lanny helping his father as translator, a service which entitled him to have his Berlin expenses charged against the company. It was Robbie's first big deal in his new field, and there were many traps to be watched out for; the long document had to be studied phrase by phrase, and several times in a day Robbie had a telephone conference with Johannes, who knew the German language, and contracts, and the Nazis.

"You see how it is," said the father. "Göring knows what he wants, and he puts down the cash and gets it. But what a difference in Washington! Our army men have seen just what Göring has seen, and they know that no plane can equal ours, yet they have to go through the farce of advertising specifications and inviting bids!"

"I admit that the Nazis' is the right way to get things done," replied the stubborn son. "But suppose it's the wrong things?"

"You can be sure it's the right thing in this case," replied the patient father. "You notice the General insists upon getting his planes ahead of any other customers. I take it that something is going to happen this spring."

VII

Lanny had promised to pay a call at the office of Heinrich Jung; that seemed a cheap return for the telephone message to the Berghof.

Of course Heinrich had told all over the place the story of his friend's visit to the Führer, and now all the staff of the Reichsjugendführung wanted the honor of shaking the hand which had shaken the Führer's hand only four months ago. It was a spiritual thing they sought, something which couldn't be affected by soap and water.

As he sat beside his friend's desk, Lanny's eye couldn't help roaming, and among the papers lying there, one gave him an inner start. A tiny thin pamphlet, three inches by four, strangely familiar to his eyes. It was lying so that the letters were upside down to him, but he could read the two biggest words, and guess the others: "ABRAHAM LINCOLN: *Sein Leben und Seine Ideen.*"

"I notice that title, Heinrich," he said, pointing. "May I look at it?"

"Surely," answered his friend, and handed it over.

"Abraham Lincoln. Are you circulating literature about him?"

"That is not our literature."

Lanny read again: "Leipzig: Deutscher Nationalsocialistischer Kulturbund."

"I have made certain that there is no such organization," explained the official. "The thing is printed by some of our secret enemies, and is designed to deceive the persons who read it."

"*Ausserordentlich!* How did you get it?"

"It was deposited in the dinner-pail of a young factory worker who has been educated by our organization. He turned it over to his Gauleiter, who forwarded it to us."

"I should think that would be a case for the Gestapo," ventured the caller.

"*Natürlich.* I called them and learned that they already have copies. We have reason to think that the thing has been printed abroad, for it has appeared near the border in several different places."

"What won't they think of next!" exclaimed the American.

"It is a particularly vicious document," remarked the official. "You start reading a perfectly sound story of Abraham Lincoln—I admit that I didn't know much about him, and was interested at once. But before long I began to see that its character had changed; it became a series of poisonous remarks—all rather vague, so that the average ignorant worker might fail to realize that he was reading treason. But he would be absorbing all sorts of doubts as to the sincerity of our regime and the reality of our achievements."

"That might be pretty dangerous, Heinrich."

"It won't take us long to track the thing down. There have been a whole series of schemes, each more cunning than the last, but they have all been detected and the criminals have been put where they can't do any harm. For the most part this propaganda is being carried on with foreign money, and our job is to find out where that comes from."

"I should think that Kurt might be of use to you in a matter like that," ventured Lanny.

"No, Kurt wouldn't have the right contacts for such work." Heinrich's bright blue Aryan eyes gazed into Lanny's brown ones with perfect candor.

"It might be that I would have. You know, I have met a lot of those people, and have some relatives among them. They talk freely in my presence, and I might pick up a hint."

"*Herrlich, Lanny!* If you hear anything, and will let me know, I'll surely make use of it, and you will earn my everlasting gratitude."

"You have earned mine already," said the American, as he laid the poison-pen pamphlet back on the Nazi's desk.

VIII

So Lanny had an interesting story to tell Trudi when he flew back to Paris. He had his ten per cent on two picture sales to put into her hands, and she had the proofs of a new pamphlet celebrating Bismarck as the founder of the modern German state. At least, it celebrated him for the first page and a half, and after that it turned into a carefully documented indictment of force as the basis of a state's progress in the modern world. Why was the Nazi regime keeping secret its budget of military expenditures? Was it hoping to deceive Germany's neighbor states, or was it the German people themselves who were not allowed to know that their government was now spending three times as much on armaments as Britain?

Lanny stopped his reading, and said: "You can make it stronger. It is five times as much as Britain and more than two and a half times as much as Britain and France combined. So Göring told my father a few days ago."

"So much the better," said Trudi. Already she was learning to take the writer's point of view!

"The comrades who are doing the distributing are to be complimented," said Lanny. He repeated what Heinrich had said, and added: "Don't ever give me a hint about those people. I might say it in my sleep sometime; but I can never say it if I don't know it."

"You might get it by telepathy," smiled his friend.

He took her for a drive, and they had lunch in a remote *auberge* by the bare and frosty banks of one of those seven rivers which meander through the plains surrounding Paris. He had laid down rules as to her eating and sleeping, and she had been obeying them, with the result that she had regained some of her lost weight and had a little color in her cheeks. She could still worry all she pleased about the fate of her husband and friends, but she no longer had to be afraid for her own physical safety, and the human creature is so constituted that this is a great relief to the subconscious if not to the conscious mind.

"My father wants me to go back to New York with him," he told her, "but I think I'll make excuses."

"You ought to go, Lanny," insisted the woman. "Your wife may have changed her mind."

"There is the mail," he responded.

"I know; but there is her pride to be considered. She doesn't want to lose her status and be taken for granted. She has to be wanted, if love is to mean anything."

"I'll go a bit later; I've promised to spend Christmas at Bienvenu and dance with my sister at a party. And besides, I have to admit that my father's conversation tries my patience. I've heard a couple of weeks' talk about destroying men and making money, and it becomes hard for me to be polite. I've done a lot of philosophizing about what seems to me a ghastly perversion of thought. My father is a good man in many ways, a man of real creative energy. He's sup-

posed to be educated, too—he went to Yale, and they taught him a
social code that might have come out of ancient Rome. He talks
about the survival of the fittest, and takes it for granted that the fittest are the most greedy. He's not at all like that himself; he's generous and considerate to his friends, and it's only when he thinks
of social classes and nations that you'd take him for another Hermann Göring."

Trudi made a curious reply: "I wonder if Göring could be like
that, too."

IX

Christmas at Bienvenu; but it wasn't the same, because there were
no children. Lanny realized more acutely that he had lost his family.
Of course there was Marceline, who remained a child even while
playing at being a young lady. He was fond of her, and glad to see
her happy; he tried to teach her something that might be of use to
her, and he kept on, even though sadly aware that most of what he
said went in at one ear and out at the other. It wasn't that she did
not have the brains; it was that she had been trained by Beauty and
Beauty's friends, including Irma. For six years she had lived in the
reflected glory of the Barnes fortune, and while she didn't admit it
to Lanny, she was dreaming of making a rich match and becoming
a *grande dame* whose doings would be reported in the newspapers.
Lanny could disturb and distress her by his antisocial remarks, but
he was powerless to change her.

He didn't want to live in the Cottage with its thousand memories
of Irma and Frances. He had a cot put in his studio, and stayed there
a good part of the time, playing the piano and reading the books of
his great-great-uncle which had decorated the walls for many years.
Also he pushed the picture business, so as to keep a stream of illegal
literature flowing into Germany—that was his excuse for living. But
he was restless, because he had been a married man and now he was
what the world called a grass-widower, and he missed what he had
got used to.

All the time there was his mother, watching him yearningly, pushing at him gently but firmly; she spoke only a small part of her thoughts, but Lanny knew them all—he was to go back to Irma, apologize and promise to be "good," and repair his dreadful blunder before it was too late. She begged him to write and say that he was coming; to pacify her, he did this. He told Irma about his trip with Robbie, and the messages that Kurt and Heinrich sent, and about the Oberleutnant becoming a Hauptmann; he told about the party in London and the one being prepared at Sept Chênes; he sent messages of love to his little daughter and promised to come and see her before the end of January. He added: "I am sorry, and I still love you"; but he didn't follow his mother's sly suggestion and mention having danced with Rosemary at his half-sister's début party.

X

Right after New Year's, Emily Chattersworth arrived, bringing her servants according to her custom. She had offered to have the party at her place, and now Beauty would have the time of her life giving the orders and going over the lists of guests with her old friend. The Riviera was a place where people came and went, and you had to study the newspapers and then telephone your friends to find out who the newcomers were; your friends would ask you to invite So-and-so, and if you valued these friends you would say Yes, and if you didn't you would make excuses, and also, perhaps, enemies. You mustn't have too long a list, because that wouldn't be *distingué;* on the other hand, if you had too few, that would indicate that you were skimping. Robbie had given Beauty a check for her services, and had added ten thousand francs for Marceline, telling the mother to go the limit, since the girl would have only one chance. There wouldn't be any need to engage "talent," since she and Lanny would provide it; but there must be the best colored band on the Riviera, and there must be food and drink without limit.

Lanny had taken part in preparations of this sort ever since he could remember; he had run errands and offered advice—at first his mother had accepted it in a spirit of play, but before long she began accepting it seriously. Now he was not merely Beauty's son but

Irma's husband, which meant that he was an authority on the affairs of the *beau monde*, and it would have been unkind to shut himself up and play the piano and refuse to take any interest in the question whether Prince Dimitrovitch was an ex-nobleman or only a sort of ex-country squire, and whether Mrs. Packingham from Chicago was socially important now that she was living here permanently on a comparatively small alimony.

Marceline had never taken any responsibility; it was her role to be beautiful, gay, and free, and this she did to perfection. Having already been launched under the best auspices in London, she was invited everywhere, and had to be advised which invitations to accept and which to evade. She wasn't told in crude language that certain persons had money while others lacked it; she was told in refined language that certain families were "desirable," and that certain *partis*—that is, candidates for matrimony—were "hardly eligible," while others were "catches." If the *parti* was European, some member of his family or else the family lawyer would make the proper approach to Beauty or Lanny; while if he was American, he waded right in on his own account. It was the duty of a girl just turned eighteen to know how to deal with these different sorts of males: which it was safe to flirt with, which must be treated with reserve, and which must be "frozen." The Riviera was full of all kinds of pretenders and parasites, impecunious noblemen and refugees from revolutions which might or might not be permanent, so that marrying off a daughter became a political as well as an economic problem.

Among many candidates was a nephew of the Marchesa di San Girolamo, who lived very modestly in an unfashionable part of Cannes. The marchesa belonged to one of the oldest Tuscan families, but there had been some scandal which nobody seemed to know about, and she had been a resident of the Côte d'Azur since before Mussolini. Just recently had come this nephew, a Fascist aviator with the rank of captain; he had led the first attack by an Italian squadron in Abyssinia, and after gloriously bombarding native troops and villages and being decorated for it he had been grounded in rough mountain country by engine trouble. He had come near to death, having crawled into hiding and been saved from the savage enemy only by the advance of Il Duce's army. As a reward for all this he had several medals, a badly scarred body, a bloodless pale face, and an empty left sleeve. From the happy days before his accident he had brought aristocratic features and a tiny sharp-pointed black mustache; also pride, romantic charm, and a devil-may-care spirit.

A dangerous person, as any competent mother would instantly perceive; and it did not escape Beauty Budd's mother-eagle eye that this *elegantissimo* was strongly attracted to her incomparable daughter. Vittorio di San Girolamo couldn't dance like the other suitors, but he could stroll on a terrace in the moonlight or sit by a gleaming fireside and tell hair-raising stories about solo flights along the sides of mountain precipices, dropping bombs upon fortresses never before seen by a white man, so close to the targets that the explosions would throw the plane into the air; plunging down into canyons so narrow that the wingtips had brushed the foliage, machine-gunning savage enemies who were accustomed to inflict dreadful mutilations upon prisoners of war.

When Marceline came home and repeated these tales, the anxious mother replied: "Don't forget, my darling, he probably has a pension of a couple of hundred lire a month—about sixteen dollars—and his aunt has to collect her income from a score of peasant families who scratch a bare living out of terraces on a mountainside."

XI

It gave Lanny satisfaction to see the British Foreign Secretary forced out of office as a result of the Hoare-Laval fiasco; but Rick wrote him not to be too hopeful. "The Tories will bend before the storm, but they won't break," said the Englishman. "Public opinion in this country can prevent some especially flagrant offense, but it is powerless to compel any sound positive action. Mussolini will go right ahead with his conquest, and in the end he'll probably get more than Hoare-Laval tried to give him."

The forces of protest in France were equally active, centering their attacks upon Laval. Lanny couldn't keep away from it entirely —he would learn about a meeting somewhere in the neighborhood and decide that he ought to know what the people were thinking and saying; he would slip in unobserved and sit in a corner, and when he found that the speakers didn't know as much as they ought to, he would yearn to get up and tell the whole truth. He would take Raoul to lunch, finding excuse to drive somewhere into the country where they wouldn't be recognized. He knew that German agents swarmed like flies over the Riviera, and he didn't want to sacrifice any part of his double role.

French national elections were due in the spring, and all the energies of the Left were centered upon getting rid of the *fripon mongol* and his gang. The Front Populaire program was now in effect and the two powerful workers' parties, Communist and Socialist, had ceased their sniping at each other. It was the thing for which an American Pink had been pleading over a period of years, and he urged his Spanish friend to stick to it in spite of all difficulties. Raoul said that those at the school were doing their best; he believed the effort would succeed, at least until after the election period, but it was hard to travel along with Communists, because they had a philosophy which justified intrigue and deception. Did any Communist ever really believe in parliamentary methods of procedure? Lanny recalled what Bess had said, and fell silent.

The elections in Spain were due even earlier, in February; and there Raoul had high hopes. The united front was working there also, and a tremendous campaign of education was being carried on among the peasants and the workers in the towns. In spite of all the jailings and beatings, nothing had been able to stop it. "My people are fierce individualists," said the school director. "Really, Lanny, you ought to go there and get to know them; it would do your heart good. A man may be in rags, and wearing sandals made of rope, but he keeps his natural dignity, and by now he has learned who it is that is exploiting his labor."

"I am expecting to leave for New York in a few days," Lanny explained. "When I come back, I might like to take such a trip. Would you care to go with me and act as interpreter?"

"I'm afraid it would be risky for me to go into Spain, Lanny; they're bound to have me on their shooting-list."

"Not if you travel with a rich American," replied the other, with a smile. "I would be an art expert, and I'd take you into the palaces of your enemies; they would tell you all their plans, just as they do here on the Riviera. I have to report the painful fact that they have no idea of submitting to a popular verdict if it goes against them; that applies to Spain as to France. If they are forced to it, they will find some man like Mussolini, to hold you down and keep their seat on your backs."

"I know," said Raoul, sadly. "That is why I try not to quarrel with the Communists in spite of all provocations. We have to bear them in mind as a sort of last resort. There may be no peaceful way."

XII

Marceline Detaze, half French and half American, had been reared in one country and got her ideas from another. She desired to live like an American girl on the Coast of Pleasure: to have her own car and drive where she pleased, to make her own dates, and above all to choose her husband without tiresome consultations with her elders. She was of an affectionate nature, but apparently that was on the surface and did not reach down to the level from which her actions were derived. She had in her an odd stubborn streak: she would listen amiably to all the warnings and exhortations—and then go quietly ahead and do what she pleased.

She liked the company of Vittorio di San Girolamo. She said that the idea of her falling in love with him was silly; she wasn't going to fall in love with any man, she was going to have a good time, and for a long, long time. She was going to have beaux, all kinds, and many of each. Since it was better for her to do her entertaining at home, Beauty invited the young airman to Bienvenu; he came to lunch and spent the afternoon, and presently it was time to dress for dinner; Marceline asked him to stay, and he was there all evening—for practical purposes a member of the family.

To Lanny this was an unpleasant development, and Il Capitano di San Girolamo a most unpleasant personality. He was only twenty-four, and hadn't read much, but there were few things he thought he didn't know. He had been filled to the brim with the Fascist ideology and his assurance that it comprehended all truth was the more annoying because it was expressed with such suavity and quiet dignity of manner. He knew that Fascismo was destined to rule Mare Nostrum—Our Sea—and the lands all about it, and he was sorry for any persons who hadn't adjusted their minds to the fact. As to his personal future he was clear: his wounds, decorations, and family position entitled him to a diplomatic career, and to become governor of a province in that new Roman Empire which Il Duce was engaged in establishing.

Sacro egoismo was the phrase; you made yourself holy by the force with which you asserted your own Godhead. The Italians were the coming race, and *Fascismo* the creation of their genius. By the right of their newly discovered power and under the guidance of their great leader they would take what they pleased, as other races had done in the past, as their own race had done more than two thousand years ago, building an empire which had endured for centuries and had been revived for yet more centuries. Vittorio had got his history out of some Fascist textbook, and apparently it hadn't informed him that the Holy Roman Empire had been pretty much a dream, and that while it existed it had been governed by Franks and Teutons, never by Italians.

This glorious bomber of barefooted black troops and mud-hovels had apparently never heard about his host's eccentric ideas; he took it for granted that Lanny believed what the other darlings of fortune on the Riviera believed, and so he talked freely. Lanny held his tongue, and, watching his half-sister, perceived that she was swallowing hook, line, and sinker; it was her first glimpse of the world of ideas and her first dream of glory. When he got her alone he tried patiently and kindly to show her how phony it was, the cheapest circus tinsel, illuminated by some kind of calcium light which would fizzle out quickly; but he found that he was getting nowhere, for the reason that Marceline had heard ever since her childhood that her half-brother was a victim of the subtle Red propaganda—and now he was trying to pass the disease on to her! No, Vittorio was a real hero, and his cause was proving itself in action. In the battle for Marceline's mind Lanny was licked before he began.

XIII

He talked to his mother about it. "The fellow looks to me like a fortune-hunter under the sign of the fasces. All this career that he's outlining depends upon money, and he hasn't the nerve to claim that his own family has it."

"But, Lanny, he can't imagine that *we* have!"

"Of course he does; he thinks we are American multimillionaires. We live on a big estate, and know all the smart people, and we're planning a grand party. What else can he suppose?"

"He should see my unpaid bills!"

"All the rich have unpaid bills; that is one of their privileges. He has doubtless heard that Robbie is launching a new industry. Above all, he knows about Irma. You are leaving your friends to suppose that she is coming back here, so naturally Vittorio imagines it's all in the family."

"What do you want to do, Lanny?"

"I ought to have a straight talk with him. He's a Continental, and expects a *dot;* he'll count it a favor if I explain that Marceline won't have any."

"Will he believe you?"

"I'll make it perfectly clear that I have no money but what I earn, that you have only the allowance my father gives you, and that I've broken with my wife and won't have a cent of her money."

"Oh, my God, Lanny!"

"You'll see how it works! The Capitano will fold up his tents like the Arabs and as silently steal away."

"But, Lanny, the scandal!"

"Whatever scandal there is we have to face, and what's the good of putting it off day after day?"

"Oh, you promised me you would go and see Irma!"

"I did and I will; but I told you that nothing would come of it, and you only deceive yourself when you cherish any hope."

Beauty began to weep. "Oh, Lanny, Lanny! We have been such a happy family! And I thought all our problems were solved!"

She had tried, but couldn't bring herself to face the cruel reality. No! No! Not a word! Keep the skeleton locked in the family closet! She would talk to the young airman herself, and tell him about the poverty which had dogged her all her life; she would tell him that she had never had a penny from Irma and never expected to have one; that the place was plastered with mortgages. "He won't be able to find out about that, will he, Lanny?"

"He can look it up any time he wants to; and then he'll think you're lying about everything."

"I can tell him that the place belongs to Robbie, and that he's threatened to turn me out and sell it. Robbie will back me up, for he certainly won't care to see Marceline married to a poor crippled Dago—that's what he'll call him!"

XIV

Margy Eversham-Watson came to occupy the Cottage for the season, and some friends of Sophie's leased the Lodge; so Beauty would have plenty of company, and a bridge four always at hand. Everybody was interested in the coming party and helped when they could. When the great evening arrived, Lanny put on his white tie and tails, and Marceline a rose-pink tulle costume bought with Robbie's money. The white-haired Emily looked stately and noble in black velvet, and the golden-haired Beauty Budd in white satin was asked if she was the débutante. Music, laughter, and the perfume of flowers filled the air of the very splendid villa. Lanny danced with light feet but a heavy heart; having created patterns in times of joy, he could reproduce them in times of sorrow. The elegant company knew nothing about the state of his heart, and applauded enthusiastically; the occasion was one of great *éclat* for the Budd-Detaze-Dingle family.

There is an old song telling about the sad things which happen after the ball is over, and it was so with the abdicating prince con-

sort. He packed his bags for the drive to Marseille, with the family
chauffeur to bring back the car. The last thing before departing he
put his arm around Marceline, led her aside, and exhorted: "Remember, Little Sister, if you marry an Italian Fascist you come under
their code, which makes woman nothing but a brood animal, and
your one duty will be to bear children so that Il Duce can have
plenty of soldiers for his new empire."

Little Sister's reply was: "*Boo!*"

17

A Fruitless Crown

I

"THE proprieties are very important to the rich"—so remarked a
character in one of Rick's dramas. "If it were not for the proprieties,
the poor would surely take their riches." And now the visiting husband discovered that the proprieties were going to rule at Shore
Acres. Irma brought the child to meet him at the steamer, and the
child provided all the warmth necessary to a proper reunion. She was
at the age where they grow fast, and half a year provides many surprises; an inch or two taller, many pounds heavier, a new vocabulary,
a set of new ideas, new questions. "Oh, Papa, why do you stay away
so long? Oh, Papa, will you stay for my birthday?"

He told her about the wonderful party they had had at Sept
Chênes, and how he had danced with Marceline. Frances had a dancing teacher, a piano and singing teacher, and told him all about
these. She prattled a little rudimentary French and he would teach
her more; in these matters she was in his hands. She had heard no
hint that there was anything wrong with him; a tragic thing that
there had to be, and both the parents, sitting in the car with the

eager little one between them, felt a tugging at their heart-strings.

At Shore Acres he found the same desperate determination that the proprieties should rule. "Mother" and Uncle Horace came to the door to greet him. "Mother" kissed him, and her brother shook him warmly by the hand. Not one of the servants must see any sign that his status was diminished. Having lived in the fashionable world for thirty-six years, Lanny was familiar with the fact that people often say one thing when they mean another; they laugh gaily when their hearts are weeping; they express cordiality when in reality they dislike you and begin to run you down the moment you are out of the room. So now in the smiling faces of this elderly brother and sister he read anxiety, in their voices he heard mock humility.

He understood the situation. He was the father of the most precious of all children, and had committed no offense which would enable Irma to deprive him of his rights. He might insist upon taking the little one away for six months every year, and no court in the world would say No. He might take her motoring and put her on board a steamer for France, and once outside the ten-mile limit, they might be forever powerless to get her back. So, bow down before him! Study his whims, ask what he wants and try to supply it, make him feel that this is his home, in which he can enjoy every privilege, and even the spiritual benefits of love and affection, cordiality and admiration. If he expresses dislike for any person, that person will cease to be invited; if he expresses an opinion as to the prospects of the market, Uncle Horace, who considers himself Wall Street's leading authority, will hasten to agree.

What in their secret hearts did they feel, and what were they hoping the young couple would do? Lanny would never know. Irma was the boss of the establishment; she would settle it, and the elders, the dowager and the derelict, would accommodate themselves as best they could. That was the way the public utilities king had decreed it when he had drafted his will; the widow down and the daughter up—and himself standing at the top of the great staircase, frowning down upon the scene, knowing that he had employed the best lawyers and that his orders would stand.

II

The little darling was sent away to her governess, and Lanny was alone with his wife in her apartment. He looked at her and she at him. "Well, Irma?" he said; and she answered: "Well, Lanny?"

"I have thought about it a lot, dear." He waited, and when she did not answer he said: "It was you who went away."

"I know; and you who have stayed a long while." So they sparred. He asked: "You haven't changed your mind?" and she replied: "Have you?"

Someone had to break the ice, and he had promised his mother to try. "I still love you, dear," he said, and she answered: "I still love you; but have you changed your mind?" He said: "No," and she at once replied: "I haven't changed mine."

So it was a deadlock, and not much more to be said. Irma had had a long talk with Robbie since his return from abroad, and Robbie, sensible fellow, had known there wasn't any use trying to fool her as to Lanny's attitude. Robbie was a man who could be trusted with a confidence, and both had trusted him; he had tried to serve as arbitrator, and the best compromise he could suggest was what they had right now. They would be friends, and be polite to each other, but go their own ways and not be husband and wife.

Irma had the suite with the solid gold bathroom fixtures and Lanny had the suite with the solid silver bathroom fixtures. Between them hung a generously proportioned door of eucalyptus wood, known in the days of J. Paramount Barnes as "Circassian walnut" and very highly esteemed. That door stayed open both by day and by night, but neither of them crossed its threshold. Lanny would lie in his sumptuous bed with the baby-blue silk coverlet, and would try to guess: "What does she really want?" The hearts of men and women are not simple, and he guessed that her emotions were mixed like his own. Did she want to be wanted, even though in vain? If he came to her bedside and tried to seduce her, would she be secretly pleased or would she consider it a breach of faith?

There was much that he might have said. "I want you to know that I haven't been making love to any other woman. I have no thought of any other woman but you." He might have said: "We have a great deal in common, dear, and for the child's sake we ought to work out some arrangement." She would have been willing to talk it out with him, but what had he to propose? Would he give up his interest in left-wing causes? Would he give up helping Trudi Schultz and others like her when they asked him? Would he say that if ever he met some anti-Nazi or anti-Fascist in peril of his life he wouldn't help that person to escape? No, he wouldn't say any of these things; to broach the subject would be to start another wrangle, of the sort that killed all love and even friendship. As for Irma, would she say: "I am willing to go on loving you, even while I know that you are doing the things I hate and fear"? Well, if she was willing to say anything like that, let her give him a hint! Any woman knows how.

III

He played the piano for Frances and watched her music lessons; he taught her Provençal songs, and danced with her to the music of a phonograph; he romped with her in the snow and pulled her on a sled. She rarely went off the estate, for it had everything a child nearing six could desire, including the children of several of the staff, with whom she played under supervision of the trustworthy Miss Addington, who had educated Marceline. Irma's friends came; they were supposed to be his friends also, and they played squash and billiards and bridge, they swam in the indoor pool, they danced in one another's homes and in roadhouses built for their entertainment. Irma had always been a reserved woman, and Lanny a queer fish, so no one suspected trouble between them. When they went in to a show, they took the old people along, which was a kindness and at the same time spared an estranged couple the temptation to intimate talk.

Lanny drove over to Newcastle and spent a while with his father's family, visiting the new plant. They were working on the planes for General Göring, also on trainer planes for the United States Army and on sport planes for the rich. Aviation was spreading everywhere and the tireless Johannes was searching out new business; flying to

Canada, where freight was being ferried to prospectors in the northern wilderness; to Central America, where planes were hopping over
jungles and up into precipitous mountains. Robbie Budd was completely absorbed in his grand new job. Esther, taking Lanny for a
confidant, reported that her husband was no longer going downhill;
he still had his whisky, but wasn't increasing the quantity, and his
substitute for the stock market was a night of poker once a week
with his cronies.

Lanny moved to the home which Hansi and Bess had bought on a
point of the Connecticut shore. The couple went into the city and
gave concerts, frequently for the benefit of refugees, or of working-
class agitators in trouble with the police; it was damaging to the
reputation of two distinguished artists, and their agent protested as
much as he dared. The granddaughter of the Puritans would answer:
"We don't have to be rich." Pretty soon she would have to retire
for a while, on account of the expected baby.

Lanny was a free man. He could go into New York when he
pleased, and didn't have to say where he had been or whom he had
met; if he wanted to spend the night, there was nobody to worry.
He could call at the office of the *New Leader,* have lunch with its
editors in the Rand School cafeteria, and listen to all the Pink talk
he pleased. He could even go to a Communist meeting in Mecca
Temple, slipping in quietly and watching the united front in action
—not altogether perfect action, he was sad to admit.

IV

One morning he read in his newspaper that Terry Hammersmith
was in town; there was Terry's picture, plump, with nose-glasses and
the most benevolent of smiles. Lanny hadn't seen this budding bu-
reaucrat since the month of June 1919, when they had been part of
a dissident group which dined together to discuss the newly concluded treaty of Versailles. They had to decide whether it was their
duty to resign in protest against its many departures from the Fourteen Points. Terry had been one of those who made evasive speeches
and decided to stay on and make the best of things; now he was

having his reward, being Co-ordinator of the P.D.Q., or whatever the alphabetical combination was which had just been formed to integrate six other assorted groups which had been stumbling over one another's initials for the past year or two.

Lanny thought: "Here's a chance to find out about the New Deal!" He telephoned, and after some difficulty got the busy official on the wire, and they gave each other verbal slaps on the back. Terry must have heard about Irma Barnes, and wouldn't fail to be impressed. "Meet me somewhere for lunch," said the prince consort, "and tell me about your job."

The guest was late, because he had been at an important conference. He was bubbling over with energy and enthusiasm. He was making over the world, and the happiness of many thousands depended upon his efforts; it gave him a sense of exhilaration. Lanny got from his talk the impression that the New Deal consisted of many well-meaning persons pulling and hauling, each against the others. Terry had just emerged victorious from a titanic struggle for power. He had managed to get to the "Big Chief," and had presented an outline for a reorganization of his own and other bureaus. "Honestly, old man, you could have knocked me over with a feather when I learned that my plan had been accepted and that I was to have full charge! Of course the problem now is whether I can manage to persuade the others to co-operate, or whether I'll have to get a new staff."

Lanny tried to find out what it was all about, but his friend described so many trees that Lanny couldn't get a clear idea of the forest, and wasn't sure if his friend had it either. Presently he was surprised by a proposal: "Listen, old boy, why don't you come in with us?"

"You mean, take a job?"

"I'd be delighted to have you, and you could be tremendously useful."

"But, Terry, I haven't had any experience!"

"Very few of us have, at this kind of work. We learn as we go along. Of course the pay isn't high, but you probably don't need it."

"I'm afraid I'm not adapted to a settled job, Terry. I'm not a particularly good judge of men, and I don't believe I'd be a success at giving orders."

"The main thing is that you're honest, and your heart would be in it. We have to train a whole staff of men in disinterested public service, and if they make mistakes on the way, that can't be helped. You know as well as I do that this thing isn't going backwards; all private industry has got to become a public service—but we can't do it until we have trained men and got them ready to take responsibility as the emergencies arise. It's hard work, but it's a lot of fun, really."

Lanny listened with one half of his brain, and with the other half he thought: "What a joke it would be on Robbie! I wonder how he'd take it!" He thought: "I wonder how I'd get along with Irma. That might be a solution of our problem; if I took a government job, it would be respectable and make an impression on her." But then he thought about Trudi in Paris, and what would she do for funds? She couldn't keep up her work on what Lanny could spare from the six or eight thousand dollars a government job would pay. He thought about Raoul and the school, and about Rick, and the other people he would never see if he tied himself down to a desk in Washington.

"I'm sorry, Terry," he said. "It all sounds alluring, and some day I may fall for it; but right now I've got a job that I think is important. I've made promises that don't leave me free. I'll drop in once in a while when I'm in America and find out how things are going with you."

V

Back at Shore Acres the young lord of the manor found a cablegram just being delivered; a message that was like a blow over his heart. It was from his mother, and read:

"Marceline eloped with Vittorio left farewell note not stating destination am prostrated what shall I do?"

It seemed to Lanny that his world was falling to pieces, stone after stone. He could think of few things worse that could have happened to one whom he still regarded as a child. His conscience smote him because he hadn't tried harder to prevent it; because he had gone away and left her in this peril. He had been neglecting all his different families, his different homes, while trying to solve the problems of a world which didn't want his help and wouldn't take his advice.

He hesitated only a few minutes over his reply. He had done some investigating into the marriage laws of the Continent while trying to get married to Irma, and he knew that Marceline couldn't get married in Western Europe without her mother's consent; also a birth certificate was requisite, and a period of delay which varied in the different countries. This ill-assorted couple would be conspicuous wherever they went and it should be possible to find them. He cabled:

"Advise you notify police endeavor intercept prevent calamity disregard scandal absolutely necessary avert wreck of child's life you alone can act."

Having sent this, Lanny telephoned his father. He had already told Robbie about the Capitano and so not much conversation was required. Robbie agreed with his son and would send an urgent message. Several hours later Lanny received a reply saying that his mother had done what he advised; so next afternoon the New York papers carried a delightful item from Cannes regarding an elopement in the highest circles of that socially prominent town. You cannot expect to bask in the limelight while you are happy, and have it instantaneously turned off when you happen to get into trouble. Having done everything possible to make herself and her daughter conspicuous only two or three weeks ago, Beauty Budd couldn't dodge the consequences now.

Being married to the eloping débutante's half-brother, Irma Barnes Budd was in the news stories, and her telephone was being rung by reporters. Having been brought up in café society, she wasn't worried by it. "After all, Lanny," she remarked, "running away with an army captain and war hero, the nephew of a marchesa, isn't exactly the same thing as if it were the family chauffeur. It's all right to try to stop them, but if you find they've got away with it, take my advice and put a bold face on it." Lanny realized that the phrase "Fascist aviator" was different in Irma's ears from what it was on his lips. To him it was a term of odium, and the performance of dropping bombs on helpless "niggers" was far from glorious; but Irma found excuses for Mussolini as she did for Hitler, and there was no use raising the issue again.

In the course of the day came another message from Bienvenu, reading:

"Couple sailed from Marseille steamer *Firenze* bound New York married at sea do meet them probably penniless."

So there was another blow over Lanny's heart. For six or seven years the story of how Irma and he had outwitted the Archbishop of Canterbury by getting on board a vessel more than ten miles out at sea and being married by the captain—that delightful anecdote had been a part of the Budd family legend. Of course Marceline remembered it, and had been able to tell her lover how to get around the stringent laws which Napoleon Bonaparte had devised for the protection of the French family and its property. The young couple had found out about an Italian steamer and had scraped together the cost of their passage. Probably they had sailed as a married couple and, after the vessel was at sea and away from French jurisdiction, they had appealed to or bribed the captain to make their presence regular. Best feature of all, from the point of view of the rascal pair, was the fact that Irma and Lanny would be completely barred from criticism; if either ventured it, they would only have to look innocent and say: "But we thought it was the right thing to do."

Chickens coming home to roost!

VI

"Of course you're absolutely bound to meet them"—so declared the mistress of Shore Acres. "I must go along—that's the only way to keep it from being a scandal."

"It's pretty tough on you, Irma," he remarked.

"I've lived in your mother's home about half my married life and been treated as a daughter. What sort of person would I be to refuse shelter to my young sister-in-law?"

"You mean to invite her here?"

"What else can I do, decently?"

"Well, it's up to you, Irma. I want you to know that I'm not asking it."

"What on earth would you propose?"

"I would make it plain to that fellow that he has to take her back to Italy and earn a living for her."

"But you say he's been wounded in the war, Lanny! Surely you can't expect him to go to work until he's had a chance to recuperate!"

"He's recuperated enough for love-making, and he's coming here because he's been told that you have a lot of money and aren't stingy with it."

"Are you sure you're not prejudiced against the man? It seems to me unlikely that a Fascist could win your approval by anything he did, either in war or peace. The fair thing is for me to meet him, and see what I make of him, and what chance there is that he can make Marceline happy."

No small joke on Lanny Budd, who had been glad to get away from Bienvenu because he so greatly disliked the *sacro egoismo*—and now the damned thing was moving in on his other home, the place where he had been hoping to enjoy the company of his little daughter. He understood and to some extent had foreseen what was happening to him—he was being ousted from his world. "Give me a fulcrum and a long enough lever and I can move the earth"—so Archimedes is said to have remarked. Adi Schicklgruber had made himself a long, long lever, and with it he had reached out and pried Lanny Budd, first from the Meissner home and then from his wife's bed. And now came the Blessed Little Pouter Pigeon with a crowbar to pry him out of Shore Acres, and perhaps later out of Bienvenu—for surely Lanny wouldn't find any pleasure in living there if Vittorio di San Girolamo was going to be the co-cock of the roost.

VII

The American heiress had visited the Führer in his eyrie, and had pledged her sympathy and support. Was it likely that so competent and tireless a propagandist as Adi would overlook this opening? Would he fail to drop a memorandum to his publicity man, the crooked little Reichsminister Doktor Goebbels, who also knew the heiress and her prince consort and had had them as guests in his home? No, indeed! Lanny had been anticipating results from that scene in the Berghof, and wondering what form they would take.

While they were waiting for Marceline's steamer to arrive, the wife said: "Lanny, I have company for dinner this evening, and I want to be sure it will be agreeable to you."

"Bless your heart!" he replied. "I'm not censoring your guest list. Who is it?"

"Forrest Quadratt, the poet."

"Never heard of him; but that may be my fault."

"He's well known in New York, I'm told; he came to me with a letter from Donnerstein."

"A German?"

"American born of German parents. He divides his time between the two countries, trying to interpret each to the other."

"Is he a Nazi?"

"I suppose you would call him that. He prefers to be known as a man of letters."

"That is understandable. Have you told him about my views?"

"Not a word. I promised, and I've kept the promise."

"Well, I'm perfectly willing to meet him. Unless you'd rather I went to town, of course."

"Not at all; I'll be interested in your reaction to him. But I didn't want to subject you to boredom without warning."

"Thanks, dear," he said. It wasn't so different from being husband and wife. "Have you any of his writings?"

"He gave me a book, but I haven't had time to more than glance into it. It's mostly about love, and my guess is you won't approve it."

"I ought to be able to stand it if you can," he replied, with a smile. She got the thin volume, *Eros Unbound.* Lanny looked at the date and saw that it was more than thirty years ago. "Is he an old man?"

"About fifty, I should guess. He has a wife and some grown children in New York." Irma didn't say whether she had met them, and tact forbade Lanny to inquire.

It was the poetry of youthful decadence, a fruit that was rotten before it was ripe. The poet sang the futility of living before he had had time to begin; he identified himself with all the empires which had fallen, with the roses which had withered before they had bloomed. He was sad beyond words, but he had chosen the words with care and knew they were right; he had the gift of melody, and sang in lilting verses the futility of singing. In short, he was the product of a society which was sick and knew nothing but its own sickness.

Forrest Quadratt in person proved to be rather small and slender, near-sighted and peering out through thick-lensed glasses; his hand was soft when you took it; his hair was gray, his manner gentle, his voice rather melancholy. It was the old-world charm which Lanny knew so well. He disliked the man, but could see that he would have an attraction for women, and that the many romantic adventures of which his poetry boasted might easily have occurred. He was widely read, had a sense of humor, and talked rapidly and nervously, as if he was afraid his witticisms might be anticipated. What did he want with a woman of half his years and very little culture? Was it that she was very rich, or was it that her husband had been absent when the visitor had called?

Forrest Quadratt took it for granted that he was among sympathizers. He explained that he had once been a poet, perhaps the greatest of his time, but the flame had burned out and he knew better than to try to rekindle it. Now he was what the world disparagingly called a "propagandist"; as the heir of two cultures, he was trying to interpret his own land to the land of his forefathers, and vice versa. He wanted to introduce Emerson to Goethe and Goethe to Emerson. Two master-peoples, each fitted to organize and guide a hemisphere; two nations which ought to be not rivals, but cooperators—and would be when they understood each other's ideals and destinies.

So it went: the old Nazi guff, but embodied in beautifully chosen words, spoken in a refined voice with no trace of accent. Lanny thought: "Goebbels has made a good choice! I wonder what he is paying for it." Lanny thought: "He'll get Irma's money, and be the guiding spirit of the salon she is dreaming about. Will he win her love, too? He'll try, of course. Wife and children won't stand in his way." From that was only a short leap of the mind to the question: "Is it my business to stay and interfere? Shall I try—or will it only mean another quarrel?"

VIII

The steamer *Firenze* came in, and Irma and Lanny were at the pier, but found that the elopers were no longer on board. From the captain of the vessel they learned that the pair were married, but the bride had no passports or papers of any sort, therefore they were being held at Ellis Island, and Marceline might be shipped back on the steamer's return. The newspaper reporters had gone down to meet the vessel in the harbor, and the couple had been stood up on deck and photographed. It wasn't long before afternoon newspapers were on the streets with the picturesque story.

Irma was indignant; she took it as an insult to her family that a relative even by marriage should be detained like a common peasant girl. She insisted on phoning her lawyer and having him go with her to Ellis Island at once; Lanny tagged along, because refusal would have been a public repudiation of his half-sister. The Fascist aviator was a hero in the eyes of most of New York's Italians as well as of all lovers of newspaper romance; as soon as the reporters learned that the heiress and former glamour girl was interested in the case, it became a front-page story, and every hour's development was followed by the press. The daughter of a famous French painter had committed no crime against the august United States government, and was a lawfully wedded wife; surely therefore she was entitled to the hospitality of her mother's native land!

The learned lawyer and the Immigration Commissioner between them uncovered an amusing set of complications. Apparently under the Italian law she was a citizen of Italy; under the French law she was a citizen of France, and under the United States law she was in a delicate and embarrassing situation. Her status was governed by the United States law of 1907, and if at the time of her birth her mother was married to her father she was a citizen of France; if, on the other hand, she could claim to be illegitimate, she could enjoy the citizenship of her mother, which was American. The fact that she had just married an Italian would not make any difference, because under the act of 1922 marriage would not affect her citizenship status. "Under that law a woman becomes a citizen in her own right and does not derive or lose her citizenship by marriage"—so declared the august Commissioner.

Lanny had to admit that he had been present at the marriage of his mother to the French painter nearly two years before Marceline was born; so the situation looked dark indeed. The only way to establish Marceline's right to enter the great port of New York was to have Congress pass an act establishing her as an American citizen. Irma was quite prepared to undertake that, but unfortunately it might take considerable time, so the legal authorities agreed. However, the skies cleared when the suggestion was made that Marceline might come in as a visitor. She and her husband could stay for six months, and that permission could be extended by the Attorney General.

Since the husband had a satisfactory passport visa, all that his wife would require would be some "travel document," and the Commissioner said he would be satisfied with an affidavit from the captain of the ship stating that the couple had been married by him. Then if Mrs. Irma Barnes Budd would consent to put up a bond of five hundred dollars to guarantee that her relative by marriage would not try to remain permanently in the country, the Commissioner would issue a visitor's visa allowing her to remain six months. "I will put up a bond for five hundred thousand if necessary," declared the haughty heiress; and so at last the persecuted young couple emerged from their island cage.

It was like a stage entrance, carefully built up; just enough un-certainty and delay to fan curiosity into a blaze. All Irma's friends wanted to meet the runaway pair; if they visited a country club everyone turned to look at them, if they entered a night-spot the limelight was turned upon them. Marceline was walking on the clouds—having suddenly come into possession of everything of which she had been dreaming. The reporters followed her up; when they learned that she was a dancer, they took more pictures of her, and she could have had a stage engagement if she hadn't been on a honeymoon. She expected Lanny to dance with her, and it would have been unkind of him to refuse.

Meanwhile here was the wounded Fascist hero, dignified, aristo-cratic, taking his honors not for himself but for the cause which he served. His talk was much like that of Quadratt, except that he had a different prospectus of the world's future. There were to be not two great empires, but three. While the Germans moved eastward to destroy Bolshevism, that would leave the Balkans and the Medi-terranean area for the newly awakened Italian race. Ultimately Ger-many would have Asia and Italy would have Africa. This would leave for the United States not merely Canada and Mexico, but the whole of Central and South America, and what more could any reasonable people want? It seemed entirely satisfactory to the ladies and gentlemen to whom the Capitano explained it, and this included the heiress of the Barnes fortune, which he had as good as married.

IX

There were now two crowbars working on the prince consort, and it seemed to him they had broken every root which bound him to this sumptuous estate. All except the poor little Frances root! Did he want to carry her off to Bienvenu and take care of her? Was he prepared to give up his other activities and devote himself to raising a child? He knew it would really be Beauty who would do the raising, and in Marceline he saw what the end product would be. The child was happy where she was, and he had no choice but to leave her here.

Lanny read in the newspapers that the Frente Popular had won a great victory in the Spanish elections; he pictured Raoul exulting over that. Also, Laval had been ousted in France, and the Front Populaire, as it was called in French, was putting up an electoral campaign which should be a spectacle. There came a note from Trudi, saying that she had new sketches to show him. He had been visiting some of his clients and obtaining orders and commissions, so there was money in sight. It was time for him to move on.

Was he going without any sort of overture to his wife? He had thought of a dozen approaches and dropped them one after another. She seemed entirely satisfied with Forrest Quadratt as mentor, and with the new brother-in-law and his bride as playmates. She found the Capitano convincing as a hero, praised him to all comers and was pleased by their approval. What fault was there to find with the man—except that he didn't happen to agree with Lanny's subversive ideas? The fact that there was a conflict between the Teuton dream and the Latin made no impression upon Irma's mind; her genius did not lie in the field of world statecraft, and she was satisfied with the vague formula that both Italy and Germany were poor nations, badly crowded and compelled to find room in which to expand.

Lanny could take his licking, of course; he could say: "I am sorry, old girl; I have been rather silly, and I'm ready to quit. I'll have to be polite to my Red relatives, of course, but I won't give them any encouragement, and I'll drop all the other people that make you unhappy." He could say that with good grace, and Irma would open her arms to him. Neither had spoken any irrevocable word, neither had committed any unforgivable act; they would be as they had been in the beginning. He might even propose a bargain: "I'll give up my Reds and Pinks if you'll give up your Nazis and Fascists. Hand the young honeymooners a check and ship them off to Italy. Tell Quadratt you are busy. Let's cut out all disputers and all subjects of dispute."

What would Irma reply? He pictured her happiness and relief. "These people mean nothing to me," she would say. "I just wanted you to see how *I* feel when I see you with people I dislike and fear." They would seal their bargain with kisses, and Lanny would be the prince consort for the rest of his life, with art experting as an agreeable side line, and security for all his family and friends. He could have a private yacht, a private orchestra, a private anything. He could go in for charity, helping the worthy poor. He could endow psychic research and perhaps make discoveries which would be of permanent importance. Anything in the world, so long as he didn't try to undermine the pillars of a public utility king's fortune; so long as he didn't impair the value of those bales of stocks and bonds hidden a couple of hundred feet below the sidewalk of one of the great Wall Street banks.

But no, he didn't believe in that fortune, he didn't believe in any great fortune or other form of vested privilege. Therefore he must abdicate and retire, and it was up to him to do so gracefully, in the modern, light-hearted manner. "Well, darling, it's time for me to be toddling. I've had a pleasant holiday and I'm in your debt. I wish I were a better husband, but you know we leopards cannot change our spots. Take good care of yourself and don't let the gobble-uns git you!" He wouldn't have to elaborate; she could guess that the "gobble-uns" were Nazis and Fascists, and she would pay just as much attention to his warnings as his "Little Sister" had done.

X

Zoltan was in London and Lanny had business there, so he cabled that he was coming and engaged a passage to Southampton. He thought of saving money for Trudi by going second cabin; but no, he had to meet the "right" people, and a steamship was as likely a place as any; if he were a second-class passenger he would become a second-class art expert, and now of all times he had to keep up his morale.

He knew nobody on board, and was content to read and to pace the windy deck and ponder his future; but others soon found out who he was, and the ladies tried to rope him in for bridge and conversation. Young ones, bright-eyed and full of chatter, or soft-eyed and shy; middle-aged ones not having given up hope; they knew that he was married, but also they knew about Reno and were willing to take a chance. A handsome young man traveling alone, and saying that he was on the business of purchasing old masters—well, they were pleased to learn about this distinguished occupation, and when he made it plain that he served only the very rich and discerning they were impressed. Before the steamer docked, he had a wealthy widow from Chicago begging to be made acquainted with great art in London, and willing to pay any price to a teacher.

Two days before leaving Shore Acres, Lanny had run over to Newcastle to say good-by and had learned that the last of the Budd-Erling P7's had left that day on a fast cargo boat for Bremen. The fat General had been so eager to get them that he had had his men in the plant watching production and begging for speed; they had dispensed with most of the customary tests and had put down the cash and taken into their own hands the job of loading the planes. Robbie Budd hadn't known what all this was about, but Lanny found out the morning he reached London, for the newspapers had placards with letters a foot high: "HITLER MARCHES!"

It was the Führer's move into the Rhineland, long planned and carefully staged; on a Saturday, as usual, so that British statesmen would be paralyzed! He had put his troops on the road at dawn, and made public announcement to his assembled Reichstag at noon. As always, whenever he made a military move, it was in the cause of peace. This time he repeated it: "Peace! Peace!" With a perfectly straight face he declared: "We have no territorial demands to make on Europe." He called upon the men of the German Reichstag to "unite in two holy inner confessions: First, we swear to yield to no force whatever in the restoration of the honor of our people, and prefer to succumb with honor to the severest hardships rather than capitulate. Second, we confess that now, more than ever, we shall strive for an understanding between European peoples, especially for one with our western neighbor nations."

What he was doing was obvious: preparing to fortify this strategic border, so that he would be able to hold the French while attacking Poland and Czechslovakia. Lanny Budd, along with every thinking person in Europe, knew that the fate of the old Continent was being decided that Saturday. Were Britain and France going to stop him or were they going to surrender to him? Under the Versailles pact, Britain, France, Belgium, and Italy were pledged to prevent this specific action. "The maintenance and the assembly of armed forces, either permanently or temporarily," was declared to be "a hostile act" against all the powers, and they were obligated to resist it. Hitler knew this so well that he had given his commanders orders to fall back at once if they met with opposition from the French; this while he was proclaiming to the Reichstag: "We swear to yield to no force whatever."

XI

Lanny was so excited that he forgot his own business, and phoned to Rick, who came to town by the next train. He tried to telephone Wickthorpe at Downing Street, but the report was that His Lordship was away for the weekend, and later that he was on his way to town. Rick wanted to send telegrams to everybody he knew; he wanted to call a meeting and make a speech, to organize a parade and carry a banner. But at the same time he was in despair; he said: "It's all fixed up. Lord Londonderry has been to Berlin, and dined with Ribbentrop, and with Göring, and then with Hitler, and they have filled him full of the idea that they mean to put down Bolshevism and are the only ones who can do it. A friend of the pater's had a talk with Londonderry just a couple of days ago, and he argues that the ratifying of the Franco-Soviet pact by the French Senate constitutes an act of aggression against Germany and releases Hitler from the Versailles and Locarno agreements."

The only hope was an appeal to labor and other anti-Nazi forces. But the trouble was, you were calling for war, and labor was pacifist and looked askance upon all "warmongers"—especially those whose fathers were selling military planes! Lanny found it in London as in Paris: the Right was militant, while the Left was using words. As if Hitler cared about their words! Hitler had thirty-five thousand troops in the Rhineland by Sunday night, and ninety thousand by the middle of the week; he paced the floor of his Chancellery, rubbing his hands with glee while the French statesmen argued in an agony of fear and uncertainty. They were afraid of German bombers over Paris; they were afraid of the several billions it would cost to mobilize the Army—and precisely while they were struggling to save the franc, and losing gold every day!

Late on Saturday night the French Cabinet announced that France was appealing to the League Council. All the world knew what that meant: Hitler had got away with it! On Sunday morning Lanny and Rick had the agony of reading the rejoicings in the Tory press of Britain, which was for all practical purposes a Fascist press and came out with editorial hymns celebrating the fact that "Locarno" was dead and "sanctions" also, and Britons were not going to die to help the ally of Soviet Russia. Several months earlier they had been rejoicing because Britons weren't going to die to open the way for the Reds in Italy. On Monday the pipe-smoking and pig-raising Prime Minister of Britain told the House: "We have no more desire than to keep calm, to keep our heads, and to try to bring France and Germany together in a friendship with ourselves."

Tragic hours for two clear-sighted men of the Left! On Monday the League Council condemned Germany's action; whereupon began a long exchange of protocols and demands upon Germany, sickening in their futility. Perfectly marvelous how many formalities and rigmaroles they could invent, how many pretexts for delay and talk, while Hitler poured his labor battalions into the Rhineland and set them to work digging fortifications day and night. You could see the white lights of the construction jobs blazing across the river, and in a few weeks they would have barred Germany away from the French armies, and the rest of Europe would belong to the Nazis. The French Premier and the Foreign Minister came to London with their staffs and got just what they had given to the British five months previously. You let us down in the matter of Lake Tsana, and now it's tit for tat. How do you like it, *messieurs les mangeurs de grenouilles?*

XII

Lanny attended to his picture business and then wrote Trudi Schultz, making an appointment in Paris. She was the first person he wanted to see, and the only one in all France to whom he could talk with complete frankness. He found her all but in tears over what had happened, and he had no comfort to give her concerning the attitude of Britain. Hard, hard men were in control of that empire; silk-hatted savages, Rick had called them. They thought about their class and their class privileges, their property and their property system, and they thought about little else in the world. Their system was threatened in every country, and they were frightened, and hated what they feared. Class had become more than country, and the enemy at home more to be dreaded than anyone abroad.

The success of Hitler's coup was, of course, a setback for Trudi and her friends, and might add years to the work they had to do. Lanny said: "It's no good fooling ourselves about it. We may none of us live to see the end of what Adi is building. This victory will make him into a master-magician to the Germans. So we've got to go back and take a fresh start, and plan a long war."

Lanny heard his friend's story of her activities, and told her the outcome of his visit to Shore Acres. Very sad, but no help for it, and that book was closed. He couldn't live in Irma's world nor she in his, and neither desired to try.

They drove out into the country, and strolled and saw the signs of spring underfoot and overhead. Life was renewing itself, even on the banks of the River Marne, which twice during the late unpleasantness had run red with blood of French patriots. It was pretty sure to happen again, Lanny said. The intelligence of men was not equal to management of the huge societies they had built; their moral sense was not powerful enough to restrain the weapons of destruction they had invented. "We social organizers are a tiny group," he said, "and we are going to be rolled over by the tanks."

What was Trudi going to do with her life? She couldn't live entirely alone, hiding in a wilderness of bricks and tiles and thinking about nothing but the composing and distributing of anti-Nazi literature. That way she would surely be an object of suspicion to her neighbors in time of stress; she would be much safer, Lanny advised, if she took up some sort of normal life as a camouflage. "Doesn't your drawing interest you any more?"

"It would," she said, "if I could do it for the cause."

"Do it without labeling it," he suggested. "Use a little cunning as our enemies do. Why not get a studio in Montmartre or over on the Left Bank and be one artist among thousands? Call yourself an Austrian, if you like, and no one will pay any attention to you, in war or peace. Now and then you can disappear for a few hours and meet your underground friends. This will be pleasanter for me, because I can come to see you when I'm in Paris and we won't have to meet on street corners."

"What are you planning to do, Lanny?"

"My home on the Cap will be a quiet place for a while," he replied. "My mother will reconcile herself to what she cannot help, and I will write letters and make as much money as I can for our propaganda. I'll spend my leisure time in the company of Beethoven and Liszt and some other old friends. I have a library of books which I've been telling myself I'd like to find time to read: Plato's *Republic* and More's *Utopia*, *War and Peace* and *Jean-Christophe*— I could compile quite a list. We've got to wall ourselves in, Trudi, and learn to hibernate like the bears; to live on our own intellectual and spiritual substance. There's a long winter ahead of us—and it may be an ice age, who can say?"

Printed in the United States
4037